Michelle Douglas [...] since 2007, and bel[...] world. She lives in [...] Australia's east coa[...] house full of dust and books and an eclectic collection of sixties and seventies vinyl. She loves to hear from readers and can be contacted via her website: michelle-douglas.com.

Hana Sheik falls in love every day, reading her favourite romances and writing her own happily-ever-afters. She's worked at various jobs—but never for very long, because she's always wanted to be a romance author. Now she gets to happily live that dream. Born in Somalia, she moved to Ottawa, Canada, at a very young age, and still resides there with her family.

WEDDING DATE IN MALAYSIA

MICHELLE DOUGLAS

TEMPTATION IN ISTANBUL

HANA SHEIK

MILLS & BOON

First Published in Great Britain 2022
by Mills & Boon, an imprint of HarperCollins*Publishers* Ltd,
1 London Bridge Street, London, SE1 9GF

www.harpercollins.co.uk

HarperCollins*Publishers*
1st Floor, Watermarque Building,
Ringsend Road, Dublin 4, Ireland

Wedding Date in Malaysia © 2022 Michelle Douglas

Temptation in Istanbul © 2022 Muna Sheik

ISBN: 978-0-263-30218-9

05/22

MIX
Paper from
responsible sources
FSC™ C007454

This book is produced from independently certified FSC™ paper
to ensure responsible forest management.
For more information visit www.harpercollins.co.uk/green.

Printed and Bound in Spain using 100% Renewable Electricity
at CPI Black Print, Barcelona

WEDDING DATE IN MALAYSIA

MICHELLE DOUGLAS

MILLS & BOON

To Newcastle Romance Writers,
for the monthly meetings and the weekly sprints,
but mostly for the fun and fellowship.
Oh, and the wine.

CHAPTER ONE

'RIGHT, SO I haven't told you about the bridesmaid yet.'

Harry raised an eyebrow as Martin concentrated on reversing his four-by-four into one of the restaurant's parking bays. What was wrong with the bridesmaid?

Was she some predatory gold-digger? Or worse still a party girl? He glanced at the harbour twinkling with a thousand lights—like a party!—and winced. Being linked with a woman like that at the moment wouldn't do his image makeover any good.

When Martin didn't continue, even after switching off the engine, Harry's gut clenched, but he pushed his shoulders back. He had every intention of taking his best man duties seriously, even if that included dealing with a difficult Bridezilla of a bridesmaid.

Though, could a bridesmaid technically be a Bridezilla? That term, by definition, belonged to the bride, didn't it?

Oh, for God's sake, Harrison, concentrate.

'C'mon, spit it out. Why'd you say "the bridesmaid" like that? As if it was in italics or something?'

He needed to know what he was up against. Agreeing to be Martin's best man was supposedly step one in Operation New Leaf. He needed to convince the world—or at least the trustees of the charity he wanted to partner with—that he was a changed man who'd given up his playboy ways.

Playboy ways that weren't entirely earned, he reminded himself.

Earned or not, it didn't change the fact that he had the kind of *reputation* entirely deserving of italics.

'You're taking a long time answering the question, Martin.' It wasn't setting his mind at rest.

'I'm just trying to think of the most tactful way of putting it.'

This was going from bad to worse!

Hold on... 'I've met Susie.' He'd met Martin's intended yesterday when he'd flown in from Switzerland. 'She's a sweetheart.' Which was true. 'I can't imagine her having a gorgon of a girlfriend, let alone choosing someone like that to be her bridesmaid.'

'Oh, Ellie isn't a gorgon. She's just...sad.'

He eased back to stare at Martin. *Sad?*

'She's the one who was engaged to Susie's brother.'

He wracked his brain. Susie's brother...?

Martin rolled his eyes. 'You're jet-lagged.'

Considering he'd only flown in yesterday from the other side of the world, he didn't feel too bad. But he had been burning the candle at both ends lately. Though *not* in the way the tabloids would suggest. He'd had a lot on his mind, but he'd have to switch gears now he was back in Australia—for both Martin's sake and the sake of Operation New Leaf.

'James died... I guess it'd be over twelve months ago now.'

He slapped a hand to his head. 'Drowned. Great guy. Awful tragedy.'

'That's the one.'

'Aw, c'mon, Martin, put yourself in her shoes.'

'I know! I know! And I don't mean to sound unsympathetic, but she's the maid of honour, for God's sake. Is it really too much to ask her to put on a brave face and be happy for Susie?'

He grimaced. His friend had a point.

'She's bringing down the whole tone of the celebrations. It's like no one can be too happy or festive around her. This is supposed be one of the happiest times of my life—*of Susie's life*—something we remember forever. Instead, it's turning into a wake.'

Harry shifted on his seat. 'Why the hell did Susie ask her, then? And if she's grieving—' if she'd been in the process of planning her own wedding '—why on earth did this Ellie agree to be Susie's bridesmaid?'

Martin raised his hands, a mystified expression on his face. 'I'm all ears if you can explain to me why women do what they do, why they make the decisions they make, when those decisions seem to defy logic. When I asked her why she chose her, Susie said, "Because it's the right thing to do." Right thing for who? That's what I want to know.'

Harry let out a slow breath. He of all people knew how difficult relationships could be.

Not romantic relationships, though. He avoided those like the plague.

'The two families are close. Susie's mum and Ellie's mum have been best friends since kindergarten. And once they married, the two couples went into business together. So Susie and Ellie grew up together. They're more like sisters than friends.'

The word sister had his gut clenching. If Susie and this Ellie were that close then they'd probably do anything for each other, regardless of the cost to themselves. That was something he understood.

'So this is where you come in, Harrison.'

He snapped to attention. 'Me?'

'I want you to do everything in your power to cheer

her up, to get her to loosen up and enter into the spirit of the thing.'

What?

'You're good at getting people to laugh and let their hair down. Nobody throws a party like you do.'

Hell. He was supposed to be shedding the Harrison 'party boy, bad boy, can't-be-serious-for-a-moment' routine. He dragged a hand down his face. God, he was so typecast.

And whose fault is that?

He'd hoped acting as Martin's best man would help him present a more responsible image to the world, not reinforce his current one.

'But I *only* want you to cheer her up. Save any other shenanigans for some other girl, all right?'

He glanced at Martin. Was he asking him to just *platonically* cheer her up?

'No hanky-panky with the bridesmaid unless—' Martin bumped shoulders with him '—you've changed your view on relationships. It comes to all of us, you know?'

That was an out-and-out lie, but he didn't bother challenging him on it. For God's sake, the man was marrying the woman of his dreams in three months. He obviously believed in true love and happy-ever-afters. But for some people that kind of long-term commitment didn't stick, the ability to go the long haul wasn't in their make-up. 'Nope, no change on that front.'

'Ellie's a hearts-and-roses kind of girl. She and James were childhood sweethearts. They'd never dated anyone else.'

Seriously?

'I wouldn't like to see her get hurt.'

He raised both hands. 'Definitely not my type. I run a mile from women like that. Best behaviour,' he promised.

'Besides,' Martin added, 'it'd cause a bit of an uproar.'

What did that mean?

'I'm relying on you, Harrison. I don't want any drama marring my wedding.' He leapt out of the car. 'Ready?'

'Ready,' he agreed, pushing out of the car.

Martin and Susie had booked out a restaurant with stunning views of Sydney harbour. They'd wanted all the interested parties—families, close friends, and wedding attendants—to meet each other before the big day.

The restaurant was small, which made it feel crowded, and it looked as if he and Martin were the last to arrive. And despite what Martin had said, the atmosphere was convivial.

He met Susie's parents and chatted with Martin's—who asked after his mother, though not his father—and a few of the couple's nearest and dearest before Martin bustled him over to a woman in the middle of a group of other women.

'Ellie, I'd like you to meet my best man, Harrison Gillespie. Harrison, this is Ellie Hawthorne.'

He found himself staring down into the brightest blue eyes he'd ever seen. They smiled into his as she held out her hand. 'It's lovely to meet you, Harrison. I've heard a lot about you.' She rolled her eyes at Martin. 'And I'm El*la*.' She stressed the second syllable.

He took her hand and found himself encompassed in warmth and…welcome. He frowned. She made him feel *welcome*. He couldn't work out how. Or why he wanted to rest in that welcome, put up his feet and just…be.

He shook himself. Jet lag, he must have it bad this time around. 'I'm pleased to meet you too, El*la*.' He stressed the second syllable in the same fashion she did, which made her eyes dance.

'You don't have a drink. Let's remedy that.'

She smiled and he immediately relaxed. Ella's entire demeanour calmed any concerns he might've had. Her expression was the same as the one that the women who always avoided him wore—the ones who dismissed him as frivolous and not to be trusted with their hearts—determinedly friendly but determinedly distant too.

Ella couldn't currently avoid him so she was doing the next best thing—putting him firmly in the friend zone. He *loved* the friend zone.

'Susie is trying to get your attention, Martin. Leave Harrison with me.' Ella took Harry's arm. 'He's in safe hands.' She turned to the assorted throng around her. 'You'll have to excuse us,' she said. 'We have important bridesmaid and best man business to discuss.'

Her hand on his arm tightened and he went on immediate high alert. Whenever Lily seized his arm like that, it meant she needed rescuing. Who the hell was hassling Ella?

He hated men who preyed on vulnerable women. He'd be more than happy to set the guilty party straight.

He searched the vicinity as she led him towards the bar, but couldn't find a likely suspect. He frowned. Perhaps her covert urgency had another cause. 'Do we have important bridesmaid and best man business to discuss?' Was there something he needed to do, a problem he needed to solve or—?

'Oh, I don't know. Probably.'

She shrugged without looking at him and continued towards the bar. She had short dark curls that danced as she walked—glossy, shiny and the colour of the icing on a chocolate éclair.

The thought made him blink. He couldn't remember the last time he'd eaten anything sweet and sticky. He wasn't much into desserts, but if someone set a chocolate éclair in front of him now, he'd wolf it down and relish every bite.

He frowned. She was nothing like he'd expected. After Martin's description, he'd pictured a pale waif with tragic eyes brimming with tears, and a general air of inertia. Not this lively woman who moved with brisk purpose.

She sent him a smile as she slid up onto a stool. 'If the truth be told, I just needed a little break from the gathering horde.'

Her smile removed any sting from the words and he suddenly realised that she no longer held his arm, although the imprint of her fingers continued to burn on his flesh. It occurred to him then that her former touch had been mercifully brief.

Or do you mean mercilessly?

The thought made him swallow.

'I mean, I love them dearly, don't get me wrong, but they can be a bit much en masse.'

Hold on, she'd been desperate to get away from…

He glanced back the way they'd come and found a large proportion of the room sending covert glances Ella's way—biting lips, shaking heads and heaving sighs.

He turned back to Ella, who wasn't looking at him but studying the wine list. She'd been desperate to get away from all of that commiseration and *pity*? Pursing his lips, he nodded. He supposed it must get a bit suffocating after a while.

She clapped the wine list shut. 'What'll you have?'

'A beer.'

'Would you like to try one of these new-fangled craft beers?'

He really didn't care and she interpreted his shrug as such because she didn't ask any other questions, merely pointed to one of the beers on tap and ordered a glass of white wine for herself.

'So…you prefer Ella?'

'I do. Not that anyone pays the slightest bit of attention.' There was the tiniest edge to her words, but before he could attempt to decipher what that meant, she sent him another of those discombobulating smiles. 'And you prefer Harrison?'

Actually, he didn't. 'I like Harry, but my parents insisted on calling me Harrison and, therefore, so did the teachers at school. And therefore so did all the kids at school.'

Their glasses were set in front of them and she raised hers to clink it with his. 'Harry it is, then.'

And something inside him unwound. Just like that. Something that felt as if it had been wound tight his whole life.

'So...'

She leaned towards him and he wondered if he'd read her incorrectly and that maybe she was about to start flirting with him.

'Do you know what Martin and—?'

A middle-aged man clamped a hand to Ella's arm, and her words stuttered to a halt. 'How are you doing, Ellie dear?'

'I'm well, Uncle Aubrey, and you?'

'It's nice to see you making such an effort for our dear Susie's sake.'

'Well, I'm very happy for Susie, and this *is* a night of celebration.'

'Och, you're a good lass.'

Uncle Aubrey patted Ella's hand as if... Harry blinked. As if she were a sad puppy!

'You're doing your parents proud.'

And then he left, and Ella turned back to the bar and gulped wine, avoiding Harry's gaze. 'That was Uncle Aubrey, who's actually Susie's dad's second cousin, so not really an uncle at all, but you know how these things are. I'd have introduced you, but...'

'He didn't really give you the chance.'

She straightened. 'So what I was going to ask was, has Martin let anything slip about…?'

Her gaze moved to a point behind his right shoulder and her words trailed off again. He swung around to find a slender woman standing there, staring at Ella with tears in her eyes.

'Hello, Adele, how are you?'

Tears fell. 'Oh, Ellie, I don't know how you can stand it. When you should be here with…well, you know.'

He found himself wanting to shout, *Her name is Ella, not Ellie!*

'No, no, don't mind me.' Adele dabbed at her eyes with a tissue. 'I'll just—'

'Oh, no you don't.' Ella slid off her stool, wrapped an arm around the other woman's shoulders and steered her to a seat between both of them. 'You're not crying on Susie's shoulder. Not tonight. Tonight is a happy night. Have you met Harry yet? He's Martin's best man.'

The tears dried up. 'Best man? Oh! So he's not your date?'

For a moment he wished he were so he could wipe the relief from this woman's face.

'We were just having a best man and bridesmaid confab.'

'Oh, then I won't interrupt.'

With that she leapt up and disappeared back into the crowd. The nosy so-and-so. She'd just wanted to find out who the hell he was.

Ella stared into her glass with pursed lips. She had pretty lips, but it was the curl resting against one dusky cheek that caught his attention. No matter how much he might want to, he couldn't reach out and wind it around his finger, and—

Stop it!

He rolled his shoulders. Old habits and all that. He just hadn't realised how ingrained they were. He was *not* going to flirt with Ella Hawthorne. He wasn't flirting with *any* woman.

Ella pulled in a big breath that made her chest rise. He averted his gaze and refused to notice *anything*. He especially wasn't going to notice the sweet curve of her chest.

'Okay, let's get the elephant in the room out of the way.' Resentment lurked in the back of those blue eyes, but he didn't think it was directed at him. 'Have you heard about James yet?'

With someone else he might've hemmed and hawed, treaded softly, but he sensed she'd prefer straight talk. He went with his gut and nodded. 'Susie's brother who died over a year ago.'

Her lips twisted. 'Eighteen months.'

That was a year and a half. 'And you were engaged to him.'

'That's right.'

He stared at her for a long moment. 'So how are you really doing?'

She stared back, her eyes not wavering from his. 'Actually, I'm doing really well.'

He believed her.

And then he frowned. From where he was sitting, Ella was doing a fine job of putting on a brave face. What was Martin's problem?

'Ellie, dear.' An elderly woman came bustling up on his other side.

Ella pasted on a bright smile. 'Have you met Harry yet, Aunt Edith?'

She introduced him as Harry rather than Harrison and he found himself absurdly touched.

'Susie's grandmother on her mum's side is one of five sisters and Edith here is the eldest.' Her smile widened. 'You can imagine what Christmas dinner is like, can't you?'

He recognised her pre-empt attempt at diversion—trying to get in before she became an object of pity and subjected to yet more platitudes. He sensed her quiet desperation returning. It didn't show in her face, but he saw the way her fingers tightened around her wine glass in the same way they'd tightened on his arm earlier.

It occurred to him then that Ella was close to her breaking point. If someone didn't do something soon, she could go off like a firecracker. If she did, Martin and Susie's celebrations would be remembered for all the wrong reasons.

And Ella would hate herself forever.

He didn't know how he knew that, only that he did. And he couldn't let it happen. He leapt into the breach. 'Five sisters? I'm guessing Christmas is rowdy. Really rowdy. And fun.' He thrust his hand out towards the older woman. 'It's nice to meet you.'

Edith frowned. 'I…'

'Are you ladies on the blue lagoons already? Way to go!' Ella leaned closer as she held up a hand to high-five the other woman and her scent—all peachy freshness—dredged his senses. 'It's clearly going to be a good night.'

She had the kind of smile that could fell a man. Not to mention gumption. She was digging deep to keep up this front. He was determined to do whatever he could to help her.

Edith heaved a gusty sigh. 'You don't need to put a brave face on for us, Ellie. We understand what you're going through. Dinner is about to be served and we've saved you a seat at our table. We don't want you feeling lonely. We widows need to stick together.'

He felt Ella flinch and in that moment he saw it all. It wasn't that Ella was so sad—it was that everyone else still was. And they were projecting it all onto her.

Damn it all to hell.

His hands clenched and unclenched, even as his heart went out to not just Ella but everyone else as well. They probably didn't know they were doing it. But trying to keep James alive through Ella—martyring her on some awful altar of remembrance—wasn't fair. It made him want to...

He rolled his shoulders. He wasn't sure. But he wanted to do something.

Ella's strength, though, astounded him. She kept her chin high, she kept the smile on her face. 'That's very thoughtful of you, Edith.'

She'd pushed all of that boiling bubbling frustration and desperation back deep down, and he winced. That couldn't be good for her.

'We're looking forward to hearing all your news, Ellie love, and talking about old times.'

Dear God. He might not be able to do anything else, but he could at least rescue her from a dreary night spent on the *widows' table*.

'I'm sorry, Edith, but I've already claimed Ella for the evening. As best man and bridesmaid we obviously have important wedding business to discuss.'

Ella had to fight an entirely inappropriate laugh at the shock on Aunt Edith's face.

'But perhaps after dessert we can join your table for a...'

He glanced towards Edith's table and the jug of bright blue cocktail sitting there, and she swore she heard him swallow, which had her fighting another laugh.

'...for a drink. I'd like to meet all of Susie's family.'

Edith hefted up her ample bosom as if to challenge him, but before she could splutter out an argument, Harry slid from his stool and took Ella's hand to help her down from hers. 'You'll have to excuse us, but Martin and Susie must be wondering where we've got to.'

He didn't drop Ella's hand as she'd expected, but led her away from Susie's flabbergasted great-aunt towards the table where Susie and Martin sat with their parents. Ella glanced back at Edith with a smile and a shrug, but it didn't stop the guilt from rolling through her.

Edith and her sisters had loved James so very much. She understood how much they missed him. She missed him too, but—

'How can you stand it?'

Harry lowered his head to murmur the question in her ear and it stirred the hair at her temples, sending prickles along her nape and raising the fine hairs on her arms. She didn't know if that was the result of the question he'd asked or the effect of the man himself.

Not that she had any intention of taking Harry Gillespie seriously. She'd heard all about his reputation, thank you very much. She had no intention of falling victim to his playboy charm. She wasn't falling for *anyone's* charm, playboy or otherwise. She barely managed to suppress a shudder at the thought.

Before she'd managed to formulate a response to his question, though, they were standing at Susie and Martin's table.

'You're joining us?' Susie's eyebrows rose and her teeth worried her bottom lip.

Ella bit back a sigh. She truly was the black widow—the kiss of death to all fun and frivolity. No wonder Edith had tried dragging her off to the *widows' table*. It wasn't that she was trying to prevent Ella from feeling lonely. It was that she didn't want Ella raining on anyone else's parade.

If they'd only give her half a chance, she'd show them that she could be the life and soul.

Well, you know how to fix that. Return to the fold—

She flinched at the thought. Tried to cut it dead. Couldn't

face it. If she surrendered her dream now, she couldn't help feeling it would be the slow death of who she was.

Except following her dream was making everyone else unhappy!

Maybe they were right. Maybe she was being reckless and selfish. She was so tired of being on the outer, of constantly having to justify her choices…of being the source of so much worry. James's death had hurt everyone so badly. Did she really have it in her to keep hurting them?

She suddenly realised she had a death grip on Harry's hand and loosened her hold. Her eyes burned, but she forced up her chin. Next week. She'd tell them next week. Monday. She'd say she'd made a mistake, would return to the family business…and to a life of dull, secure monotony.

But deep inside her a voice whispered that she shouldn't have to surrender all her dreams simply to make everyone else happy.

'Auntie Edith told me she was organising for you to sit with them.'

Had there been phone calls prior to this evening's gathering about how best to handle Ella? She'd bet there had been. Why couldn't they acknowledge that she was making an effort? They'd all lost James. Not just her.

Pulling in a breath, she let it out slowly. She knew how much they were hurting, and she'd do anything she could to change that. But it was as if whenever she was in the room the family didn't see her any more, all they could see was James's absence.

She was trying to do her best by and for Susie. Why couldn't Susie return the favour? Unlike Ella, the family was letting *her* move on. Didn't she have it in her to extend some of that grace to Ella? Rather than relegating her to the *widows' table*?

Ella did what she could to beat down the resentment.

Susie had idolised James. Losing him had blown her world apart. It had blown all their worlds apart. In the grand scheme of things sitting with the great-aunts was a small sacrifice to make. And if she was honest she couldn't care less where she sat.

So why the pang at the thought of not sitting with Harry?

Because, for all his playboy ways, he was a breath of fresh air. In the same way anyone who hadn't known James would be a breath of fresh air.

She opened her mouth to say she'd go and sit with Edith, but Harry spoke first. 'Susie, your bridesmaid is too young to be banished to the great-aunts' table.'

It felt odd to have someone going into bat for her. Odd but nice.

His mouth hooked up in a crooked grin and she saw the charm that must've won him at least a thousand hearts over the years. 'That said, I can see you and Ella making up your own great-aunts' table in another fifty years and getting up to all sorts of shenanigans.'

Just for a moment Susie's eyes met hers and they shared a grin—a 'before James had died' kind of grin. Ella pointed at her. 'We are *not* drinking blue lagoons.'

'What will we drink instead?' Susie asked.

'Champagne, of course. We'll be on the bubbles, darling.'

But the smile had already started to fade from Susie's face. It was the same with everyone. They'd enjoy a brief moment with her, and then feel guilty because James was no longer here. In this instance, though, Susie's smile became a frown. Her gaze lowered, and with a start Ella realised that her and Harry's hands were still linked.

'Mind you—' Harry craned his neck towards Edith's table '—they've just ordered another jug of blue lagoon. *That* could be the party table. You up for it, Ella?'

Her cheeks burned and she tugged her hand free. She hadn't realised she'd left her hand in his. It'd just been so nice to let someone else take charge for a moment that she'd let herself wallow in it.

Dangerous.

It struck her then how tired she was. Which meant she was getting closer and closer to her breaking point. And she had to guard against that with everything she had.

Martin shot to his feet. 'Of course you should sit with us.' He gestured to the spare seats at the end of the table, but he didn't meet Ella's eye. He never met her eye.

Wine was poured and the conversations continued around them, but nobody invited them into said conversation because…black widow…kiss of death.

She wondered how soon before she could excuse herself, go home, climb into bed and pull the covers up over her head.

She sipped her wine and glanced at Harry, found him watching her with a frown in his eyes. She didn't know how to answer the question there, so she merely shrugged. 'You'd have had more fun this evening if you'd surrendered me to Edith and her gang.'

'You're wrong. You and I have Very Important Things to discuss.'

He said the words as if they should have capitals. 'Oh?'

'The thing is…'

He leaned across the table towards her and it felt as if not just the table shrank but the entire room. It was possible that every eye in the room was on them, but in that brief moment she didn't care.

Which was also dangerous, but so damn freeing she couldn't help glorying in it. She reminded herself about the playboy thing.

'What *is* the thing?' she found herself asking. Her pulse was *not* racing and her breath was *not* hitching.

'You and I need to make a deal. Wedding attendants have to stick together. It's the *rules*.'

She fought a smile. 'The rules, huh?'

'Exactly. Which means I hereby solemnly swear to save you from the great-aunts' table as long as you promise to save me from the scary ladies' table.'

She glanced in the direction he indicated and a laugh shot from her. A little too loudly, obviously, because it suddenly felt as if the entire room stared at her.

'Susie's cousins,' she said, trying to school her features. 'And I guess you could call them a little scary. But rumour has it there's not a scary ladies' table in all the land that holds any fear for you.'

He wagged a finger at her. 'Wrong answer. You haven't promised me yet.'

She choked back another laugh. 'Okay, okay, you have a deal.'

'Thank you!'

He sounded heartfelt.

'I could kiss you. Except I'm off kissing and romance and all of that nonsense.'

'Oh, ho! Another drink for the gentleman, please.' She seized a wine bottle and topped up his glass. 'Colour me intrigued. This is a story I have to hear.'

'It's not as interesting as it sounds.'

She couldn't work out if he was mock rueful or whether the regret was real. 'Why don't you let me be the judge of that?' It had to be more interesting than her life at the moment.

He sat back, gave a shrug. 'Well, for reasons...'

Ones he obviously didn't want to go into.

'I need to clean up my image. I have to channel less of the party boy and more of the clean-cut role model.'

She glanced at the scary ladies' table. 'So you're trying to stay away from temptation.'

He huffed out a curiously mirthless laugh. 'That's the problem: it's what everyone thinks—that I'm constantly on the prowl. Wherever I go, even if it's just a quiet dinner with friends, compromising pictures of me somehow get leaked to the press, as if it's a game. In reality they're not compromising. In reality it's usually just some girl who's had too much to drink throwing her arms around me, and her friends snapping a picture.'

Was he serious? But…that was awful!

His eyes narrowed. 'And experience tells me that the women on the table over there would find something like that a hoot, a great joke. And I'm tired of being the butt of everyone's jokes.'

'Oh, Harry.' Her chest burned. 'I'm sorry.'

'Not your fault.'

'Yeah, well, I could've been more sensitive rather than jumping to conclusions.'

'Conclusions fed by the press.'

She stared at him, wishing she could make him smile again. 'We shouldn't believe everything we read.'

'Yeah, well, I'm not saying I'm a saint either.'

It sounded like a warning. 'I never thought that for a moment.'

His gaze sharpened. 'You and I—' he gestured between them '—are on the same wavelength.'

She took in that square jaw, the white-blond hair and those ridiculously broad shoulders and a pulse started up inside her.

She pulled back. She had no intention of viewing Harry in *that* kind of light. But with his soulful brown eyes and wicked-as-sin grin, he was the kind of man who *oozed* sex appeal, and she'd be a fool to let her guard down around him. He might say he was trying to clean up his image but that could just be a line he was spinning. Or a promise he wasn't capable of keeping.

And she wasn't in the market for anything like that. 'What makes you think we're on the same wavelength?'

'You can't breathe a word of this to another soul.'

She wasn't breathing too much of anything to anyone at the moment so she crossed her heart.

'Before we came into the restaurant, Martin told me you were sad and asked me to cheer you up.'

She sat back, stung, though his words shouldn't have surprised her.

'But it took me less than half an hour to work out that you're not sad.'

He knew that? *How?* And how could she convince everyone else of that fact?

'You're not sad, but everyone else is.'

His words speared into all the sore places in her heart. It took all her strength not to lower her head to the table and close her eyes.

'So *I* don't need to cheer *you* up. What *we* need to do is find a way to cheer everyone else up or this wedding is going to be about as much fun as…'

'Balancing the books?' she offered. The thought of spending her life balancing books made her want to scream. Really loudly.

'There's a certain satisfaction in having balanced the books. No, this wedding is in danger of becoming a—'

He broke off. 'A wake?' she said softly.

He grimaced. 'Sorry.'

'Don't be daft. No apologies necessary.' She didn't want him walking on eggshells around her.

His gaze held hers and it felt as if he plumbed her very depths. And then he nodded and she let out a breath, realising he'd taken her words exactly as she'd meant them, that he'd accepted she wasn't some delicate flower in danger of breaking.

He sent a pointed glance at Susie and Martin and then hitched his head at the rest of the room. 'We need to do something to fix this.'

She'd been trying to, but her best efforts clearly weren't good enough. But with Harry's help…

Maybe he was right. Maybe they were on the same wavelength. She leaned towards him. 'I'd love to cheer everyone up, Harry. I'd love to make this a wedding Susie could look back on with pride, one not marred by grief.'

'Then we're on the same page.'

She chewed the inside of her cheek. 'Speaking of the wedding, do you know what they have planned? Something's afoot and—'

'Can I have a bit of shush?' Martin chose that moment to rise to his feet and tap his wine glass with his knife to get everyone's attention. 'Susie and I have a rather important announcement to make.'

CHAPTER TWO

ELLA SLUMPED AT the bar and glared into her diet cola, wishing it were something *much* stronger. She barely glanced at Harry when he slid onto the stool beside her. 'They're gone?'

'Every last one of them,' he said with a cheerfulness that set her teeth on edge.

Don't begrudge him his good mood. You should be sharing it, you ungrateful wretch.

She made herself straighten and send him a smile. 'Quiet at last.' She closed her eyes and pretended to relish it. Not that much pretence was necessary. 'How's the serenity?'

When she opened her eyes she saw her oblique reference to the iconic Australian film *The Castle* had made his lips lift.

Which, it had to be said, lifted her spirits a fraction too, so there was that.

She dragged her gaze away before it could become anything more. She didn't want him thinking she was in the market for anything like that. And if he wasn't looking for anything of that nature either—and he hadn't said or done anything to give her reason to think otherwise—she didn't want to be lumped in with the scary ladies.

'I'll have what she's having,' he said when the bartender came over.

'It's diet,' she warned.

'But not diet,' he added, before glancing back at Ella. 'You look like you'd prefer something stronger.'

She pointed a finger at him. 'Perhaps we are on the same wavelength after all.' Rather than emerging light and teasing, though, an edge of bitterness laced her words, making her wince. 'But you know... I need to get home in one piece, so it's time to switch to the soft stuff.'

His nostrils flared fractionally. Harry really did have the most classically handsome nose to go with that classically handsome face. He had the kind of face that a girl could enjoy staring at for a very, *very* long time.

'Are you driving?'

The question was carefully asked, but she sensed the disapproval behind it. 'Oh, Harry, that wavelength thing just took a bit of a battering. Of course I'm not driving. I'm always far too tempted at these things to have one glass too many. Also, driving from the southwest of the city to the northeast on a Friday afternoon in peak-hour traffic is not my idea of fun. It was quicker to take the train and taxi it from the station.'

'Sorry, I should've realised.'

There was absolutely no reason he should've realised anything. Despite what he said, he didn't know her from Adam...or Eve.

'Oh!' She straightened. 'Were you hoping for a lift home?'

'Of course not.'

He said it too quickly and then she saw what this was and her chest clenched. 'You've been co-opted into Ella duty, haven't you?'

His grimace gave him away. For God's sake, she didn't need babysitting!

'I promised your dad I'd see you safely home.'

'I'm a grown woman.'

'I don't feel good about it either, but…'

She raised an eyebrow.

'I had the distinct impression it was either promise that, or they'd…'

'Babysit me?'

'Shepherd you back to the family home for the night. I thought maybe this was the lesser of two evils.'

He had a point.

One deliciously broad shoulder lifted. 'If it bugs you that much, I won't, though.'

She straightened. 'You mean that?'

'I'd hate not keeping my word to your dad, but I'm not into forcing my company onto women who don't want it.'

She believed him. Harry Gillespie might have the face—and body, don't forget the body—of a God, but he didn't have an ego that went with it.

'That said, I'd like to see you home, Ella. But not on the train. Let me spring for a taxi. Everyone knows I'm loaded, and what's the point in being wealthy if you can't make things comfortable for yourself and your friends?'

Were they friends? She took a deliberate sip of her cola, before setting her glass down. 'I won't be inviting you inside once we get there.'

'Even if you did,' he said gently, 'I'd refuse your very kind invitation.'

His words shouldn't sting. They'd been uttered far more graciously than hers. It made no sense. The lack of sense, however, didn't temper the sting.

'I do have an ulterior motive, though. I want the skinny on everything and everyone. So you might as well ride in comfort while I pump you for information.'

She laughed, but she sensed he wasn't joking.

'And it means we can both have that one last drink we're

dying for rather than this—' he flicked a finger at his glass '—lolly water.'

Did he think another drink would get her rolling drunk? She hadn't drunk anywhere near as much as everyone thought she had. This would be her third glass of wine for the entire evening. Oh, different family members had poured many more for her, but she'd left those glasses in various out of the way places and had sipped water instead.

His lips twitched. 'I'm not trying to get you drunk so I can take advantage of you.'

Her face suddenly burned. 'I never thought any such thing.'

'Liar.' But he grinned as he said it.

'Well, not in the way you think,' she admitted. 'I meant in the "alcohol is a truth serum" kind of way. Another glass of wine isn't going to get me drunk. It'll put me over the limit for driving, it'll give me a pleasant buzz, but it won't have me throwing caution to the winds, dancing on the tables, and divulging all of my deep dark secrets…or anyone else's.'

'I don't want secrets.' He frowned. 'At least I don't think I do.'

'What do you want, then?'

'I'll have another of those,' he said to the barman, pointing to the tap of craft beer she'd ordered for him earlier, and then raised an eyebrow at her. 'Sémillon?'

Whether it was wise or not, she nodded.

She didn't know if she ought to be on her guard around Harry or to trust her instincts and take him at face value. One thing was in his favour—he was Martin's best friend. While Martin might not be able to look her in the eye at the moment, he was still a good guy. Her dad trusted him enough to ask him to see her home. The family were all driving her mad at the moment, but if anything about Harry had rung alarm bells for them, they'd all be sitting here playing guard dog.

She raised her glass in salute and took a sip before saying, 'Grill away. What do you want to know?'

He gazed into his glass, lips pursed.

He had nice lips. They seemed to be forever on the verge of spilling laughter and—

She jolted back to earth. Swallowing, she spread her hands. 'You have to give me something to work with here, Harry.'

He turned more fully towards her. 'I don't think the two of us should tiptoe around each other. Agreed?'

Suited her just fine. She was tired of everyone walking on eggshells. 'Agreed, especially if we're to save this wedding.' He looked a little too serious, though, so she added, 'Besides, there's the wavelength thing to consider. If we're so attuned to each other, you'll know when I'm lying, right? So it'd be pointless.'

The thought made her frown. While she'd been turning the wavelength thing into a joke, making light of it, a ribbon of truth threaded beneath it. In some odd way, she did feel connected to Harry. It wasn't the most comfortable thought she'd had all evening.

She huffed out the smallest of laughs. It wasn't the most uncomfortable one either, though, so there was that.

He spread his arms. 'See? Friends at first sight.'

She made herself laugh, made that laugh sound as if she thought him ridiculous. But that didn't stop her heart from thump-thumping or prevent warmth from curling in the pit of her stomach.

'So no faffing about or beating around the bush,' he ordered. 'Our policy is to be upfront and honest. We've a lot of work to do.'

'Agreed.' They shook on it.

'So first of all, I want to know why you hate the thought of an all-expenses-paid week in a luxury resort in Malaysia.'

Ah.

He leaned in closer. She had no idea what aftershave he wore, but she caught hints of leather and smoke, amber and resin. She wondered if they sold that scent in candles. If they did she was buying ten of them first thing tomorrow.

'You hated the idea so much you weren't able to convince a single solitary person in the room otherwise, even though you said all the right things and made all the right noises.'

Guilt bit at her. 'Was it really that obvious? You sure that's not the wavelength thing talking?'

'Not the wavelength thing. *Very* obvious.'

She swore.

'What's the story?'

'It's not Malaysia. I've nothing whatsoever against Malaysia. The resort sounds fantastic. And even though I shouldn't take too much time off work at the moment...' Except she could now, couldn't she? If she was going to turn her back on it all and return to the family business.

A howl started up at the centre of her.

'Then what is it?'

His eyes didn't leave her face, and he asked the question so gently it took all her strength not to drop her head to the bar and weep. 'It's the week they've chosen.'

Susie and Martin's wedding would now take place in one month's time—on a gorgeous Malaysian beach—and the bride's and groom's families were paying for everyone present at the restaurant this evening to attend. In theory it sounded like dream-come-true stuff. In reality...

'A month is long enough for us to work our magic, if that's what you're worried about,' he assured her. 'We can turn this thing around and make it the funnest damn wedding that ever was.'

She didn't want to make it the funnest damn wedding ever. She wanted to rant and rail and tell them all she was sick to death of the way they were trying to control her. She wanted to throw the bridesmaid towel in and tell Susie to find someone else for the job.

She couldn't of course. That would be overreacting. She pulled in a breath to the count of six, released it again just as slowly. 'In one month's time, on that exact week, I'm supposed to be showcasing my business at a fashion expo. It was a major step in getting my name and brand out there. I've been working on this for more than six months.'

'You're a fashion designer?'

'Of sorts. This is an alternative fashion expo, showcasing sustainable garments and practices. Sustainable sewing is gaining mainstream traction and—' she shrugged '—it's something I feel passionate about. So while I do some designing and take the odd commission—' because people were prepared to pay an insane amount of money for what they considered a couture one-off item '—I'm building towards the launch of my own online sewing school.'

Except none of that mattered now if she planned to return to the family business, did it?

He leaned in closer as if utterly intrigued. 'So you're a seamstress, fashion designer, sewing teacher and environmental crusader?'

She sent him a weak smile. 'Just call me Wonder Woman.'

'You made this?' He handed her off her stool and made her pirouette.

'Both skirt and blouse are thrift-store refashions.'

'They're amazing. You look amazing.'

There was a *but* behind his words. She slid back onto her stool. 'But?'

He grimaced.

'You were the one who said we needed to be upfront and honest,' she pointed out.

'It's just…the colours aren't very cheerful.'

She glanced down and blinked. He was right. She had a wardrobe full of colourful clothes, and yet she couldn't remember the last time she'd worn any of them. Had she been channelling her gloom and resentment into her clothing choices? Because the family was making her feel *less* at the moment? Less capable. Less than she was. Less *everything*.

'Okay, observation noted and taken on board.' That was definitely something she could work on.

'You're not offended?'

'Nope.' She sipped her wine.

'I didn't mean I don't like the outfit. It's fabulous. You look great in it.'

'Relax, Harry, I'm not offended.' She gestured at her outfit. 'And as you can see, I'm good at what I do.' Her lips twisted. 'I just need to get the word out there.'

'Does Susie know about the fashion expo? Because—'

'She knows.'

She hadn't challenged Susie about it tonight because… She swallowed. Because she hadn't been honest with Susie in recent times, and if she started now it might lead to questions. An ugly ball of darkness twisted in her stomach. Questions she didn't want to answer.

Still, how could Susie do this to her? It was all she could do to stop her hands from clenching. It'd serve her right if Ella told her to find a new bridesmaid. The next moment, though, her shoulders slumped. She didn't mean it. If she did that it'd break Susie's heart, and while Ella might be angry enough to scream she wouldn't hurt Susie for the world. She knew the family would've railroaded her en masse to choose this particular date for the wedding. Susie wouldn't have been able to withstand them.

Dark blond brows lowered over throbbing brown eyes. Ella shrugged. 'They all know.'

His frown deepened. 'What am I missing? If everyone knows about the expo, knows how important it is to you, then why…?'

'Because they don't support what I'm doing. They don't believe me when I tell them that running my own online sewing school is the dream of my heart and what I want to do with my life. They think it's a reckless decision I've made in response to James's death.'

'But it's not.'

It wasn't a question but a statement. It felt like a recognition—that he saw what it meant to her and implicitly trusted in that. 'The problem is, I hadn't told anyone about it before James died.'

He blinked. 'Not even James?'

'Oh, no, James knew.' They'd been fighting about it. He'd hated the idea as much as everyone else appeared to. Her heart squeezed in her chest. The knowledge that his final days would've been happier if she'd never raised the topic with him could still make her wake up in a cold sweat in the middle of the night.

'So—' he tapped a finger against his half-empty glass '—it feels as if it's come out of the blue for them.'

'More like a bomb that's exploded.'

His frown deepened. It took an effort not to reach up and smooth out the lines on his forehead.

And maybe she ought to stop drinking right about now.

'What were you doing prior to being a seamstress extraordinaire? What do they think could possibly top that?'

On second thoughts… She gulped her Sémillon. 'I was working in the family business—business consultancy and management.'

His jaw dropped. And then he swore. 'Ella, you're in a right pickle, aren't you? Because they're not going to think anything can top that.'

Bingo. 'A rock and a hard place,' she agreed.

They sipped their drinks and were silent for a bit. 'This is deliberate sabotage against your business.'

'That's not how they'd phrase it. They'd say they were saving me from myself.'

'It's crossing a line and it's not fair.'

'Don't I know it. And if I'm not careful I'm going to explode soon, Harry.' She'd say things she shouldn't. She'd say things she'd regret. She'd say things she could never take back, and they'd been hurt enough. 'I don't want that to happen. I know they're hurting—that this is all tied up in their grief for James.' She stared down at her hands. 'I've started to think I should just keep the peace and return to the family business.'

'You can't do that!'

It was nice of him to sound so outraged on her behalf, but—

'Ella, you *can't* do that.' He rested a warm hand on her forearm and squeezed gently until she met his gaze. 'You'll regret it forever. Worse, you'll resent them for it. It might look like a short-term quick fix, but in the long run…' He shook his head. 'Don't do this to yourself.'

Your dreams are just as important as everyone else's.

Maybe they were. Maybe they weren't. But, God, she was *so tired.*

'I honestly think we can turn things around and have everyone enjoying the upcoming celebrations. I think we can make this a wedding that will be remembered for all the right reasons.'

She stared. 'You're not just saying that?'

He pressed a hand to his heart. 'I believe we can do it.'

His expression was all fierce focus, and beneath it she saw the determination that had won him several world championships.

He leant down until they were eye to eye. 'I know you're feeling overwhelmed, you've had to deal with all of this on your own for far too long, but you have help now.'

She had help... Some unknown weight lifted off her shoulders. 'I could kiss you for saying that. Except, you know, you're off kissing. And so am I.' It seemed prudent to add that last bit.

He grinned. 'See? You're already entering into the spirit.'

She was?

'We just need to find a way, or ways, to stop them worrying about you. Once we show them it's okay to laugh around you again, not only will we be able to rescue the wedding, but we might even prove to them that you're in charge of your own destiny—that your sewing school is an excellent plan.'

Her heart thumped all the way up into her throat. 'I want to believe that so badly.' She wanted to believe her family could be happy again. She wanted to believe that she didn't have to sacrifice her dream.

'Then believe it. And don't make any drastic decisions about your business until after the wedding. Deal?'

A month? It didn't seem like too much to ask. If, at the end of that time, the family were still unhappy with her choices... She swallowed. Well, she could give her dream up then. In the meantime she could hold it close. She nodded. 'Deal.'

Damn! No wonder Ella's discontent at Martin and Susie's wedding plans had been so transparent. Her entire family as well as Susie's—and it appeared they were pretty much one and the same—were conspiring against her. In her shoes he'd—

What? an inner voice mocked. *Rebel?*

He rolled his shoulders. Maybe not, but he'd be chafing in the same way Ella chafed, while trying to be as careful with everyone's feelings as she was trying to be.

He scratched both hands back through his hair. She'd had a lot to deal with over the last eighteen months. She deserved a break.

And Martin and Susie deserved a great wedding.

He bumped shoulders with her. 'Before we start brainstorming ways to cheer everyone up, there's an issue we need to clear up first.'

She raised one finely shaped eyebrow. *Nice* eyebrow. Nice eyes—*so* blue. Actually, she had a nice face. *Really* nice and—

Focus, Harrison.

He shook himself. 'Right, why not go to the expo instead of attending the wedding?'

She grabbed hold of the bar as if she were in danger of falling, her mouth opening and closing. 'Harry, Susie is practically my *sister*. I can't *not* go to her wedding. That'd be—' She broke off and shook her head. 'That's not even remotely an option.'

'Sorry, I just thought…' He grimaced. 'I was speaking with my practical business hat on. My family aren't like yours and Susie's.' *Obviously.* He could feel his lips twist, even though he tried to stop them. 'In my family, business always comes first.'

Blue eyes frowned into his. 'I know I'm losing patience with them and feeling resentful. But family comes first Harry. *Always.*'

How different would his family have been if—?

Don't even go there.

He slapped a hand to the bar. 'Okay, then we need to work out how to get your business represented at that expo. You must have an employee you trust enough to act as your representative.'

Amusement turned her eyes even bluer. 'Oh, listen to you, world champion skier and super-successful business-man.'

'Former world champion,' he corrected.

'No wonder you've been so successful with a won't-say-die attitude like that.'

He stared. And then he swallowed. She'd focussed on his success, rather than his wealth. That was...

'What?'

'Nothing. I just...' He trailed off with a shrug.

'You're a problem solver. I get that. But I'm a one-woman band, Harry. I don't have any employees, trusted or other-wise. Sew Sensational currently comprises...me.'

He felt the size of a pea. Not everyone had the money he had. What an entitled jerk she must think him.

'I only struck out on my own six months ago. Until I start turning a decent profit, I'm going to remain a one-woman band.'

He read between the lines. James had died eighteen months ago. She'd given herself over to the family busi-ness for the twelve months following his death.

Because she'd been too grief-stricken to think straight?

Or because she hadn't wanted to create too much up-heaval in her family's life all at once?

She'd said the family business was business consulting and management. 'You have a business degree?'

She nodded.

'It's not like you've gone into this venture of yours blind or with blinkers on, then.'

'Absolutely not.' She twirled her glass around slowly, staring at the golden liquid inside. 'I'm fully versed in the traps that lie in wait for the unwary. I've spent over a year building a platform on YouTube, establishing a clientele, and running sewing classes at the local community college. I have a stall at the local monthly markets. I've focussed hard on building a solid base, and I make enough money to pay the bills from the activities I now engage in. The expo was supposed to launch the second phase of operations. While it's only a small boutique-style event, it's been garnering interest in all of the right circles. To have my sewing school's name linked to it, get it endorsed by the right people…'

She trailed off, her shoulders drooping. He was shocked at how much he wanted to make her smile again.

'If it went well, it was going to provide me with the right credentials to launch the school with the appropriate fanfare.'

And he could see that her vision for the sewing school was the passion that powered all the rest.

He clapped his hands. 'Right, then. What we need to do is find you someone who can represent you at the expo and—'

'No.'

No? What did she mean, *no*?

'This is my problem, Harry, not yours. I don't want you offering to invest in my business or to lend me a trusted employee or three of your own or…anything. It's my company and if I'm going to keep going I need to find my own solutions.'

He really wanted to help. But her need to feel in control of at least one aspect of her life was far more important than anything he might want. Very reluctantly he raised his hands. 'Okay, but I hope you'll let me know if there's anything I can do.'

She frowned, as if his sincerity surprised her.

'Look, I'm considered a successful businessman.'

She huffed out a laugh. 'You're stating the obvious now.'

'But I didn't start from nothing. Not like you. I inherited a trust fund and had backers.'

His company dealt in adventure ski holidays. They helicoptered their clientele to some of the most remote ski fields in the world, where they stayed in chateaus whose luxury was unsurpassed. He'd spared no expense on any of it. The very rich were prepared to spend an exorbitant amount of money for the very best. Especially when it was endorsed by a former alpine ski champion.

Her soft laugh warmed him from the inside out. 'Nobody handed you those world titles on a silver platter. You worked hard for them all on your own.'

'That's not exactly true. I had a team surrounding me—coaches, managers, physios. Plus,' he added when she opened her mouth to argue, 'my parents were wealthy enough to indulge the ski lessons and clinics I wanted. I was fortunate.'

'And unnecessarily humble.'

She reached out and clasped his forearm. 'I appreciate the offer, I really do.' She dropped her hand again almost immediately, but her touch sent a flicker of heat licking along his veins. His pulse pounded and his heart thudded. The curve of her lips when she—

No! He would *not* develop an inconvenient attraction to this woman. His stomach churned. She was exactly the kind of woman he avoided. Women like Ella got hurt by men like him. And it was clear she'd been through enough in the last eighteen months.

Ella stared into her nearly empty glass with pursed lips,

completely oblivious to his turmoil. Which was good. Perfect, in fact. He didn't want her aware.

He just needed to master the wilful compulsion that now gripped him to shake her out of her complacency and force her to see him as a man. Talk about self-destructive impulses! He ground his back molars together, reminded himself of all the reasons it was important to win the confidence of the trustees of the Bright Directions charity, reminded himself that he wasn't his father!

Seizing his beer, he drained it before slamming it back to the bar. 'Ready to hit the road?'

She blinked. 'I…yeah, sure.'

If his abruptness startled her, she was far too polite to say so.

But as the taxi wove its way from the harbour towards the address she'd given the driver, the silence in the cab grew oppressive.

'Look, Harry, I'm sorry if I offended you.'

The air was scented with peaches—probably her shampoo or body wash—and it was oddly alluring. He tried to not breathe in too deeply. 'Offended me?'

'By not accepting your offer of help.'

'I'm not offended!'

Those finely shaped brows rose. He ignored the desire to reach out and trace a finger across one delicate arc. 'Two things. The first is that I flew into Australia yesterday from Switzerland and jet lag has started to kick in. So my responses are probably off kilter.' He sure as hell felt off kilter.

'Uh-huh.' She didn't sound convinced.

'And two, I'm outraged on your behalf at this stunt The Family have pulled on you.'

Her lips twitched. 'The family capitalised?'

'If the shoe fits,' he murmured.

She pushed a stray curl back behind her ear. 'Okay, so missing the expo is a setback, but if I'm going to forge ahead with Sew Sensational…'

She *had* to. She couldn't give up her dream.

One slim shoulder lifted. 'Then I can't let things like this derail me. So please, Harry, forget about the expo. At the moment we have bigger fish to fry. We need to focus on the wedding.'

'The fish we have to fry are pretty big,' he agreed. The task before them suddenly felt gargantuan. And the stakes were high. But if they could pull this off, then maybe Ella wouldn't abandon her dream. He couldn't explain why it mattered so much. Only that it did.

He stifled a yawn and she smiled. For one heart-jerking moment he thought she meant to pat his arm, but she lowered her hand back to her lap before it had a chance to reach him. He couldn't believe how much he wanted to drag her into his arms and kiss her. He clenched his hands. He really needed a good night's sleep.

'However, we don't have to come up with a plan right now,' she said. 'Why don't you rest for a while—get some shut-eye while you can?'

There wasn't a hope in hell he'd get a moment's sleep sitting this close to her, but he could pretend. And pretending was definitely the wisest course of action at the moment. 'Promise you'll wake me when we get to your place?'

'I promise.'

He closed his eyes and although he'd thought he'd continue to prickle and burn, her undemanding presence and the scent of peaches were oddly soothing. He didn't fall asleep, but to simply be quiet and have a chance to allow his body to adjust to the time zone felt like a gift.

He immediately opened his eyes, though, when the taxi stopped. He didn't want her shaking him awake. He didn't want her touching him at all. Not now he'd lulled the slathering beast inside him into a semblance of slumber.

She gestured out of the window. 'This is me.'

He stared and then he straightened. 'You live in a warehouse?' That was cool. Seriously cool.

She blinked, at whatever she saw in his face. And then smiled. Oh, God. *Don't focus on those lips.* 'These are my business premises. I live in the flat above. I know it's not particularly grand, but—' she frowned, turning back to stare at it '—it's not just a glorified garage either.'

He stiffened. 'Who called it that? I'll bop them on the nose.'

She raised one of those ridiculously beautiful eyebrows and he let out a slow breath. Her family. That was who. The people who should be supporting her dreams. Didn't she have anyone to share the excitement of all this with?

'These digs are cool, Ella. Seriously cool. I'd love to see inside.' He jerked back. 'But not tonight! That's not what I meant.' He didn't want her thinking he was a sleaze. 'I just meant in daylight hours when I could appreciate it properly and—'

He broke off with a groan, but she just laughed. 'Relax, I know what you meant.' She bit her lip. 'If you're serious…'

'I'm serious.' He was definitely serious.

'Do you have a busy weekend ahead of you?'

'Nope.'

'Then why don't you come to lunch on Sunday? Middayish? And I'll give you the grand tour. And maybe we can throw around a few ideas for how to pep everyone up and give Susie and Martin the wedding of the year.'

'I'll bring a bottle of wine and my imagination.'

'Perfect. It's a date.' She'd started to turn away to open her door, but froze before glancing back over her shoulder.

'I didn't mean *date* date. It was just a turn of phrase, a figure of speech, not—'

'Relax, Ella, I know what you meant.' He got the message loud and clear.

'No, no, stay there,' she said when he made to get out of the taxi to walk her to her door. 'Jet lag, remember. There's a sensor light that'll come on. Just wait until I get inside and you'll have performed your duty admirably.'

He couldn't kiss her. This wasn't a date. 'Goodnight, Ella.'

'Night, Harry, sleep tight.'

And then she was gone, but heat continued to thread its way through his veins with an insidious viciousness that made him scowl as the taxi turned around and took him back towards the city centre.

CHAPTER THREE

Ella heard a car draw up outside, probably heralding Harry's arrival, but she forced herself to remain at her sewing machine, rather than rushing to the door to check. She'd already spent far too long today—and yesterday—thinking about Martin's best man.

And the last thing she needed was to start obsessing over some guy. Lord, talk about a glutton for punishment!

Besides, it'd only be a displacement activity and she couldn't afford one of those. Not if she planned to cling to her sewing-school dream. Harry's words on Friday night had given her hope. They'd reinvigorated the fire in her belly.

To drive her point home, she concentrated extra hard on sewing her seam utterly, perfectly and divinely straight. When she was done, and only after she'd snipped the thread, did she answer the prickling at the back of her neck and turn her head.

Harry stood in the open doorway, and the breath hitched in the back of her throat. The sunlight pouring in behind him left his face in shadow, but the lean, broad height of him was backlit, showcasing the muscular power of a body in its physical prime.

Dear God. She'd known on some level on Friday night that he was fit and athletic—*hello, former world cham-*

pion—but she'd been too dazzled by his grin and easy manner—and the fact he hadn't known James—to pay attention to much else.

She had to swallow before she could speak. 'Harry, it's nice to see you again. Come on in.'

When he strode into the large room, the overhead lighting revealed that chiselled jaw, sculpted cheekbones and… dear God, *that grin*…and she immediately forgave herself for not noticing anything else on Friday night. She'd thought perhaps she'd exaggerated his, uh…assets because she'd been so desperate for a little respite from her family.

But, no, the man was a hundred and ten per cent pure male perfection.

'You're working?'

His words snapped her back. 'I'm always tinkering.' She leapt up to take the bottle of wine he carried. 'The thing about my work is that it never feels like work.' She glanced at the bottle's label, and something warm slid beneath her guard. He'd brought a Sémillon. He'd remembered what she liked to drink?

A hot guy was a temptation she could resist. But a hot, *considerate* guy…?

Stop it. Obviously she had every intention of resisting one of those too, but… It struck her then that she liked Harry. As a person. He was a good guy.

'Is there something wrong with the wine?'

She started. 'No! It's great. I…you remembered what I was drinking the other night.'

He looked suddenly discomfited, as if worried she'd read too much into it.

Oh, for heaven's sake, Ella, it's just a bottle of wine.

'It's very thoughtful of you, and puts us on a par, because I remembered you drank beer and I got some in specially,' she tossed over her shoulder as she moved towards the kitchen.

He immediately relaxed. 'See? I keep telling you we're on the same wavelength.'

The kitchen was situated to one side of the main doors, separated from the rest of the room by a large counter with glass sliders. There wasn't enough room in the kitchen for a table but she'd set a table on the workshop side of the counter the very first day she'd moved in.

She stowed the wine in the fridge. Harry trailed along behind her. 'Your kitchen and bathroom are downstairs?'

'The upstairs flat has its own kitchen and bathroom, but I find myself eating down here more often than not.'

'Because you're working so much?'

There was no censure in his voice, as there would be in her mother's if she'd asked the same question. 'Well, it's true that you can whip up a seam or two while something's simmering on the stovetop or heating in the oven, but more often than not in the evenings I just like to play around with an idea or two and...fiddle for the hell of it.'

His lips twitched. 'Which you don't consider work.'

Her lips twitched too. 'Of course not! It's play. And as there's far more room down here than upstairs...'

'It's a no-brainer.'

But he raised an eyebrow and she found herself laughing. 'Okay. If you want the pure, unadulterated truth—' she gestured at her workshop '—I know it's not exactly what one would call pretty, but...' She tried to put the feeling into words. 'It makes my heart sing. It makes me ridiculously happy to look at it and realise it's mine—my own little kingdom. So I eat down here more often than not because in those brief moments of downtime I get to relish that feeling.'

She hadn't tried to articulate that sentiment to anyone

before. It surprised her how easily she'd been able to express it to Harry now. Brown eyes the colour of a deep smoky topaz turned to her, an arrested expression in their depths, and an itch started up between her collarbones. She shrugged—a stilted movement that made her feel suddenly graceless. 'I don't know. Maybe that sounds a little pathetic and sad, but—'

'*No!* Hell, Ella, you're living your dream, making that dream a reality. You should be milking every drop of joy from it that you can. Some people go through their whole lives never feeling this way. It's not sad and it's not pathetic. It's glorious and empowering. And it's all yours.'

Her eyes prickled and she had to blink hard. She should've known he'd understand. The man was a former world champion. He'd obviously had a dream once too. Hers seemed so much smaller in comparison.

'Please tell me you're not giving this up without a fight.'

Her dream might not be huge and lofty, but it didn't make it any less worthy. She pushed her shoulders back. 'I'll fight. I know the family can't see it, but I'd be miserable if I had to go back to business consultancy. If I can make a success of my online sewing school…' Her heart pounded. 'Eventually they'll start to worry less.' Wouldn't they?

'Especially once they realise how happy you are.'

Therein lay the rub. It was hard to be happy around them when it felt as if they were continually waiting for her to crash and burn.

A knock sounded on the door. 'Harrison? Hello?'

Harry shot out of the kitchen. 'Lily? What's up?'

'You're lucky I love you. You dropped your phone in the car. I jumped out of my skin when it rang. I thought you'd probably need it.'

The woman's words made Ella blink.

'And now I'm going to be late so—'

She broke off when she saw Ella.

He glanced at Ella and gestured. 'This is my little sister, Lily.'

Sister? She refused to acknowledge the relief rippling through her. It was entirely unworthy of her.

'And, Lil, this is—'

'Sew Sensational's Ella! *Oh, my God!*' She leapt forward to pump Ella's hand. 'I subscribe to your YouTube channel. I think you're amazing.'

Harry's brow pleated. 'You mentioned you had a YouTube channel.'

Ella tried to contain a grin. She had a fan? A real bona fide fan?'

Lily glanced around at the workshop, hands clasped beneath her chin. 'And this is where the magic happens?'

Magic? Oh, had she ever had a nicer compliment? 'It is. Do you sew, Lily?'

A shadow fell across the other woman's face. 'No, but…'

She heard that 'but' a lot—*but* I want to…*but* I wish I could…*but* I don't know where to start. There were endless variations.

'God, this room! It…'

'It what?' Harry demanded, a frown lurking in his eyes.

Lily swung back. 'It reminds me of my mother.'

Harry froze.

'She had a sewing room.' She sent Ella a smile. 'Obviously not on this scale. She was going to teach me, but…'

She heard a lot of those 'buts' too. And everyone knew how successful Harry's mother was. Claudia King was CEO of the mining dynasty King Holdings. Had she become too busy to teach her daughter to sew?'

'Do you run sewing classes? Please say yes.'

Ella did her best to project a professional image, but inside a huge smile stretched through her. 'I'm in the process of setting up an online sewing school. I'm hoping to take it live in the next few months.'

'Oh, that's perfect.' Lily clapped her hands and bounced. 'Absolutely perfect.' Her gaze continued to rove hungrily around the room, and her eyes widened when they landed on Susie's wedding dress on the mannequin. She pointed. 'That's breathtaking.'

'It's for a beach wedding so it's a little less formal than a lot of wedding gowns. For my friend Susie…' She gestured at Harry and herself. 'The wedding we're best man and bridesmaid for.'

Lily reached across and gripped Ella's hand. 'You and I really need to talk.'

She blinked. 'I… Okay.'

'Why?' Harry barked, staring from Lily to the wedding dress and back again. He pointed. 'You are not…'

It sounded like an order rather than a question, but Lily merely rolled her eyes and ignored him. 'Would you consider giving one-on-one lessons?' she asked Ella.

'I…' She hadn't thought about it.

Lily's phone pinged and she grimaced. 'I have to go, but—' She transferred her grip to Harry's arm. 'You have to bring Ella to dinner some time soon. Promise?'

He glanced at Ella and raised an eyebrow. She nodded. Dinner with a fan? Yes, please! That could be the boost her flagging spirits needed.

'Okay, okay, I'll bring her to dinner. Now stop manhandling her, Lil, and get out of here. And drive safe!'

'It was so nice to meet you,' she said with a wave at Ella. 'Wait until I tell Viggo.'

'Her boyfriend,' Harry murmured as Lily shot out of the door.

Then he turned to her more fully. 'What magic have you woven to captivate my little sister so completely?'

She shrugged. 'I...'

He frowned. 'What do you think she meant?' He gestured towards Susie's wedding dress.

'Are she and Viggo serious?'

'No!'

He glared, and she did what she could to choke back a laugh.

His glare became a scowl. 'What?'

'You're hilarious, you know that? All overprotective, bristling big brother,' she teased.

He grimaced but humour lightened his eyes. 'Old habits.' And then he frowned. 'I had no idea she wanted to sew.'

'Your mother never had the time to teach her?'

He gazed at her blankly for a moment, and then his face cleared. 'She was talking about her mother, not mine. Lily and I aren't really siblings, we're first cousins. Her parents died in a car accident when she was six and she came to live with us. Her father and my mother were siblings. I've always told her, though, that she's my little sister.'

Oh, that was nice. See? He really was a good guy.

'Tell me about your YouTube channel.'

'It's called Sew Sensational—spelled S-E-W—and I film sewing tips and tricks, give mini tutorials.'

He rubbed a hand across his jaw. 'You're obviously good. Lil's a damn fine judge of these things.'

She feigned surprise. 'You doubted it?'

That made him laugh. 'Not for a moment.' He glanced at Susie's wedding dress. 'You're making Susie's dress?'

'Susie's and mine. And the mums' outfits as well.'

He opened his mouth, closed it and then shook himself. 'Let me get this straight. Your family don't believe in your sewing business, yet they still want you to make their outfits for the wedding? That doesn't make sense.'

'They know I'm a good seamstress. They just don't think

there's any money to be made in running an online sewing school,' she corrected. 'They consider sewing a hobby, not a business opportunity. They think it safer and smarter of me to remain in the family business.'

He was silent for a moment, but when he glanced up his gaze had sharpened. 'They want to keep you close because James is no longer here.'

That old heaviness descended on her. 'Do you think it's ungrateful of me to—?'

'No! What they're doing is unfair and selfish. Understandable because of their grief,' he added before she could defend them. 'But it'd be a grave mistake to submit to it, Ella.'

His words helped lift some of her heaviness.

He shook himself and grinned, and suddenly there was no heaviness at all. 'Is lunch in danger of spoiling—it smells great, by the way—or do you have the time to give me the grand tour first?'

She gestured at her workshop. 'Well…this is it.'

'Nonsense. I want you to show me everything from go to whoa.'

She tried to slow the swirling excitement that had taken up residence in the pit of her stomach. Was he serious? Was he interested or just humouring her?

'Take me through the process if you were making a… I don't know—a dress.'

And in that moment she didn't care if he was truly interested or not. It was just exciting to share all of this with someone willing to listen. Nobody had shown this level of interest in what she was trying to do. *No one.*

She had a feeling it could become addictive.

Well, don't let it go to your head. And don't go overboard.

Two walls of the workshop were set up with her sewing

machines and overlockers, while a series of built-in cupboards made up the third. In the centre of the room was her cutting table. She started by showing him her fabric stash, where he fingered some of the material and chuckled at some of her prints—particularly the ones with a sewing theme. When they moved to her drafting and cutting table, he inspected her various rulers and gauges, before she took him across to her sewing machines—six in total—and her two overlockers.

He gestured at the ironing board she had set up, a question in his eyes.

'It's good practice to press as you go.' And then she opened the doors beneath the drafting table.

He let out a breath. 'You have thread in every shade known to man. They look amazing. It makes you want to reach out and touch them.'

She felt the same way. Walking around, she opened a drawer on the other side. He followed to gaze at her neatly ordered rows of ribbons, buttons, lace trims, zippers, bias binding and cording. 'I don't even know what most of those things are called.'

'Notions.'

He opened the drawer nearest and pulled out an object, lifted it towards her in question.

'That's a tailor's ham. It helps press darts and contoured fabric patterns.'

'I don't even know what half of the words you're using mean. It's like a foreign language.'

And she could see that he wanted to understand it. That he liked to know how things worked.

'I do, however, know what these are.' He picked up her favourite pair of fabric shears. He hefted them from one hand to the other. 'They're heavy. You use these?'

'Every day. And don't even think about it,' she added

when he went to cut through a piece of nearby scrap pattern paper. 'Nothing touches those hallowed blades except fabric.' She plucked a piece of cotton sateen from her offcuts bin and tossed it to him.

He cut along the sateen's length and a strange expression lit his face. 'God, that feels satisfying.'

She knew exactly what he meant.

'Oh, my God.' He set the shears down and raced across to the far corner. 'Now, this looks like fun.'

She laughed and stroked a finger across the casing of the sewing machine, its innards spread across the table. 'I service my own machines.'

His head whipped around. 'No way.' He stared at the assorted pieces. 'No wonder you've impressed Lil so much. You can do it all.'

He straightened, stuck his hands in his back pockets. 'You wouldn't let me help you put this back together by any chance, would you?'

She stifled a smile.

'It's just…this is an Aladdin's cave. I loved building stuff when I was a kid. Pulling a sewing machine apart, giving it a grease and oil change, and putting it back together could be fun.'

She stared at him for a moment. 'You can't help on this one because it requires a rather complicated repair and I'm waiting on a part, but…'

He leaned towards her. 'Yes?'

'Two of my machines are due for a service, so, if you're serious, after lunch we can take a machine each and I'll walk you through it.'

'You just became my new favourite person!'

She laughed, and went to tell him he was a cheap date, but choked the words back. This wasn't a date.

'And I want to know what you were working on when I arrived. You looked totally engrossed.'

Yeah, totally engrossed in trying not to look totally engrossed with him. But that reminded her...

'Not only am I making Susie's wedding dress, but I'm making the waistcoats for the groom and best man.'

'Martin and me?'

'I've Martin's measurements already, but do you mind if I grab yours now?' She seized her tape measure and a nearby pad and pencil. 'It should only take a sec.'

'Sure.'

'I was making a *toile*—a mock-up—of Martin's waistcoat when you arrived. I'll have him to try it on, so I can make any final adjustments to it before making the real thing.'

'Makes sense.'

She moved behind him and stretched the tape measure from shoulder to shoulder. A spasm convulsed through her the instant she touched him. The heat of him beat at her through his long-sleeved tee and crept beneath her skin. Heat and need and want flooded every atom of her body... And she didn't know what to do with any of it.

The moment Ella's fingers brushed his shoulders, air hissed from Harry's lungs. It was the lightest of touches, but, light or not, Ella's touch seared a path to his very bones and heat began to bubble in his veins. He gritted his teeth and silently started to recite the seven times table. The woman was simply doing her job, for God's sake.

Seven times four is twenty-eight. Seven times five is—

Her fingers moved from measuring the breadth of his shoulders to measuring shoulder to waist. Everything in between started to prickle and itch, while other parts—lower and higher—like his groin and his jaw, clenched.

He could hear the scratch of her pencil as she jotted the measurements down.

She moved in front of him, not meeting his eye.

Why would she meet your eye? She's not measuring your eyes. She's a professional. You're not a body to her but a series of measurements.

That last thought bolstered neither his strength nor his mood.

'Arms out,' she instructed, demonstrating.

He did as she asked, gritted his teeth as she measured him from armpit to waist. It drew her in closer and the scent of peaches rose up all around him. In that moment he'd give anything to sink his teeth into a sun-warmed peach. It wasn't the season for them, but maybe he could—

Stop! Fixating on peaches wasn't helping.

Seven times six is forty-two. Seven times seven—

She slipped the tape measure around his chest and… His nipples hardened. He bit back a groan. It was July. Winter in the southern hemisphere. Cold. The cold made nipples pebble. No big deal.

But the sun shone brightly outside and it was a mild nineteen degrees, not a frigid minus five on some alpine ski slope.

She moved away and he let out a breath, lowered his arms. *Seven times seven is forty-nine. Seven times eight is—*

'Nearly done…'

He closed his eyes and told himself to keep breathing when she slipped the tape measure around his waist. Her fingers brushed the top of his belt buckle and his eyes flew open…to stare into eyes so blue they transported him to Lake Geneva on a crystal summer's day. A pulse thundered in her throat and her lips parted as if to drag air into lungs that didn't want to work.

Ella might be a professional, but she clearly wasn't as

immune as he'd thought. The realisation made him want to swear. The only thing standing between him sweeping her off her feet and into bed was Ella's resolution! If she caved…

No. Operation New Leaf. He *could* resist temptation. He clenched his hands to fists. He *would* resist temptation.

It didn't stop him from wanting to cup her face and exploring that sweet rosebud of a mouth with a slow thoroughness until he'd memorised every millimetre of its enticing lushness.

As if she could read the intent on his face, she swayed towards him. They hovered between breaths, eyes locked…

Then she blinked.

And snapped away.

And the tension holding him tight slackened, and he sagged.

She slipped the tape measure around his hips and he immediately straightened again. 'Fifty-six!' He practically shouted it out.

But she'd already moved away before his groin could thoroughly disgrace him and embarrass them both.

'Fifty-six?' she said, her back to him as she jotted the measurement down.

He rolled his shoulders, stretched his neck to the left and then the right. 'Just a sum I was doing. I was, uh…cooking the books this morning and left a few loose ends.'

'Want me to write it down for you so you don't forget?'

He couldn't look at her. He pulled his phone out with a shake of his head. 'I'll make a note and email it to myself.'

He did too.

The email read: Get a grip!!!

'I thought it might be a forty-two thing.' She turned with a smile that didn't reach her eyes. 'You know—the answer to the ultimate question of life, the universe and everything? From *The Hitchhiker's Guide to the Galaxy*? Douglas Adams?'

He gaped at her.

She stowed the jotted-down measurements in a drawer.

He picked up his jaw. '*The Hitchhiker's Guide to the Galaxy* is my favourite book.'

She swung back. 'Mine too.'

What were the odds? 'Right. First item on the "lunch-time topics of conversation" agenda is favourite sci-fi and fantasy books.'

And just like that she laughed and everything was fine again. 'Let's eat.'

He followed her to the table she'd laid with the prettiest linen cloth embroidered with purple flowers. 'You made this?'

'Repurposed. I found it in a thrift store. The original piece was four times as big as this, and pocked with various holes and stains. I salvaged this piece to make a small tablecloth.'

'Clever.'

She traced one of the purple flowers. She had small hands, but he knew from the equipment she'd just shown him how capable those hands must be. He could imagine…

No, he couldn't. He couldn't imagine anything.

'The embroidery is beautiful. It deserved a second life. Just because something is old and out of fashion or imperfect doesn't mean it should be thrown away.'

He had a feeling that could be a metaphor for life.

'Wine or beer?' she asked him.

'Wine.'

She handed him the bottle to open while she served up a winter vegetable and chorizo frittata that smelled heavenly, along with a green salad and crusty bread. His mouth watered as he gazed at it all.

They ate.

'Dear God, that was good,' he said half an hour later, pushing his plate away after polishing off a second slice of the frittata. 'You're a woman of many talents—a seamstress extraordinaire, a business guru *and* an excellent cook.'

She laughed, and he wanted to make her do it again. It seemed to lift some weight inside her. She'd had so much grief and sadness to deal with in the last year and a half. To now have to battle her family's disapproval of the direction in which she wanted to take her life… His chest clenched. It was too much.

'I'm a lazy cook,' she corrected. 'My MO is to make up a big batch of something and then freeze the leftovers to have for dinner for the rest of the week.'

He stiffened. He shouldn't have had that second slice of frittata. He should've filled up on bread and salad because they wouldn't keep whereas she could've eaten the frittata for—

Her laugh snapped him back. Laughter turned those blue eyes even brighter. 'You need to school your face a little better, Harry. You're too transparent.'

Nobody had accused him of that before.

'Don't feel guilty because you had two slices of the frittata.'

But it could've been another whole night's dinner for her.

'I'm glad you enjoyed it. And notice I said I was lazy, not that I'm penny pinching. It was nice to—'

She broke off with a frown. He stared at that frown and his gut clenched. Nice to *what*?

The furrow in her brow deepened and she shook her head. 'I just hadn't realised—'

She spoke as if to herself and her murmur raised all the fine hairs on his arms. 'Hadn't realised what?'

She started. 'Oh, nothing.'

He raised an eyebrow.

She grimaced. 'Fine! I hadn't realised how circumscribed my life had become.'

'What do you mean?' he said carefully, neutrally. 'Do you mean you've been too focussed on your work?' Or was she talking about the lack of romance in her life?

'I was talking about my social circle.'

The defences he'd started to stake into place wavered.

'The Hawthornes and the Mayberrys—my family and Susie's…'

He noted she said Susie's family, not James's.

'Well, we live in each other's pockets; we're each other's social circle. My mother and Susie's mum have been besties since kindergarten. A tradition James and I continued when we became besties from the cradle.'

Best friends who'd become lovers. He and Ella might share a similar sense of humour, love the same books, and have the same drive and ambition to reach their goals, but it was clear they had wildly different expectations where love was concerned.

'Our parents went into business together before we were born and…' she shrugged '…we consider each other's aunts, uncles, cousins and extended families our own.'

'I guess it's nice,' he offered. 'But I guess it means everyone is in each other's business too.'

One slim shoulder lifted. 'And it's not entirely true that I hadn't realised how limited my social circle had become. I just hadn't realised until today the kind of impact it's had on me. I mean, obviously I have friends outside the family, but most of them have moved away in recent years for work, so it's a weekend trip to visit them. At the moment, The Family—' she said it as if it were capitalised '—almost exclusively makes up my social circle.'

No wonder she felt so suffocated. No wonder she feared

she was going to explode. Her life wasn't just circumscribed. It had become too *small*.

She glanced up and forced a smile to her lips. Though he didn't know how he could tell it was forced.

'So today has been a rare treat. To enjoy a meal with someone who's not tied up in knots of grief, or treading far too carefully around me because I've lost my fiancé and they're worried they'll say the wrong thing. It's really nice to be around someone who didn't know James. I'm sorry if that makes me sound hard-hearted, but—'

'You don't sound hard-hearted.' His chest tightened. 'You've every right to enjoy a simple meal with a friend. And every right to enjoy setting up your own business. You shouldn't feel guilty for moving on.'

She glanced down at her hands. 'I know. It's what I tell myself in my more sensible moments.'

It had to be hard, though, when she was surrounded by a family of mourners who couldn't imagine a life for her that didn't involve James.

'It doesn't mean you loved James any less or miss him any less. But sacrificing your life and happiness to grief would be a sad homage to pay to a man who sounds like a pretty special kind of guy.'

She nodded. 'The funny thing is—'

The twist of lips told him it wasn't funny at all.

'The thing I most miss about James is our friendship. He really was my best friend.'

Most women would have a best friend to help them through the loss of a partner. She'd lost partner and best friend in one fell swoop.

'I need to start making some new friends. I've been so focussed on getting Sew Sensational off the ground that I keep putting off overtures of friendship from people in the sewing community—other teachers at the community college, stallholders at the markets, other vloggers. I've been telling myself I don't have time, but this—' she gestured at what was left of their lunch '—has made me think I need to make the time.'

In that moment he wanted to be her friend more than he could remember wanting anything. He wanted to be her new *best* friend. He opened his mouth—

Don't.

He snapped it shut again. He had to stop being impulsive. He had to tread carefully. He couldn't do anything that would ruin this wedding. He couldn't do anything that might hurt this woman. He couldn't give the press anything more to talk about.

So he made himself straighten and be sensible. 'I think that's wise. On a lot of levels.'

'Oh?'

God, that eyebrow could slay a man! 'We all need work colleagues. They're the people we bounce ideas off, who help us feel part of a community, whose feedback lets us know if we're on the right track.'

'When we have a wobbly day,' she said slowly, 'they're the ones who remind us of all the reasons we love what we love.'

She'd had no one to help her through the wobbly days. He couldn't even... 'I'd never have won a world championship without the support of my team—people who believed in me.' Some days he'd kept going simply for them. They'd all worked as hard as he had.

She stared as if his words were gold. He ordered himself not to let it go to his head. 'Also, if the family sees you making new friends, it'll show them you're moving on in positive ways.'

Behind the blue of her eyes her mind raced. 'And then

they'll worry about me less…might focus more on Susie and the wedding. And maybe…'

'And maybe it will help them move on too,' he finished for her.

He could tell from the expression in her eyes how much she wanted that for them, wanted to see them happy again.

'We don't do this haphazardly, Ella. We create an agenda.' She needed to broaden her world.

Two beats passed, before she gave a wary nod. 'Okay.'

'How's this for a start? Some time during this coming week drop into conversation with your mother that you had lunch or something with one of your fellow sewing teachers—and make sure you have that lunch. Maybe you can tell Susie you attended a gathering of fellow vloggers or…'

'A sew-along held by the local sewing guild,' she said, taking up where he left off. 'I've been a member forever, but I haven't attended an event in…' She trailed off. 'I should be making connections with anyone who might be interested in my sewing school.'

She sent him the smallest of smiles, but it shattered every single barricade he'd tried to put in place.

'Plus it'd be fun.'

And it was clear she'd not had enough of that in her life in recent times. When it came to fun, he was the master. He sent her a grin that made her blink. 'Speaking of fun… Can we go pull those sewing machines apart yet?'

CHAPTER FOUR

ELLA WALKED HARRY through the servicing of the sewing machines, and his genuine enjoyment further lightened the weight that had been pressing on her heart for eighteen long months.

She was beginning see the missteps she'd made. For a start, she shouldn't have given those twelve months after James's death to the family business. She should've confided her plans to the family *much* sooner. Maybe then they wouldn't have misinterpreted her growing restlessness as a sign of grief.

She'd then spent too much of her leisure time with them in an attempt to reassure them they weren't losing her. Harry was right. They needed to see her moving on and being happy rather than stressed and resentful. They needed to see her making friends and laughing more, settling into her new world. Once they could see her doing that, maybe they'd start to trust her.

'You know, it's not just me—'

She started at the same time as he said, 'You know what else I think you should do?'

They broke off at the same time. 'You first,' she said. Everything he'd suggested so far had been solid gold and she was curious to hear his next suggestion.

'I think you ought to start dating again.'

His words shocked her so much she leapt out of her chair and strode around the drafting table. 'No way.'

He folded his arms. 'Why not?'

'So many reasons.' She strode back and took her seat again, because pacing seemed like an overreaction. 'So *so* many reasons.'

'Give me one.'

'I'll give you three.'

He leaned back and folded his arms as if he had all the time in the world. 'Hit me with the first one.'

She fought an entirely alien urge to thump him. 'I'm not ready.' How was that for starters? She and James might not have been seeing eye to eye in those last few weeks, but it didn't mean she wanted to start seeing someone else.

His face gentled. 'Ella, it's been eighteen months.'

'I know how long it's been, but it doesn't change the fact that I'm not ready to fall in love again.' There had been days when she'd missed James so much she'd thought the ache would kill her. She didn't want to think about men, she didn't want to think about relationships. She didn't want to think about any of it.

'Who said anything about falling in love?'

The pulse in her throat missed a beat.

'Dating doesn't have to be about falling in love. It can just be about having fun. I'm living proof of that, aren't I?'

If it was so much fun, why didn't he look happier about it?

'Dating can be a casual thing, a social outlet.'

She pursed her lips. 'Casual?'

He nodded, though she suspected he was trying not to laugh at her consternation.

She glanced away, wrinkling her nose. 'The thing is, Harry, I haven't dated casually in my life. I don't even know how that works.'

He stared at her before pursing his own lips. 'That's right, childhood sweethearts.'

Bingo.

'It's easy.'

Sounded damn terrifying to her.

'You bump into someone—maybe at the markets—it might even be someone you sort of know or have seen around. Anyway, you share a joke or a stray comment about the goods for sale, and he—or she—asks if you'd like to go for a cup of coffee some time. You say *That'd be lovely*, and you exchange phone numbers. You set a time, meet for coffee and have a nice time.'

He made it sound easy.

'What if that person wants more? What if they're look-ing for a serious relationship?'

'During that first coffee date, you make it clear what you're looking for and where you stand.'

She mulled that over. 'So if he's looking for serious he doesn't ring me again. And if he isn't...' She frowned harder. 'We what? Become friends?'

A low laugh shook through him. 'You really are new at this, aren't you? If you enjoy each other's company and like the look of each other...'

He stared at her expectantly...spread his hands. She shot back out of her chair. 'Oh, God, you're talking about sex.' She stalked around her drafting table, twice.

'Is it really so shocking?'

'Yes.' She glared. Though it wasn't. Not really. She'd been thinking about sex a lot. Even though she'd been doing her best to ignore it.

He studied her, lips pursed. She felt like a butterfly on the end of a pin. 'Do you find sex without commitment morally reprehensible?'

'No.' She sighed and took her seat again. 'Casual sex

sounds great in theory.' She nibbled the inside of her cheek. 'Really great,' she murmured. And then shook herself, straightened, ordered her cheeks to stop burning. 'It makes me feel guilty though, because…' She trailed off with a grimace.

He nodded to let her know he understood.

She forced herself to take a slow deep breath, in a measured *adult* way. 'But I'm young and healthy and in my sexual prime. It's normal for someone my age to miss sex and want—'

Too much information! Harry was no longer looking at her. He didn't need, or want, to hear this.

She folded her arms. 'Okay, you've made your point.' Time to move on. 'Reason number two.'

He motioned with his hands. 'Hit me with it.'

'Me dating would send the family into a spin. They'd find it confronting.'

His eyes narrowed. 'The family doesn't get to decide when you're ready to start dating again. That's your decision.'

'And yours apparently.' She rolled her eyes. 'It's clearly what you're pushing me towards.'

'Not pushing, just reminding you of the benefits.'

Sex.

She stared at him and then reefed her gaze away. Played with a spare bobbin she hadn't packed away yet. She definitely shouldn't think about sex and Harry in the same sentence.

'The thing is, Ella, they *don't* get a say in it. The other thing is…'

She glanced up.

'One day you will meet a guy who makes your heart beat faster, who you can imagine settling down with and—'

'*Not* going to happen!' The words emerged more violently than she meant them to, and his eyebrows shot up. Her shoulders ached and her temples throbbed. Maybe the family were right and she ought to mourn James forever. Maybe that was the right thing to do.

He studied her for several long moments. 'You might not be able to imagine it at the moment, but… What about kids? Don't you want those? I mean, I know you don't have to be in a committed relationship to have them, but the single-parent route is tough.'

She'd be lying if she said she didn't want children.

'I think, at some point in the future, white picket fences will feature on your horizon once again. The family might find that difficult to accept at first, but you'll be making this hypothetical guy's life a whole lot easier if you date a few transitional guys first.'

'Bring home a few frogs for them to scare off first?' The thought made her smile. She wasn't in the market for love right now, and maybe she never would be. Yet Harry's strategy was still a sound one.

'What's reason number three?'

She gestured at her workshop. 'My main focus is getting Sew Sensational established.'

He folded his arms. 'You can still find the time to date.'

'I could find the time if I *wanted* to date, but I don't. This is going to sound selfish, but I don't want to pander to any guy's ego at the moment. I only want to focus on what's important to me.'

'And that's building Sew Sensational?'

She hesitated. 'I've had first-hand experience at the kind of curveball life can throw at you, Harry.'

He lifted a hand as if to reach across and squeeze hers. Instead, he picked up a nearby spool of thread and turned it over and over in his fingers.

She forced her mind from his fingers and back to the

conversation. 'If I can make a success of Sew Sensational, that means I'll always have something in my life that's mine, that can't be taken away from me.'

'Something you can fall back on if life goes pear-shaped again.'

She nodded. He did understand. 'Sew Sensational, Susie's wedding, the family…' she chewed the inside of her cheek '…and making a few new friends are all I have time for at the moment.'

Those fingers tapped against the spool of thread. 'Guys can be friends too.'

He almost sounded as if he were putting himself forward for the job. She folded her arms, but she didn't know if it was to protect herself from that thought or to temper the pounding of her heart. 'We've talked an awful lot about me, Harry. Can we talk about you for a moment?'

He rolled his shoulders, shifted on his seat. 'What do you want to know?'

'You said you're currently giving dating and romance a wide berth.'

'That's right.'

His eyes narrowed and he said the words carefully… and clearly. Was he worried she might challenge him, try and change his mind? He shouldn't. She'd meant it when she said she didn't have room in her life for any guy at the moment.

'I've shared why romance won't be featuring on my horizon any time in the near future, but what's your reason?'

He continued to stare at her with narrowed eyes and she suddenly realised why. She sat back. 'You don't trust me.' The realisation stung.

'It's not personal.'

Seriously? How else was she supposed to take it? She kept her chin high. 'I suppose you've had more than one woman sell a tell-all exposé to the tabloids. I guess you've learned to be cautious.'

Which was sad and awful.

'My gut tells me I can trust you.'

But it was clear his gut had led him astray in the past.

He swore softly. 'It feels mean-spirited to not answer your question when you've been so open with me.'

She waved that away. 'Don't worry about it.'

'No. I *am* going to trust you. I'm not an idiot. I can tell when a person is genuine or not.'

Her gaze speared back to his.

His eyes flashed. 'I'm not going to let them take that away from me. Sometimes it's worth the risk—even if you do find yourself mistaken and disappointed. I refuse to turn into some sad and lonely cynic.'

'That would be a tragedy,' she agreed, a smile lifting through her. 'I won't tell the world your secrets, Harry. They're safe with me.'

His gaze didn't waver from hers. 'I believe you.'

Something in her chest hitched. What was it about this man that made her feel so empowered?

'I'm wanting to partner with a charity called Bright Directions. It helps teenagers struggling with depression. My plan is to set up ski clinics to give these kids a chance to experience a week on the slopes, and an opportunity to build new skills that will boost their self-esteem.'

She stared at him, momentarily lost for words. 'That's… it's a gorgeous idea.'

He gave a half-grin—a little abashed and a lot self-conscious—and she had to fight an impulse to hug him. 'Lily's going to head the programme up for me, and she's really excited about it.'

'Of course she is.' Who wouldn't be?

'But the charity is pretty conservative, and the trustees

are wary about partnering with someone who has developed a reputation as a playboy. They want their name to be synonymous with respectability, and anyone they partner with needs to be role-model material.'

Ah.

'I mean, I have the connections in the skiing world, and I have the money…'

'But I'm guessing pictures of you with what seems like a different girl on your arm every week, looking as if your entire life is a party, isn't exactly convincing them that you're serious.'

'No.'

'But if those pictures were to stop…you might be able to convince them that you've turned over a new leaf?'

'It's the plan.' And then he shook his head. 'It's my own fault. I've played up my reputation to the tabloids because I've found it amusing.' He leaned back, expelled a breath. 'The thing is, I've never been interested in having a serious relationship. I love playing the field and can't imagine settling down with one woman.'

He actually shuddered. Clearly white picket fences were the stuff of nightmares for him.

'So I've exaggerated certain aspects of my behaviour to send that message loud and clear.' He was silent for a moment. 'I'm not built for the long haul. Some people aren't, you know? I think it's best to be honest about these things.'

'Absolutely,' she agreed. 'But now all of that exaggeration has come back to bite you on the nose.'

'So it would seem.'

'And that was your reason for avoiding the scary ladies' table on Friday night.'

'That's exactly the kind of table I need to avoid if I'm to rehabilitate my image.'

'Are you finding it hard?'

'Not in the way you think. I don't crave a new woman on my arm every week, and I don't need a calendar full of parties. People seem to forget that I run a successful business, that I work hard. Most of the events I attend these days are for business purposes.'

That made sense. 'So what *do* you find hard about it?'

'Staying on my guard. No longer teasing the media—that's hard to resist. It had become a bit of a game, a bit of fun.'

Because at heart he was a fun-loving guy who didn't feel the need to explain himself to anyone.

'Martin's wedding is a godsend. It's pulled me out of the limelight and is giving me the chance to prove myself.'

She tapped a finger against her lips. 'And if we're to drag this wedding out of the doldrums, you're going to be too busy to be snapped doing much else.' She straightened. Tit for tat. 'Well, Harry, if there's anything I can do to help, let me know.'

He blinked. 'That's nice of you.'

Guys can be friends too.

She moistened her lips. 'Well, as I said… I need a few new friends.'

His eyes throbbed. 'If you believe what the papers say, I can't just be friends with a woman.'

'I don't care what the papers say. I care what you say. Can you just be friends with a woman?'

He leaned in close and she saw he had lighter flecks in his irises, the colour of gold. 'Yes.'

'Then maybe we can be friends.' In the short term. It wouldn't last. She wouldn't see him once the wedding was over, but he could be…a transitional friend maybe.

One side of his mouth hooked up. 'I'd like that, Ella, but I'm not going to be your new BFF. You have priors for falling in love with those.'

Her jaw dropped. And then she choked back a splutter of laughter. *'Once!'* She held up a single finger. 'Once does not make me a serial faller-in-love with my BFFs. It's not a pattern.'

He grinned and held out his hand.

She grinned back and shook it.

CHAPTER FIVE

'OKAY, SO TELL me how it went.'

It was Friday night, and Ella watched Harry as he unpacked a Chinese takeaway—honey prawns, Mongolian lamb, fried rice and stir-fry vegetables all appeared on the table before her.

'Which part?' And then she gestured at the food. 'How many people were you planning to feed?'

'I couldn't decide what I wanted. And I figured you'd find a use for any leftovers.'

She grabbed plates and cutlery and tried to not dwell on the fact that it was sort of sweet of him to make sure she had leftovers.

There was nothing *sort of* about it. Harry *was* a sweet guy, period.

'As I told you on Wednesday night—' when they'd chatted on the phone '—it was lovely.'

After teaching her class on Tuesday night, she'd gone for coffee and dessert with two of her fellow teachers at the community college. 'We talked shop, and our bigger creative goals, and it was...'

'Yes?' he prompted, a spring roll halfway to his mouth.

Spring rolls? Where were they? Spotting them, she reached for one and bit into it, trying to find the right words.

'Invigorating. Freeing. Guilt-free. Well, not if you count the chocolate lava cake I had.'

He huffed out a laugh that warmed her to her toes. 'You don't need to worry about your weight, Ella. You look great.'

For a fraction of a moment their gazes caught and clung. They both looked away at the same time. She rattled back into speech. 'I told them about my Sew Sensational plans and they asked intelligent questions, challenged me on a few points.'

He set his spring roll down, his brow pleating. 'Challenged?'

She pointed at his plate. 'You want to eat that while it's warm. They're really good. And, yeah, challenged. Joy teaches advertising and thinks I need a more distinctive logo. Aleeta is an artist who immediately started doodling potential logos…and said she could create a banner for my website and YouTube channel too. Neither of them liked my current one.'

He thrust out his jaw. 'What's wrong with it?'

'No, they're right. It's an amateur job—just something I whipped up as a placeholder that I've never got around to updating.' She helped herself to the honey prawns. 'We're going to work out a quid pro quo arrangement where we can help each other out without cash actually changing hands.'

'Sounds great.'

'We're making Tuesday dessert night a regular thing.' She handed him the prawns. 'I'm really looking forward to next week. I enjoyed it more than I have any outing in a long time.'

If it hadn't been for his prodding, she'd have missed out on it. Catching her eye, he sent her a grin—one that made the right side of his mouth hook up in a devil-may-care kind of way, and her pulse did a little jig.

Be sensible. Harry. Friend. That's all.

'And yesterday I popped into one of my favourite fabric warehouses and bumped into one of the stallholders from the markets. We started chatting and ended up hunkering down in the pattern section for an hour.'

He ladled food to his plate. 'That's not something you'd normally do?'

'No.' She frowned. 'And now I'm wondering why not. I can't remember why it always seemed so important to get back to the workshop asap. It was nice to connect creatively with someone on a work level.' It had reinforced her love for what she was doing. It had helped to strengthen her belief in herself, confidence that her family's scepticism had battered. 'Not only was it fun, but creatively instructive.'

'Sounds brilliant *and* productive.'

It had been.

His gaze raked her face and he gave a nod. 'You look better. More relaxed.'

She refused to read anything into the warmth of his eyes. Harry had made it very clear he wasn't interested in her in that way. And she wasn't interested in him either.

'I feel better,' she admitted. 'Not so tightly wound…like I might explode at a moment's notice.' Which was a relief. 'I hadn't realised I'd fallen into such a negative holding pattern. No wonder the family have been so concerned about me…and sceptical about what I'm trying to do here.' Her frown deepened. 'You've been a godsend, Harry.'

He stared and then laughed. 'You could try and look a bit happier about that.'

'Oh, I didn't mean—'

'I know what you meant.'

He grinned and she couldn't help grinning back.

'Did you manage to slip the dessert date into conversation with your mother.'

'And Susie too.'

'Way to go, Ella.'

They high-fived. Both her mother and Susie had been surprised, but they'd made all the right noises. There'd been consternation threaded beneath the encouragement too, though. She reminded herself this was a process—change didn't happen overnight.

They ate in silence for a while. Eventually she pushed her plate away and patted her stomach. She'd eaten far more than she should have. 'So I've had a bit of inspiration on the cheering-them-up front.'

He pushed his plate away too. 'I'm all ears.'

'Beer?'

'Love one,' he said, rising to help her clear away.

She grabbed a beer for him and a soda for herself. 'It occurred to me that if I hadn't realised the negative patterns I'd fallen into, maybe they don't realise their own. I know them seeing me being more cheerful and relaxed and enthusiastic is going to help ease their worry—' she crossed her fingers '—but we need to shake them out of their negative ways too.'

'You have some thoughts on how we can do that?'

'What if we get them doing the things they used to love doing? Things they've stopped doing since James died.'

He straightened. 'I like it. What kind of things are we talking here?'

'Karaoke.'

His eyes lit up. 'No way.'

'Yes way. The whole family is crazy about karaoke.'

'You can sing?'

That made her laugh. 'I didn't say that.'

'What else?'

'The dads used to love going to the baseball.'

'Right.' He clapped his hands. 'I know Martin and Susie

said they didn't want hen and stag parties, that the week in Malaysia is going to be one big party and more than enough.'

Ella rolled her eyes. 'Yeah, and like a whole week of partying doesn't put the pressure on us or anything.'

He grinned at that. 'We're up for the challenge, Ella.'

He made her believe they were—that *she* was.

'But now I'm going to organise a boys' day to the baseball prior to flying out and I think you should host a girls' day. What do Susie and the mums love?'

'Susie is mad about musicals.'

He tapped idle fingers against his glass. 'Don't you have dress fittings for Susie and the mums soon?'

'Not until the weekend before we fly out.' Which was only three weeks away.

'You could do the fittings and then have a party afterwards, play soundtracks from musicals during the afternoon, host a musical-related trivia game. You want to play songs from the upbeat musicals, though, not the mournful ones.'

Susie would love it. And it could be fun. '*Grease* and *The Sound of Music*,' she murmured.

'*Hairspray* and *Mamma Mia*.'

That made her grin. 'I love a man who knows his musicals.' Dear God, why did she have to go and use the L word? She rushed on, hoping he hadn't noticed. 'We'll have champagne and nibbles…and I'll organise something fun.' She'd have to put her thinking cap on, because she didn't want it to be anything that reminded anyone of James.

She twisted her hands together. 'I want to ask you something. And I need you to tell me the truth.'

He crossed his heart, instantly alert.

They'd known one another for such a short time, but she trusted him. It made her frown. *Be careful, Ella.* She couldn't come to rely too much on Harry. She couldn't replace one set of negative behaviours with another.

She pressed her hands together. 'I've long suspected that, before any group event, certain family members put their heads together and come up with a plan for how to manage me.'

He'd had his right ankle resting at his left knee, but his foot slammed to the floor now. He stared at her.

'Do you think I'm wrong?' She wanted to be wrong.

He mulled her words over. 'The widows' table…it was planned?'

'I think so.'

He set his beer to the table. 'It's worse than I thought.'

'I'm thinking of turning the tables on them. I'm thinking of ringing Mum and Auntie Rachel the day before the dress fittings to tell them we need to make sure it's a fun day for Susie.' She chewed her lip. 'But…is that mean-spirited?'

His brow pleated. 'You want Susie to have a fun day, don't you?'

'Of course!'

'And you want the mums to help you achieve that.' He shook his head. 'That's just you stating the outcome you want. And it sends them a subtle message that they no longer need to *manage* you. It's neither mean-spirited nor unkind.'

His words gave her heart.

'The thing is, Ella, while they're focussing on you, they don't have to address their own sense of loss.'

Her eyes started to burn. She knew how much they were hurting. She wished she could wipe all of their pain away. 'I just want to see them happy again.'

He reached across and gripped her hand. 'You will.'

She clung tight to that promise.

He abruptly released her and she had an awful feeling

she'd been gazing at him in adoration. She swallowed. If she had been, it had only been on account of her family, *not* for any other reason.

'Ready to try your waistcoat *toile* on?' She was looking forward to seeing the look on his face when he saw it.

'Lead the way.'

She took him across to the cutting table and whisked off the cover on her dressmaking model.

His jaw dropped. And then a grin threatened to split his face in two. 'Where did you get this?'

He reached out to touch the fabric—cartoon skiers made their way down snowy slopes on a light blue background. The fabric was fun, light-hearted and she'd thought of him the moment she'd seen it. She hadn't been able to resist.

'This isn't a mock-up. It's brilliant!'

'There's nothing fancy about it,' she warned. 'The fabric is an inexpensive cotton. It's what we call a wearable *toile*. The wedding waistcoats will be in fine wool and patterned silk—the sort of fabrics I'd prefer to not handle too much, which is why I want to get the fit right on these first. Now let's see if it fits.'

He'd worn a white button-down business shirt as she'd ordered, and he shrugged off his jacket—black leather, of course—to don the waistcoat. She couldn't help but laugh when he turned. 'It suits you. Now let's check the fit.'

She walked around him, smoothing the fabric across his back. 'I thought I might've made it a little big across here.' She tried to ignore the heat scorching her fingertips, but it was impossible. Harry's heat was a living, breathing thing that took on a life of its own. She swallowed. 'But the fit looks good.'

She walked around him again, ordered her gaze to not linger on taut buttocks in form-fitting jeans. She risked smoothing a hand across his shoulders again. The man felt like heaven.

She curled her fingers into her palms. *Stop it*. The guy was off limits. *She* was off limits.

She told herself to look away, but her eyes refused to obey. His chest looked so very broad and muscled—the most inviting thing she'd seen in a *very* long time. She could imagine being plastered against it and—

She took a hasty step back, hands on hips—her fingers digging into the fleshy area just below her waistline with a death grip that would probably leave bruises. *Be professional.* 'How does it feel? Any spots where it feels too snug or a bit loose?'

He shook his head. 'It's perfect.'

He didn't look at her, stared instead at the fabric, and she dragged in a breath. While she might be in danger of getting all het up, he was completely oblivious. Which was just as well.

A bad taste coated her tongue all the same. The simple truth was she wasn't the kind of woman to tempt a man like Harry.

Also—*hello*—he had a noble goal. She couldn't do anything that would mess that up for him.

And she couldn't afford any more slip-ups that would give her family further reason to think her incapable of making a sensible decision. She gestured. 'There's a full-length mirror in the corner.'

He marched across and stared at her handiwork, moving this way and that before meeting her gaze. 'You're a magician.'

That made her laugh.

He froze, and then he swung around, his entire face coming alive. 'Can you make me more of these? Ski themed, but suitable to wear with business suits? And maybe an even fancier one for evening wear?'

She shrugged. 'Sure.'

He turned back to the mirror, tugged gently on the hem of the waistcoat. 'Because these will attract attention.'

Attention?

He raised an eyebrow. 'I'm not normally one to toot my own horn, but I am an A-lister...'

She suddenly realised what he was talking about. Her heart thudded so hard she could barely speak. 'You'd...? No way!' He'd endorse her brand?

'You might not get your fashion expo, but there are other ways to get your name out there.'

Her mind raced. This was ten times better than the expo! Once the press took photos of Harry in those waistcoats she'd be flooded with orders, and the Sew Sensational brand would be established.

If her family could see Sew Sensational making a splash, could finally see its potential, that would help alleviate their anxiety levels where she was concerned, surely? And free them up to focus on happier things like Susie's wedding.

'I watched some of your YouTube videos through the week.'

She bumped back to earth, wiped suddenly damp palms down her jeans. 'And?'

'You're a natural on camera—personable, enthusiastic, super encouraging...' His eyes darkened. 'And a little bit flirty.'

Her mouth dried. 'Flirty?'

'You're like the Nigella Lawson of the sewing world. Your passion for your subject shines through.'

Flirty? Did that mean he thought her just the tiniest bit sexy?

'You're a born teacher.'

A lump lodged in her throat. He really thought so?

'For God's sake, you made me want to learn how to sew!' That made her laugh.

He shifted his weight from one foot to the other. 'You sometimes have guests on your channel.'

He raised an eyebrow and spread his hands. Her pulse went haywire. 'No way,' she breathed.

'Yes, way.'

If she had him on as a guest, her ratings would sky-rocket.

'You could do a segment on waistcoats featuring me— we could talk about how the idea for them came about. And I'd be your model.'

Her mind raced as ideas dive-bombed her. 'Oh!' She glanced at him. 'Wouldn't it interfere with your image makeover?' Because no matter how good this would be for Sew Sensational, she wasn't doing anything that would hurt his charity efforts.

'I can't see how. It'd probably help. I—' He broke off and eyed her warily. 'I mean, as long as I keep my shirt on. I…'

'I'm not going to ask you to go shirtless, Harry.' No matter how much she might want to. 'It's not that kind of channel.'

'You interested, then? Do you think it'd help?'

'I think it's inspired, and it's a sure-fire way of getting my name out there.' It was a lot to ask, though. 'As long as you don't mind?'

'Are you kidding? I mean, I get free bespoke waist-coats, right?'

She found herself grinning. 'You absolutely do.'

He grinned down at her. 'I'm on a roll; here's another great idea. I'm attending a swish do in a couple of weeks' time where I'll be schmoozing with the trustees of Bright Directions, and doing my best to prove I'm someone they want to be associated with. That's where I want to wear one of the waistcoats.'

He leaned down towards her and she could smell leather and amber and every good thing.

'Ella, if you went as my date, you'd be able to talk about your work to the kind of people who set, not just fashion trends, but all kinds of trends.'

Her heart hammered into her throat and she couldn't utter a word.

'Interested?'

'Very.' She couldn't get her hopes up though, because… 'Again, what about your no-dating policy? Won't the media and the trustees get the wrong idea if you turn up with a woman on your arm?'

'That depends on the woman, and I suspect dating a woman like you will only help my image, not harm it.' He gave a single hard nod. 'Right, that's a date, then.' And then he waggled his eyebrows. 'But not a *date* date.'

Absolutely not a *date* date.

'Can I ask another favour?'

She started to laugh then. This man was helping put her brand on the map. 'You really truly can.'

'Will you teach me to sew?'

She had a feeling her grin was in danger of splitting her face in two. She gestured across the room. 'Choose your machine, my friend.'

Friend. She repeated the word over and over in her mind.

CHAPTER SIX

'THIS IS WHERE you live?'

Harry bit back a grin at Ella's astonishment. Holborn House was pretty impressive. 'It belongs to my mother— it's where she stays when she's in Sydney.' He punched in the security code for the double wrought-iron gates. 'I have my own place in Woolloomooloo.' But Holborn House was where Lily currently lived.

'It's been in the family for three generations.' A drive lined with date palms led to an enormous Victorian mansion with expansive views of the harbour. 'This is what a mining empire buys you.'

He'd meant to say the words with wry mockery, but an edge of bitterness tinged them too and he could've kicked himself when the weight of Ella's gaze settled on him. She didn't ask a single question, though, didn't probe or pry. He rolled his shoulders. 'My mother works too hard to enjoy the spoils of the family's wealth.'

He parked the car. In the sudden silence the engine clicked and ticked as it started to cool. 'This was where I grew up before my parents divorced. Afterwards, my mother threw herself into running the family's holdings.' And had become a virtual stranger.

'And your father?'

'Couldn't be seen for the dust he left in his wake.' It had

been demoralising how hard and fast his father had run. 'Lily and I were shunted off to boarding school.'

It had felt as if he and Lily had lost both parents in one fell swoop. His hands gripped the steering wheel so hard his fingers started to ache. Lily had lost not one, but two families. It had sent her into a spiral that had almost resulted in her death. That was what this house represented to him now. He forced a smile to frozen lips, rolled his eyes. 'They were the very best schools, though, of course.'

One soft hand curled over his on the steering wheel, and he found himself turning, found himself in danger of falling into clear blue eyes. 'All the wealth in the world is no comfort when your world comes tumbling down, Harry. You lost your whole way of life through no fault of your own. It must've been the most awful time.' She stared at the house. 'My family is driving me batty at the moment, but I'm incredibly lucky to have them.'

He squeezed her hand before leaping out of the car and racing around to open her door. 'Come and see the view,' he said, changing the subject. 'It's glorious.'

Lily met them on the terrace. Taking Ella's hand, she tugged her inside. 'There's something I'm dying to show you.'

He trailed behind. And then pulled up short at the sight that greeted them. Spread across one of the large sofas in the formal living room was *a wedding dress*!

What the hell…? His hands clenched and unclenched. He'd sensed Viggo was trouble from the first moment he'd met him, but Lily couldn't be hoping to marry the guy. And even if Viggo were serious, surely Lily wouldn't contemplate…

'It's my mother's wedding dress.'

Her mother's? He sagged.

'Aunt Claudia sent on some of my parents' things from

the Brisbane house last week, this among them. The moment I saw it…'

She trailed off with a shrug and he wrapped an arm around her shoulders. 'That's a hell of a find. It must be nice to have it.'

'It is.'

She leaned into him and some of his anxiety eased.

'But there are a few marks and tears, and I don't know what I ought to do about it. I was hoping Ella could point me in the right direction.'

Ella inspected the dress. 'It's exquisite,' she said eventually, reverence in her voice. 'The damage is only minor. This could easily be restored to its former glory.' She swung to them with a smile that made his heart beat hard, her curls dancing all around her face. 'It's pure nineteen-eighties over-the-top fabulousness, probably influenced by Princess Di's dress.'

'Would you like to see a picture of my mother in it?'

'Yes, please!'

Harry fixed drinks while Lily raced off to get the photo. 'I'm sorry Lily wants to talk shop. You probably get sick of people asking you about stuff like this.'

'Nonsense! I live for stuff like this.' She gestured towards the gown. 'It's a real privilege to see something like that. The workmanship is out of this world.'

Lily returned with a framed photograph and the two women oohed and ahhed and he couldn't say why, but those two heads bent close together—one dark and one fair—had a strange warmth stretching through his chest.

'Okay, so I want to ask your advice on one point, and then I'll stop pestering you about sewing stuff.'

'I *love* sewing stuff and you're not pestering me.'

She was utterly glorious, he decided in that moment—enthusiastic and warm. And kind.

'Would it be possible, do you think, to rework this dress into...' Lily's hands fluttered. 'Into the dress of my dreams?'

'Why all this sudden interest in weddings?' he barked.

Lily glanced at him and rolled her eyes. 'Maybe because my mother's wedding dress has suddenly turned up and started me thinking about such things.' She peered at him. 'Why, what's wrong?'

Her question made him feel like an idiot. He grimaced. 'In my head you're still fifteen and...'

'Oh, Lord, you're hilarious,' Ella said. 'I bet he was a nightmare when you first started dating, Lily.'

Both women laughed and turned back to the dress, ignoring him. He had a feeling he deserved to be ignored.

'Tell me about your dream dress,' Ella said.

'I do love the old Edwardian style.'

'Ooh, me too.'

They started throwing around ideas, discussing pros and cons. He looked up Edwardian wedding dresses on his phone, because he had no idea what they were talking about. He stared at the pictures and nodded. Nice.

'Now, say if this is too much,' Lily said, 'but Harrison told me about the waistcoats and it's what gave me the idea.'

He immediately transferred his attention back to the women.

'Ella, would you consider helping me to make that dream dress...and in return we could film the process for your channel?'

Ella went ramrod straight. 'Are you serious? Lily, I don't have specific expertise in this area. You could take it to a couture designer and—'

'I don't want some big-name designer. I want you. I want you to teach me how to make that dress myself. It might sound strange, but it'll make me feel closer to my mother.

And one day when I do get married, wearing this dress will make me feel like a part of her is with me.' She blinked a few times before rushing back into speech. 'I watch your YouTube channel religiously. I saw the episode where you made that formal gown. I saw the wedding dress in your studio. I love the way you teach and I know with you I'd have the confidence to tackle something like this.'

'That's a lovely thing to say,' Ella whispered.

'Please say you'll do it.' Lily leaned towards her, hands pressed together in an unconscious plea.

Harry held his breath and waited for Ella's answer. *Please say yes.*

'Oh, Lily, I'd be honoured.'

Lily threw her arms around her and Harry couldn't get the grin off his face.

They shared a delicious roast dinner and the conversation didn't have a chance to flag. Ella asked about the plans they were hoping to make with Bright Directions, and Lily described their programme in detail. When she told Ella that she'd had an eating disorder in her teens and that was why working with this particular charity meant so much to her, he nearly swallowed his tongue. She so rarely spoke about it.

His hands clenched about his cutlery. He had to make this partnership with Bright Directions happen.

'Between the two of you I'm sure you'll win them over. It's a brilliant initiative.'

Ella's smile made him feel as if he could achieve anything.

'Now tell me about Malaysia. Harrison tells me the plans were sprung on you both without notice.'

Ella told her about the upcoming wedding and the scheduled week in Malaysia. She even told her that it meant she'd now be missing the fashion expo she had such hopes for.

Waistcoats…? Wedding dresses…? Harry suddenly clapped his hands. 'Could you turn Malaysia to your advantage?'

Both women turned to him.

'Could you do some Sew Sensational filming on location? A special feature on…' He grappled for an idea. This world was so new to him. 'Something beach themed?'

'Oh, my God,' Lily squealed. 'Do a couple of your Fast Fashion sessions on…'

'Three things to make from a sarong,' Ella said, her whole face coming alive. 'Everyone has a couple of old sarongs in their wardrobe.' But a moment later she sobered. 'There won't be time. Not with the wedding and—'

'We could stay an extra week.'

Lily bounced. 'Say yes! And let me join you for part of it. I could be your guinea pig learner sewer who shows everyone how easy it can be.'

Ella bit her lip. 'I really shouldn't take so much time off.'

'You won't be taking time off. You'll be working,' he pointed out. 'What will you be missing here?'

She tapped a finger to her lips. 'It'll be mid-semester break at college, which means no classes for a few weeks, and I'd miss one market day.' She paused. 'But for something like this…'

Please say yes.

She glanced up and must've seen that command in his eyes because she grinned, excitement alive in her eyes. 'Let's do it.'

He wanted to punch the air in victory.

'I meant to ask earlier. How did the family barbecue go on Sunday?'

Harry glanced briefly at Ella before turning his eyes back to the road. The evening had been one of the most enjoyable he could remember. She'd assured him she'd be happy to catch the train home, but he'd insisted on driving her. Just as he'd insisted on collecting her earlier in the evening.

'Um…'

He stiffened.

'There were some…*uncomfortable* moments.'

'Okay…' He didn't know whether to press her or not.

'The first was when Dad made a comment about what I was wearing—said something about it being bright and cheerful.'

He'd seen what she'd planned to wear, primarily because she'd been in the process of making the skirt the last time he'd had a sewing lesson—a long velvet number in the most astonishing shade of yellow. She'd planned to team it with an apple-green long-sleeved tee.

'And I made the mistake of saying, "Harry told me all I needed was purple shoes and an orange belt and I'd look like a rainbow vomited over me."'

He barked out a laugh. When Ella decided to do colour, she *really* did colour. He might tease her about it, but those bright colours suited her.

'So then came the third degree—when had I seen you and why? How much time were we spending together?'

'What did you say?'

'Told them the truth—that we were bridesmaid and best man and as such needed to put our heads together about certain things. It sort of eased their minds.'

It'd *sort of* do them good to start thinking about Ella seeing other men, but he didn't say that out loud.

'Sounds like you handled it well.'

'Maybe, maybe not.'

Her sigh speared into his chest. He glanced at her again. 'If that's the worst the afternoon held—'

'I told them James knew about my plans to strike out on my own with Sew Sensational.'

His hands tightened around the steering wheel at the mention of James. 'Wow, okay.'

'I didn't plan to. I just *blurted it out*. I wanted them to know my decision hadn't come out of the blue. So then came another third degree—why hadn't I told them this before? What did James think about it?' From the corner of his eye he saw her fold her arms. 'I told them he was disappointed, that he didn't want me leaving the business.'

He winced.

'And I told them he also knew I had my heart set on it.'

She stared straight out to the front, her lips pressed in a tight line. He wanted to take her hand and offer her comfort. 'What happened then?'

'They all went quiet. So I added that I've never felt more vocationally fulfilled as I have these last six months and I wish they could just be happy for me.' She swung to him suddenly. 'Do you think I've wrecked everything? Do you think I've ruined the wedding and—?'

'Absolutely not!' She might've shaken them up but… 'You're refusing to allow them to keep casting you in the role of tragic victim. Confronting for them, no doubt, but also positive as it removes you as a constant source of concern. You don't need to feel guilty for any of that, Ella.'

She rubbed a hand across her chest. 'I hope you're right.'

He moistened his lips. 'James's accident…what happened? Do you mind me asking? I know he drowned, but…'

She was quiet for a moment. 'He sometimes swam laps in the mornings before work. We lived in a little flat in Cremorne and he'd use the nearby ocean baths.' She paused, her hands gripped tightly in her lap. 'As far as we can make out, he slipped and hit his head on the rocks…knocked himself out before falling into the water.'

His heart burned.

'It was still dark…nobody saw it happen…'

And a life was snuffed out, just like that. He reached across and squeezed her hand. 'I'm sorry.'

'Me too.' She squeezed back and then straightened. 'Now, enough about me. Lily had an eating disorder. That… I can only imagine how hard that must've been for her.'

He felt her turn towards him, but he kept his eyes on the road.

'It must've been hard for you too, Harry.'

'It was the worst time of my life,' he found himself admitting. She'd just been so open with him. It felt wrong not to be equally open.

He parked outside her workshop, but neither of them made a move to get out. He knew she wouldn't ask him in. He tried telling himself he was glad about that.

'I thought we were going to lose her.' His heart clenched, as he remembered the darkness of that time.

'But she pulled through.' That quiet voice pulled him back from the abyss. 'You helped her do that. Your strength and your patience, she told me it made all the difference.'

He turned to stare. When had she told her that? It must've been when he'd popped to the cellar for another bottle of wine. 'I didn't do anything—just held her hand, nagged her to not give up, to keep going…to keep fighting.'

'You were there when she needed you. She knows you're one person she can always rely on. Don't downplay it. It's a big thing. She worships you, you know?'

He met her gaze in the dim light of the car's interior. 'She means a lot to me too. I'm still angry that my parents weren't there for her. That they were too caught up in their own mess to see what was happening.'

She frowned. 'I know you said your father headed for the hills, but surely for something as important as this…?'

'I contacted him.' He hadn't wanted to. He hadn't for-given him for tearing their family apart, but he'd have done anything to help Lily. 'You know what he said? He said Lily wasn't his flesh and blood and, therefore, no concern of his.'

Her hand flew to her mouth, horror reflected in her eyes. He nodded. 'Charming, right?'

'I can't…there aren't even words for that.'

There were, but she was too polite to utter them. 'About the only good thing to come from Lily's illness is it shook my mother out of her self-indulgent martyrdom. She raced home and organised the best treatment possible, sat with Lily almost as much as I did.'

'So…she *was* there for Lily.'

'Eventually. But it took the shock of Lily nearly dying to make her realise what was important!' He dragged both hands through his hair. 'To make her remember she still had children who were relying on her.'

'Oh, Harry, I'm sorry.'

'Don't waste your sympathy on me, Ella. I was fine. During all of the ugliness of the divorce I still had my ski-ing to focus on.' He'd been making a splash on the junior circuit by then. 'But Lily…' The old guilt and anger rose through him. 'She must've felt abandoned by us all. She'd already lost one set of parents to a car accident—'

'None of it was your fault, Harry.' She seized his hand, shook it until he looked at her. 'None of it! You were a child yourself.'

She was wrong. He should've seen what was happen-ing with Lily.

'It's in the past now. Lily has become a lovely, vibrant young woman who wants to make her mark on the world. She got through it. You all got through it.'

A breath eased out of him, and he nodded. He was de-termined that nothing would ever upset Lily's equilibrium like that again. He squeezed Ella's hand and then released it. In the stillness and the darkness his physical awareness for her grew, and he needed to keep it in check.

'It's why sealing this deal with Bright Directions is so important. And why I'm determined to never make the same mistakes my father made.' Rock hard resolution settled in his chest. 'It's why I'll never become involved with any woman long term.'

She shook her head. 'Bzzz.' She made the sound of a game-show buzzer and raised her hand. 'I'll have to stop you there, Mr Gillespie, and ask you to explain. I don't see how that second statement follows the first.'

He hauled in a breath. 'I know it's not fair to blame my father for Lily's eating disorder, but he let her down—badly. She thought he loved her, she trusted him, and she blamed herself when he turned his back on her, blamed herself for the divorce. She said her coming into the family unit created the extra stress that broke my parents' marriage.'

Ella's eyes shimmered with sympathy. 'Poor Lily,' she whispered.

'The thing is, I knew about my father's infidelity. I confronted him about it when I was thirteen.' A year before the divorce. 'He told me he felt suffocated—that the only way he could remain married to my mother was by having extramarital affairs. He said as long as my mother never found out about them, they couldn't hurt her. He said that as long as we maintained the status quo, our family would survive.'

'Of all the—'

She broke off, but even in the darkness of the car he could see the way her eyes flashed.

'He emotionally blackmailed you into keeping his secret!'

And he had kept the secret. Not that it had made any

difference. Not in the end. His father's lies had torn their family apart.

'Harry, you have to see that wasn't fair. And it doesn't make you like your father. You were only thirteen!'

'I saw what his betrayal did to my mother and Lily. I'm never doing that to a woman. *Ever.* I refuse to be responsible for hurting someone so badly.'

'Harry, you're *not* your father.'

'I loathe my father, Ella.' Acid burned his throat. 'But apparently I'm my father's son. That sense of suffocation he described to me?' He turned and met her gaze. 'I feel it too. As soon as a woman becomes too clingy, it's like I can't breathe and am going to die a slow and horrible death.'

She stared at him with wide horrified eyes. She'd started to shake her head, but broke off, her fingers going to her throat.

'What's worse—' he forced himself to continue '—when I feel like that, I don't blame him for running.'

She pressed a hand to her mouth. Those blue eyes filling with tears. 'Oh, Harry.'

His jaw ached he clenched it so hard. So did his hands. 'I won't make the same mistake he did. I won't mislead any woman into thinking I can offer her anything lasting or substantial. Some people are made for the long haul, and some aren't. I'm not, and I refuse to pretend otherwise.'

CHAPTER SEVEN

'THE PARTY'S *HERE*?'

Ella did her best to not look too awed when they pulled up outside of one of Sydney's most elite venues.

'Stop fidgeting,' Harry said when she touched nervous fingers to the gathered straps of her sleeveless gown. 'You look great.'

'You haven't even seen me properly yet.'

He'd sent a driver to collect her *in a limousine no less* before it fetched him from his Woolloomooloo town house.

'I'm sorry. I got held up at the office and—'

'Harry, you're doing me a favour. Don't apologise.' She peered out of the window. 'I'm nervous, that's all. What if I get in there and become star-struck and stupid?' That wouldn't impress the trustees of his charity.

'Celebrities are just people too.'

She snorted.

'You weren't star-struck by me.'

'No, but...' She'd had a lot on her mind the night they'd met. She'd barely given his fame and celebrity a thought. It was his humour and empathy that had made an impact.

'We're making a deal—we're sticking close to each other tonight, okay? I'll save you from any star-struck moments, and you'll save me from any scary women. Deal?'

'Deal.'

He reached out and squeezed her hand. 'Ready?'

'Ready.'

'Wow!' he breathed when he handed her out.

He stared at her with the strangest expression and her stomach dropped. She glanced down, praying she hadn't somehow stained the fine satin of her dress.

'You look like a film starlet from the…'

'Nineteen-forties.' She wore a nineteen-forties-inspired evening dress in pale blue satin.

'You look *amazing.*'

She glanced back up and her heart started to gallop. He looked as if he wanted to *devour her.*

In that moment she was perilously close to offering herself up as a five-course banquet. Speaking of delectable things, Harry's crisp white shirt and bow tie made him look like a prince while his waistcoat hugged his powerful form in a way that—

Don't!

She couldn't let this go to her head. Flirting came as naturally to Harry as breathing. She forced herself into speech. 'When you said it was black tie, I thought this would be suitable.'

'This is one of yours? You *made* it?'

He continued to survey her with far too much male appreciation. 'I, um…don't own any floor-length gowns that I haven't made myself.'

She skimmed her hands along the gathered hipline and ordered herself not to babble about the five outside radiating darts—he wasn't interested in any of that. 'It is okay, isn't it? You don't mind that I'm wearing one of my own designs?' Had she inadvertently made a faux pas?

'It's perfect.'

But the smile he sent her was tight and she couldn't help feeling she'd got something wrong. Unless…

Dear God. Had he seen the effect he'd had on her? Was he starting to feel the jaws of that awful suffocation he'd described closing around him? The thought that *she* could make him feel like that…

She pressed her hands to her stomach. She couldn't think of anything worse!

She entered the ballroom on autopilot, her mind weaving in drunken circles as she searched for ways to put his mind at rest, but then he started pointing people out to her, explaining who was connected to whom, the deals going down and the latest celebrity gossip, becoming as warm and easy as ever again, and she was able to let out a sigh of relief.

The event was pure over-the-top glamour. Women she'd only ever seen in the society pages strutted beneath gleaming chandeliers in gowns that dazzled. Wait staff in spotless white uniforms circulated platters of oysters. Tables laden with the most sumptuous delicacies stood at one end of the room, while at the other a five-piece orchestra crooned swoony music. A glass of champagne was placed in her hand and she and Harry made a slow circuit of the room. She met the trustees of Bright Directions and their partners, and it all seemed ridiculously convivial. Wait until she told everyone about this tomorrow!

The moment Harry absented himself to procure her a plate of food, she found one of the trustees at her elbow. Donald was a former politician and she doubted the timing was an accident. 'Are you enjoying yourself?' he asked, introducing his wife, Rita.

'I'm having a lovely time. It's such a treat to be here.' She leaned in close to whisper. 'I feel as if I've stepped into another world.'

They both laughed. 'You look a vision yourself,' Rita said. 'Your gown is divine.'

'While we men are desperately jealous of Harrison's waistcoat.'

It was her turn to laugh. 'It suits him, doesn't it?' Tiny mountains were picked out in silver thread on a midnight dark background. There was no denying he looked fabulous in it.

'He's inordinately proud of it. And your gown. He's been handing out your business card to all and sundry.'

He was doing *what*? 'Good Lord, where did he get those from?' She pressed a hand to her waist when Rita pulled one from her purse. 'They're old. I'm having them redesigned—'

The older woman patted her arm. 'As long as the contact details are correct, nobody will care what your card looks like.' She popped it back into her purse. 'What the two of you are wearing is advertisement enough.'

'That's very kind of you,' she managed, touched that Harry was going to so much trouble for her.

'My dear,' Donald started, 'please don't take this the wrong way, but I'm surprised to find a woman like you on Harry's arm.'

'Donald!'

Rita sent him a scandalised glare, but Ella only laughed. 'You mean an old-fashioned girl like me?'

She straightened. Maybe she could repay Harry all his kindness.

'You shouldn't believe everything you read in the papers. Harry's not a saint and I'm not saying he is, but he's not the playboy he's made out to be either.'

'Are you and he…?'

'We're very good friends,' she told him firmly.

She stared from Donald to Rita and made a sudden decision. 'Harry has been helping me through a rather difficult time. Eighteen months ago my fiancé died in a terrible accident. Harry has helped me turn my face towards the future. He's made me realise it's the only positive thing to do, that anything else would be a sad homage to pay to a man I loved.'

And she had loved James. Dearly.

'Oh, my dear.'

Rita's eyes grew suspiciously bright and Ella waved a finger at her. 'Don't you start or you'll set me off. Obviously what I just told you isn't something I publicise, but I know what Harry's trying to achieve by going into partnership with you.'

Donald blinked.

'I think someone with Harry's empathy and enthusiasm is a perfect fit for your charity.'

Donald's gaze sharpened and she saw the shrewdness that had made him such a successful politician. She held his gaze. She had nothing to hide. She'd meant every word.

Slowly the older man nodded. 'It was the conclusion I was coming to myself, but it's nice to have it confirmed. And speak of the devil…'

She turned to find Harry approaching. She spread her hands. 'Where's my promised delicious delicacies?'

'Australia's leading starlet intercepted me on the way over here and said, "It's simply too good of you, darling," and whisked the plate from my hand.'

They all laughed.

Those whisky warm eyes rested on her. 'Would you like to dance instead?'

'One dance,' she told him, working hard to keep her voice light, refusing to dwell on how she'd manage to maintain her equilibrium in his arms. 'And then I'll be venturing forth to find my own food.'

'Before you go—' Donald clapped Harry on the shoulder '—I'm convinced we could do something special together, Harry.'

Harry straightened. 'So am I.'

'Can you meet with me first thing Monday?'

'Absolutely.'

'Bring your lawyers and let's see what we can thrash out. I'll look forward to talking more.'

The older couple ambled off and Harry swung to her. 'What did you do?'

She tried to rein in her grin, but couldn't. 'Oh, you know… Promised him half a dozen waistcoats and threw in an evening gown for his wife. Just common run-of-the-mill bribery.'

His jaw dropped.

'Joking,' she said, taking his arm and leading him towards the dance floor, and away from a famous pop singer who'd started to bear down on them with a determined glint in her eyes. 'Scary lady at nine o'clock.'

He immediately took her in his arms and she found herself enfolded in his scent and his heat. Being pressed against the long lean length of him fired every cell in her body to aching life.

'Tell me what you said to Donald.'

His breath disturbed the hair at her temple, sending a curl brushing against her ear. An electric thrill arrowed straight to her nipples. She could feel them harden and press against the satin of her dress. If anyone was looking… She swallowed. She was never wearing satin near Harry again!

'Ella?'

She had to swallow before she could speak. 'I told him his organisation should be proud to associate themselves with a man like you.'

He eased back, raised an eyebrow.

'Someone with your compassion and enthusiasm.'

His mouth fell open. Firm sculpted lips and—

She forced her gaze over his left shoulder, did what she could to ignore the yearning that swamped her. 'I told him you were the kind of person who helped others find joy in life again.'

His hand tightened about hers and she glanced back up. And found herself in imminent danger of falling into the depths of his eyes.

Would it matter if she did?

The thought slid beneath her guard, making her heart hammer. *Would* it matter? She'd been celibate for eighteen months. She was young and healthy…and sex for fun was something she could really get behind at the moment.

Her body hummed its approval. She sensed that making love with Harry would be exhilarating, extraordinary. And so, *so* satisfying.

Stop! He's trying to clean up his image. After everything he's done to help you, you want to repay him like that?

She dragged her gaze away, moved back until she could feel air between them again, ruthlessly ignoring her body's protest. 'I merely confirmed his own opinion, so it's nothing. And I think we're being watched so we'd better be on our best behaviour for the rest of the evening.'

She glanced up to find a puzzled smile on his lips. 'It's not *nothing*. You're amazing, you know that?'

'Don't be silly.'

'I knew bringing you tonight was a good idea. I just hadn't realised how good. I'm very grateful, Ella, and—'

'Me too.' She sent him a tight smile and tried to temper her curtness. In less than thirty seconds the song would end and she'd be able to breathe again. 'Besides, quid pro quo and all that. You scratch my back and I'll scratch yours.'

Don't think about fingernails and naked backs.

'I heard what you've been doing,' she added. If she kept talking maybe it would help her keep everything else in check. 'Handing out my business card.'

He blinked and frowned.

'If we stay on the straight and narrow, we'll both get what we want.' The song ended and she promptly moved out of his arms. 'Excellent.' She'd managed to not ravish him on the dance floor. 'Let's go get some food.'

Neither she nor Harry had wanted a late night—they were holding their pseudo hen and stag parties tomorrow—so they made a strategic retreat at midnight. He insisted on seeing her home, and they were literally only around the corner from the venue, when he swung to her. 'What did I do wrong?'

'What do you mean? You didn't do anything wrong.' She frowned. Had she missed something? 'Donald and Rita said goodnight to us very warmly. I don't think—'

'Not with them, with you. What did I do wrong with you?'

Her heart started to thump. 'I've no idea what you're talking about.'

He slid the privacy screen up between them and the driver. 'On the dance floor…something happened. You changed.'

It took her last reserve of strength to not press cool hands to burning cheeks. All evening she'd thought she'd hidden her emotions, but she hadn't fooled him for a moment. 'Harry, I promise. You did nothing wrong.'

'Was it Donald and Rita, then? Did they say something to upset you or—?'

'No!' She couldn't let him think that. She dragged in a deep breath. 'Will you please just let the subject drop?'

'No.'

She closed her eyes.

'Ella, we're friends. Will you please tell me what's wrong?'

Ella turned positively green and Harry's stomach lurched. 'Are you ill?' Did she need to see a doctor?

She shook her head, turning to stare out of the window. 'Adults,' he heard her murmur. 'We're adults.' As if she was giving herself a pep talk.

Before he could ponder that further, she squared her shoulders and turned back. 'It's not you, Harry. It's me.'

His brows wanted to shoot up towards his hairline, but with a superhuman effort he forced them not to. When her eyes narrowed, though, he realised his brows now lowered in a frown. He did what he could to smooth his face out. 'This sounds ominously like a break-up speech.'

'We're not a couple so we can't be breaking up.'

'You can break a friendship up.' It hit him then that he didn't want her breaking their friendship up. He enjoyed spending time with her. She made him laugh. When he was around her he could relax…be himself.

'This isn't a break-up speech. I'm not trying to break anything up.' Her gaze slid away. 'Look, let's just drop this and—'

'Not a chance.' He sat up straighter, aching to fix whatever was wrong. She'd had enough to deal with for the last eighteen months. She could abdicate responsibility to him.

She barely moved a muscle, and yet he could've sworn she wanted to drop her head to her hands. She didn't. Instead she lifted her chin in his direction, but her gaze didn't meet his. 'This hardly needs saying, Harry, but you're a very attractive man.'

He hated how tense she'd become. 'Are you sure this

isn't a break-up speech?' he teased. 'It's sounding more and more like one.'

The corners of her mouth twitched, just for a moment. 'Can't you be serious for ten minutes?'

Sure he could, when he had to be. But he really wanted to hear her laugh.

Her mouth pressed into a firm line. 'No falling in love. No breaking up.'

'That's my motto.'

'Except I've been celibate for eighteen months, and...'

He couldn't begin to imagine it. 'And?'

She grimaced. 'And in those eighteen months the closest I've been to a man who isn't related to me was this evening on the dance floor with you.'

Her meaning hit him then. He rocked back in his seat.

'See?' she hissed, clearly misinterpreting his reaction as shock, rather than what it truly was—excitement. 'So when I said it wasn't you, that you did nothing wrong, I meant it. It was me—all me. And this would've been better left unsaid. It would've saved us a lot of embarrassment.'

'Ella—'

'Look, I know it's normal, all right? So, please, no platitudes.'

Platitudes were the last thing on his mind.

'And I get that I should find it...*unsettling*. But you want to know what I find really confronting? You invited me to the party tonight out of kindness.' Her bottom lip wobbled. 'And maybe pity.'

He stabbed a finger to the leather car seat between them. 'Not pity.'

'But you did it to introduce me to influential people and help get my name out there. You didn't have to do that.'

'I did it because I believe in you.'

'See?' She lifted her hands as if he'd said something

dreadful. 'You're this great guy who's trying to do meaningful things with a seriously worthy charity, and I promised to act as a kind of shield tonight because I knew how important it was for you to present a wholesome image. But little did I know you'd need a shield against me!' She met his gaze. 'But when we were out on the dance floor, Harry, I didn't care about any of that. All I could think about was what it'd be like to get naked with you and—'

He pressed his fingers to her lips. 'Not helping,' he ground out, trying to get the thundering of his blood under control.

She stared at him and her eyes widened as they raked his face. 'No,' she whispered.

But it sounded less like a refutation than a revelation.

'No,' she said again, shaking her head. 'I'm not the kind of woman you'd find attractive.'

He blinked. 'What kind of woman would that be?'

'Beautiful.'

Dear God. This woman.

He undid his seat belt, slid across to the middle seat and put that seat belt on instead.

Her eyes went wide. 'What are you doing?'

'You are beautiful, Elle.'

'Don't be ridiculous.' Her throat bobbed. 'And what did you just call me?'

'Did you not look at yourself in the mirror tonight?'

The limousine was roomy, but this close they couldn't help but brush thighs and arms. And every touch fired a shot of energy and desire through his blood. He knew it did for her too from the way she tried to shift away to avoid—how had she phrased it?—feeling unsettled by the rush of feelings they evoked in each other. The rocking of the car, though, made it impossible, and he had no desire, or intention, of avoiding it.

He wanted to touch all of her. He wanted to explore her every inch with his hands and mouth. He craved to know what would give her pleasure, and he hungered to feel those small clever hands on his body—

He hauled himself back, appalled at how consumed he'd become by the fantasy he'd started to weave. They had a couple of things to clear up first. 'You are beautiful,' he repeated, 'but, like every other woman on the planet, you're going to say, *Oh, but this part of me is too big, and this part is too small, while that bit is too wide, and there's a blemish there...* Yada-yada-yada.'

'"Yada" being a technical term, I suppose?' But her breath hitched as she said it and he knew her equilibrium was hanging by a thread. Just like his.

'You *are* beautiful, Ella, but you also have an inner fire that lights you up from the inside out, and it's drawing me like a proverbial moth.' He wanted to dive right down into the middle of that flame.

Playing with fire is dangerous.

He shook the thought off. He was adept at not getting burned and making sure nobody else got burned either.

She stared at him as if she hadn't properly seen him until this very minute.

'I really want to kiss you,' he said, his heart thumping with need. 'I've wanted to kiss you since I first saw you in the restaurant when you barely registered who I was.'

Her chin shot up. 'I registered!'

'Can I kiss you, Elle?'

She swallowed. 'God, when you call me that...' Desire-drenched eyes met his. 'I want you to kiss me so badly, I think I might die if you don't.'

As they spoke, they turned more fully to each other. He cupped her face, revelling in the softness of her skin and the fine bones beneath his fingertips. Her fingers closed about his lapels and they pulled each other closer as if they each had a magnet drawing the other nearer and nearer. Millimetres from each other's lips, they paused—as if to breathe each other in, as if fixing the moment in their minds—and then their mouths came together and there was nothing tentative about that.

For a brief moment he felt unbalanced, as if he'd hit ice on his skis and was in danger of crashing down a mountain, but at the last moment Ella's mouth opened beneath his and everything suddenly righted itself.

He couldn't put together a single coherent thought after that. Sensation pounded through him—glorious, exhilarating and better than any damn race he'd ever run. Ella's mouthed moved against his, just as hungry, just as demanding, driving him to new heights, filling him with a wild, desperate need.

Lips, teeth, tongue—all teasing inevitable rhythm. Her hands on his jaw, fingernails scraping lightly across the designer stubble he swore he wore for just this purpose. But it had never felt this good before. Small strong hands that moved from the sides of his neck to splay across his chest, pushing aside his waistcoat, to glory in his heat and the muscled strength of his torso.

Dear God, it wasn't nearly enough. He needed more. Where the hell was the zip on her dress?

He found it—a side zip—and lowered it, before bringing his fingers back up, knuckles brushing against the side of her breast. He caught her shocked cry in his mouth, and the electric ripple of her body flowed through him too. Pressing kisses to her throat, he lowered the bodice of her dress until her breasts were proudly exposed in the sheerest of white lace bras.

He brushed his knuckles down the sides of both breasts and again that shocked gasp and electric shudder ripped through her. Leaning forward, he drew one erect nipple into his mouth and laved it with his tongue. She arched into him, her hands partially lifted as if to tunnel into his hair, but her arms stopped short, pinned to her sides by the bodice of her dress, and a primal roar of satisfaction filled him.

When she was lying half reclined like that, lips kiss-swollen, hair mussed and her breasts exposed for his delectation as she gazed up at him, eyes drunk with arousal, he felt like a king or sultan. And every time he ran the backs of his fingers along the sides of her breast, another electric jolt shook her.

Her nipples grew harder and tighter. He drew her other nipple into his mouth, and continued the knuckle brushing down the sides of her breasts until she was sobbing with need. Could he make her come just from this? He'd love to try and—

'Harry.'

Her voice, threaded with need, drew him back and he suddenly froze. Was he really in danger of taking her in the back of his car like some randy teenager? She hadn't made love to a man in eighteen months. *Eighteen months!*

She deserved to be wooed and cherished…made to feel like a queen. She deserved fine champagne, a king-size bed, and Egyptian cotton sheets. She deserved a man who would make the experience memorable.

He dragged in a breath before lifting his head. 'Spend the night with me, Ella.' He'd take her back to his place and give her everything she wanted—and everything she didn't know she wanted. He'd shower her with so much attention it'd turn her head.

She stared into his eyes and he saw the desire, the yearning, the temptation all reflected there. She wanted him every bit as much as he wanted her.

And then she closed her eyes, her face screwing up tight. 'We can't, Harry. Oh, God, we can't.'

Every muscle screamed a protest. He wanted to argue. He wanted to kiss her until she stopped thinking and started feeling again…until she begged him not to stop.

Instead, he pulled the bodice of her dress back up, and slid back into his original seat to try and give them both the air they desperately needed, averting his gaze as she drew up her zipper and tried to straighten herself back out again.

'Why can't we?' he asked when he was sure he could control his voice and ask the question gently. She didn't deserve his frustration. She deserved his understanding.

She remained silent for so long he didn't think she was going to answer. 'I won't do anything that could cast a shadow over Susie's wedding,' she finally said. 'It wouldn't be fair.'

He opened his mouth.

'I know you don't think it's fair that the family has any say in my sex life.'

'You don't *have* a sex life, Ella.' And she wasn't likely to get one if she continued to let her family have any say in the matter.

'When I do start dating again it's going to cause a ruckus. I'll deal with that as and when I have to, but the lead up to Susie's wedding definitely isn't the time.'

He dragged a hand down his face. She had a point. Had he completely forgotten his promise to Martin? He had a duty as best man to ensure the wedding ran as smoothly as it could.

'And anyway—'

He could feel the heat of her gaze.

'What happened to your no romance rule? I know you don't want to do anything to jeopardise your deal with Bright Directions. Why risk that for a quick fling with me?'

Ice stepped down his spine and slowly but inexorably filled his chest, spreading out to his limbs until they felt like frozen lead. The charity deal was so important to Lily, meant so much to her. Was he really so selfish that he'd endanger it?

His lips thinned. He was exactly like his father. He'd been fighting it all his life, but what further proof did he need? And that meant he had to stay away from a woman like Ella. 'You're right. I'm sorry. I lost my head.'

'I'm sorry too.'

He had to close his eyes against the need that threaded her whisper.

They barely spoke again until the car pulled up in front of her workshop. He slid out first and offered her his hand, but she ignored it. He didn't blame her. Touch was a torment. He didn't offer to walk her to her door. 'I'll wait here until you're inside.'

She glanced up. 'I'm—'

'I'll see you Sunday,' he cut in. 'Good luck tomorrow. I hope the day is a roaring success. We'll compare notes on Sunday.'

She dragged in a breath and nodded. 'Goodnight, Harry.'

CHAPTER EIGHT

WHEN HARRY'S CAR pulled up outside her workshop on Sunday morning, Ella didn't bother pretending that she hadn't noticed. She stood in the doorway as he strode towards her, those long legs covering the distance with a loose-limbed ease that had all the feelings he'd evoked in her on Friday night roaring to instant life.

Don't think about Friday night.

Of course, she hadn't been able to think of anything else since.

Then think of Susie.

That, at least, had her pushing her shoulders back and pasting on a smile. One glance into his face, though, had her gaze sliding away. 'C'mon in, it's turned chilly.'

This time Tuesday they'd be on a plane winging their way to the balmy climes of Malaysia, leaving the winter chill behind. *It'll be fun.* She gritted her teeth and tried harder. *It'll be fun!*

'Did you want another sewing lesson while we compare notes about yesterday's events?' Yesterday had been their unofficial hen and stag parties.

'Love one.'

She'd put an inordinate amount of thought into this meeting, hadn't wanted them to sit awkwardly at the table, staring at each other while nursing mugs of coffee. It'd be easier to talk if they had something else to focus on.

She moved to the sewing machines. 'You've mastered the main construction of the boxy tops I make for the markets.'

The tops were ridiculously easy to make—nothing more than a back and front, sewn together, with simple cuff sleeves. But she made them in such breezy bright fabrics that they flew off the racks. Inexpensive to make, and she priced them to sell.

'Those sleeves were tricky.' He took a seat at what had become *his* machine.

'But you got the hang of them.' He'd insisted on unpicking one sleeve three times to get it perfect. His determination had impressed her. 'There're just two more things to do before your top is finished.'

He swung to her. 'No way!'

'Yes way. And the first of those is to bias bind the neckline.' She pointed. 'The bias binding is the long thin piece we cut.'

She'd set his work in progress beside his workstation and grabbed a finished top from the pile she was working on. 'This is what we want our finished product to look like.'

He took it and studied the neckline thoroughly. She swallowed at the intensity of his gaze. Dear God. If she'd said yes to spending the night with him on Friday evening, all of that amazing focus would've been squarely concentrated on her and—

She rattled back into speech. 'This is how we attach it.' She showed him how to pin the binding to the neckline. 'And we sew along there.'

'Fiddly,' he muttered.

That was the plan—to keep his attention focussed elsewhere rather than on her. 'The sleeves were fiddly too, but you managed those. Just take it slow. Cuppa?'

'Maybe later.'

Damn. She'd hoped for a break from the enticing scent of leather and amber. Seizing one of the unfinished tops from her pile, she started sewing. She'd attached bias binding to necklines so often she could do it on autopilot. Gritting her teeth, she did exactly that now.

'You are demoralisingly fast.'

She glanced across to find him staring at her with a frown in his eyes. She straightened. Did he think she was showing off? 'Oh, Harry, I've done this so many times I could do it with my eyes closed. Not recommended, of course. Needles are sharp. You don't want one going into a finger.'

He leaned fractionally closer. 'You've done that?'

'Only the once.'

That made him laugh and the laugh lightened something inside her. She gestured at her sewing machine. 'The equivalent would be if you put me on a pair of skis. I've never skied in my life, and I promise you don't want to see that. I'd spend more time flat on my face than upright.'

'You're wrong. I would like to see that.'

'Ha! So you could get a few cheap laughs.'

The colour in his eyes became richer and deeper. 'So I could watch you master the necessary skills,' he corrected. 'I think you'd love it. There's nothing like the freedom of flying down a mountain, the air crisp and cold, the sky blue and everything dazzling white and sparkling like crystal.'

She almost said, 'When can we go?' She gulped the words back. 'How did the boys' day go yesterday?'

He was quiet for a moment, but when she glanced at him, he'd turned back to his machine. 'It was great, really relaxed.'

'Even the dads?'

He nodded and she let out a breath she hadn't known she'd been holding. It occurred to her in that moment how grateful she was to him. For *so* many things.

'After the baseball—which was a real hit, by the way—it was back to mine for burgers and beer and games of pool. It wasn't a particularly late night, but it was nice to kick back.'

'Sounds perfect.'

'Your turn.'

She gave up all pretence of sewing. 'It was mixed. The fittings were fun. Everyone loves their outfits. And as you suggested, I played the soundtracks from *Grease*, *Mamma Mia* and *Dirty Dancing* while we did that. The mums were in good form and we all hummed and swayed along in good moods. Susie couldn't stop smiling.'

'So why aren't *you* smiling now?'

She moistened her lips. 'I hadn't realised our picture made the society pages.'

He grimaced. 'Ah.'

'And neither did the mums or Susie. However, Cousin Adele…remember her?'

'The tragic one?'

She nodded. 'When the larger party arrived, she took a lot of glee in showing said society page around.' She'd had to endure a series of pointed questions. 'I told them it was a work thing.' Which was exactly what it had been.

'Did they believe you?'

'I think so, but Auntie Rachel was quiet for the rest of the day.' Which meant her mum had been quiet too.

She'd organised a painting party. A café in the city held social painting evenings, and it had become all the rage. She'd spoken to the artist who ran the events and she'd agreed to run a private party for them. Set up with easels, canvases and paints, they'd endeavoured to paint Susie in a silly mock veil. Susie had loved it.

The mums had said they'd had fun, but that hadn't stopped them casting perturbed glances in her direction whenever they thought she wasn't looking. They'd felt betrayed. She'd seen it in their eyes. Not only had she left the family firm, but she'd also gone on a date with a man who wasn't James. And even if that date had been platonic, it was still a milestone. Another infinitesimal shift away from James.

'They need to get used to the idea of you moving on, Ella.'

His words pulled her back. 'Yes, but not the week of the wedding.'

'Not this week.' His mouth tightened and he turned back to his sewing machine. But his words didn't sound like agreement. They sounded like a warning. 'Not this week,' he repeated as if to wedge them in his mind.

Her eyes narrowed. If she didn't know better, she'd think he was up to something.

He straightened. 'Did I tell you I spoke to the resort manager? He's making sure everything we requested is on hand.'

'Excellent.' They'd come up with a range of group activities to keep things light and fun for the week, to help everyone get into the holiday spirit; to give Susie and Martin a week they could look back on with pride for the rest of their lives. Ella crossed her fingers.

'What now?'

She snapped to. What did he mean?

He held the top towards her and she realised he was referring to the sewing.

She scrutinised his stitches. 'What are you? Some

child sewing prodigy?' She handed it back. 'That's amazingly neat.'

'I'm hardly a child, Ella.'

His lips twisted, and every moment of Friday night with her dress down around her waist and his hands and lips on her breasts rose up between them. She tried to drag her gaze from his, but he held it captive.

'This isn't working,' he bit out, gesturing at the sewing machines.

She didn't bother misunderstanding him. 'Well, I don't imagine talking about it is going to help either, so if you have any other bright ideas, I'm all ears.'

'Oh, I'm full of bright ideas.' He slid across on the castor wheels of his chair, closing the distance between them with a speed that had her gulping. His hands went either side of her on the table, his bulk and his heat crowding her in. 'Here's one—we race upstairs right now, make mad passionate love until we've had our fill and get this thing out of our system.'

Had she ever been more tempted by anything in her life?

'Just say the word, Ella, and I'm there. Or if you don't want to speak, just nod.'

Her heart tried to hammer a path right out of her chest. She couldn't think when he was this close. Planting a hand on that broad, hard chest, she gently pushed. He gave way immediately. 'There are too many flaws with that plan.'

He folded his arms. 'Hit me with them.'

'They'll know.' The mums would know.

He looked suddenly tired. 'Ella…'

She thought her heart would break at the expression in his eyes. 'I know! I know!' The family had no right to judge her. She had nothing to feel guilty about. 'But I won't do anything that could cast a shadow on Susie's wedding. She lost a brother she dearly loved, Harry. This is a new beginning for her and I don't want anything to mar it.'

'And when do you get your new beginning?'

She gestured at her workshop. 'I'm making a start.'

He dragged a hand down his face. 'What other flaws are there in my plan?' he eventually asked, pointing upstairs as if to remind her of the plan.

As if she could forget it! She swallowed. 'I don't think once is going to be enough to get this thing out of my system, Harry.'

He shot out of his chair and raced around the drafting table until its bulk stood between him and her. He braced his arms against it as if to stop from…what? Hauling her into his arms and kissing her?

Her pulse went mad.

'Eighteen months is a long time to…' Today it felt like an eternity. 'And I don't want to start something now that's in danger of spiralling out of control for the next week and—' She broke off, refusing to let her mind dwell on tropical beaches and balmy, starlit nights. 'My focus needs to stay centred on the wedding.'

She risked glancing across at him. Both his hands and eyes were clenched and he was dragging in deep breaths as if he was counting. She wanted to yell at him to find someone else to torment if he was feeling all hot and bothered, but the thought of him with another woman…

She flinched.

He pointed a finger at her. 'As soon as we're back in Australia, you and I are going out on the town, Ella. I'm going to wine and dine you and shower you with attention and spoil you. At the end of the evening I'm going to do my utmost to seduce you. And I'm going to do it again and again until you've had your fill.'

Best plan ever! She wanted that so badly, but…

Don't be an idiot.

She made herself laugh. 'We're from such totally different worlds, Harry. You're a successful high-flying millionaire and former world champion while I'm a nobody who barely has two brass tacks to rub together at the moment. We run in different circles.' She rested an elbow on the table and brow in her hand. 'I've absolutely no expectation of seeing you again once we return to Australia.'

The words tasted bitter in her mouth, but she forced herself to say them, forced herself to face the reality. It was better to face that reality now than later. 'No expectations at all,' she repeated.

Harry froze at Ella's words. Very slowly he straightened. 'You really believe that?'

She lifted her head and it looked as if it took all of her energy to do so. Lines of exhaustion fanned out from her eyes, but he hardened his heart. 'If that's what you think friendship means to me then you're right, we've nothing else to talk about.'

He shoved his arms into the coat he'd shrugged off when he'd arrived. 'I'm glad to have found this out now, though, rather than a week or two down the line, because I make it a rule to not sleep with women who have such a low opinion of me.'

She shot to her feet. 'Oh, Harry, wait. I—'

But he'd already started for the door. A white-hot anger he'd not experienced since he was a kid had him in its grip and he knew he had to get out of here before he unleashed its full force on her.

Had anyone ever offended him quite so fully? Had he ever felt more disappointed in his life? How had he got her so wrong?

He sensed what he was feeling was out of proportion to the crime, but he couldn't think straight.

Before he lashed out, he needed to think straight.

'Harry, I—'

He swung around. 'Once we return from Malaysia, I expect you'll have no trouble whatsoever finding someone to help you scratch whatever itch you need scratching. For as long as it needs scratching.'

She paled and took a step back.

He stalked out of the door and didn't look back.

Harry did everything to avoid Ella at the airport on Tuesday. He'd taken her call yesterday, but only because he'd thought it might have something to do with the wedding. When she'd tried to stutter out an apology, he'd cut her off with a curt, 'Not now, Ella,' and had hung up.

She'd evidently got the message, because other than a nod and quiet, 'Hello, Harry,' in the airport lounge, she'd kept her distance.

Which was exactly what he wanted!

But he was now crammed into a window seat beside second cousin once-removed Uncle Aubrey, while Ella was hemmed in in a middle row with the great-aunts.

The wedding group were all roughly seated in the same section but scattered about in pockets. The benefit of that meant there was plenty of seat-hopping. The downside was that Adele—the tragic one—kept casting glances in his direction. With Ella no longer running interference for him, he knew the moment Aubrey vacated his seat Adele would fill it.

Harry did everything he could to avoid the Adeles of the world. She was the kind of woman who'd claim she only wanted a bit of fun, but that clearly wasn't the case. She'd want everything—love, marriage, babies. It wouldn't matter how often he said he wasn't interested in any of that, she'd be certain she could change his mind.

All hell would break loose when she realised he was in earnest. There'd be scenes. He'd be accused of misleading her, of taking advantage. Sweat broke out on his top lip. He'd promised Martin he'd keep things running smoothly. He couldn't afford that kind of scene.

Serves you right for not accepting Ella's apology.

If only he could catch Ella's eye... But he was pressed up hard in his window seat while she was in that darn middle row, several rows ahead of him. He could see her dark curls from time to time. He fancied that they drooped rather than bounced, and he cursed silently.

Why the hell had he taken such offence on Sunday anyway? If the papers were anything to go by, he was a fly-by-night who didn't have a serious bone in his body. Why should she trust him? What true signs of friendship had he actually given her?

He'd offered her business his support. And then he'd pressured her for sex! He'd told her he was off dating and romance, and yet he'd kissed her and asked her to spend the night with him. Why *would* she trust him?

As if his imagination had conjured her, she walked past on her way to the restrooms. She didn't spare him a single glance. He didn't blame her. He cursed himself for not thinking quicker and finding a way to make her stop and talk to him and Aubrey.

Aubrey broke off his monologue about the three months he'd spent in India forty years ago—a reminiscence that thankfully required very little input from Harry—to say, 'I hope you're not thinking of messing with our Ellie.'

He wanted to tell the other man to go to hell. The savage urge made him blink. Alpha confrontations and testosterone-driven beatings of his chest had never been his style.

It made too many ugly headlines. Humour and charm had always been his weapons of choice.

'I like Ella a lot. And I respect her. We're friends. I can't imagine anyone here having a problem with that, can you?'

'I guess not.' But the older man looked dubious, and in that moment Harry realised the seating arrangement hadn't been a happy accident. It had been managed by the family.

He shuffled upright. *Game on.*

He nodded towards the great-aunts. 'I believe Edith has been trying to catch your eye.' He paused. 'She's a fine-looking woman, don't you think?'

'I… Well…' Aubrey straightened and squared his shoulders. 'She has an admirable sense of style.'

'If you want a tip from me, and I have quite the reputation with the ladies…'

He watched the older man struggle with his dignity before capitulating. 'Let's have it, then, son.'

'If you'd like to charm that entire row of women, order them all a pina colada, and then go join them.'

'But I hate those sweet sticky things.'

'You don't have to drink one. You go sauntering up there with something manly in hand, like a Scotch and soda or a brandy. But what will really win their admiration is if you go back to them with gossip…about me.'

His eyes narrowed. 'But I don't have any.'

'You could make it up the way the newspapers do. Or,' he continued when Aubrey started shaking his head, 'I could give you some. And I will. On the condition you make sure Ella takes your seat when she comes back from the restroom. The thing is…' he leaned in closer '… I really need to avoid Adele. She has a gleam in her eye.'

'I thought you'd like that! She's a pretty girl and a woman with a gleam in her eye isn't to be sneezed at.'

Was Adele a set-up? He filed the thought away. 'Normally I would, but I need to clean up my playboy image for business reasons, and Ella has been helping with that—acting as a kind of shield to keep other women at bay.'

'Well, I'll be! You've had us all worried.'

'Of course, Ella and I aren't spreading that around. We want the focus of this coming week to be on Susie and Martin.'

'Naturally.'

'We need to make sure that the bride and groom have a week they'll remember for the rest of their lives. In a *good* way. Ella and I have been putting our heads together to come up with ways to make sure that happens.'

'So *that's* what all this has been about?'

'Absolutely.' People went to hell for lying as well as he did. 'We've been thrown together due to the wedding prep, so we decided to make the most of it. I'm helping endorse her business, and she's helping keep problematic women at bay. Win-win, see?'

'Well, I'll be.'

'Here comes Ella now.'

Aubrey immediately stood, moved into the aisle, and all but manhandled Ella into his seat. 'The poor lad needs protecting from Adele,' he said. 'You look after him, now, you hear?'

She gave a mock salute. 'Aye, aye, Captain.'

Aubrey gestured to a steward and put in his order for five pina coladas and a brandy, and then followed in the steward's wake as they were delivered.

Ella turned towards Harry but didn't meet his eye. 'If you want me to find another seat, I can organise for one of the boys—'

'I asked Aubrey to make sure you sat here.'

She eyed him warily. 'You did?' Then she stiffened. 'Is

something wrong? Do we need to go into emergency containment mode or—?'

'It's nothing like that.'

She eased back, pursed her lips. 'So...you'll let me apologise now?'

He nodded, his head suddenly heavy. 'Yes, but—'

'Oh, Harry, I'm so sorry! What I said to you on Sunday was truly offensive. I didn't mean it to be. It came out all wrong. And honestly, it's more of a reflection on me and my insecurities than it is on the kind of man you are. You've shown me nothing but consideration and kindness. And I had absolutely no reason to doubt you.'

'I think you've every reason for those doubts, but we'll get to that in a moment. What do you mean it's a reflection of your insecurities?' The vulnerability in her eyes made his chest hitch. 'What insecurities?'

She stared at her hands. 'I want new friends so badly. I mean, I told you that already. And I'm making them, which feels great.'

He was with her so far.

'I worry, though, that I want it—' Her nose wrinkled. 'This is going to sound so self-absorbed. I worry that I want that more than the people I'm becoming friends with want it.'

His heart lurched. *Oh, Ella, sweetheart.*

'The thought of being too needy and making people uncomfortable... I mean, that'd be awful. When you spoke about clingy women making you feel suffocated.' She shuddered. 'I don't want to be like that.'

'You're not coming across as needy, Ella, I swear.'

She pulled in a breath. 'You've done so much, Harry. You've helped me find my belief in myself again, helped me see that what I'm doing is what I should be doing.'

She glanced up. 'You're helping me find my feet with the family again.'

Except that last item was still a work in progress. The conversation he'd just had with Aubrey was proof of that.

'You've gone out of your way to endorse my brand. I just… I can't see— Please don't take this the wrong way, because I know friendship isn't about what you can get, it's not a financial transaction, but… I can't see what possible benefit my friendship is to you.'

Could she seriously not see her own awesomeness?

'At the moment we're working towards a common goal. We want to make sure this wedding is wonderful. But once we no longer have that point of connection…'

'You thought I'd wash my hands of you.'

She grimaced. 'I had that wrong. I can see now you value friendship every bit as much as I do. What I said on Sunday was me trying to put up a wall so if it did happen and I never saw you again—it would help temper my disappointment.'

He couldn't speak.

'Harry, will you please accept my apology?'

'Utterly and wholeheartedly.'

She sagged. 'Thank you.'

Her words were so heartfelt he suddenly felt small. He didn't deserve them. 'Your honesty slays me.'

'We promised to be upfront with each other. Besides, I was so ashamed of myself when you stormed out on Sunday that nothing less than a full and frank confession would suffice.'

'Do you want to know why I value our friendship, Ella?'

Raising both hands, she shook her head. 'Don't pander to my insecurities. It's not your job to make me feel better about myself.'

'It's because my status, my money, and my accomplishments don't impress you at all.'

'Yes, they do! I—'

'What impresses you is how hard I've worked to achieve what I have. You don't care about the trophies and the trappings.'

Her eyes gentled. 'It sucks that you have to be on your guard around people because you can't trust their motives.'

'Ferociously,' he agreed. 'But you like me for the same reasons I like you—we value the same things, we have the same drive and the same sense of humour, we make each other laugh. And we have the same sense of adventure.'

Her mouth fell open. 'Adventurous, me?'

'What else would you call going out on your own to create Sew Sensational?'

She sat up a little straighter.

Adele chose that moment to amble over. 'Want to swap seats, Ellie? Uncle Derek was hoping to catch up with you.'

'Oh! Harry, we haven't started comparing notes yet on our schedules.'

He grimaced. 'My fault.'

Adele frowned. 'Schedules?'

'We've organised a few activities for the week,' Harry said, pretending to go through his phone. 'I need to tell you about the chat I had with the concierge, Ella.'

'Don't tell me he hasn't been able to organise all the things I asked him to.' She glanced up. 'Give us an hour, Adele.'

Adele drifted away. 'What happens in an hour?' he murmured.

'I fall asleep and you bury yourself in work emails.' She turned more fully to him. 'Speaking of work, did you close the deal with Bright Directions yesterday?'

'I did.'

'Yay! Congratulations. I'm so pleased for you.' She danced in her seat before high-fiving him. 'Lily must be so happy.' She pulled herself back into straight lines. 'Right, so when Adele comes back, hold a finger to your lips to tell her not to wake me and stage-whisper that you've a lot of work to get done.'

'Devious.'

'You're rubbing off on me.'

He settled back in his seat and everything suddenly felt perfect with the world.

CHAPTER NINE

BREATHLESS, ELLA CLAPPED and laughed, as did everyone else on the dance floor. Her father grinned. 'Who knew square dancing could be so much fun, eh, pumpkin?'

It was the end of their first full day in Langkawi, Malaysia, and the first of the planned activities that she and Harry had organised. None of the activities were compulsory. They were simply fun, light-hearted diversions designed to help everyone get into the holiday mood and make the most of their time here. Nobody, however, had sat the square dancing out.

Ella raised an eyebrow and her father laughed again. 'Okay, you and Harrison were inspired. How on earth did you know Aubrey was a square-dance caller?'

'He told Harry when they were sitting together on the plane.' It had seemed a fun way to bring the generations together and create a sense of community among the wedding guests.

'You and Harrison are doing good work here, poppet. I'm proud of you.'

Her old nickname had her eyes filling. 'Thanks, Dad. Susie deserves her dream wedding without the shadow of James's death hanging over it.' She'd never spoken so bluntly before and she held her breath, but her father only nodded.

'You're right. It's time to move on.'

And for the first time in a very long time, it felt possible. They'd always miss James, of course, how could they not? But they could also begin to live their lives again. They could allow themselves to be happy.

'Who are you dancing with next?' he asked, when Aubrey called for everyone to swap partners. 'And where should I set my sights?'

The rules were that you couldn't dance with your spouse or fiancé, and you couldn't dance with the same person twice.

'How gallant are you feeling, Dad?'

'*So* gallant. You've never met anyone more gallant.' He pressed a hand to his chest, his eyes twinkling, but then he sobered a fraction. 'I'm totally on board with what you're doing here, Ellie. I'll be as gallant as you need me to be. It's just…'

Her heart beat harder. 'What?'

'It's hard for your auntie Rachel, honey. She wants to give Susie the best wedding, and yet she's afraid we're all going to forget James in the process.'

'That's never going to happen.'

'And she's grieving so hard for all he's missing out on… the life he should've had.'

Her chest clenched. James should've had that life. He'd had the world at his feet. She swallowed the lump wanting to lodge in her throat. 'Which makes it hard on Mum, because it tears her up to see her best friend grieving, and she feels disloyal for wanting to move on…for wanting me to move on.' She pulled in a breath. 'I think Auntie Rachel needs to see a grief counsellor, Dad. And I think Mum should be suggesting it.'

'You could be right. In the meantime, we work on keeping everyone out of the doldrums and having fun.'

Exactly.

'So who do you need me to be gallant to? Who needs some cheering up?'

'Adele.'

His grin widened. 'That girl always needs cheering up. It'll be my pleasure. Oh, and look, here's young Harrison now.'

He clapped a hand to Harry's shoulder, intercepting him from what looked like his next target—Great-Aunt Edith. Wow, that was going above and beyond. Martin was going to owe him big time after this week.

'It must be time for the two of you to actually relax for ten minutes and enjoy yourselves. No doubt you have notes to compare. Keep up the good work.' With a wink, he waved to Adele. 'Look lively, young Adele. I want to see if you youngsters can keep up with a spring chicken like me.'

Harry's mouth hooked up. 'Am I mistaken or did your father just order me to dance with you?'

'Scandalous, isn't it?' she agreed, her pulse picking up pace as they took their place in a square.

'Your dad's right, though. It *is* nice to be able to let the guard down for a bit. Don't get me wrong, I'm having fun, but—'

'All of this vigilance is exhausting,' she agreed.

They hadn't planned to dance together, the memory of the dance at the ball too fresh in their minds, but... 'This is probably good,' she said as they do-si-doed. 'It might've looked odd if we hadn't had at least one dance.' And they'd agreed that they didn't want to do anything that would draw attention to them as a couple.

It shouldn't have been comfortable dancing with him, not when her body came alive at his touch, and heat pooled in places she hadn't known she had as he swung her around and they promenaded. But they had to concentrate so hard on Aubrey's directions, and they laughed so hard when they made a mistake that it… It just felt like letting out a big pent-up breath. 'Extraordinary,' she murmured.

'What is?'

'Just talking to myself,' she said as they led a chain. Before he could question her further, she said, 'Were you about to brave Great-Aunt Edith before my father co-opted you for my dance card?'

'We're a few men short and some of the great-aunts are taking on the men's parts. I thought I'd give them a break.'

He really was a nice man. She squeezed his hand as they went round and round. 'Now I know what Adele and I are doing in the next set.'

His eyes twinkled. 'You're brilliant, you know that?'

Those whisky dark eyes looked at her with so much warmth it made her feel like a million dollars. That was the moment when she really believed that, between them, they could pull this off. They could make sure that Susie and Martin had the wedding of their dreams, and in the process they might even help the family turn their faces towards the future.

They truly were in paradise. Ella moved out onto the deck and down into the shadowed coolness of the garden beyond. A low moon hung in a navy sky, a silver path lighting a sparkling trail to it on an equally navy sea.

'Paradise,' she whispered, welcoming the balmy warmth of the air against her bare arms. She wondered if it ever got cold here.

A few steps brought her to the beach and she kicked off her sandals to dig her toes into the sand, relishing the sensation, relishing the peace.

Not that it was particularly quiet. The hum of crickets and frogs, the chatter of monkeys and an occasional squawk from a night bird filled the air. But behind it was the supremely peaceful sound of water sighing on sand, and the treetops rustling in the breeze.

A figure emerged from the undergrowth to her left, making her start.

'Everything okay?'

Harry. Pressing a hand to her heart, she nodded.

He moved towards her with that long-limbed ease that made her mouth go dry. She ordered herself to not focus on the moonlight, or the fact this was one of the most romantic locations she'd ever been in. 'All's well. I just stepped out for a moment of quiet.' She gestured towards the recreation room and their party. 'It gets a bit much after a while.'

'You want to be alone? I'll leave you to it and see you back inside—'

'No, no, it's as good a time as any to compare notes.'

They turned to survey their party. One wall of the recreation room was glass, allowing them to see inside, though a proportion of their group had also spilled outside to the deck. Everyone looked as if they were having fun—some dancing, some playing pool. 'I think Susie and Martin are having a good time, don't you?'

'They're having a great time. Your dance lesson was inspired.'

She'd organised for a professional dancer to come tonight and teach them a dance routine to a medley of Susie's favourite songs. 'A few people wanted square dancing again, but it didn't seem fair for Aubrey to miss out on all the fun, and I don't want to wear the poor man out. The dance lesson was the next best thing and right up Susie's alley.' She shrugged. 'It was more of a hit with the girls than the guys, though, so the pool and darts was a nice idea.'

'It's official. We're the best damn bridesmaid and best man on the island.'

They high-fived.

'Right, tomorrow's agenda.' She rubbed her hands together, trying to appear calm and pragmatic…trying to rub away the tingling caused by the palm-on-palm contact. 'We have lots of lazing by the pool or on the beach, plus kayaking for those who want something more energetic. And we need final numbers for the river cruise. So—'

'Before we get to that… How do you think everyone's doing? I mean *really* doing? Susie and Martin are happy, but what about your mother and your auntie Rachel?'

Through the glass wall, she watched her parents move to a table, both holding glasses with little umbrellas in them, to join Uncle Derek, who was nursing a beer. They all looked a little flushed and smiling. 'The break has been really good for my parents.' She cocked her head to one side. 'And Uncle Derek too, I think. I haven't seen any of them looking this relaxed in a long time.' She rubbed a hand across her chest. 'They deserve to have some fun. To be happy.'

'And your auntie Rachel?'

His question speared into all of the sore places in her heart. She searched what she could see of the room and deck. Where was Rachel? She should be there with Ella's parents and Uncle Derek.

Was Rachel in her room in the dark, unhappy and grieving? Ella swallowed. 'She's doing her absolute best to make this a happy time for Susie, but she's not happy. She hadn't been happy since—' A lump stretched her throat into a painful ache. 'Oh, Harry, James wouldn't want this for her, and I don't know what I can do to help.'

Harry turned more fully towards her, his expression grave. 'And how are *you* doing, Ella? You've been putting on a brave face, but it can't be as easy as you're making out.'

Unbidden, tears burned the backs of her eyes. She stared at the room full of happy, smiling people and the world tilted as grief blindsided her. It had been like this in the early days. In those moments when she'd briefly forget James had died, and then remember again. It had always felt like a physical blow. She'd thought she was over the worst of it, but…

'James should be here.' Her voice came out low and vehement, as she gestured at their party. 'He should be in there proud as punch of his little sister and teasing her for her appalling taste in music. He should be in there good-naturedly ribbing Martin and cleaning up at pool. He'd have loved this, and it's so *wrong* that he's not a part of it.'

She gulped back a sob, breathing hard.

Closing her eyes, she counted to five before forcing them open again. 'He should be here but he's not. And that can't be changed. Dwelling on it does no good. And he wouldn't want us to be miserable. If he thought we were moping around it'd horrify him.'

It was the truth and she'd tried to honour that, but… 'He'd want us to be happy. He'd want us to get on with our lives. He'd want us to remember the good times instead of resenting the fact we no longer get a chance to make new memories with him. If we don't move on…' She shrugged, not sure she could explain it. 'It feels as if we'd be break-ing faith with him in some weird way and not honouring his memory.'

She pressed her hands to her cheeks, mortified to find them wet. She closed her eyes again. 'I'm sorry, Harry. I haven't…not for a while and…'

He squeezed her shoulder. 'Grief's like that, Ella. You've nothing to apologise for.'

Oh, but she did. *So much.* He had no idea.

'Tell me a good memory.'

She lifted her eyes to the night sky. She'd not allowed herself the luxury of sifting through those, hadn't thought she'd deserved them, but couldn't resist the lure now. A sudden smile shifted through her. 'When I was thirteen, I wanted to make the girls' under-fourteen representative soccer side. James spent three months training with me every afternoon after school. Even though he hated training.'

'Did you make the side?'

'Yep. He made it onto the boy's rep team too, even though he hadn't planned to trial.' She laughed. 'I nominated him without him knowing. He loved to play, but loathed the training. It took him a long time to forgive me for that.'

Harry's chuckle filled the air, and it warmed her in ways that no man—not even James—had done. She reached for another memory. 'Whenever I had a cold he'd make me eat a bowl of chicken soup, and once I'd eaten it he'd then go out and buy me a bag of hot chips, because that's what I craved whenever I was under the weather. He'd then watch my favourite rom coms with me without complaining. It always made me feel cared for.'

She turned to meet his gaze. 'I have a lot of good memories, Harry.' Could she find a way to remember them without dwelling—?

'Whenever James was feeling under the weather, you'd sneak him chocolate bars and would play endless games of whatever his latest favourite computer game happened to be.'

She swung around. *Auntie Rachel!*

Oh, my God, how long had she been standing there? Had they said anything that might've hurt her? 'I—' She swallowed. 'If anything we just said upset you, I'm really sorry. We—'

'I have a feeling it's me who owes you an apology, Ellie. I've been so resentful towards you for making plans that don't involve James, that I… I've lost sight of some important things.' The older woman stared down at her hands. 'I haven't been fair to you. After all, what else are you expected to do? Stay stuck in some kind of grief rut for the rest of your life?'

She moved forward to brush her thumbs beneath Ella's eyes and dry her tears.

'I'm ashamed to admit it, but a selfish part of me hasn't wanted you to move on. I haven't wanted anyone to move on. But that has to stop. It's not fair to you, it's not fair to your mother. And you're right, it's not fair to James's memory.'

Did she mean that?

'I'd been afraid that you were forgetting James and if you forget him—'

'How could I ever forget him?' She seized Rachel's hands—this woman had been a second mother to her. 'He'd been a part of my life forever. I loved him.'

Rachel pulled her into a fierce hug. 'And a part of me has always known that, Ellie, I promise you. It's just been unbearable to me to consider my life without James in it.'

They eased apart. 'He was your son. Of course it's hard to move on.'

Rachel ran a hand over Ella's hair. 'You said sadness isn't what James would wish for us, and you're right. I don't want to move on without him, but as I heard you talking just now I realised that if I don't I'll be in danger of losing the good memories, and all the good times we shared. If that should ever happen, that's when I truly lose my son.'

'So…' Ella bit her lip. 'You're okay?'

'Yes, my darling girl.' Rachel hugged her again. 'I'm going to be just fine.' She released her and gestured towards the party. 'I'm going to join the group. You?'

A howl started up at the centre of her and she didn't

know how long she could keep it in. 'I'm going to take a moment to catch my breath. I actually wouldn't mind an early night.'

'If I don't see you for the rest of the evening, then sleep well.'

Something about the way Ella held herself, the way she pressed her arms tightly to her sides as she watched Rachel return to the party, told Harry all was not well.

The air around her trembled and simmered, and his every muscle tensed. What had he missed? That conversation with Rachel had indicated a turning point. Something Ella had fiercely wished for. She should be happy.

He leaned in close, the scent of peaches filling his nostrils. 'Ella?'

She started as if she'd forgotten he was there, turned with wild eyes. And then she spun away and sprinted down the beach.

What the hell…?

He stared and then set off after her. He understood her need to be alone, but they were in a strange place. What if she got lost or hurt herself?

Her sprint eventually slowed to a jog, and he kept easy pace beside her. Once they reached the end of the beach, she halted and rested her hands on her knees, winded. More from emotion than exercise, he suspected. Eventually she straightened to stalk across and plant herself on a flat rock and stare out to sea.

It was a large rock and he sat down too, uninvited. He knew from experience with Lily that sometimes sitting quietly beside someone could be the comfort they needed. Grief defied logic. He didn't try to press her for an explanation or the reason for her flight.

'I'm such a fraud, Harry.'

His every instinct told him to tread carefully. It was instinct that had saved his neck more than once as he'd negotiated the best route down a mountain, and it was instinct that had won him several world championships. He listened to instinct.

In this instant he metaphorically gripped it around the throat and held on tight, because it felt as if this moment mattered more than any race he'd ever run. Which was an odd notion. He pushed the thought aside. He'd work out what it meant later. 'I think you're one of the most genuine people I've ever met. What makes you say you're a fraud?'

She glanced up and the exhaustion in her eyes made his chest ache.

'Harry, James and I were going to break up.'

He had no hope of keeping the shock from his face. All of this time he'd thought they'd been this mythical golden couple and yet…

'All this time I've been playing the role of bereaved fiancée and it's been a lie.'

He closed his eyes.

'But how can I tell them that? It'd only cause more pain.'

He forced his eyes open. 'He died before the two of you had a chance to tell anyone?'

Her entire frame shook as she drew in a breath. 'James died before the two of us could have that conversation.'

'Hold on.' He shook his head to try and clear it. 'You and James hadn't discussed it yet?'

'I know how it sounds, but I knew James almost as well as I knew myself. When I told him I wanted to leave the firm to set up Sew Sensational…'

'You disagreed.' He remembered her mentioning that. 'But, Ella, some people are risk-averse and it takes them longer to—'

'It made us both realise that we wanted different things

in life, Harry.' She met his gaze once more, her smile heartbreakingly sad. 'And I realised I couldn't sacrifice my dream so he could have peace of mind and security.'

She stared back out to sea. 'And I know he was wrestling with all of that too. He'd always dreamed of running the family firm with his wife and passing it on to his children— a real *family* business.' She stared down at her hands. 'He always swam more when something was troubling him. He said it helped to quieten his mind—like meditation—and that in the quietness he could get to the heart of a matter. Find a way forward.'

Skiing could be like that too. His heart burned, though, that this was Ella's final memory of a man who'd obviously loved her as much as she had him.

'If he hadn't been so troubled about us, he wouldn't have been out swimming at such an early hour.'

'He was a fool to be swimming when it was still dark and there wasn't anyone else around.'

She stiffened. 'Lots of people do it.'

'Doesn't make it right. He should've taken more care.'

She spun on the rock. 'It was an accident. He didn't mean for it to happen!'

'Exactly.'

He saw the moment she registered his meaning. She turned back to stare at the sea, her lips pressed into a tight line.

'Ella, James's death wasn't your fault either. You need to stop blaming yourself.'

She still didn't turn.

'And I'll tell you another thing. You hadn't had the *"Are we staying together or breaking up?"* conversation with James yet, so, while you might've known him as well as another person can know someone else, you can only hypothesise on how the conversation would've gone. You can't know for sure.'

She turned back. 'I—'

'What if those early morning swimming sessions were him finding a way to work your new dream into your lives? What if he was reimagining your futures so you could both have what made you happy?'

'You can't know—'

'Neither can you!'

She blinked.

'Oh, Ella, do you really think the man who, as a thirteen-year-old, trained with you for three solid months so you could reach the dream you had then, was really going to ask you to give up your adult dreams? Do you truly think he wouldn't have done all he could to make sure you could follow your Sew Sensational dream?'

She swallowed.

'No doubt you took him by surprise and threw him for a loop, but do you truly think he was ready to throw in the towel?'

Her face crumpled and with an oath he pulled her into his arms as sobs wracked her body. 'Oh, sweetheart.' She'd been bottling these awful thoughts up and her guilt had been eating her alive.

He held her close, stroked her hair, and murmured meaningless nothings in the hope they'd soothe her. He'd do anything to take away her pain. Eventually the tears subsided, but she didn't move—she remained in his arms as if she didn't have the energy to move.

And God help him, but he loved the feel of her there, her warm weight pressing against him, the scent of peaches rising up all around him.

'Thank you,' she whispered.

She eased away and he immediately missed her warmth.

It took an effort not to pull her back against him. 'You don't need to thank me. I—'

'You've given James back to me.'

He stilled.

'And you've no idea what that means. Everything you just said is so true. I've been playing worst-case scenarios, tormenting myself. The thought that I'd somehow blighted his last days has haunted me. I…' She shook her head. 'Just like Auntie Rachel, I'd lost perspective.'

She met his gaze. 'I don't know if James and I would've made it as a couple or not, but you reminded me of one crucial fact. James was my best friend, and I was his. We wanted the best for each other. And that's one thing we never lost.'

He traced a finger down her cheek, and her breath hitched. 'He wouldn't have wanted you haunted in any kind of way.'

'No,' she agreed, her gaze dropping to his mouth and hunger stretching through her eyes.

Her face filled his vision, and roaring sounded in his ears. It was as if a strange force gripped him, one he had no control over. Their gazes met and held, he lowered his mouth towards hers—need, desire and craving flooding his every atom. Their breaths mingled, the air sawing in and out of their lungs, only a few centimetres separating them…

He froze. What the hell was he doing?

Look where you are. You're on a public beach.

Anyone from their group could walk by!

He shot to his feet.

She blinked and then stood too, one hand pressed to her ribs, just beneath her breasts as if she were trying to catch her breath. She glanced from him and then quickly out to sea. 'I'm sorry, Harry. Talk about sending you mixed messages.'

There'd been nothing mixed in what he'd read in her eyes. She'd wanted him with a fierceness that thrilled him. 'No apologies necessary. It's been an emotional evening.'

She turned, hands on hips, chin set at a defiant angle. 'The things that have happened tonight, Harry…they've freed me. I no longer feel guilty for wanting you. And I do want you. I'm tired of pretending I don't. I want to spend the night with you.'

He tried to wrestle the temptation back under control, tried to stop it from dragging him under. 'Two things,' he ground out.

She folded her arms. 'Okay.'

'We're not spending tonight together.'

Her face fell.

'If you were to regret it in the morning, I'd feel like a heel. You're vulnerable right now. I can't take advantage of that.'

She opened her mouth as if to argue, but then her shoulders slumped. 'While I think you're wrong. I don't want to make love with you if you're worried about that. It wouldn't be fair.'

Damn, he liked this woman.

'And the second thing?' she asked.

'The wedding.'

She turned away, raked both hands through those glorious curls.

'I know your auntie Rachel turned a corner this evening, but if word was to get out that you and I had…'

'It would cause…consternation.'

'And we don't want to do anything—'

'To ruin the wedding,' she finished, turning back to him.

He took a step towards her. Her eyes widened and the pulse in her throat fluttered like a wild thing. It took all of his strength not to press a kiss there. 'But come Monday, everyone leaves and we're here for another week. If you still feel the same way then…'

'I'll still feel the same way,' she said with a flattering swiftness that had him needing to anchor his feet more firmly on the sand.

He bent so they were eye to eye. 'Then you and I are going to spend some serious one-on-one time together in my cabin come Monday and I'm going to make you come so hard and so often you're going to cry Uncle.'

She leaned in closer until their breaths mingled. 'Challenge accepted. And we'll see who's actually crying Uncle by the end of the week.'

He went so hard he saw stars, and then he laughed. 'In the meantime I'm going to need a lot of cold showers.'

They walked back to the resort and had barely set foot on the deck when Ella's mother came racing up. 'My darling girl, Rachel told us about the conversation the two of you had. She's turned a corner and I'm so grateful.'

She folded Ella in a hug. Her eyes narrowed when she pulled away and stared into her daughter's face. 'You've been crying!'

'I'm fine, Mum. It's just been an emotional night, and poor Harry here copped the brunt of it. I'm sure I soaked his shirt.' She shrugged. 'I hadn't known I'd needed to turn another corner too, that's all. But I feel better now.'

Harry found himself enfolded in a hug then too. 'Thank you for being there for my daughter, Harry.'

She'd called him Harry not Harrison. He swallowed an unexpected lump. 'It was nothing. Ella is special. I'm proud to call her my friend.'

'And we're sorry, sweetheart,' her father said, moving to stand with them. 'From now on you get our unconditional support for Sew Sensational. We want to support you in anything that makes you happy.'

Ella's eyes filled. 'Thanks, guys, that means a lot.'

They shared a three-way hug and he could feel a grin—no doubt ridiculously goofy—break across his face.

'We're heading to bed,' Mr Hawthorne said. 'We'll see you in the morning.'

They watched the older couple stroll through the garden in the direction of their cabin, arm in arm, and Ella swung round to him. 'Just…wow. I'd have never achieved all of this on my own, Harry. Thank you. Thank you to the power of a million!'

She hugged him then and it made him feel like Superman.

CHAPTER TEN

EVEN THOUGH ELLA was minutely aware of Harry during her every waking moment, and, if her tangled sheets every morning were anything to go by, her every sleeping moment too, the next couple of days passed in a blur of fun and laughter and sightseeing.

Not that she and Harry saw those sights. For both the kayaking on the lagoon and the boat tour to explore the inland river system that they'd organised, more people turned up for the events than who'd registered interest, meaning they had to give up their slots.

'Don't even think about it,' she told her parents when they realised what had happened.

'But you organised it and your mother and I know you were looking forward to it.'

'There'll be time for sightseeing next week,' she told them.

The older couple exchanged glances. 'We were going to save this for when the wedding was over, poppet, but I think now is as good a time as ever. We've paid for you to have a beachside cabin next week. We thought the extra room would come in handy for your filming. It's our way of apologising and to let you know we truly do support you.'

'Oh, but—' Ella stared from one to the other. 'That's too generous. It's—'

'Nonsense!' Her mother hugged her, and so did her father. Ella had to blink hard when they eased away.

'Now don't let her go back to her room and sew, Harry,' her mother ordered. 'She deserves a holiday too.'

'I'm going to stretch out on that gorgeous beach with a magazine, and I plan to spend at least an hour bobbing about in the sea. I might even have a snorkel,' she told them.

'Sounds fabulous,' Harry said. 'Count me in. A lazy few hours is exactly what the doctor ordered.'

'The two of you have been working so hard behind the scenes. Don't think it's gone unnoticed. Ask the kitchen staff to pack you a picnic.'

Harry grinned and it made her heart beat too fast for comfort. 'This is sounding better and better.'

They waved everyone off and headed back to the resort. 'Where are you going?' Harry demanded when she turned in the direction of her room.

'I thought that with everyone out of the way, I might…'

He folded his arms and raised an eyebrow.

Okay… 'Harry, after last night and how…um…*tense* things got, I thought maybe you wouldn't want to spend too much one-on-one time with me.'

He straightened. 'Are you worried I won't be able to control myself?'

She sent him a self-deprecating grin. 'Unfortunately, I know you can.'

He spluttered out a laugh and then sobered. 'While we plan to become lovers, don't forget we're friends too. I enjoy spending time with you, Ella. I don't feel as if I'm treading water or biding my time. The plan you just outlined to your parents sounded like a fine one to me.'

Oh. She couldn't find her voice at all.

'You need to learn to live in the moment, learn to make

the most of your downtime. Becoming a workaholic won't help Sew Sensational in the long run.'

He had a point.

He nodded in the direction of her quarters. 'So where are you going?'

She swallowed. 'To grab my towel, a hat, my magazine and the sunscreen.'

'Perfect. I'll meet you back here in five.'

She couldn't believe how easy the next few hours were. She and Harry read, swam, chatted, swam some more, and ate a delicious hamper the resort's kitchen staff had whipped up, and for the first time in weeks, maybe months, she felt herself truly relaxing.

'I had no idea Malaysia was so beautiful.'

Palm trees lined a white sand beach, and they reclined in the shade of one now. Behind them was the lush greenness of the tropical rainforest where long-tailed macaques—small mischievous monkeys—waited for opportune moments to try and raid their picnic hamper.

Their conversation moved to the beautiful places they'd visited, and she listened spellbound as he described his favourite alpine locations. He made them sound like magic. Maybe when Sew Sensational was making a tidy profit she could visit them for herself.

After lunch they snorkelled the shallow bay, marvelling at the brightly coloured fish, and for the life of her she couldn't remember a more perfect day.

As soon as everyone returned from their excursions they were 'on' again. Cocktails by the pool and dinner were followed by an evening of trivia. There was a *Susie and Martin* category and a lot of joke prizes that kept everyone laughing.

Friday had been deemed a rest day—in preparation for the wedding the following day—so more lazing by the pool ensued, but she and Harry had concocted plans for a water fight. As prearranged, he threw the first water bomb, hitting Ella squarely in the chest as she reclined on a banana lounge. Martin's shot went a little wide of Susie, but when it burst it splattered both Susie and her cousins, making them all shriek.

Ella handed out oversized water guns and the older folk strategically retreated to an upper level of the veranda. From their positions above, Edith and Aubrey acted as generals, shouting out instructions to the group as the girls waged war on the guys. Of course, everyone ended up in the pool playing a rowdy game of volleyball.

From the other side of the net, Harry winked at her. She grinned back.

Friday night, however, was their *pièce de résistance*—karaoke. Family night karaoke. There wasn't a whole lot of rhyme or reason to it. Everyone and anyone could join in with whatever song they wanted. Uncle Derek sang The Temptations' 'My Girl' to Susie, making everyone sniffle. Susie and Martin started up *Grease*'s 'Summer Nights' and nearly everyone joined in—the women behind Susie, skipping and dancing, while the men lined up behind Martin, strutting and acting cool.

Ella fanned herself afterwards. Harry could really move when he…um…wanted to.

When the mums led everyone in 'Dancing Queen', though, Harry and Ella, who'd retreated to the back of the room for a breather and to sip their sodas, high-fived each other. It was a moment of perfection, everything she'd hoped for and more. When Auntie Rachel gestured for her to join them, she pushed her drink into Harry's hand and ran up onto the makeshift stage to dance with them, aware of Harry's gaze on her the entire time, warm with desire.

She danced for him, and couldn't wait until Monday came and they were finally alone.

'How do I look?'

Susie turned from the mirror to face Ella and the mums. All three of them drew in audible breaths. The mums' eyes filled. Ella blinked hard. 'You look like perfection, Susie. Utter perfection. You're going to knock Martin's socks off.'

She fussed, adjusting a strap, smoothing the skirt at the back. The dress was simple—shoestring straps, a ruched bodice of white silk encrusted with crystals. The skirt fell in soft folds to Susie's feet and the sheer chiffon overlay drifted around her when she walked. With her hair piled on top of her head and falling around her face in ringlets, she looked beautiful.

Oh, James, I wish you could see her.

'Thank you, Ellie. For everything.' Susie grabbed her in a fierce hug. 'This week has been everything I dreamed it would be.'

Ella hugged her back. 'There's nothing to thank me for.' She eased back and winked. 'And I hope this coming week exceeds all your dreams too.' After this evening's celebrations, Susie and her groom were being whisked off to their own private honeymoon hideaway on the other side of the island for a week.

Susie grinned, her cheeks going a delicious shade of pink.

The ceremony was beautiful, and as the happy couple exchanged vows Ella shared a glance with Harry. He smiled, those whisky eyes warm with approval. She could practically read his thoughts when he nodded towards Susie and Martin—*We did it*. She sent him a surreptitious thumbs-up from where her hands were wrapped around her bouquet.

Then they both turned to the front with huge grins and watched their dearest friends exchange rings.

Saturday afternoon and evening were a time of joy and celebration.

Sunday was a day of rest and relaxation. And packing. Everyone except Ella and Harry was leaving the following day. Though Ella packed up her room too in preparation for moving to the beachside cabin. The cabin had separate living and sleeping quarters, which would make it perfect for setting up the two sewing machines the resort had sourced for her.

By mid-morning Monday, she and Harry were finally alone. As they waved everyone off, she felt unaccountably shy. He turned to her with a grin. 'I've organised a surprise.'

He had? Before she could grill him, he said, 'You'll need your swimmers, a hat and decent walking shoes.' And just like that, her nerves vanished.

Half an hour later she found herself standing at the bow of a privately chartered boat, sailing along the Kilim River, staring in awe at the towering treetops that passed either side of them. Her guidebook had told her that the area was rich with mangrove swamps, lagoons, pristine beaches, and rock formations, but to experience it first-hand was magical. Wildlife was abundant too and their guide pointed out swimming macaque monkeys, hairy-nosed otters, and sea eagles.

When they emerged into a bay and a vertical limestone formation rose up in front of them—ancient, majestic and breathtaking—all she could do was stare. Its sheer cliffs towered above everything, dominating the landscape. 'Thank you for this, Harry,' she whispered. She'd remember it forever.

'You deserved a treat. For the last week you've been looking after everyone else—organising tours and activities, spa treatments and banana lounges, cocktails and can-apés. You've made sure that everyone has had the most wonderful time.'

'You worked just as hard.'

'I knew how much you wanted to explore the river. It didn't seem fair you should miss out.'

She had to swallow before she could speak. 'You didn't need to—'

He pressed a finger to her lips. 'Humour me. For the next few days I don't want you to worry about a thing. It's time you let someone spoil you.' He leaned closer. 'And I believe I'm the perfect person for the job.'

Harry watched the expressions dance across Ella's face—surprise, awe, delight—and was fiercely glad he'd organ-ised the river tour. The hungry, ravening part of him had wanted to drag her off to his lair and make love with her all day, again and again, until they were both too drunk on pleasure to move.

But Ella deserved more. She deserved to be wooed. And while he recognised the answering hunger in her, she didn't deserve to be rushed. He'd sworn to take his time.

They were going to become lovers, but they were friends too and that friendship was important. They'd take their week here, they'd make love and he'd be her transitional man, help her move on to the next stage of her life, and when they returned to Sydney and normality, they'd still be friends. He wanted her to know that, to feel it in her bones and trust in it. He wanted Ella in his life for good. She'd become the best damn friend he'd ever had.

They ate their lunch on a deserted beach, sitting on a blanket on the sand in the shade of the forest. Ella's eyes widened when she saw the label on the bottle of champagne. 'Harry! That's a little extravagant.'

'Not today. Nothing's too good for today.' He poured two glasses and handed her one, raised his own. 'To us.'

She touched her glass to his, her lids fluttering in appreciation when she took a sip. 'Oh, my. It's delicious.'

He stared at the wet sheen the champagne left on her lips and heat rose inside him hard and fast. He anchored one hand in the sand and gestured towards the picnic hamper with the other. He *would* go slow. 'More deliciousness awaits.'

She lifted the lid. 'Right, so… We have some gorgeous sourdough bread, prawns and shellfish…salad.' She stilled. 'Mangoes and little strawberry tarts.' Her gaze lifted to his. 'All my favourite things. How did you know? Who did you grill?'

He stretched out his legs, tried to stop her expression from sneaking under his guard and doing weird things to his heart. 'I didn't have to grill anyone. I've simply paid attention.'

Her eyes grew suspiciously bright. She blinked fiercely, stared back down at the food he'd ordered. 'You should've added a creamy Havarti, crackers and olives, and salt and vinegar chips.'

She'd been paying attention too?

'Thank you.' Those bright blue eyes held him momentarily captive. 'It's been a long time since anyone went to this much trouble for me.'

He would *not* ravish her. Swallowing an oath, he reminded himself that she deserved finesse, and Egyptian cotton sheets, and a king-sized bed. She deserved a man who would go slow.

He *could* go slow.

He *would* go slow.

He eased away from her a fraction. 'I want you to be able to look back on this week with…'

'With?'

'Affection. I want the memory of it to always bring a smile to your face.'

'And will you? Will you look back on this week with affection as well?'

Her words made his mouth dry, though he didn't know why. 'Every time I hear the word Malaysia, it's going to make me smile, Ella. That I can promise you.'

It was a day of diamonds and gold.

As Harry dressed for dinner that evening, though, he found it harder and harder to bridle the passion that rampaged through him. He'd hopefully given Ella a day she'd remember forever. He couldn't spoil it now. He *would* be patient while they shared a candlelit dinner, he *would* be controlled while they danced to something sweet and smoky. Only then would he bring her back to his cabin and lavish her with the single-minded attention she deserved.

He pulled in a long breath, fixing his purpose in his mind.

He turned at the tap on his door—open to take in the glorious view outside. Ella stood in the doorway. 'Can I come in?'

'Of course.' He gestured her in, trying to banish the image of the king-sized bed in the neighbouring room from his mind.

She wore a silk shift dress in bright turquoise and when she walked it moved over her body like water, highlighting the curves beneath. He bit back a groan. 'You look lovely.' He swung away before he lost his mind, dragged her into his arms and kissed her senseless. 'Drink?'

He marched over to the bar fridge. Would it be inappropriate to go take a cold shower? Was there even water cold enough in the world to dampen the heat rising through him?

When she didn't answer, he glanced back, and instantly straightened. The way she bit her lip and twisted her hands... What was wrong? How could he help?

He froze. Had she changed her mind? Acid burned his stomach. If she had, he'd act like an adult.

The frown in her eyes deepened. 'Do you mind if I say something?'

'Not at all.' His voice emerged too low and gravelly, but he couldn't help it. If she'd changed her mind he'd behave like a gentleman. He clenched his jaw. She deserved nothing less.

'It's just that we've fallen into the habit of being honest with each other and...' She shrugged. 'I like that. I like that we don't play games with one another.'

His shoulders unhitched a fraction. If nothing else, he had this woman's friendship. He valued that friendship, trusted in it in a way he rarely trusted anything. He wouldn't allow sex, or the lack of it, to come between them.

'It means a lot to me too,' he assured her, moving to take her hands. 'So tell me what's on your mind.'

He had a feeling that she wanted to remove her hands from his. His fingers instinctively tightened. *Finesse. No pressure.* He loosened his grip and then didn't know what to do. He couldn't bring himself to release her completely. He settled on continuing to hold her hands lightly instead. If she wanted to break the contact, she could. He wouldn't stop her.

'Harry...'

He loved the way she said his name.

'If you're having second thoughts...'

What?

She winced and he realised he was crushing her fingers. He immediately relaxed his grip.

'I just wanted to say that if you are, then I understand

and you don't need to worry about hurting my feelings. We're both adults and—'

'*No.*'

She eyed him uncertainly. 'No, we're not adults? Or no, you're not having second thoughts?'

She pulled her hands from his and pressed them to her abdomen. It pulled the silk at the front of her dress taut, highlighting the rise and fall of her breasts. He couldn't wait until he could run his fingers down their sides again to elicit those breathy, needy gasps. He let his gaze linger and heat, and her nipples beaded in instant response.

Only then did he lift his gaze back to hers. 'I'm not having second thoughts, Ella. Are you?'

She shook her head, pink flushing her cheeks, but the frown in her eyes remained. 'Then why the withdrawal?'

'I haven't withdrawn! I'm simply trying to keep a rein on my baser instincts. I want to make this week special for you. I don't want you to feel rushed or *stampeded.*'

'Oh, for pity's sake,' she murmured under her breath, before pulling herself up to her full height. Which still wasn't all that tall, but it didn't stop her from looking as regal as a queen. 'I know you've had a lot more experience at this kind of thing than I have, but we're still equal partners, right?'

'Of course.'

'I have as much a say as you in what happens here?'

'Absolutely.' How could she think otherwise?

'Good,' she said, before turning and walking to the door. Hold on! Where was she—?

She closed the door and he swallowed as she leaned back against it, an unconsciously sensual temptress.

'The thing is, Harry, I don't want to wait any longer.'

She pushed away from the door and reached under her arm to draw down the long side zip of her dress, and the sound of it lowering filled the sudden hush of the room.

His breathing sounded loud in his ears. She shimmied the dress over her hips and it fell to pool at her feet in a splash of colour.

His groin hardened in instant approval, his nostrils flaring as he greedily surveyed her lingerie.

She moved towards him. 'Do you approve?'

Approve what? No longer waiting? Of the lingerie? Either way, his answer was the same. 'Wholeheartedly. You look…' There weren't any words to do her justice. 'Beautiful.'

Beneath her turquoise jewel of a dress she wore a lace bra and panties in a vivid tangerine, and the sight made his mouth dry. She'd been fake tanned to within an inch of her life—her words—earlier in the week, and she glowed with a golden good health that had his every atom firing to life. He stood rooted to the spot as she hip-swayed towards him with the grace of a tropical nymph.

Halting in front of him, she slipped a finger beneath one bra strap. 'I made these with you in mind.'

She'd *made* them?

'The colour is called Tropical Heat. It's how you make me feel, Harry—like I'm on holiday one minute and then as if I'm going to burn up the next.'

He couldn't resist her then. He caught her mouth in a raw greedy kiss that spoke of his need, and she kissed him back with a hunger that set him on fire.

Deep drugging kisses.

Hands dragging at clothes.

She pulled back, breathing hard. 'Do you mind if I…?' She gestured at his shirt.

He shook his head. She could do whatever she damn well pleased.

Gripping his shirt in those small strong hands, she pulled

and the buttons popped and flew all around them. She gave a delighted laugh. 'I've always wanted to do that.'

How many other button-down shirts had he brought with him? He made a mental note to buy at least another twenty from the resort gift shop tomorrow.

'I'll sew them all back on tomorrow.'

Not a chance. He meant to keep her far too busy for anything as mundane as sewing on buttons.

All thought fled then when her hands ran across his chest, revelling in the feel of him. Before he could lose all the strength in his legs, he swept her up in his arms and strode into the bedroom. Laying her down, he immediately covered her body with his.

'Trousers,' she gasped. 'You need to lose the trousers.'

He didn't answer. Instead he took one nipple into his mouth and laved it with his tongue as he ran the backs of his fingers down the sides of her breasts and back up again. She gasped and arched into him, his name dragging from her throat.

He moved his way down her body, learning all the things that made her gasp and moan and arch into his touch. Only then did he shuck the rest of his clothes and seize a condom. She went to take it from him as if to sheath him herself, but he shook his head. 'I'm hanging on by a thread here, sweetheart.'

'Please tell me that means you're not going to make me wait any longer?' she said, her voice threaded with need.

He settled himself back over her. 'No second thoughts?'

'None whatsoever.'

He entered her in one smooth stroke and her mouth opened on a long sigh, her body arching up to meet his. Their gazes caught and clung. 'That was definitely worth waiting for,' she whispered.

He huffed out a laugh. *She* was worth waiting for. All

thought fled then as she moved with him in a rhythm that seemed all their own. Her muscles gripped him, tightening as the heat and need built, until she cried out and they were flung out into the abyss, finding release together.

CHAPTER ELEVEN

ELLA DIDN'T KNOW how long she lay there afterwards, her fingers entwined with Harry's, a kaleidoscope of colours dancing behind her eyelids as she waited for the world to resume its normal course on its axis.

On the pillow beside her, she felt Harry turn his head to look at her. She opened her eyes and turned to meet his gaze.

'That was—' he said.

At the same time she said, 'Wow!'

Chuckling, he pulled her to him and she curled against his side, her head on his shoulder and her hand making patterns across his naked chest, her fingers revelling in the firm, vibrant feel of him.

He pressed a kiss to her hair. 'Are you okay?'

'Absolutely!' Why wouldn't she be? She felt alive in a way she never had before. She lifted her head. 'Are you?' Was there some post-coital etiquette she was unaware of because she and James had never had any other lovers and, hence, had made the rules up as they'd gone along?

He grinned and she let out a breath because he certainly looked okay—all sated smugness…happy and relaxed.

He twirled one of her curls around his fingers, brought it to his lips. 'I love these.'

That made her smile.

'I'm *very* okay. I'm about as okay as it's possible to get.'

The way he looked at her did crazy things to her breathing.

'But I also know I'm the first man you've made love with since James, which makes this a milestone of sorts. And milestones shouldn't pass unacknowledged.'

The man looked like a Greek god, he made love with an intensity that could become addictive, but it was his kindness that really caught at her. 'Oh, Harry.' She pressed a kiss to his chest. 'It's past time I moved on— we both know that. These last couple of days, all of the attention I've had left that the wedding hadn't taken from me has been focussed on you. There's not been any other thought in my head.'

His eyes darkened at her words. She reached up and smoothed a hand across his cheek. 'I know how much effort you've put into making this experience wonderful for me—and you've achieved that. I'm never going to forget this for as long as I live. Whenever I do think of it—' she had a feeling she'd be pulling this memory out a lot '—it's *always* going to give me a happy shiver.'

She pretended to frown.

'What?' he demanded, his muscles bunching beneath her fingertips.

'And hot,' she added. 'Very, *very* hot.'

He instantly relaxed, that grin hooking up one side of his mouth and sending her stomach tumbling. His grin disappeared, though, when her fingers danced down his abdomen, her hand drifting lower and lower.

'Ella.'

She didn't know if it was a warning or a plea. 'You're an excellent lover, Harry. You swept me away completely, had me mindless with pleasure as you explored every inch of my body. I didn't get the opportunity to explore every inch of you.'

His groin twitched back to admirable life. She stared at it, her mouth going dry. She forced her gaze back to his. 'And I'd very much like to.'

He blinked as if she'd surprised him. His expression gentled as he reached out a finger to trace her cheek. 'I want to make you happy, Ella. I want you to have whatever you want this week. But you don't have to—'

She closed her fingers around him and his words ground to a halt and a guttural groan ground from his throat. She grinned, and a lascivious heat licked along her veins. 'Then how about you lie back and think of England while I...explore?'

His breath hitched as she pressed a path of kisses across his chest and down his stomach, across firm muscle and hot male flesh. His hands clenched in the sheets. 'Ella!'

She paid him no heed. Her mouth closed over him and his hips jerked. She took her time before lifting her head. 'Whatever I want, you said. Do you want me to stop?'

His eyes had turned smoky and slumberous. She recognised the desire darkening his eyes and pulsing in her hand. 'No, but I want to make this good for you and—'

He broke off with a low groan as she resumed her ministrations. 'You can let me take care of that, this time.'

She took the lead, taking her time exploring him with the same slow focus that he had her, and when she finally sheathed him and straddled him, she was as hungry and needy as him. His hips surged upwards as if he were unable to control his need and her muscles clenched around him. They found a rhythm that all too soon had her crying in release and wonder, his cry following immediately after.

He caught her when she collapsed to his chest in sated exhaustion. Holding her to him, he rolled them to their sides with a surprised oath that sounded like an endearment.

The following day they were boated out to spend the day on a tiny uninhabited island—just the two of them in an idyllic tropical wonderland. They returned in the evening to a candlelight dinner on the beach. The day after, he took her to a local village where they spent the morning with batik artisans. She returned with so much batik fabric she'd need to buy another suitcase to get it all home.

And they made love. She hadn't realised before the many different moods lovemaking could take—playful and spontaneous, raw and needy, intense…and loving. The first time they'd met, Harry had told her they were on the same wavelength; that never felt more true than when they were making love.

He looked after her in every way imaginable. It was as if he wanted to fill her with every good thing—infuse her with joy and strength and wonder—so that when she returned to the real world she'd have the resources to move forward with her life with confidence.

In odd moments she'd wonder how, once they returned to Sydney, they'd return to being just friends—wouldn't they continue to burn for each other with the same fire they did now? But she'd push the thoughts away. Harry had done this before, and he didn't seem to have any qualms.

No doubt work and the ordinary world would consume them once again, and they'd find their friends' footing once more. And even if that didn't happen seamlessly, they were adults, and their friendship meant a lot to them. They'd work at it.

Harry hadn't become a world champion by giving up. And she wasn't the kind of person who surrendered the things that mattered either. Sew Sensational proved that. They'd find a way to make it work.

'Lil said she'd be here at six p.m.'

Lily had texted Harry from the airport and he'd organised dinner for the three of them at eight o'clock, but he'd wanted to greet her when she arrived. His closeness to his sister touched Ella. She'd tried to absent herself, had thought it'd be nice for him and Lily to have some sibling time, but he wouldn't hear of it.

'Lily's expecting to see you too. She's so excited about the filming.' He sent her a smile that made her blood fizz. 'Thank you for indulging her.'

'I'm as excited as she is.'

From inside the foyer, they watched as the resort minibus pulled into the circular driveway. 'This should be her now.'

He started for the foyer door, but pulled up short when Viggo emerged from the minibus behind Lily. Ella's gut clenched at the expression on Harry's face. He didn't like Viggo? 'Smile,' she ordered. She'd ask questions later.

His eyes swirled with turmoil. 'Did you know about this?'

'No, but, regardless, you don't want to disappoint her.'

His nose curled. 'I suppose you're right.'

'And you don't want to make Viggo feel uncomfortable.'

'I don't give a damn about Viggo,' he ground out, just as the new arrivals marched into Reception. The moment Lily clapped eyes on Harry she flew into his arms.

And then she hugged Ella too. 'Isn't it wonderful? I talked Viggo into joining us.'

'This is a surprise,' Harry said, offering his hand to the other man.

'But a good one, right?' Lily said, hanging off Viggo's arm and practically dancing where she stood.

Ella surreptitiously kicked Harry's ankle. He straightened. 'Absolutely.'

But some of the excitement drained from Lily's face as if she sensed Harry's mood. Ella jumped in. 'We've arranged to have dinner on the beach at eight o'clock. I hope that suits. It gives you nearly two hours to freshen up and get into holiday mode.'

Lily started to dance again. 'Sounds wonderful.'

'We'll let the kitchen know to set a fourth place. So, we'll see you soon.'

'Can't wait,' Lily said as Ella practically dragged Harry away.

'What is wrong with you?' she said when they'd reached his cabin, planting her hands on her hips. 'You know the two of them have been dating. And I know you're protective of her, but she is a grown-up.'

He paced to the door and scowled out at the beach. 'I don't trust that guy.'

She moved to wrap her arms around his waist, nuzzled his neck, and he rumbled his appreciation. 'Why not?' she asked. 'He seems like a nice guy—a little reserved, perhaps, but from the little I've seen he treats Lily like a queen.'

He turned to wrap his arms around her, drawing her closer, and her body came to instant eager life. 'You think I'm being an overbearing big brother.'

'I think you're being a tad overprotective. You need to loosen up, though, or you're going to put her back up.'

He let out a breath that caught at her. 'I don't want to see her get hurt.'

'Of course you don't. But you don't get to tell her who she can and can't date. Besides—' she pressed herself more fully against him '—she's entitled to a bit of fun, a bit of R & R, just like we are.'

That made him grin. 'What time did you say dinner was—eight p.m.?'

She nodded.

'That gives us over an hour. What could we do in an hour?'

She cocked her head to one side and pursed her lips. 'Hmm… I wonder.'

He laughed low in his throat and kicked the door shut. 'Let's find out, shall we?'

They made it to their table on the beach at three minutes past eight, Ella slightly breathless, to find Lily and Viggo already seated. 'Isn't the resort and the island gorgeous?' Ella said, sliding into her chair.

Lily's gaze shifted from Ella to Harry and back again, and her eyes started to dance. In that moment Ella knew any hope she and Harry had of trying to keep what was happening between them a secret had just flown out of the proverbial window.

'It is the epitome of a tropical hideaway,' Viggo said in his heavily accented English.

'Magical,' Lily agreed. Her smile turned mischievous. 'The air here certainly seems to have agreed with the two of you.'

Ella's cheeks heated and she hoped the gathering darkness hid her blush. 'It certainly has. It's been far too long since I had a holiday and my mind is buzzing with ideas for our filming. Though that will only take an hour here and there. You'll have plenty of time to explore the island and get some R & R.'

Lily leaned forward, her lips curving in excitement. 'Viggo and I have managed to extend our holiday. We're now staying a full week.'

Her original plan had been to stay for only three nights.

Harry blinked. 'I thought you were swamped with work.'

'I was, but I made time because…'

'Because?'

Something hard had entered his voice. Ella glanced at Lily's shining face, and then at Harry's frown and an awful portent gathered beneath her breastbone.

'We have the most exciting news, Harrison. Please be happy for us. Viggo has asked me to marry him. And I've said yes.' She gave a happy squeal. 'We're engaged to be married!'

Wow. Before Ella could offer her congratulations, Harry leaned forward and stabbed a finger to the middle of the table. 'Are you out of your minds?'

He shot to his feet and the smile dropped from Lily's lips. Viggo rose too, calm and stern, moving to stand behind Lily, his hands on her shoulders in a show of comfort and solidarity. The expression on his face informed anyone who cared to look closely enough that he wouldn't allow anyone to upset his intended, not even her overprotective big brother. 'We hoped you'd be happy for us, Harrison.'

Ella tried to tug Harry back into his seat, but he was as immovable as a snow-covered mountain. No, not snow. The heat rolling off him was the antithesis of winter. At the moment Harry was more a seething volcano.

'Harry,' she whispered, hoping to break through whatever red mist had descended over him.

He ignored her. 'Have the two of you thought about this? *Really* thought about it? It means— You know what it means and—'

'Yes,' Lily and Viggo said in unison.

'But—' He broke off, glanced at Ella, frustration twisting his features. With an oath, he turned and wheeled away, disappearing into the thick foliage of the garden.

Ella stared after him, her mouth dropping. Snapping it

closed, she swung back to the happy couple. 'I'm really sorry about Harry,' she said as Viggo resumed his seat. Not that it was her place to apologise for him. 'But a huge congratulations to you both. I think it's the loveliest news.' She filled their glasses with the champagne sitting on ice and proposed a toast. 'To the two of you—may you have a long and blissfully happy life together.'

Lily's eyes misted with tears. 'Thank you.'

They drank.

'You're not going after him,' Lily whispered.

'Absolutely not!'

'But the two of you seem…close.'

She pondered that. 'This might sound crazy, but in the short time I've known Harry, he's become—' she shrugged '—the best friend I didn't know I needed.'

She hoped Lily got the message. She and Harry might've become lovers, but they were friends first and foremost.

'So?'

She pushed her shoulders back. 'So he just behaved badly.' *Why had he behaved so badly?* 'And I've no intention of pandering to it.'

She pasted on her best smile. 'Besides, I'm hungry and the seafood here is amazing. I suggest we have a lovely dinner to celebrate your gorgeous news. And I want to hear all about Viggo's proposal. Was it romantic? Tell me all.'

Lily's face lit up. 'Oh, Ella, you've no idea. It was *so-o-o* dreamy.'

Harry paced the living room of his cabin, glaring at the clock. Ten p.m.! Where the hell was Ella? He'd checked her cabin twenty minutes ago, but she hadn't been there.

He seized his phone from the nearby counter to check it for the umpteenth time. No text messages. He slammed it back down. *Damn*. He thought they were friends! Apparently, though—

A knock on his door had him swinging around. Ella stood framed by the light in a deceptively simple dress with some kind of sheer overlay that floated on the breeze. Every cell in his body responded, roaring to life with hunger. He did what he could to ignore it. 'Where the hell have you been?'

It came out more savagely than intended. Not that she flinched. Not that she gave off much of anything. He couldn't stop pacing.

'I take it that means I can come in?'

'You don't need an invitation, Ella. Not after everything we've been getting up to these last few days. We'd agreed you could treat this place as your own.'

She moved inside, sat on the sofa with teeth-gnashing calm. 'You asked where I've been. I've been doing what you should've been doing. I was having dinner with your sister and celebrating her lovely news.' She stood again. 'But rather than gritting your teeth and pretending you were happy for her, you flew off the handle like an idiot—'

An idiot!

'—who bitterly disappointed her.'

He swallowed.

'And hurt her feelings.'

His stomach churned.

'And marred something that was precious and special.' She strode across and poked him in the chest. 'You were rude, ungenerous...' she hesitated '...and unkind.'

The bottom dropped out of his stomach.

She moved to the refrigerator and grabbed them both cold sodas. 'You might not approve of her chosen man, but you don't get a say in who she marries.'

'But—'

'No buts. If you don't want to materially hurt your relationship with Lily, you'll find her first thing tomorrow and apologise. And try to find some reasonable explanation for why you behaved so badly.'

She'd taken a seat on the sofa again and he fell into the one opposite. 'You really thought I was unkind?'

'Uh-huh.'

He could tell she was disappointed in him and that stung, mattered more than it ought to. 'Look, Ella, there are things you don't know.'

'Like the fact Viggo is minor royalty of a small Scandinavian kingdom?'

They'd told her? *Wow*. 'Minor? Damn it, Ella, he's third in line to the throne.'

'But once both of his older brothers have babies, he'll drop further down the line of succession pretty quickly.'

She leaned forward, elbows on her knees. Her neckline fluttered in a delicious vee that hinted at the shadow of her breasts. He forced his gaze upwards.

'Lily thinks you were angered by her news, but I know better. That wasn't anger. It was fear. What I don't understand is what you're afraid of.'

His jaw dropped. What the hell…?

She gestured between them. 'It's the wavelength thing.' Her frown deepened. 'So what gives?'

All of the anger seeped out of him, leaving him spent. 'If Lily marries a man like Viggo, she's going to be thrust into the spotlight. We know what the papers are like. They don't judge women by their accomplishments or what they achieve, but by what they wear and how well they present themselves. For most of her teenage years, Lily battled demons surrounding her weight and what she looked like. This is the last environment I would wish for her.'

'Oh, Harry.' Every sign of reserve drained from Ella's

face and she flew across to sit beside him, her eyes warm with sympathy and her hand warm on his arm. 'I should've realised. You're worried that being thrust into the spotlight will trigger all of her old insecurities.'

He tried to smile, but he couldn't, not when his insides were twisted with so much *fear*. If he were to lose Lily… He closed his eyes. He didn't think he could bear it.

'Harry, you're forgetting something important.'

He forced his eyes open.

'Lily is an adult now.'

'Do you really think that makes a difference? Ella, when my parents divorced, it nearly destroyed her. She idolised my father, and I thought he idolised her too—loved her. Hell, I thought he loved me, and I was pretty damn gutted when he cast us off like last year's fashions. But I was older, had started to work out the kind of man he was.' And he hadn't liked what he'd discovered.

He dragged a ragged hand down his face. 'We were supposed to be her haven, Ella. She'd been through so much. We were supposed to be something she could believe in again. But we let her down.'

Ella's eyes filled with tears. 'Harry, you didn't let her down. You've never let her down.' She placed her hand over his heart. 'I know you're worried that Viggo might break her heart the way your father did. And that if he does it'll send her spiralling into despair and depression.'

Exactly!

'But do you think wrapping her up in cotton wool and hiding her away from the world is the answer?'

'Of course not.' He rolled his shoulders to stop her words from settling there. 'It's just…if anything goes wrong it'll be ten times worse if it happens when she's in the public gaze.'

'And what if it never happens?'

He leapt up to pace again, agitation making his gut churn. 'There are too many variables and—'

'And there are some constants you're not taking into account.' From her spot on the sofa, she held her hand out to him. 'Come and sit again.'

He hesitated, but did as she bid.

'Lily is an adult now and that does make a difference. She's learned strategies to cope with those old insecurities. She knows now that she's not to blame for the breakdown of your parents' relationship. She's not that same scared and confused teenager. And the fact she wants to head up your initiative with Bright Directions proves that.'

Her words made sense, but—

'There's always a risk when falling in love, but it doesn't mean the risk isn't worth taking. And, Harry...' She paused until he met her gaze. 'She loves Viggo. Truly loves him.'

That fear speared into his gut again.

'But Viggo loves her too. Fiercely, I believe. This is a risk for him as well. And he's not a rash man.' She hesitated. 'You're mistaken if you think he's ignorant of her past. I'd bet you a million dollars that they've discussed it.'

Did she think so?

'One more thing and then I'll shut up. Whatever your thoughts, feelings and opinions are on the subject, you're not going to change her mind about this. Or Viggo's.'

He felt the truth of those words in his very bones.

'So if you don't want to alienate her...'

'I need to apologise.'

'Grovel is the word that immediately leaps to mind.'

He winced.

She leaned in until their eyes met. 'More importantly, you need to tell her why you behaved the way you did, and what it is you're worried about.'

He groaned, dropping his head to his hands. 'God, I

made a real hash of it tonight, didn't I?' He lifted his head. 'But I can do a really good grovel.'

'Good to know.' But there was a smile in her eyes too.

She was right. If he wanted Lily to forgive him, she needed to know why he'd acted like such a brute. Seizing his phone, he sent Lily a text. An answer pinged back almost immediately. 'She's agreed to meet me for a walk before breakfast.'

'Excellent.'

'And, apparently, if that goes well, I can join her and Viggo afterwards.'

'Where you can finally toast the happy couple.'

He pressed his lips together tightly and nodded. Tomorrow he would think before he spoke.

'You were right!'

Harry burst into Ella's cabin the next morning. She glanced up from her laptop and her eyes lit up—at the sight of him or his news, he had no idea. 'Everything went well, then?'

He picked her up and swung her around. 'Very well. All three of us spoke very frankly and—'

He broke off to drag a peach-scented breath into his lungs.

She thumped his arm. 'And?'

'They're setting strategies in place in case it does start to feel too overwhelming for her. Viggo has a palace full of staff at his beck and call, including counsellors of the highest calibre. The palace is happy to let him and Ella take a back seat in terms of royal duties now that his older brother has married and the first grandchild is on the way. Viggo and Lil plan to focus on their charity work and to divide their time between Scandinavia and Australia.'

'Sounds perfect.'

'I was an idiot to fly off the handle the way I did.'

'You were an understandably concerned big brother,' she said staunchly.

Her loyalty touched him.' He twined one of her delectable curls around his finger. 'You told Lil I was your best friend.'

She blinked as if surprised she'd come up in conversation. 'I know we've only known each other for a short time, but…well, that's what it feels like. Harry, you bolstered my confidence in Sew Sensational at a time when I was considering surrendering that whole dream. You helped me help make Susie's wedding dream come true. You helped me encourage the family to turn their faces towards the future. And…'

She dragged in a breath that made her entire frame shudder. 'You've helped me move on too—helped me stop feeling guilty about James, helped me to embrace my own—' her cheeks went pink '—needs. I'm free and happy, and that's all down to you. I'm lucky you came into my life when you did. So, yes, Harry, you're my best friend. I don't know what else you'd call it.'

Sincerity shone from her eyes and he couldn't utter a single damn world, an odd lump blocking his throat. So he did what he ached to do. He leaned down and kissed her.

CHAPTER TWELVE

THE NEXT COUPLE of days were a revelation. Ella hadn't realised the creative rush one could get when three other intelligent people were invested in ensuring her videos were the best they could be. What she thought would only take an hour, often blew out to encompass an entire morning or afternoon due to everyone's enthusiasm.

They filmed a series of fifteen-minute workshops on how to repurpose old sarongs to make a beach caftan, a sweet little shirt, and a beach bag. Lily sewed alongside her to demonstrate the simplicity of the makeovers, but to also highlight where the inexperienced sewist could become unstuck. Harry and Viggo discussed how to get the best lighting and what were the best camera angles.

It was a ridiculous amount of fun.

Everything had worked out so *perfectly*. She'd been so disappointed at missing the expo, but the promotional work Harry had done for her—wearing the waistcoats, introducing her to the kind of people who set trends, not to mention guesting on her channel—had more than made up for it. The filming she was doing now with Lily, coupled with the networking she'd embarked upon herself, would consolidate all of that hard work.

Her name was getting out there, Susie had had the wedding of her dreams, and now Ella could attend the expo next year *with* her family's blessing. A month ago she couldn't have envisaged such a happy outcome.

When they weren't working on her videos, the couples went their separate ways—exploring the island or lazing on the beach—coming together for dinner each night.

And the nights themselves were… She swallowed, a familiar heat rising through her. The nights were a revelation.

Making love with Harry was utterly exhilarating. Maybe it was the short-term nature of their liaison that had her embracing it with a zeal reserved for once-in-a-lifetime events. Whatever the reason, it felt as if the stars had aligned. She felt as if she was on the path she'd always been meant to travel.

And if thoughts intruded for how they would go back to being *just friends* when they returned to Sydney, she pushed them out again. They had no place in the week, and she refused to let them mar what little time they had left.

'Ella, I've had a thought.'

She glanced up as Lily skipped into the cabin.

'What if we were to film a kind of preview here in Malaysia that you could release once Viggo and I announce our engagement officially? Viggo doesn't want to appear on camera, but I could talk about the engagement, my mother's wedding dress and how you're going to help me alter it to make it mine? It'd be fun, don't you think?'

Ella's jaw dropped. 'You still want me to work on your dress?'

'Of course.' Lily frowned. 'Why wouldn't I?'

Harry sat up from where he loafed on the sofa. 'Maybe because you're going to be a princess, Lil, and the palace will no doubt want a say in everything to do with the wedding.'

'They can content themselves with dressing Viggo,

choosing the church and the guest list. *I* get to choose my own dress and who I want working on it.'

This would catapult the Sew Sensational brand into the stratosphere. 'Lily?' She leaned towards her. 'You're sure about this?'

'Positive.' Lily hugged her. 'You've given me a vision for the perfect dress—*my* perfect dress—and I'll feel as if I have my mother there with me on the day, and that means so much to me.'

Viggo had walked in behind Lily and stood leaning against the walls in the shadows. 'She wants to film this right away, so when the palace sees it—and when the people see it—they will want her to wear this dress too. She wants to create a human element that will have them all falling in love with her.'

Lily lifted her chin. 'I just want people to see I'm an ordinary girl who's excited about her wedding and marrying the man of her dreams.'

Ella recognised the flicker of concern in Harry's eyes as they rested on Lily and wanted to ease it. She also wanted to bring Lily's vision to life—not just the dress, but how she wanted Viggo's fellow countrymen to see her. Lily wanted to take control of her destiny and Ella would do everything she could to support that.

She thought hard, her business training coming to the fore. 'Okay, let's not overthink this. How about we start with a basic conversational format? I'll start us off by asking you some questions and we'll see how we do. We'll keep going even if we stumble—we can edit those bits out later—and we'll see what we come up with.' She glanced at Viggo. 'We can edit out anything the two of you decide you'd rather not have go to air. I'm happy for the palace to vet it too if need be.'

Viggo waved that away. 'I trust you, Ella. I know you won't sell this to the tabloids.'

'We all trust you.' Harry grinned at her with so much warmth it made her feel the centre of the world.

She dragged her gaze away to survey Lily. 'You're camera ready.'

'I came prepared, hoping you'd say we could do this now. You, however, need a lick of mascara, a little powder on your nose…and go put on that gorgeous wrap dress.'

With a laugh, she did as Lily bid.

Half an hour later, they were well into the interview. It had been so ridiculously easy. Lily was so happy she shone, and Ella tried to stay as much in the background as she could as Lily spoke of her engagement and Viggo's romantic proposal.

Slowly, though, the tables started to turn when Lily confided to the camera that the first time she'd met Ella, she'd fan-girled all over her. 'I'm so grateful we met, and it was just by chance because of my brother.'

Ella smiled into the camera. 'Some of you will remember Harry from the feature I did on waistcoats. We were best man and bridesmaid at our dear friends' wedding, which is the whole reason we're in Malaysia now.'

'Harrison is one of the kindest people I know,' Lily said. 'He's been one of the biggest influences in my life. I honestly don't know where I'd be without him.'

From the corner of her eye, she saw Harry straighten. *Way to go, Lily.* Between the two of them, they could further rehabilitate Harry's reputation in a piece of video that had the potential to go viral. 'I couldn't agree more. He has a heart of gold.'

Lily pulled in a breath. 'He helped me through one of the most difficult times in my life.' And Lily then spoke of her struggle with the eating disorder she'd developed at the age of twelve, and how Harry's strength and patience, and his unwavering belief in her, helped her to win that battle.

It was the perfect lead into a discussion about Harry's partnership with Bright Directions, but first… Ella moistened her lips. 'He helped me through a really difficult time too, reinforced my belief in myself and my dream of opening a sewing school at a time I was on the brink of surrendering that dream. I owe him so much. He's become one of my dearest friends.'

She was about to steer the conversation around to Harry and Lily's joint charity work when Lily said, 'I think he's more than a friend, Ella. I think you're in love with him.'

The shock of those words doused her in ice, held her immobile for several long seconds. Seconds that felt like years. She wasn't in love with Harry. She couldn't be. *No!*

Then she recalled that the camera was rolling and forced a laugh. 'I will confess that I might have a teensy crush.' She pressed her hands to her heart. 'Those shoulders!'

They both laughed and Ella steered the conversation to the wedding dress and twenty minutes later they finished up.

She glanced across at Harry. He'd moved to stare out of the window, and even from here she could see the tension that had his spine rigid and shoulders stiff. She winced.

Damn!

Damn. Damn. Damn.

'Ooh, can we look now?' Lily said, bouncing over to Ella's laptop. 'We could—'

'We have other plans for the rest of the day,' Viggo said, taking her hand, evidently aware of the undercurrents in the room. 'We're going snorkelling off the reef.'

'But—'

'I'll send the raw file to you right now to watch whenever you want. You can suggest edits and we'll take it from there,' Ella managed. 'Have a nice time out on the reef.'

The silence that descended when Lily and Viggo had left had her breaking out in gooseflesh. She rubbed her arms, trying to lift the numbness that had her in its grip. She swallowed. 'Harry?'

If possible, he went even more rigid. *Oh, God!* He was feeling suffocated, wasn't he? They'd been having so much fun and because of her stupidity he now couldn't breathe. And due to his innate kindness—that soft heart he did his best to hide—he now felt guilty and responsible and just like his father.

He swung around. 'Is it true?'

If there'd been a single doubt in her mind that he might feel the same way, it died a swift death now. She rubbed a hand across her chest, but it did nothing to ease the ache that gripped her.

'We promised each other honesty, Ella.' Those whisky eyes flashed. 'Have you fallen in love with me?'

'Yes.'

He flinched, his face draining of colour.

'I didn't realise until the moment Lily said it. I suppose I'd have worked it out once we were back in Sydney, but...' She trailed off. There didn't seem to be much more to say.

'You promised!' he burst out. 'You told me just because you'd fallen in love with one friend didn't mean you'd fall in love with another.'

'I didn't mean for it to happen! I didn't *know* I was falling in love with you.'

He paced the room, flinging his arms out. 'How can you not know you're falling in love with someone?'

'I don't know,' she shot back, stung. 'Why don't you try it some time and then maybe you'll be able to explain it to me.'

Her words made him freeze.

'Of course, that's never going to happen because the moment you start to feel something real for someone, you head for the hills.'

His head reared back as if she'd slapped him.

'I will, however, tell you one thing, Harry.' She folded her arms tight across her chest to stop from reaching for him. 'I have absolutely no expectations of you.'

His gaze speared to hers.

'I'm asking nothing of you, so you've absolutely no reason for all of this outrage. I might've fallen in love with you but I'm not *clingy*. I've zero expectations of you falling in love with me.' Her heart clenched. 'And from the expression on your face I'm not holding out great hopes for our future friendship either.'

His head rocked back again.

She dragged in a breath. She wouldn't cry. Not yet. 'This thing between us ends right now.' If he couldn't promise her friendship, she didn't want any of the rest either. *Liar.*

'Darn tootin', it does.' But his voice lacked its earlier heat.

She thrust out her chin. 'And if you think I'm going to curl into a little ball and hide my weepy self from the rest of the world you're going to be sadly disappointed. I've a lot to look forward to, and a lot to keep me busy. This is just a…*bump*. I already know broken hearts mend.'

Oh, she was going to cry buckets and buckets over this man, but he didn't need to know that.

'And just for the record,' she added, 'I don't regret a single second of—' she gestured around '—any of this.'

She wanted to tell him that if he had the courage to unlock that heart of his for more than five minutes, he might discover that for himself. But what was the point? He wouldn't believe her.

'I know you think you're a carbon copy of your father, Harry, but you're not. It's just a lie you tell yourself to keep your heart safe.'

His jaw dropped.

She reached across to grab her beach bag and towel. 'If you'll excuse me, I'm going to go lie on that gorgeous beach and make the most of what's left of this holiday while I can.'

She turned and left, not lifting a hand to brush away the tears that had started to fall down her cheeks, in case he watched. She had no intention of letting a single gesture betray how shattered and broken she felt. He already felt bad enough. She didn't want to add to his guilt and regret.

Harry stared after Ella as she walked away and tried to make his mind work.

Damn!

He swore hard and loud and with a vehemence that shocked him. How had he not seen what was happening? How could he have *let* it happen?

His hands clenched and unclenched. He needed to go for a run and clear his head. Actually he needed to ski at breakneck speed down a mountain, but there weren't any convenient Alps in the vicinity. And even if there were, it was August.

You could book a flight for Switzerland this afternoon. There'd be a dribble of snow somewhere.

It was what he'd normally do—head for the hills as quickly as he could.

But if he did that he'd ruin—

Ruin what? There's nothing here left to ruin. The thought made him want to drop his head to his hands and yell out his frustration as loud as he could.

Go for a run.

He turned to leave then stopped and glanced around. Ella had walked out without packing up any of her computer equipment. Anyone could walk in and take it. He shifted his weight from one leg to the other, before moving across to her

computer. He emailed the raw video files to Lily and Viggo…
and himself, before shutting her computer down and placing
it in the safe in her bedroom, along with her purse and phone,
neither of which she'd taken to the beach with her.

Only then did he let himself out of her cabin to go pull
on a pair of running shoes.

He ran hard and long. He might no longer be in the peak
physical condition of a world champion, but he could still run
hard and fast. For a long time. Even in heat and humidity.

But he couldn't outrun his thoughts.

So he dived into the sea and tried to outswim them, but
that didn't work either. Eventually he stumbled up shore to
collapse against the trunk of a coconut palm and wait to dry
off, wait for his heart rate to slow.

Why hadn't he taken more care where Ella was concerned? She wasn't built like him. He'd always known that.
For pity's sake, she'd had one other lover—the man she'd
meant to marry! He'd always made it a rule to never get involved with a woman like that. Why the hell had he made
an exception this time around?

Because he'd thought they were on the same wavelength.

His nostrils flared. Because he'd *wanted* to believe they
were on the same wavelength.

He dragged both hands through his hair. He'd been so
damn selfish. He'd let desire override everything else. In
exactly the same way as his father.

The realisation had him battling nausea. For more than
half his life he'd worked hard to be the opposite of his father.
When he'd discovered that the same restlessness resided in
his veins, the same antipathy to commitment, he'd made
sure to not become involved with anyone who would read
anything more into sex than a temporary release.

And he'd succeeded.

Until Ella.

And Ella was the last person who should have to deal with heartbreak. She'd had enough to deal with for the last year and a half, and she had big plans. She needed all her energy to see those plans through. If he'd done anything to derail them…

He leapt up and started to pace.

Seizing his shirt and sneakers, he trudged back in the direction of his cabin. Was there some way he could fix this? Could he mitigate the damage somehow?

A growl sounded in the back of his throat. He'd do anything!

He showered. He lay on his bed and stared at the ceiling fan going around and around. Endlessly. Going nowhere. And wondered if he'd ever felt more wretched.

Smothering a curse, he seized his laptop and downloaded the video file, watched Ella in action. It hurt just to look at her.

The thought of losing her friendship had a ball of pressure building beneath his breastbone that threatened to break him in half. He clenched his hands and forced himself to keep breathing, forced himself to watch that moment when Lily had claimed Ella was in love with him.

The stricken expression in Ella's eyes, so brief, when she realised the truth stretched his throat into a painful ache. 'I'm sorry, sweetheart.' He brushed a finger across her face on the screen. 'I'd have not hurt you for the world.'

At some point he fell into an uneasy sleep. He woke with a start to pounding on his door. The shadows in the room had lengthened, and he sat up, groggy in the semi-dark, his eyes feeling scratchy and his skin hot and tight.

'I know you're in there, Harrison!'

Lily. He fell back against the pillows to stare at the ceiling again. He made no move to get up and open the door. He didn't want to talk to Lily. The only person he wanted to talk to was Ella.

Lily gave up and left.

The only person he wanted to *see* was Ella.

He froze. In the past, whenever a woman told him she'd started to develop feelings for him, the claustrophobia would descend, smothering him in a suffocating blanket that sucked all the joy and light from his world. He'd have to throw it off as quickly and efficiently as he could or risk losing his sense of self.

But that sense of suffocation hadn't descended over him this afternoon.

His phone pinged. A text from Lily: You're an idiot!!!

'Tell me something I don't know,' he muttered.

Setting the phone down, he tried to work out why he hadn't felt smothered and trapped by what had transpired this afternoon. He switched on the bedside lamp, but it didn't help shed any light on the dark places inside him.

Ella hadn't begged him to give them a chance. She hadn't tried to change his mind about love and commitment. She hadn't tried to curtail a single one of the freedoms he considered essential to his happiness.

She hadn't apologised for falling in love with him, but she had told him she hadn't meant to. She'd said she didn't regret a single thing that had happened between them. And she'd told him he was nothing like his father.

His hands clenched. If he weren't like his father, none of this would have happened in the first place!

I wouldn't have hurt your mother for the world.

Hadn't he thought the same thing about Ella?

Then fix it. Don't hurt her.

The thought made him flinch. As if that didn't have disaster written all over it. He hauled himself off the king-sized bed and headed for the shower again. Cold water might help clear his head. He couldn't risk doing to Ella what his father had done to his family. Ella wanted children and if—

The image of a curly-haired little girl lodged in his mind, making him ache.

You're not like your father.

She believed that. They'd never lied to each other. He lifted his face to the cold jets of water. She was wrong, obviously—

He stilled, his mind suddenly whirling.

But what if she wasn't?

He turned off the jets, stood there dripping.

He hadn't thought of another woman since he'd met Ella. It was odd, but true. Despite his supposedly infamous wandering eye, the only woman he'd noticed in the last six weeks had been her.

He'd expected to have to work hard to toe the celibacy line—and obviously he hadn't managed it. But where previously he'd have been captured by one bright smile here and the flash of a different pretty thigh there, that hadn't been the case. He hadn't been tempted by countless lovely women…just one.

He seized a towel, blotted his face. He'd only wanted Ella's attention. He *still* wanted Ella's attention. Even after she'd told him she loved him.

He rubbed the towel over his hair. Did he really think he'd eventually get bored with her? Ella was the kind of woman a man could know for a lifetime and she'd still manage to surprise him. She'd still be able to make him laugh in twenty, thirty, fifty years.

And feel cared for.

He halted. Ella had always made him feel cared for. And that feeling… It was the best feeling in the world. Even better than flying down a mountain at breakneck speed. Did he really mean to cut himself off from it?

It hit him then. He hadn't felt suffocated when she'd said she loved him. He'd felt cast adrift when she'd walked away.

CHAPTER THIRTEEN

LILY'S PHONE PINGED with an incoming message and Ella tried to not look too relieved at the brief respite as Lily checked it. She, Lily and Viggo were all trying to maintain a bright flow of conversation over dinner, but all Ella wanted to do was crawl back to her room and hide under the covers. When she'd tried to bow out of dinner, though, Lily had been so crestfallen she'd found herself backtracking.

Ella hadn't mentioned Harry once, but clearly she hadn't needed to. Lily had taken one look at her face earlier in the afternoon and had read it all. 'I'm so sorry,' she'd said. 'I shouldn't have said anything. I just wanted to shake Harry up.'

Well, she'd certainly done that.

'I just want him to be as happy as Viggo and I are. And, Ella, he *is* happy with you.'

Not in *that* way, though, and the knowledge sliced at her with the cold precision of a rotary blade. 'What we had was always temporary, Lily. I knew that.' She'd gone into their arrangement with eyes wide open. 'Besides, people find happiness in different ways. You need to let Harry find his own happiness.'

Lily's eyebrows rose now as she read her message, and

then she sent a quick message back before setting her phone face-down on the table. 'I'm sorry. I always promised myself I wouldn't be *that* person—the one glued to their phone at the dinner table. I promise not to look at it again.'

Ella forced a smile to uncooperative lips. 'What do the two of you have planned for tomorrow?'

Viggo and Lily exchanged a brief glance. 'We haven't decided yet.'

Oh, no, no, no. She wasn't letting them look after her. She might have a broken heart, but that made her neither feeble nor helpless. 'After hearing how much the two of you enjoyed exploring the reef, I thought I'd head out on the snorkel boat tomorrow.' It was one of the many activities the resort offered. 'Weren't you thinking of chartering a yacht?'

A waiter placed their entrées in front of them. The food smelled delicious, and the presentation couldn't be faulted, but her stomach gave a sick roll. She doubted she'd be able to force down a single bite.

She set her napkin on the table. 'I'm really sorry, guys, but I have a splitting headache. A touch too much sun, I suspect. I think I need to lie down in a dark room and let it pass.'

Before she could rise, however, Harry strode into the restaurant…in a dinner jacket, no less. The sight held her immobile. *How unfair!* How was she supposed to maintain a modicum of equilibrium—and pride—when the man looked like *that*?

He spotted them and started directly for their table. Ella glanced at Lily. 'The text you just received. It was from Harry?'

Lily picked up her phone and showed her the conversation.

I AM an idiot.

Told you so.

Are you in the restaurant? Is Ella with you?

Yes, and yes.

Harry *wanted* to see her? Now that was something she hadn't expected. She pressed her hands together in her lap to stop them from shaking. It didn't mean anything. This could just be his attempt to save their friendship.

But as she watched him stride closer, she suspected her feelings were far too strong for her to settle for friendship. She had a feeling she couldn't settle for anything less than Harry's heart. But giving his heart to any woman was a concept that was totally foreign to him.

He halted at the table, but he didn't sit. 'Hello, Ella.'

'Harry.'

Viggo took Lily's arm and rose. 'I believe this is our cue to leave.'

'Oh, but—' Lily spluttered.

'Thank you,' Harry said, over Lily's protests. 'I appreciate that.' His gaze met Ella's again. 'May I take a seat?'

The gentleness of the question had tears burning the backs of her eyes, and she realised that Lily and Viggo were waiting for her to answer before they made their exit, so she nodded. 'Of course.'

As soon as Harry said what he needed to say, and she'd heard it like the adult she was—she gritted her teeth and repeated the word *adult* over and over in her mind—she'd plead a headache and retire for the night. She *could* manage that much.

He leaned across the table towards her. It had seemed

like a perfectly respectable-sized table when she, Lily and Viggo had been sharing it, but it shrank now. 'I owe you an apology.'

She glanced out of the window with its glorious view of the beach—palm trees silhouetted against a full moon, no less—and her hands clenched. 'Do we have to do this, Harry?'

'Yes.'

Fine. Then… 'You don't owe me an apology. What happened this afternoon shocked us both. Neither of us meant for it to happen. You're not responsible.' He might never see it, but he wasn't his father. 'I harbour no anger towards you.'

Please let him be satisfied with that.

'I harbour anger towards myself.'

She stiffened. She was tired, cranky and, whether he'd meant to or not, he'd broken her heart. 'You want *me* to make *you* feel better? Seriously? I'll amend what I just said—I *do* harbour certain…hostile feelings.'

His brows rose. 'Hostile feelings?'

Was he laughing at her? She shot to her feet, clenching her hands so hard she shook. She knew she was drawing glances but she didn't care. 'I'm not hungry so I suggest we take this outside where I can yell at you properly.'

He immediately rose. 'Whatever you want.'

Ha! That was a joke. What she wanted wasn't on the table.

Without another word, she whirled on her heel and marched to the nearest exit. Which, of course, led down to that ridiculously romantic beach with its silver sand and those rotten palm trees, big moon and all of that starlight. It made her want to scream.

Kicking off her sandals when they reached the sand, she left them where they fell to march down to the waterline, needing to stay in motion.

'Tell me about these hostile feelings of yours.'

She rounded on him. 'Are you laughing at me?'

'No, I swear. But let me have it, Elle. Don't hold back.'

She wanted to tell him not to call her that, but she loved the sound of the diminutive on his lips. The way he said it sounded like an endearment…and then she saw her sandals—silly strappy things—dangling from his fingers, and all the fight went out of her.

He'd picked up after her?

He noticed her staring at them and shrugged. 'They're pretty. I figured you wouldn't want to lose them.'

She'd never be able to wear them again. They'd always remind her too strongly of this moment.

'Tell me why you're angry with me. I think you should be angry at my general cluelessness, for not seeing what was happening.'

She turned away. Then she'd have to be angry with herself too.

'And for the infantile way I reacted this afternoon.'

She turned back, planting her hands on her hips. 'You know what really offends me? The fact that you think I'm going to fall apart because I have a broken heart. You think I'm going to go off the rails like poor Lily did when she was twelve. But guess what, Harry? I'm not a child and I'm not without resources.'

She hiked up her chin. 'I'm strong.' She swallowed. It might not be easy, but… 'I will get over you. In the meantime I'm going to make a roaring success of Sew Sensational, I'll spend time with new friends, and eventually I'll even start dating again and—'

'No!'

'My life will be full and happy and every good—' She broke off, her eyes narrowing. 'What do you mean…no?'

'I mean I don't want you dating anyone else. I only want you to date me.'

Her heart thudded so hard she feared it'd leave bruises. Had he just said…?

'I love you, Ella.'

She took a step back. Didn't he know lying to her was a hundred times worse than anything else? 'Don't you do this. Don't you dare.'

'Do what?'

To his credit he did look suitably confused.

'You have such a horror of being like your father, you'd be prepared to shackle yourself to a woman you didn't love to ease your conscience and prove—'

'I'm nothing like my father!'

She rocked back on her heels. Fire flashed from his eyes and he mangled the straps of her pretty sandals in his fist. She suspected he was rendering them unwearable, but she couldn't care less about her shoes. She cared about the fire in his eyes.

'All of my adult life I've done everything I could to not be like my father, without realising the very impulse rendered me the antithesis of who he is.'

Wow. Okay. That was progress. 'I'm glad you can see that.'

'And you know what else? I finally realised that my animosity wasn't due to the fact that he divorced my mother and broke up our family. Divorce happens, people change, and I wouldn't wish a loveless marriage on anyone. But he constantly betrayed her, was unfaithful to her—not just once, but many times. Infidelity is…' He shook his head. 'It's a terrible thing to do to a person who trusts you.'

She agreed wholeheartedly.

'Worst of all, though, was the way he abandoned Lily and me. Shed us like an old suit he had no use for any more. He made no attempt to fit us into his new life.'

Her shoes dropped to the sand as he took several steps away. Her heart burned at the slump of his shoulders, at the way he raked both hands back through his hair.

'He didn't *want* to fit us into his life. He didn't love anyone but himself.'

She rested a hand against his shoulder, aching to offer him some comfort. 'I'm sorry, Harry.' The man should be hung from his thumbs.

He turned. They stood too close. She should take a step back, but the expression in his eyes held her immobile, his heat and scent twining around her, casting a spell in the moonlight.

He thrust out his jaw. 'But *I'm* not like that. I love Lily. I love my mother. I love a lot of people—the team I trained with for years and friends like Martin.' His eyes danced. 'In a manly, masculine kind of way, of course.'

'Of course,' she said, her lips twitching and her heart lightening at the expression in his eyes.

'And I love you, Ella. Not just as a friend. I love you with all of my heart.'

Her breath hitched and she took an involuntary step back, but his eyes didn't waver from hers.

'I know I panicked earlier.'

He could say that again. She folded her arms, but she didn't know if it was to protect herself against his words or her own violent reaction to them.

'But it wasn't because I felt suffocated. And it wasn't because I couldn't breathe.'

She found that she was the one who now couldn't breathe.

'It was because I thought I'd hurt you and the thought sent me mad. I couldn't think of any greater crime I could possibly commit.'

She wanted to weep. She didn't want his guilt and remorse. And that was all this was, and—

'I wasn't thinking of me. I was thinking only of you.'

Which was the antithesis of his father. She understood that. But it didn't mean he loved her.

'And when you walked away, Ella—and don't get me

wrong, I don't blame you for walking away—it wasn't relief that flooded me, relief that you'd given me an out and had let me off the hook…all without creating a scene. I felt…'

He paused until she met his gaze once more.

'I felt lost.'

Her heart all but stopped.

'It took me a while to work out what it meant. You said you hadn't realised you'd fallen in love with me, so you can't hold my own cluelessness against me. I've always thought my restlessness and lack of interest in settling down meant I wasn't designed for the long haul, but I was wrong. It just meant I hadn't met the right woman yet.'

Did she dare believe him?

He leaned in close. 'You're my best friend but you also send so much heat flooding through my veins that there are times I can't think straight. But I'm thinking straight now.' He touched a finger to his temple and then hers. 'The same wavelength, that's us. You and I have never played games and I'm not playing games now. I want it all with you, Elle— the friendship, the sex, but most of all the love. Every single day of our lives together is going to be an adventure—the best adventure I could ever have imagined.'

She couldn't breathe, couldn't move.

'So what do you say?' He gave her one of those devilish grins. 'Do you dare take a risk on a guy like me? Because make no mistake about it, Ella. I'm talking forever here. And I know there are still a few hurdles in our way. We'll have to take things slow for your family's sake—let them get used to the idea of you having a new man in your life. And the press won't believe that I've settled down and will try to cause mischief.'

He'd thought about this. Really thought about it.

'But we just need to wait those things out. And, together, we can do it. I know we can.'

He pulled in a long steady breath. 'Here's the thing. I'm through with being a coward with my heart.' He straightened and spread out his arms. 'It's all yours if you still want it.'

She didn't hesitate. She stepped into those arms and stood on tiptoe to stare into his eyes. 'I love you, Harry. I will always love you. And I promise to keep your heart safe.'

He grinned—one of those huge numbers that did that crazy thing to her pulse. 'There's not a doubt in my mind. You?'

'None,' she breathed, pulling his head down so she could kiss him with all the love in her heart before she burst from it.

He kissed her back with a wonder and joy that had tears pricking her eyes.

His phone pinged. 'Lily,' they said in unison.

He dug it from his pocket and showed her what it said: Well?

Ella took the phone and typed back: He's not an idiot any more. He's perfect. Ella x.

With a chuckle he slipped it back into his pocket, before reaching down to retrieve her sandals. '*I'm not an idiot any more.* I think that's the best compliment I've ever received.'

She took the hand he held out towards her, and they strolled along the water's edge revelling in the moonlight and the stars.

'Something just occurred to me.'

She glanced up.

'Martin and Susie owe us big time. I mean, we *did* give them the wedding of the year.'

She blinked and then grinned. 'You're thinking that at some point in the future they have to return the favour?'

'Exactly! See?' He pointed at her, his eyes dancing. 'I always said we were on the same wavelength.'

Which of course meant she had to kiss him again. And then there was no more talking for a very long time.

* * * * *

TEMPTATION IN ISTANBUL

HANA SHEIK

MILLS & BOON

For my mom and dad, and my sisters.
Love you all, always and for ever.

CHAPTER ONE

"WHAT DO YOU MEAN, the nanny won't leave the airport?"

Faisal Umar shrugged his suit coat on, Bluetooth in his ear, and his fast strides carried him out the door of his office. He was running late, he knew that. Though now he had his head of security and trustworthy friend Burak reporting that his effort to get out of his office building might be *too* late.

"She's refusing to leave. Says that she expected you'd be here, in my place," Burak explained.

Faisal scowled as he passed through the reception area of his office. His capable executive assistant, Rukiya, sprang out of her chair, but a curt shake of his head dismissed her services. As much as he appreciated her work, he was aware she had a full schedule of tasks and milestones for him to complete. He could take the lift by himself. Use that fraction of time to take a much-needed pause. And he asked for any meetings and calls to be put on the back burner while he handled this latest task on his unending to-do list.

Pushing the button for the lift doors to close, he said to Burak, "But you told her that the time and place of the meeting has changed. That I got caught up with work."

That I hadn't purposely stayed shut up in my office all day.

"She doesn't care."

Cursing softly, he dragged a hand through his thick curls. It was one problem after another. He couldn't catch a break. "Okay, I'll be there shortly."

Burak didn't mask his surprise. "You're actually coming?"

What choice did he have? The nanny had his seven-year-old daughter, Zara, with her. Zara was coming to live with him now that he had full custody. Her mother and his model-actress ex, Salma, had called him a few weeks earlier from her opulent multilevel mansion in Los Angeles with an ultimatum. Either he took Zara in, or she would be sent to live with Salma's parents in the Netherlands. And though he had no problems with Salma's family, it hadn't sat well with him that anyone else should raise her. He was her father, after all. Wasn't it his duty to step in?

Besides, Zara and Salma had lived with him for the first three years of Zara's life. His little girl had been born in Istanbul. It wasn't like this was his first time parenting.

Just my first time doing it alone.

Faisal shook off the icy doubt shadowing that thought and said, "Give me half an hour," before ending the call.

As he tipped his head back to watch the numbers close in on the ground floor, he allowed his thoughts to meander back to his office. The workload that would be waiting for him later caused a shudder to run through him. He couldn't quash the fear that was roiling through his stomach. Months of planning and weeks of wooing a potential partner in the natural gas and oil industry. To finally see the finish line blasted off any lingering hesitation that his hard work might have been for naught.

All he'd wanted was to take his billion-dollar venture capitalist firm, Umar Capital Group, to the next level. But to give back *and* do that?

A dream come true, he thought with hope burgeoning in his thundering heart.

If all went according to plan, he would be partnering with this Turkish natural gas and oil company and bringing them much-needed investment. And in turn he secured the promise to helm the largest offshore development in the Indian Ocean, off the coast of oil-rich Somalia. His home long ago.

Even thinking of his plans now roused a smile.

He'd actually be helping boost Somalia's economy, particularly for the people who needed it the most: impoverished families. Building an offshore rig would do that. Real jobs that would offer training, livable wages and transferable skills into other industries. New export opportunities, more fundamental import of food and medications, tourism and infrastructure. The beneficial effect was what refueled his passion on his worst and most trying days.

But now it's almost here.

By tomorrow afternoon, to be precise.

The elevator came to a halt, and the doors opened on the lobby. Outside his office building, the cloudless blue skies and blinding white sunlight promised a good day. A hopeful one.

"To the airport," he said to his driver before ducking into the back of his Maybach.

Everything will be fine. I have to believe it will be.

Just as he believed this meeting with Zara's nanny would be like nothing he had ever experienced.

"Mr. Umar left the office and will be here soon."

Maryan turned to the brawny, tall man standing over her, his lightly accented English reminding her she'd flown thousands of miles to Istanbul. He had introduced himself as Burak, head of security for the Umar Capital Group.

There were three other men with him, and they all wore the same dark clothing, earpieces and shades to mask their eyes. Anyone who glanced at them knew they were security detail. Their attempt to blend in failed.

Even Zara leaned in at one point and whispered, loudly, "Why are they here?"

Maryan didn't know how to answer her seven-year-old charge.

She eyed the broad-shouldered Burak, and she had to guess he was looking at them, too. She couldn't tell with his sunglasses blocking his eyes. Unsettled but not feeling as though she should be worried about Zara's safety or her own, she wrapped an arm around the little girl's shoulders and hugged her to her side.

They waited on Zara's father.

Faisal Umar.

The multibillionaire CEO known throughout Europe and Asia for his playboy antics. It turned out he was a workaholic as well. Not that the media ever focused on that. Too boring. Why report about him working long hours when the world could gab about his fast and furious lifestyle in VIP clubs and on massive super yachts?

She had met him a few times, but it hadn't been enough to judge his character.

Maryan had taken a fine-tooth comb to his background on the plane. Poring over every detail she could learn about him. Adding it to what Zara's mom, Salma, had told her. So far Maryan knew Zara was born in Istanbul, and Salma and Faisal co-parented for a few years. Then Salma landed her first leading movie role and moved to Hollywood to be closer to the heart of the star-studded action.

It did feel a little wrong digging into his background. But she couldn't afford to feel ashamed. Zara would be living with her father now, but Maryan had been her primary caregiver for four years. Naturally, she was concerned. And her concerns encouraged her snooping.

Zara needed a parent who would be present. Maybe not always, but enough that she shouldn't have to feel like a burden.

And as far as first impressions went, Faisal wasn't giving a good one.

She had anticipated he would be there to greet them when their plane landed. Instead, his security goons had swarmed them. They would've whisked them off to meet Faisal wherever he was, but Maryan was fatigued from the flight and mightily annoyed that Faisal hadn't shown up. Putting her foot down had been too easy. She wouldn't budge with Zara, she'd explained to Burak. Not until Zara's dad put in an appearance. She wasn't asking Faisal to bid his company away. And yet that was how his security had treated her demand. Coolly appalled by her request, Burak had turned away to phone his boss.

Luckily, Faisal saw it differently.

Now he had only to show his face and they could be off. *But what if he's a brute? What if it's clear that Zara won't be safe with him?*

Then she'd have to cross that bridge when they came to it.

"How long do we have to wait here?" Zara tugged on Maryan's hand, her tiny palm sticky with sweat. "Is my daddy coming?"

He'd better be.

Out loud Maryan said, "Not much longer, hopefully," and she eyed Burak while she said it to make the point clear.

Zara lowered her head. "Does Daddy not want me?"

Her heart seized painfully at the warble of unease in Zara's small voice. Dropping to a crouch before her, she took Zara's hands and squeezed comfort into her. Without needing to think it over, she assured her, "Of course he wants you. You're here, aren't you?"

"But he's not here," the little girl rejoined with the most plaintive of whines.

"That's because he's a very busy man. Sometimes when adults have to work, they forget the time, but they don't forget their love for family."

Zara nodded, but she looked glum even after, and Maryan's heart broke ten times over.

Finally, when she couldn't take the torture of watching Zara's downheartedness, she left her to stalk over to Burak. Steam must have been misting out of her ears, because she could've sworn he drew up to his full height. As though she posed him *actual* danger. Mentally rolling her eyes, she marched his way. She didn't reach him before a knock on the pocket doors to the VIP room turned all their heads.

Burak scowled and signaled for the others to draw in. They fell into a tactical maneuver, one they must have practiced many times judging by how quickly and efficiently they moved as one unit and one team.

Meanwhile, Maryan retraced her steps to Zara.

"What's happening?" Zara whispered, hugging Maryan and leaning into her.

She wasn't given the chance to smooth over Zara's fear.

Burak opened one of the sliding doors and disappeared through. A few slow and tugging heartbeats later, he returned with someone else.

Maryan recognized Faisal instantly.

So did Zara.

"Daddy!" She shot up from her chair and bounced eagerly, her excitement unmistakable.

Faisal broke off from chatting with Burak, a wide and brilliant smile breaking over his ruggedly handsome face.

He dropped down to a knee and opened his arms to Zara.

Zara looked up at Maryan, her eyes asking if she could go to him. She wasn't about to stop the father-daughter moment from happening. She had her qualms about Faisal, true. And at some point she planned to bring them to his attention. But there was a time and place for everything. Here and now wasn't it.

With a smile and a nod, Maryan gave her blessing.

Zara beamed and didn't wait for any other confirmation.

"Daddy," she squealed, and ran to him.

Faisal caught her, laughing and pretending that Zara had the strength to topple him.

"Zara," he breathed into her hair, hugging her close. "I missed you."

They remained like that for a long while. Maryan hung back, seeing no reason to interrupt their reunion. It didn't matter that her heart was in knots when Zara clung to her father. Faisal had to disentangle her small hands from the back of his neck to get her to look at him. She strained to hear Zara's whisper, pushing off her heels to lean in and eavesdrop over the dull ringing in her ears.

"I thought you weren't coming," Zara said quietly, her head dropping low. Dejection coming off her in waves. Any joy she had displayed at seeing her dad disappeared.

"I'm sorry. I know I promised to be here when the plane arrived, but I'm here now. And I'm not going anywhere else." He pulled Zara into his arms again. From over Zara's shoulder, he finally looked at Maryan.

She could have sworn his eyes widened a fraction.

And he stared a long time. Too long. To the point of making her squirm, and not with an unpleasant and unwanted feeling.

In reality, his staring couldn't have lasted for more than a few seconds, and yet his gaze seared through her. She hugged her arms around her middle, feeling the oddest sensation of having been branded, which was ridiculous because she didn't know him. She couldn't presume through one look that he would somehow desire her.

Of the handful of times Faisal had come to visit his daughter in Los Angeles, Maryan couldn't recall anything more than pleasantries exchanged between them. It wasn't as though their worlds collided regularly.

He lived and worked in Istanbul and was an excessively wealthy bachelor.

They couldn't be more different.

While she struggled to balance paying off her student debt, her rent and her car loan, he had more money than most people ever saw in their lifetimes. And no matter how close she felt to Zara, she had always known that one day her job as nanny would come to an end. Envy that Faisal had the rest of his life to spend with his daughter coated her thoughts and cooled the flare of attraction warming her lower belly. At least most of it by the time Faisal broke eye contact and concentrated on comforting Zara.

Maryan tightened her arms over her flip-flopping stomach.

Faisal stood and clasped Zara's hand as he walked her back over.

"Are you okay?" Maryan asked, her attention lowering to Zara.

The little girl bobbed her head, but with a sullen air.

She opened her mouth to ask again, her heart stuffed in her throat, when Faisal spoke and redirected her focus.

"Nice to see you again, Maryan. Sorry for arriving late. I've been working through a business deal that's been stealing too much of my time."

She supposed his charmingly sheepish smile was meant to be an apology.

Disappointment dropped like a stone in her stomach and squashed the beginnings of a silly crush on him.

She should have been grateful. Catching feelings for him wasn't on her agenda. Instead of gratitude, she felt empty. Until the anger flooded in, fast and abundant.

It took everything in her to accept his handshake. She exhausted her energy pushing the fiery emotion down and packing it away. *Later*, she vowed. When they were alone, just the two of them, and where she couldn't hurt Zara with any harsh words to Faisal.

"I hope you can forgive me?" he said.

He had made his daughter wait—made her believe that she was forgotten. That she was unwanted and unloved...

She looked down pointedly at Zara and then up again, finding herself no less immune to his thoughtful brown eyes. Those striking gray hairs swimming in with the rest of his long night-colored curls. His flaring Nubian nose, sculpted cheekbones, clean-shaven square jaw, and too-wide, too-full smiling mouth.

Maryan swallowed at the first blush of renewed heat coursing through her body, humming a siren song she didn't like at all. Not for one second.

She snatched her hand away before she realized what she'd done.

Faisal lowered his hand slowly, confusion written openly on his face.

Zara piped up then with perfect timing, "I'm hungry."

"Good, because we're having lunch together," Faisal told her, his befuddlement erased and his devastating smile back with a vengeance. "I have everything prepared. We'll leave now and make it in time before traffic plagues the streets."

She held his stare when he looked to her, resisting the

urge to glance away or trace her fingers over her palm and the phantom sensation of his larger hand engulfing hers.

"One more thing," he said. "I hope you're both all right with boats."

CHAPTER TWO

THE NANNY DIDN'T like him.

Faisal got that at the airport after she scalded him with a quiet but fiery look. She hadn't even wanted to touch him. He rubbed his palms together, clammy with sweat. Nerves getting the best of him was uncharacteristic. Sinking back into his leather seat, he turned his head to glimpse his guests behind.

He sat up front with the driver, something he rarely did as he preferred to be chauffeured around.

Now Maryan and Zara replaced him in the back seat. And they had to be the quietest people he'd been around in a very long while.

Given the shaky reunion at the airport, he shouldn't be shocked.

Zara looked out the darkly tinted car window, appearing far smaller in the spacious tan leather seating. A stark image of her downcast face at the airport came to mind. A familiar sinking helplessness tugged on his insides all at once.

He blinked and focused on Maryan.

Like Zara, she gazed out the car window at the glass-and-steel skyscrapers and smattering of mid-rise buildings clustered around the Levent. Istanbul's city and business center. From their speeding position on the freeway, he spied the distinct architecture of his office building. The U-shaped edifice of Umar Capital Group was difficult to miss. And a bit too on the nose. But what kind of billionaire would he be if he didn't sprinkle his ego around once in a while?

"That's my office over there," he announced.

"Which one?" Zara asked and leaned as far into Maryan as her seat belt would allow. "I can't see."

"That one," Maryan said, pointing now too.

"It looks like a big *U*," his daughter assessed.

"*U* for Umar, right?" The nanny fixed him with a level look. Surprisingly with none of the hostility from the airport swimming in the shadows of her eyes.

"Yeah, that's right," he said thickly.

Maryan turned back to his building and the skyline of infrastructure, leaving him with the sense that he'd been dismissed now that she had an answer.

There were two things he had been fast to realize about Maryan: she cared deeply about Zara, and she wasn't the type to hide her feelings.

How did he know this? Because he *knew* people. He had to in his business.

Maryan was only sitting in his car because Zara's mother, Salma, hadn't been able to bring their daughter herself. Her career kept her as occupied as his job did him.

Salma hadn't smothered her skepticism about this arrangement with him, either. Her words flooded back. They were as loud as if she were saying them to him all over again right there and then…

My mom and dad want Zara. They'll be good to her. They raised me, didn't they? Salma had inhaled briskly. *But you don't trust them.*

She's my daughter, too, he'd said, his thumb and forefinger pinching the bridge of his nose.

He'd been alone in his dark office, the floor completely cleared out for the evening. Not even the cleaners had been around to witness his rising headache and his sorry attempt to squelch it before his temples throbbed. Before his heart ached.

She's my daughter, he'd repeated desperately. Not even sure if she was on the other end of the line anymore. He wouldn't be surprised if Salma had hung up on him. She was used to getting her way. It was how Zara ended up with her, halfway across the world.

And way too far from him.

He missed Zara.

Now Salma had dropped this chance to live with and raise his daughter unceremoniously in his lap, and she wanted to snatch that hope away just as suddenly?

I'm her father. Wouldn't it be natural to want her with me?

Then you should have left Turkey and come to live near her!

Salma's low blow had stung more because she hadn't stopped there.

Let's be honest with ourselves, Faisal. I struggled to do it on my own these last four years. Truthfully, the wonderful nanny I hired should be taking credit for us both. You know that Zara knows more about her nanny than either of us? She cries whenever Maryan has a sick day, which almost never happens. They've bonded. A brittle laugh and then, *We haven't been the most attentive of parents. I'm always working and you're...well, I bet you're holed up in your office right now, aren't you?*

He'd tightened his lips and cut his narrowing gaze across his spacious workspace. Though he'd wished he could tell her she was wrong, he hadn't had the heart to lie.

Yes, he'd gritted out, frustrated with them both.

More cool laughter from Salma. *And you're insisting*

*that Zara be in your care. You let her go once. Why can't
you do it again?*

He'd only done that because Salma wouldn't be argued
with. She would've taken him to court. Made it a messy and
lengthy custody battle. And he'd thought of Zara being put
through all that, witnessing her parents fighting over her.

So, Salma was right. He had let his daughter go, but she
was twisting his reasoning for it.

He'd sighed heavily. *Does the past matter? I'm more
than prepared now.*

Quick as always, she'd lashed out, *But how can you be
so sure that you're ready?*

He wanted to answer truthfully now as the bitter memory faded away.

I'm not sure.

Like Salma, he was married to his profession. Showing up late at the airport proved that. But by tomorrow he
hoped he could answer differently. Once this partnership
was actualized with signatures, he would be a freer man.

Maryan would see that.

Which brought him to the second thing about the nanny.

She was…breathtakingly beautiful. *Gorgeous.* Radiant
even, as though a golden light were shining under her dark
brown skin and illuminating her from the inside out. Her
beauty had struck him in the VIP room of the airport, and
he hadn't shaken it off. The light hadn't stopped glowing
around her, either.

It suffused her in the shadowy interior of his car. A halo
around her whole form.

He traced a mental sketch of her facial profile and committed it to memory. The line from her forehead to her up-
turned nose down to the swell of her mouth and the curve to
her small chin. Normal and plain enough features. He had
seen inhuman and alien beauty in supermodels like Salma.

Maryan wasn't that. What she had was far, *far* better. That inexplicable extraordinary light of hers swept in and enhanced the little, perhaps inconsequential quirks that were so very clear to him.

How her forehead creased when her eyebrows shot up at something Zara said.

How her nose twitched in time with short spurts of air as she coolly exhaled.

How her lips moved rapidly with speech he tuned out as he focused solely on her.

Glancing back to her eyes, she was watching him now, brow furrowing over them. Slowly, warily.

He looked ahead abruptly. Blushing before he recognized the heat scoring his cheeks for what it was. Embarrassment. Lust. More than a bit of both. His fingers had been tapping out his agitation on the console between him and the driver. Forcing them still, but too late as he caught the curious gaze of his driver.

To his credit the driver said not a word.

"You never answered me about the boats."

Maryan stopped stretching and tugged down the hem of her airy long-sleeved shirt where it rode up her stomach. Faisal hadn't been looking there, but having his eyes on her affected her nonetheless as though he were.

As if it were the two of them out and about the sprawling city. Like on a date.

We aren't on a date, though.

"I've never been on one," she confessed. Her home in Santa Monica was close to many beaches, but she never had the chance to experience the Pacific on a sailing craft.

"So, you're not averse to boats," he said with a searching look.

"I wouldn't know."

Zara exited the car and immediately clutched her hand, the touch reminding her of the little girl and her needs.

"I'm hungry," she said meekly, a frown tipping her small pink mouth down.

Shame flooded Maryan. She squeezed Zara's hand and blurted, "Your dad was just telling me all about the delicious food he had prepared." He hadn't been, but she figured now could be a good opportunity to witness another interaction between him and his daughter. Because she'd given his reunion with Zara at the airport another once-over during their thirty-minute car ride. Maybe she had judged him too early.

Everyone was deserving of a second chance, weren't they? One last window to get it right?

She thought of this lunch as his.

Change my mind. Make me trust you'll be good for Zara.

"I promise this will be the best lunch you've had." Faisal paused and smiled. "Okay, maybe not the *best* lunch. I don't want to set myself up for failure. But it'll be a unique one."

He led them to the curb and grabbed Zara's free hand. "We'll cross first."

The traffic was steady on both sides of the street. The noise of the lively city coming at them from all directions, much like the sun bearing down over their heads. For mid-May, it felt more like summer. She didn't know if that was unusual or not for Turkey. It was hot even by her standards, and she was hardened by temperatures in the high nineties.

Stinging heat wafted from the paved sidewalk. Sweat frizzed the baby hairs sprouting from her hairline. She had her hair tied up in a ponytail, and yet dampness slickened the nape of her neck. She was frying. A look at Faisal in his tan slim-fit suit had her wondering how he did it. How did he manage to appear cool, suave *and* incredibly handsome when she felt as messy as she probably looked.

She glanced away when his head turned to her. Last thing she wanted was for him to catch her ogling him.

The cars slowed at one point, and Faisal found a break for them to slip through between bumpers. They emerged on the other side safely and walked the strip of pavement adjacent to the waters of the famed Bosporus strait. She recognized it from online images, although seeing it in person intensified the experience.

"That feels nice," she said of the cool spray of water carried on a breeze. Tilting her head into the momentary respite from the heat, she sighed.

"It's really pretty," Zara commented, awe widening her eyes as she looked around Maryan at the Bosporus.

She had to agree; the sparkling waters of the strait were a breathtaking foreground to the other side of the natural boundary bisecting Istanbul…it'd make for the perfect place for a selfie. Something to post on her social media for her friends and family to enjoy.

Faisal must have read her thoughts, because he asked, "Did you want to stop and take a picture?"

She slowed at his request, the lovely Bosporus forgotten momentarily.

"I can snap it for you." He already had his phone in his hand and waved it. His phone case gleaming like it was made of liquid gold. She noted it was a showy new model of a foldable smartphone. As well as a pricey one, if she recalled correctly. He shook the phone temptingly, that heartbreakingly handsome smile drawing his lips up at the corners.

She nearly agreed to his offer, but then remembered she looked far from photo-ready. She had barely managed to brush her hair and dab on her lightweight concealer to hide the dark crescents under her eyes before the plane landed.

Now most of her painstaking work had been undone by unprecedented humidity.

"Can we?" Zara asked with a little gleeful hop.

Maryan stifled a groan. She'd forgotten Zara loved taking photos, camera-ready or not. She blamed Zara's mother. Salma was an internationally renowned model. Not Tyra Banks or Iman levels of well-known, but she was well-traveled and fully booked for the most notable fashion shows. She was an actress now, too. A few small roles in big Hollywood movies featuring A-list stars exploded her film career.

Like her mother, Zara was conditioned to glow in front of a lens. Any lens.

She posed for her dad now, making faces of all sorts. Posh ones, adorable ones and downright silly ones.

It had made Maryan worry in the past. Children could be exploited in the industries that Zara's mother worked in. But right then she knew that a few photos with Zara in front of the one-of-a-kind Bosporus meant something else…

It would be one of the last times she would get to be with Zara like this. In two weeks, she'd no longer be her nanny.

Maryan turned her eyes to the wondrously blue skies. When the lashing heat of tears abated, she blinked, and her gaze alighted on Zara and Faisal. Her heart kicked at the sight of their smiling faces, and at the sound of their bubbling laughter whenever Zara's humorous expressions were unignorable.

I hope you stay like this forever.

She didn't know who the prayer was for. Both of them, she decided thoughtfully. She didn't know Faisal as well as she did Zara, but watching him now with her, he looked immeasurably happy.

"Feel free to jump in," he said.

Zara waved for her to join. "Come on, Maryan. It's so much fun!"

She believed it. So why was she hesitating? "I should take the photos," she said softly, swiping her hands down the sides of her legs. Her faded light-wash jeans absorbed evidence of her nerves.

That was when he directed his lens at her and snapped a shot. There was no flash, but she knew he had taken a photo of her. At least one. He assessed his screen quietly until Zara rushed to his side and jumped up to see what he was looking at.

Maryan stood rooted to her spot, her veins running sun-bright hot and fiery cold.

"What do you think?" Faisal murmured, seeking Zara's opinion in the most serious of tones. He held the phone lower for her to view.

Zara studied it with a neutral thinking expression. "I don't know…"

"Is it good enough to keep?" he asked.

Maryan squirmed as they both looked at her now. Trepidation glued her tongue to the roof of her mouth, so she couldn't ask what was wrong. Did she really look as horrible as she imagined?

She blew the breath she was holding when they grinned in unison.

"I like it," Zara said. "But Maryan's always beautiful."

Faisal didn't say anything…but he didn't have to. She saw his silent opinion overtaking his face. A hungering look darkened his brown eyes and softened his lips into parting slightly. Seeing the change in him warmed her from head to toe in a way that the sunlight and summerlike heat of the afternoon would never.

She pretended that her blush was due to Zara's compliment, though.

"Fine, you've convinced me." She palmed her hair in a quick effort to jam any frizzy curls under one of half a dozen black bobby pins and fanned a hand to Zara. "Let's make a memory together."

A memory she fully understood included Faisal.

"Watch your step," Faisal said half an hour later as he steadied Zara on the other side of the walkway and looked back at Maryan on the pier. She wore a similar life jacket to Zara. He had assured her she wouldn't likely need it once aboard, but she insisted. And he realized why when Zara felt more comfortable wearing hers when she saw Maryan was as well.

In solidarity, he strapped into a life jacket, too.

"Your turn," he told her.

She walked the short boarding plank more quickly than Zara and gripped his hands for grounding for less time, but what he saw in her face when she touched him, what he felt blooming inside him, left him rattled for longer than he was used to. That would be the second time she stole a breath from him.

Maryan guided Zara safely up the stairs to the teak deck of the sun lounge. Sunlight washed over the small pool and the lounge chairs circling it.

"Wow! I can see everywhere!" Zara's exclamation rang with more of her innocent awe.

Joining her at the railing, Maryan tipped her head and closed her eyes, her alluring face relaxing.

Faisal stepped up beside her. "I don't get to go sailing as much as I'd like to, but when I do, it makes my day."

She opened her eyes. "I can see why."

"Can I go put my feet in the water?" Zara asked them, losing interest in their conversation as naturally quick as any young child would.

Faisal said, "Yes, but be careful."

Zara skipped for the pool.

"We walk on the boat, Zara," he warned, and she switched to walking slowly and carefully and with a sheepish smile flung over her shoulder at him and Maryan.

"You don't like me," he said evenly, his attention on Zara by the pool. He wanted her out of earshot for what he had to say to her nanny.

"I don't know what you mean," she replied.

"At the airport. I saw it in your eyes."

And I felt it in your hands.

He flexed his right fist and clearly remembered the touch of her…and how he liked it too much. "Though *dislike* might be too strong a word, you *do* have some issue with me."

"I care about Zara." She had her back to a stunning water view of the city he loved deeply. Completely disregarding it to supervise Zara. Because of that he believed what she said.

"And you think I don't. Is that it?"

"You were late," she said instead. She might not have answered his question, yet her nonanswer confirmed his suspicion: she was upset with him.

"I'm aware Salma sprang this custody change on you very last minute," Maryan continued.

"It's affected you, too. You won't be Zara's nanny any longer."

The thought of offering her a job had crossed his mind. Although now there was his attraction to her to navigate.

If I ask her to stay, will it be for Zara or for me?

Therein lay his problem. He didn't know whether selfishness motivated the suggestion. It had been a long while since he lived with anyone. Almost as long a time as when he had dated seriously.

"What will you do in two weeks?" he probed gently. Curious as to her plans after she left him and Zara.

"My aunt and uncle own a restaurant, and I'll be helping them more on a full-time basis."

"Somali cuisine?" he asked.

"Mostly," she said with a slow nod and an even slower wistful smile. "I'll miss Zara, of course. It won't be the same without her. That's why I want what's good for her." She pinned him with eyes shuttered to her emotions. A beautiful poker face.

It unnerved him, and yet he knew she waited on him to convince her *he* was good for his daughter. Never one for failing a test, he leaned into her unspoken challenge.

"Do you have kids?"

She scowled immediately. "No, but that wouldn't give me any special authority on the matter. We're not discussing other children; we're talking about Zara. I've been her nanny a while now. That gives me an opinion."

A brisk wind toyed with her curly ponytail, her long black tresses helpless in the gust buffeting the top deck. As helpless as he felt when his fingers itched with a longing to reach out and pull the raven strand plastered to her cheek behind her ear.

He fought against the misleading instinct and said, "I'm asking because I had to know what got under your skin before my tardiness did."

"Excuse me?" she snapped.

Faisal rested fully on the support of the railing. The boat's motor, now on and running steadily, purred through to his bones. The familiarity of his position calmed him despite delving into deeper and more personal territory.

He'd thrown open the door to it. He couldn't turn back now.

"I thought it might be me. Sometimes I rub people the wrong way before I meet them. They make assumptions about who I am based on my wealth."

She squinted at him and shaded her eyes with a hand. "Are you finished accusing me?"

He shook his head, flabbergasted. "I wasn't—"

"Weren't you though?" She cut him off, her irritation smacking into him like a wall. Hard. "It's true I didn't like that you were late. But that's entirely because Zara had noticed your absence. She…she felt like you didn't care."

Shock turned him into a pillar.

And when he thawed he jerked his head to Zara and watched her with a fast-growing ache in his heart.

She thought I didn't care?

"How?" he rasped. *Why?* What had he done to make Zara feel that way? Didn't she know that he loved her unconditionally and endlessly? Hadn't he made that clear enough? And now that he knew he hadn't, how did he go about undoing any damage he'd unknowingly wrought?

He *truly* believed he could be there for his little girl.

Salma's words reverberated through his head. *How can you be so sure that you're ready?*

Swallowing his self-disgust, he asked Maryan, "Is that all?"

His ears had grown hot, and a whining buzz filtered out the lapping waters along the gleaming white hull of his midrange sailing yacht. He swayed in place and shifted to his side with a hand steadying on the rail.

Maryan eyed him. He could've sworn a shadow of regret passed over her face.

"Is that all?" he repeated through gritted teeth.

"It's fine. I told her you were late for good reason. She's young, but she's learned from having lived with her mother why some adults could be busier. Why her parents are, specifically."

She had stood up for him? The nanny *defended* him.

So much for his theory that they had started off on

the wrong foot. They *had*, but maybe not as badly as he assumed.

"It's not fair Zara ended up with us for her parents," he said, voice gruff with guilt and shame. The memory of speaking to Salma about this very topic at the edge of his mind. Doubt fisted his poor defenseless heart. "I wanted her to live with me. To do it, I had to get around Salma's plan to send Zara to her grandparents."

Maryan didn't show an ounce of surprise at that news.

"But you knew that because she told you."

"She's a good talker, and I'm a good listener," she offered, a ghost of a smile on her lips.

Faisal returned it with what felt less like a smile and more a grimace as he delved deeper into the sticky, suffocating bog that his fear was growing into.

"As hard as I was fighting for Zara to come live with me, I also could appreciate Salma's doubting my abilities." He hadn't given Salma a reason to place trust in him. It was true, he hadn't striven harder to stop her from taking Zara away the first time. It made him wonder if he'd changed all that much. If he was ready to take on the challenge and reap the rewards of single fatherhood.

"Do you feel like you can't do it?"

Maryan's query centered him in the present. He was there and now with her, and not sinking faster and succumbing to his apprehension. It helped clear out the muddle his thinking had devolved into.

"I *want* to try."

"Then that's all that matters."

A "but" curled through his thoughts. There had to be more, surely. Was it that simple? It felt like it was. The odious burden roosting on his shoulders and pulverizing his heart eased off like a summer storm, here and gone, its booming thunders, black clouds and gloom saved for another day.

"Just to be clear, I don't dislike you. I don't even know you."

That was nice to hear. The first part admittedly more than the last, but the reassurance was kind of her.

"Also, I know how it feels to be seen only when someone needs you." She tightened her lips together, a flintiness catching the dark of her eyes.

"Boyfriend?" he guessed. He didn't expect her to nod curtly.

"Ex," she stressed.

"Out of the picture?" he wondered, but not for himself. He wasn't marking his territory with her or anything. He only hoped that if this guy was bad enough to warrant her cynicism, he wasn't in her life anymore.

She brushed flyaway strands from her face and studiously kept her focus ahead and on Zara. "Yeah, he is."

"Good." Satisfied, he smiled fully, his heart beating faster when she flickered a shy glance at him. It loosened his tongue into returning the favor. She had shared a part of her bravely, and he wished to do the same. "By this time tomorrow, I'll have signed a possibly world-altering deal."

"Is it really that?" She looked as she sounded: unconvinced.

He chuckled. That earned a smile from Maryan. "I'll be working with a Turkish natural gas and oil company to begin drilling in the Indian Ocean off Somalia's coast. With the blessing of the federal government of Somalia."

"It sounds like it'll be a lot of work, but I'm guessing it's good for bringing jobs and stability to people who desperately need it."

"That's what I'm hoping," he said before switching to Somali, "I want to give back to our home."

"It's good of you." Her Somali was soft and unaccented, and achingly comforting to hear.

They lapsed into a natural silence until the steward came up to report from the captain that they would be moving now. Faisal cleared them to leave port and gave instructions for their lunch to be served in the dining room below deck.

Almost alone again, Faisal asked her, "Will you be staying at my home?"

"I booked a hotel in the Fatih district." She gave him the name of the hotel.

A stone's throw from the Eminönü pier. The boutique hotel she picked was a reputably good option in one of Istanbul's ancient quarters. She'd have the luxury of unrivaled historic sights within walking distance and the assurance of a good night's sleep.

"Can I convince you to change your mind?" He asked without giving it much thought. Once he realized what he'd done, there was no taking it back.

Maryan stared at Zara quietly and long enough that he presumed she might not have heard him. Or he might not have even asked after all.

Finally, she regarded him with a slow tilt of her head. "I won't feel comfortable living with you, even temporarily."

He understood that and countered with a solution.

"I have guest quarters outside of my home. I'd be happy to move out temporarily." This way he was convinced he wouldn't feel like a complete troll for forcing more distance between Maryan and Zara. They'd be parting eventually. It was inevitable. He would fight to keep Zara. He needed the nanny to know that. Both his drive to be Zara's father and his commitment to make Maryan's stay in Istanbul— *with him*—as good an experience as it could be.

"I won't be putting you out?" Her wavering commitment to the hotel put wind under the sails of his hope.

"Not one bit, or I wouldn't have suggested it." He presented her a smile to sell the idea on her. And just to add pressure, he remarked, "Zara will like having you with her, I bet."

She hummed with a sharp look in her eye that hinted she was onto him and his tactics.

Despite that, his efforts worked when she agreed, "Okay. I'll have to call and cancel the reservation."

"I'll reimburse any nonrefundable deposit," he pitched in.

She slung a blithe smile his way. "That won't be necessary," she said before striding over to Zara, leaving him standing awkwardly alone to watch after her for far longer than his sudden feverishly warm body could seem to handle.

And he had invited her to his house. Damn.

CHAPTER THREE

FAISAL SPENT THE next two hours on his yacht fretting low-key about having Maryan at his home for her two-week stay in Istanbul.

He continued to worry right up to the point that they docked and disembarked onto dry land. They entered the awaiting car and headed toward his home.

In the back seat, Zara was alert and asking questions about where they were headed next. "Are we going on another boat?"

Maryan answered her patiently, hesitant when she said, "No, we're going to your dad's home."

Faisal heard what she left unsaid. That his home was Zara's home as well now.

He wondered if she was still upset with him. They had talked on the yacht. And he'd gotten the profound sense she cared for Zara even more than he initially presumed. He'd also shared more with her in a short time of knowing her than he'd done with any stranger or acquaintance in a long while. Faisal pondered why that was, and then when his temples began to throb, he stopped. No point in driving himself to a headache over why he'd spilled his guts. Or why Maryan hadn't kicked him when he'd been down. All this time he had been telling himself that what the nanny thought didn't matter...

And then she made him feel good.

Guess that means I do care what the nanny thinks.

Maryan had been in Zara's life more than he had up until this point. She knew his daughter better than he did. For that reason alone it mattered what she thought. These next two weeks could either go well with her…

Or go terribly, he thought with a grim finality.

Faisal couldn't rid himself of the image of Maryan reporting back to Salma and ending any chance he had of keeping Zara. He told himself it was silly. Maryan hadn't shown any signs of deceit when they'd talked on the yacht. Her blunt honesty had calmed his nerves. Someone that frank couldn't plot behind his back.

His driver turned the car onto the private road leading to Faisal's house. They climbed higher up the forested hillside to his home, and he listened as Zara "oohed" and "aahed" from the back of the car.

Her innocent awe brought a smile to his face and lightened the load pressing over his heart.

"Are we there yet?" she asked.

Faisal looked back, his eyes snagging Maryan's gaze before he turned to his daughter. "Almost." He pointed out the window at a break in the trees and their full foliage. "I love looking out at the city from up here."

Zara pressed her small hands to the window and exclaimed, "Look, Maryan! We can see *everything*!" When Maryan didn't move fast enough, she tossed a look back over her shoulder at her nanny. "Are you looking, Maryan? You're going to miss it!"

Caressing Zara's braids lovingly, Maryan hummed. "I'm looking, honey. It's a pretty sight, isn't it?"

Faisal beamed. Pride puffed billowing heat through him. It was worth craning his neck back and straining against his seat belt to experience the moment with them.

The car climbed higher and higher, slowing on the incline's final leg before leveling in front of an impressive set of iron gates. The gates lurched open after Faisal swiped the entry code into his phone. The driver moved the car past the barrier up and around the circular driveway. They stopped before the three-car garage. His mansion sitting ahead of them, in all its shining white stone glory.

"Wow," Zara exclaimed, her seat belt flying off and her hands gripping the back of his seat. She was close enough that her elation rang shrilly in his ear. "Is that your home, Daddy?"

"Not just my home, Zara. It's your home now, too," he said slowly, carefully.

He caught Maryan's eyes then. She held a guarded expression. None of her stunning features hinted as to her thoughts. He couldn't help but hope he hadn't crossed her by his statement. It was the truth. For now, this was Zara's home. And he wished it would remain that way forever. Maryan's blessing would be the cherry on top, that was all. At least…that was what he convinced himself this was. That he cared what Zara's nanny thought because Maryan was important to his daughter. She was attractive, but that wasn't his driving force.

"Can I get out now?" Zara looked eagerly between them, her eyes practically sparkling when she looked outdoors and spied her new home.

Maryan didn't lift her stare from him. Almost as if she waited on his word for their next action.

Knowing exactly what he'd like to do next, Faisal smiled and said, "Yes, let's start the tour."

The tour of the apartment above his garage ended half an hour later with Zara asking, very sweetly, whether she'd be allowed to watch television in his bedroom.

Faisal had a ninety-eight-inch flat-screen in his room complete with a top-notch home theater system. The walls were soundproof, too, so he could blast his music or Turkish dramas from the comfort of his bed knowing that he didn't have to worry about what lay beyond his spare bedroom.

He knew that wasn't what interested his little girl. She'd seen the large TV screen and goggled at it. When they had stepped out onto the balcony off his bedroom she had momentarily forgotten the television. But now that they'd re-entered the room and apartment, she had looked pleadingly up at him to watch her cartoons.

"Sure, why not?" Indulging her, he set her up on the bed and showed her how to control the home theater using the same remote as the television. And when he asked her to show him what he'd taught her, she huffed and rolled her eyes comically.

"Daddy, I know how to do it!"

Trying not to laugh, he said, "Show me anyway."

She humored him and demonstrated perfectly that she did in fact know how to work the remote and the myriad commands installed in it. "See," she scoffed, her ego sounding like it took a hit. "Mommy has three big TVs, too. One for me, one for her and one for anyone who visits."

Of course Salma did. She wasn't a billionaire, but she had plenty of wealth from her modeling and now her acting.

"Okay, sweetheart. Call me or Maryan if you need us." He dropped a kiss atop her head and walked out of the bedroom.

He headed for the kitchen, where he'd left Maryan when she opted out of the tour of his apartment. Wondering again if she disliked him, he strode toward her with less confidence in his swagger as to where he stood with Zara's beautiful nanny. He gulped subtly when she turned away from the electric kettle she was plugging into a wall outlet.

The kitchen island stood between them.

She grasped the sparkling white Calacatta marble countertop. Rich gold veins streaking uniformly through the marble. It had been delivered from Italy as a gift from an Italian investor who owned commercial property in the Calacatta region. What would have cost a hefty purse had cost him nothing, and now Maryan's hands explored the counter's edges nervously.

"I've put on tea," she said softly.

"I'd love a cup of *çay*." Some people preferred coffee; tea was his fuel. He blamed his Somali heritage. His mother and father *loved* their tea. And, of course, tea was a staple in Turkey. It was built into both cultures, Somali and Turkish. Steeped into their routines, traditions, stories and lives. He was taught to never refuse a cup of tea when offered.

"Çay?" she echoed.

"Sorry, that's just 'tea' in Turkish."

She nodded her understanding before drumming her fingernails on the counter, her grasp on it not looking any less nervous.

He didn't like that she was tense around him. And he didn't know why he should care, but he did and wanted it to stop.

"Did you find the tea leaves? Or do you prefer bags?" He had both, mostly for convenience. Sometimes the ritual of preparing tea was pleasant. Other times he was entrenched in a business meeting and popped out for a quick cup of tea. The simpler and faster the better.

She turned to mind the kettle, replying over her shoulder. "I found loose leaves."

"My stash," he said with a grin, blushing when she looked back at him, her hands holding two mugs.

"Stash?"

Face warming a little more, he murmured, "Yeah. I keep

tea stocked always, here and in the main house." And as she likely noticed, he stocked a variety, too. His tea preference changed with the weather, the seasons, even his moods. Not every occasion could be black tea—even if his parents preferred traditional black tea as most Somalis often did.

"Were you hiding it? Your stash, I mean," she clarified. "Because I might have had more trouble if you hadn't had everything labeled so very neatly." She lifted the kettle, poured hot water into the two mugs and replaced the kettle on its stand before turning back and finishing with the mugs. "Do you prefer sugar?"

"No, I add honey. I'll grab it," he said, and helped her by fetching a tray and depositing a jar of clover honey on it. He placed the tray on the kitchen island and waited on her to finish with the tea and face him again. What he desired most right then was sitting down with her and finishing their conversation on the yacht. He wanted to know more about her. More about how she'd come into Zara's life when she looked to be in her mid-to late twenties. Young enough to be living out her own life, not tying herself to big responsibilities.

"Seriously speaking, I've never appreciated a kitchen before, but yours is tidy and put-together and very unlike anything I have seen. I can't imagine what the main house looks like."

Maryan's praise triggered a breezy laugh from him. "You'll have to thank Lalam. She's worked her magic here and almost everywhere else in my home."

"Who?" She eyed him funnily, suspicion leaking into her voice.

And he had a guess as to why. She suspected he had a woman in his life. He didn't know whether to be slightly irked by her unvoiced assumption. It wasn't as though he couldn't date and have a woman over for fun. Though that was all it would ever be. Fun. Nothing serious. Romance had never been a serious subject for him. Right then it was the last thing he'd think to do, especially now that Zara had arrived to live full-time with him.

"My housekeeper, three times a week. You'll like Lalam. She speaks enough English, too, so you won't need me to translate."

The aromatic smell of herbal *çay* flooded the kitchen soon after. It lured him from around the kitchen island closer to her with the tray and jar of honey. There was something about her being in his space. The sight of Maryan making herself at home in his kitchen tempted him to disrupt her tea-making process.

She noted his nearness when she glanced up. Unable to hide her startle, she gazed wide-eyed at him for a handful of heart-stopping seconds before looking away shyly.

He read her shyness clear as day and as bright as the afternoon sun shining through the open blinds of the picture windows across the room. Normally he would've taken that as a sign to charm her. But he wasn't flirting. He shouldn't want to flirt with her, either. Maryan was leaving in fourteen days. She would no longer be Zara's nanny when she boarded her flight home to California. And he wasn't *really* planning to hire her, so…

I won't sleep with her.

That would be cruel. To him, to her and probably to Zara most especially. If they did make love, that was all it would be. The intimacy never left his bedroom, not with anyone—not even Zara's mother. They hadn't married as Salma hadn't wanted to, and he didn't believe in love all too much. At least, love felt like it could happen for anyone *but* him.

As if pounding it into his head and tattooing it into

his flushed skin and beating heart, he thought, *no kissing and no sex.*

Nothing remotely romantic with Maryan. He wouldn't tease himself with a friendship, either. Though he hoped they could be amicable during her stay. He could pick her brain about Zara. After all, that was all he should be worrying about: whether his daughter would be happy in his care.

Even as he thought that, his mind wandered to Maryan. He studied her.

Aboard his yacht when they got to talking, she displayed a sharp, bright mind, a fierce protective instinct and a keen perception that had him standing taller before her. And not even a boardroom full of his most important stakeholders and external board directors could do that to him.

Maryan managed it in less than the few hours he'd been in her company.

It was a remarkable feat. One she'd never know about, as he would have to reveal the degree to which she affected him.

"It's ready," she said, setting the mugs on the tray.

He lifted it and walked them to the breakfast table across the kitchen and beside the large windows with their sublime views. His garage apartment was one of his favorite spots to relax. Later, he planned to show her his backyard and the treats it held. But now he'd enjoy this cup of tea made by her and ease them into another enlightening conversation.

Last time he had learned about her ex-boyfriend and her aunt and uncle's restaurant. This time he wanted to hear more about her.

Her and Zara, he corrected.

Her phone pinged as he opened his mouth to speak.

Maryan mumbled, "Excuse me," and checked her phone. She frowned prettily and tapped a button before setting her phone facedown on the glass table. "Sorry," she said.

"Don't be," he told her, and held out the honey jar after he'd stirred the clover honey into his minty herbal tea. Their fingertips touched when she accepted the jar from him.

He sipped his mug and hummed his approval. "Sage tea. Good choice."

Her phone went off again. Chiming once, twice, three times. He lost count after that and remained quiet, observing her discreetly while imbibing his tea and savoring its honeyed earthy notes while wishing he had a slice of lemon on the side with it. By the umpteenth chime, though, his nosiness got the better of him.

"Your family?" he wondered.

"My friends," she replied with an abashed frown. "I'm sorry. I posted the pictures from earlier."

He pieced the rest together. "Of us, you mean."

"One of all three of us, yes. You, me *and* Zara." It wasn't his faulty hearing; she emphasized Zara's presence in the photo.

Smirking nevertheless, Faisal asked, "Did you tag me in it?"

"No. I didn't want to send the vultures your way." A beat passed, and then she sheepishly added, "They're really nice, actually. *Normally.* Except when they scent drama."

He laughed. Hard. Belly-heaving gusts of laughter. One, because she compared her friends to scavenging birds of prey. And two, because she looked adorably frazzled. It went at odds with the levelheaded persona she had when she confronted him about being late for the airport pickup.

"I'm glad you're having a laugh at my expense," she grumbled, though he caught a thread of humor belying her tone.

"Tag me. I can handle their questions."

"No way," she said quickly. She clutched her phone in both hands now like she worried that he'd take it from her and tag himself in the photo. Calming down, she lowered her hands and muttered, "Trust me. I'm saving you the grief of handling them."

"You're close, then."

She nodded. "Friends from high school and college."

"How much do they know about…?" He fanned a hand between them, the other clutching the handle of his mug.

"About me being here with Zara? Mostly everything…"

He chuckled when she shyly trailed off. Reading between the lines, he made an educated guess as to what she hadn't elucidated for her friends. He could have left it there, but he felt devilish and—despite firmly being convinced he wasn't flirting—he teased, "What don't they know?"

She sipped her tea, commenting, "This *is* good."

"I'm waiting," he joked, seeing through her delay tactics. She wasn't getting away with it.

Sighing, Maryan confessed quietly, "I haven't told them about staying here."

"At my place." He nodded thoughtfully. "But up until a few hours ago, you were booked into a hotel."

"True, but they're asking for pictures of the hotel room."

"Feel free to take photos of your guest room. Or any part of the house, for that matter." He waved in the direction of the main house. He planned a tour of it as well when he showed her to her room, after they'd finished their tea and pulled Zara from the TV.

"That's kind of you, but it doesn't feel right lying to them. I'll just ghost them for now." She shut her phone off and placed it on the table again.

No sooner had she closed her phone did his vibrate. It hummed in his palm as he pulled it from his pocket and regarded the caller ID.

"It's my mom." He rose to his feet. "Do you mind if I take the call?"

She shook her head, excusing him to answer the incoming call from his mother.

He had a feeling he knew why she was calling, but it wasn't until he answered and barely squeezed a "salaam" in before his mom pelted him with questions about Zara.

"Yes," he said as he walked away from Maryan, casting a glance back when he added, "she arrived safely with her nanny."

Faisal stepped into another room. Not the bedroom where Zara was watching her cartoons, the sound of the television spilling out into the hall. He walked into a room that looked like a study. Bright white bookshelves built into the walls and a wide, L-shaped mahogany desk formed the glimpse she saw before he closed the door for privacy to take his call from his mother.

She drank her tea, ruminating on the events that had brought her here. Anything to keep her from wondering what he had to be telling his mom.

A horrifying notion struck her then.

What if he tells her I'm staying here?

The mortifying thought stuck with her long enough for her tea and his to grow cold. Deciding to reheat their mugs, she walked them over to an expensive-looking microwave drawer. She figured out how to reheat and set a timer for a minute. Pacing alongside the island table, she found her eyes swiveling back to the door Faisal was behind, her mind racing over the embarrassing thought she'd had. The squalling beep of the microwave startled her.

And if that wasn't enough, Faisal's smooth, deep voice floating up from behind her added to her jumpiness.

Realizing he'd spooked her, he raised his hands up with palms facing out. "Sorry. I thought you heard me." Then he noticed the spill on the countertop. Noted her clutching her hand. "You scalded yourself."

"Nothing I can't fix." She clenched her teeth for a semblance of a smile and stuck her hand under cold running water briefly.

He fetched her a paper towel, but before that he took her hand, surprising her with his gentle touch and wrinkled brows emanating his worry. Faisal stroked his thumb lightly over the stinging, reddened skin on the back of her hand. Splotchy with angry color from where the hot tea had spilled onto her.

Maryan already hadn't expected his touch.

She wasn't even prepared for when he lowered his head and blew cool air over the heated surface of her sparking flesh. The shiver quaking through her was a force that shut down any rational thought and sharpened her primal senses. She stared at the top of his bowed dark head, his flawless deep brown skin and his slightly parted lips as he concentrated on the task of cooling her hand down.

She could probably let this go on longer.

She knew better, though, and stammered, "It's f-fine. Really. The redness should fade."

"And the pain? How's that?"

She gave it a thought. It stung a bit, but no more than she believed it ought to. "I'm used to working in a restaurant. At worse it's a little burn, at best a night's worth of discomfort."

"So, no first aid kit?"

Maryan gave him a headshake. "But an ice pack would be nice."

"You mean my blowing didn't help?"

She watched the teasing grin overtake his worried look; his handsomeness dialed up to high in the span of a heartbeat.

"It was nice…" She trailed off, and he picked up the ball she dropped.

"It's not an ice pack, though." Chuckling, he released her hand to open the freezer and pull out an ice pack. Wrapping it with the paper towel, he handed it to her.

"I'll grab our tea. Go ahead and sit down."

She heeded his instruction, her chest tight but not in an unpleasant or alarming way. Even if she wanted to argue, it would be hard to do it around the thickness closing off her throat, making breathing harder than it normally should be.

All because he touched me, blew on my hand, flirted with me?

He wasn't flirting, though. He'd *joked* with her and been kind enough to help her ice the burn on her hand. Allowing her brain to spin the moment into a big yarn would be foolish.

Foolish and a waste of time.

She had two weeks starting today to settle Zara into her new life with her dad. What she should be doing was getting to know the man who would be taking over her role as caregiver, not weighing every gesture and every look as a gateway into a passionate fantasy starring him and her.

She had to leave her fantasizing at the door until this trip was over.

"It's my fault the tea got cold. My fault you got injured." He joined her at the table with their freshly reheated mugs.

"I was going to reheat mine anyway. It made sense to do the same for you."

"Well, thank you," he said, lifting his mug to his lips and pausing to blow over its surface before a sip.

The memory of his lips hovering over her hand and his cooling breath skating over her sent a fresh shiver through her.

"My mom says hello."

"You told her about me." She wished she didn't sound so squeaky, but her nervousness was amplified at the thought of him telling his mother of their living arrangement.

Reading her mind, he replied, "I left out mention of your staying with me and Zara."

Maryan had trouble masking her relief, because he laughed low and sexily.

"Worried?"

"A little," she admitted blushingly. "I know how Somali parents can be."

Faisal laughed louder this time. "Mine are no different. My mom's especially keen for me to be married."

"Aren't most Somali *hooyo* like that?" It felt natural slipping into their native tongue with him. She'd done it on his flashy boat, and she was doing it now in his equally impressive home. Something about him lowered her normally sky-high thorny defenses.

"You mentioned your aunt and uncle. Your parents?"

"In Hamar—er… Mogadishu." She was used to calling her Somali home city by its local moniker, Hamar.

He grinned wide. "I thought I heard an Hamari accent."

"I must not have gotten rid of it." She'd lived more than half her life in the States. Somalia should be well in her rearview by now. A fond thing she pulled from her memory vault when nostalgia swayed her in that direction, much as she would a childhood toy or book. It wasn't like she ever planned to uproot her life to move back home. And yet it *was* home. Her family lived there. Her mother and father, and brothers and sisters. They made it impossible to fully label her childhood in Somalia as a thing of her past.

"Do you visit?" Faisal asked, taking a bigger gulp of his tea and prompting her to imbibe from her mug.

When her mouth was clear, she said, "I haven't since I moved away. What about you?"

"My family doesn't live in Istanbul. After retiring, my mom and dad left the city for a quieter life in a small town. My younger sister lives with them. I don't get to visit often, but I do try to get away from work for big family occasions. Birthdays, my parents' anniversary, the last days of Ramadan and both Eids."

"Does Zara know her grandparents?" She'd lived with her father and mother in Istanbul for a few years. She must have gotten to know Faisal's side of the family then.

"Oh, yeah. They love her. It's why my mom called. She was pushing for me to bring her soon. We'll likely go after you leave, though."

Of course. That would make sense. It wasn't like he could invite her to go with them. What would his family think?

"But that's not a problem today. Right now what I'd like to know is what do you want to see most in Istanbul?"

What *did* she want to see in Istanbul?

A myriad of answers came to mind. The Asian side of Istanbul, the city's many mosques, the gilded halls and salons and crystal staircases of Dolmabahçe Palace.

The famed Hagia Sophia.

"I'm still technically on the job," she said, dampening the excitement his question unfurled in her.

Salma hadn't stopped paying her. In fact, she'd offered an overly generous severance bonus to Maryan after she agreed to take Zara to her father. The financial incentive hadn't been what motivated her. Being with Zara for a little longer was all the motive she needed to pause her life in California temporarily and hop on a transatlantic flight to Istanbul. But she also wasn't unhappy to see the extra zeros on the bonus check. Especially after what had happened with her ex, Hassan.

Thinking of him annoyed her. Knowing that she'd

wasted three and a half years on him boiled her blood. All of that didn't compare to what he had done to her *and* her aunt and uncle at the end.

It was one thing to be angry at her, but her Aunt Nafisa and Uncle Abdi had done nothing to deserve being robbed. And by their sous-chef of all people.

The jerk.

She stewed in her chair and looked away from Faisal, afraid he'd see her anger and ask questions. She wouldn't be able to handle any of them with grace. Talking about her thieving ex-boyfriend infuriated her. She'd told Faisal enough already about the subject. Saying any more would be assuming that he was interested in hearing her rant.

"Okay, but I'm not tethering you to the house," he said with a frown. "You're free to go where you want. Take Zara with you. I'd like her to see Istanbul."

"And where will you be?" She ignored the alarm bell clanging in her head and the tightening mix of panic and ire pressing down onto her thumping heart. Leaping to a conclusion wouldn't do her any good.

"As I said, I'll be busy closing this partnership deal for my company. But by tomorrow afternoon, my schedule is free." His face relaxed, his frown softer and his eyes less troubled. The dark beginnings of a beard raked his jaw and climbed to his high-boned cheeks. He palmed the lower half of his face, his nostrils twitching with an audible sigh.

Suddenly the air around him shifted.

He smiled charmingly. "I was thinking a city tour might be a good way to celebrate the closing of this deal. If that's something you'd be interested in? I'm a pretty good tour guide."

His smile unleashed a fluttering in her stomach and a rush of heady warmth over her body.

"I think Zara would like that," she said.

"And you?"

She heard the rest of his question. *Would* you *like it?*

After drinking down to the dregs in her cup, Maryan placed it on the tray and watched as Faisal mirrored her with his mug. She stood and grabbed the tray handles, her eye contact with him unsevered and stronger than before. He tensed his shoulders slightly as if anticipating her rejection. Even so, his smile remained sunny on his too-handsome face.

"I've always wanted to see the Hagia Sophia."

It took a few seconds, but his bright teeth flashed at her. "Then we'll add it to the tour." He stared at her afterward, his smile edging on playful and his eyes dropping to her mouth.

"Sounds good," she agreed.

"It's a date," he added.

She couldn't unglue her tongue from the roof of her mouth to give him a comeback. So she did the next best thing. Bobbed her head, lifted the tray with their empty mugs and walked away from him before she combusted from blushing too much.

CHAPTER FOUR

MARYAN ANTICIPATED ONLY one thing from her second day in Turkey. It wasn't her usual morning routine of stretching, doing yoga poses and squeezing in a shower. It wasn't even her break from that routine when she spent half an hour longer than usual on her makeup.

It was Faisal taking her and Zara out to tour the city.

She lowered her makeup brush from the apple of her cheeks, the creamy blush adding a glow to her face and her contouring more perfect than usual. Even her experimentation with eyeshadow colors turned out beautifully. She'd worn less makeup having taken into account that they'd be walking and touring Istanbul. A summerlike breeze wafted into her grand guest room from the open balcony doors and had her appreciating her choice of adding sunscreen beneath her sheer tinted moisturizer. After their tea, Faisal had showed her to her room in the main house. If she had thought his apartment was luxurious, the main house was near palatial, her room being no exception.

She stared at the woman gazing back at her in the reflection of the wide, beautifully framed dresser mirror. Maryan barely recognized herself, but in the best way possible.

Liking what she saw, she uncapped her setting spray and closed her eyes. She spritzed around her face twice and opened her eyes when the satiny mist rested coolly over her skin.

Refreshed from her morning routine, she stood to close the balcony doors. Instead of stopping, though, she ventured outdoors, the sun-warmed stone of the balcony heating the soles of her bare feet. She stopped before the balustrade to be awed by the vista once again. She'd done it plenty of times since Faisal showed her to the room.

"Breathtaking," she whispered, her lips drawing up into a smile.

Her thoughts meandered from verdant treetops, the swooping valley and the panoramic city scene bisected by the shimmering strip of the Bosporus as the sun crept higher over the horizon. She wondered what her aunt and uncle could be up to right then. It was late for her family and friends in California. Nearly midnight. But she knew that was when Aunt Nafisa and Uncle Abdi sat in the living room winding down from another long day at their restaurant. They were late sleepers yet early risers for as long as she'd been living with them.

Fifteen years this fall.

Fifteen years since she'd left her parents and younger siblings and flew from the only home she'd once known in Mogadishu to live with her maternal aunt and her husband. Now Aunt Nafisa and Uncle Abdi were the only family she cared to recognize.

Scowling at the thought of her mom and dad, Maryan breathed deeply and pushed down the flush of anger threatening to rise. She'd been holding on to it for so long that bottling her resentment had grown to be a natural instinct.

They hadn't asked if she wanted to leave for a life in America. In their eyes, feeding seven children had become too much. They could convince themselves they'd given her a better chance to live, but the truth was her parents had been poor and desperate enough to push one of their children from the nest. As the eldest, she was the unlucky child.

But then I wouldn't have met Aunt Nafisa and Uncle Abdi.

Her aunt and uncle were the one bright spot in all this. Bright enough to blast the frosty anger that tended to grip her whenever she deigned to think of her parents. And she knew it wasn't their fault they were poor, but…

If they had asked, it wouldn't be like this.

She wouldn't feel something suspiciously close to *hate* every time she thought of how they'd made a life-altering decision for her.

She'd been twelve. Plenty old enough to make a choice for herself.

Or at least feel like they included my feelings in their decision-making.

Maryan blew out the breath she'd been holding reflexively.

Forcing her thinking away from her parents, she remembered what Faisal had told her yesterday on his sailing yacht about his plan for striking oil in Somalia. His earnest expression and voice came flooding to mind.

I want to give back to our home, he'd said.

It was an impassioned statement and a bold one at that. For his sake she prayed it worked out. There were plenty of families in Somalia—poor ones like hers who could use a change in fortune like Faisal's promising business plan. A boom in oil would lift up the whole nation and might even put it more firmly toward a direction of steadier and more rapid economic development and progress.

If she saw anyone being capable of doing it, it was Faisal Umar. Billionaire. Successful tycoon.

Single dad.

That should have stopped her fantasizing about Zara's handsome father.

But thinking of him made her wonder what he had planned for their city tour. It wasn't her imagination that made her heart thump a little faster and a jitteriness swarm her empty stomach. She would've chalked it up to needing breakfast, except she wasn't thinking about food.

She was still fixated on Faisal.

And if she wasn't careful, she'd forget why she had come to Istanbul in the first place.

Zara is why I'm here.

All thoughts of Faisal and his unwarranted effect on her vanished when she turned her head sharply from the view out on her balcony. Someone was knocking on the guest room door. It couldn't be Zara. She had checked in on her ten minutes earlier and she'd been sound asleep in the room next door.

Believing it to be Faisal, she crossed into the room and answered the door.

The tall, fair-haired young woman on the other side wasn't him.

Her rosy-cheeked smile invited Maryan into asking, "Are you Lalam?"

"I am, Miss Maryan," Faisal's highly praised housekeeper said, her glowing, lightly freckled face adding to her youthful appearance. She held a serving tray and explained in lovely, lilting English, "I bring you breakfast. I hope it's okay?"

"It's more than okay, thank you, and it's just Maryan." She reached for the tray, but the housekeeper pulled away.

"I carry." Once she was inside the room she veered for the bed. "Is here okay?"

"Evet."

Lalam turned to her, her sunny smile growing larger. "You learn Turkish?"

Maryan blushed. She'd been practicing. Since Faisal planned to give her and Zara a tour of the city, she had wanted to immerse herself in the language and experience both. The newly installed Turkish-learning app on her phone was helping. "A little," she told the housekeeper, cringing. "Is it bad?"

Looking to be on the younger side of her twenties, Lalam placed the breakfast tray on the folded duvet cover and spun to her. She hoped it wasn't to tell her to quit practicing Turkish because hers was awful.

"Your Turkish is *çok iyi*. In English: 'very good.'"

Maryan laughed. "Yes, I learned that one early." Faisal predicted she would like Lalam, and she'd have to let him know he was right.

"You like Istanbul?" Lalam gestured to the open balcony doors and what they could see of the metropolis from Faisal's home.

"I haven't seen too much, but from what I have it's a lovely city. Busy like most cities are, but lots of history to it."

"Very busy city, yes. I move to Istanbul for school. Now I live and study here all the time."

Her English wasn't hard to understand. Maryan was relieved she spoke it at all. Her Turkish wasn't going to magically improve by leaps and bounds in the span of two weeks. And she had a feeling talking to Lalam would give her breaks for some real adult conversation. Something she had a sense she wouldn't get from Faisal too much. Even though he had promised his schedule would be clear this afternoon.

Thinking of him prompted her to wonder, "Is Faisal still sleeping in his…"

She trailed off when Lalam furrowed her brow. Realizing it was possible the housekeeper wasn't aware her boss had spent the night in the swanky garage apartment, she phrased it differently.

"Is he out?"

Lalam clasped her hands in front of her spotless white apron. Her black T-shirt and black jeans must have been part of a uniform. The ensemble did make her look more efficient than Maryan already suspected she was, simply from observing how pleasingly tidy the house was.

All of that was forgotten when Lalam reported, "Mr. Umar is at work, yes."

"Work?" Maryan parroted.

The housekeeper pointed to the breakfast tray. "Mr. Umar leave a message for you."

She noted a small folded paper tucked under the covered plate. The note was in a loopier scrawl than she envisioned Faisal was capable of. The men she'd come across and the ones in her life tended to write blocky and hard print. Like they had a point to prove.

I promise I'll be back in time.

For their tour, he meant.

"When did he leave?" She looked up at Lalam, catching the housekeeper walking for the bedroom door.

She turned back. "Very early. I start work. He leave for work. We have little time to say salaam."

Staring down at the message, Maryan barely noted Lalam's departure until she looked up a little while later and found herself alone in the room. The door was closed again like nothing had transpired.

The privacy was welcome, though. She gazed down at his message again, her heart pounding and her anticipation to see him after he finished with his work walking a tightrope. It was enough to ignore the nagging doubt that she should be worrying more about his commitments and his ability to juggle his business *and* his fatherly duties to Zara.

He was running late to meet Maryan and Zara again.

Faisal sped up his walk and jogged the final paces to one of the entrances of the Grand Bazaar. Burak was exactly where he said he'd be waiting. His head of security greeted him with one of his stoic nods, his face devoid of any telling emotions. It was perfect for the job, but this wasn't a job. Faisal had asked him to kick off the city tour in his absence.

That was two hours ago.

And now he was late and preparing to grovel and give the best excuse to Maryan.

"Tell me honestly: How bad is it?" If he went in armed with the knowledge, he might be able to reverse the damage he'd done to Maryan's impression of him.

Burak crossed his arms and grunted.

"That bad?" He sighed, knowing he had only himself to blame. After promising Maryan he'd have his schedule free earlier in the day, and not explaining why he had ended up working longer, he expected nothing short of a frosty reception from her. Especially considering she hadn't shied from sharing her opinions before.

He anticipated being chewed out by her. And he was stalling because of it.

"Was she that angry?" he asked in Turkish.

"She hides it well like most women, but it's there. The quiet ones are the scariest. You'll see what I mean soon enough." Burak flung him a wry smile and switched to English, "I don't envy you, boss."

Faisal laughed, a hollow sound.

"I'd warn you to keep your distance, but she knows you're here. I told her when you left the office."

"Yeah, maybe I'd take your advice," Faisal drawled, "but keeping my distance is what got me into this mess." To be specific, the time apart from his daughter. He had no doubt Maryan would hold it over his head like the sword of Damocles.

He hoped she wasn't closed off to his legitimate excuse for being late.

Burak walked him into the bazaar before he stopped and said, "Good luck, boss."

"I'll need it," Faisal rejoined with a sigh.

He pushed forward alone. His gait purposefully slowed as he neared the small covered shop that Burak had pointed out. The shop Maryan and Zara were inside. Beautiful handmade jewelry and wood-carved trinket boxes lined the shelves. The shopkeeper was a young woman wearing a hijab. She greeted him from afar where she helped Maryan behind the glass counter.

Zara saw him first.

"Daddy!"

He opened his arms to catch her embrace and ground them before Zara's exuberance toppled them back into a display stand of cheaper-looking necklaces and bracelets. The more authentic gems and jewelry were guarded under lock and key behind protective glass cases.

Standing, Faisal grasped Zara's hand and listened to her cheery rehashing of how her day with her beloved nanny had panned out thus far. He walked her back to Maryan to face the music. And seeming to understand exactly what he planned, Maryan swung her attention back to the shopkeeper.

"Can I have a look at that mother-of-pearl bracelet?" She touched her finger to the top of the glass counter at her bracelet of choice.

As soon as the shopkeeper was preoccupied with the

task, Faisal seized the window to squeeze in the first of what he anticipated would be many apologies today.

"I'm sorry I didn't call or text earlier. I was in a meeting—"

"I get it. You were busy," she interjected in Somali, sounding far from understanding. With a breezy shrug, and still avoiding eye contact, she said, "Zara and I were doing just fine here."

The "without you" hung in the electrified air between them. She needn't have spelled it out for him. She was just as piqued with him as he expected. Burak had given him a fair warning, too.

But it didn't prepare his body for the abject disappointment hardening her voice when she snapped, "You didn't have to rush over on our account. Don't let us stop you from working."

Her words struck his heart.

With a smile that rang fake to him, she then accepted the bracelet from the shopkeeper and switched to English again to thank her.

Realizing that he wouldn't get anywhere with her in their current setting, Faisal held back from saying any more. He allowed Zara to lure him to a part of the store away from Maryan. Their backs turned to her, Zara pointed out a series of beautifully rendered necklaces, anklets, brooches, bracelets, earrings and even cuff links. Gold, silver and copper metal formed the bases, and alluring precious and semiprecious gemstones were inlaid in the metallic frames.

"I like that one," Zara said, smiling toothily up at him.

"This one?" He tapped the glass showcase at the stunning amber necklace. Inlaid into a simple rose-gold case, the polished honey-colored amber was the size of his thumbnail. The threads of pink gold holding the amber pendant looked too fragile for a seven-year-old. But this was a momentous experience. He had Zara living with him now. She was his daughter, and he could do everything he ever dreamed of doing with her since he had stepped in Salma's delivery room and gotten his first peek at Zara inside her bassinet.

"Do you like it that much?" he asked her.

She nodded enthusiastically. "It's so pretty, Daddy!"

He glanced over his shoulder and caught Maryan's darting gaze. She'd been looking at him. Possibly glaring holes into the back of his head from her warranted annoyance.

"Excuse me," he called to the shopkeeper in Turkish. "Can you wrap this one up for me?"

Maryan stubbornly cast her eyes everywhere but at him as he approached her once more. This time to do business with the shopkeeper. Zara bounced up and down in place while she watched her necklace be lovingly packed into a jewelry box and inside a shopping bag. The shopkeeper held it out to her from across the counter, and as soon as she had it she showed Maryan.

Her nanny indulged her with a warmer, genuine smile. Something she hadn't been able to muster for him when he entered the store.

The sterling silver chain bracelet with its iridescent mother-of-pearl stones was on the glass counter where Maryan left it to shower Zara and her new necklace with attention and affection. Deftly he plucked it up by its thin chain and held it out to the shopkeeper.

"Add this too, please." He spoke Turkish, knowing full well Maryan and Zara wouldn't be able to understand.

The shopkeeper did as he requested and quickly packed the bracelet up without alerting Maryan. She smiled knowingly when he tapped his card to pay her for the service. All of this happened in the time that Maryan was looking away.

When she turned, she confronted a second small shopping bag identical to Zara's on the counter over the exact spot that she'd left the bracelet.

She looked at him instantly, her lips parting, her eyes holding a question...*and* an argument to return the purchase.

He made a silent show of tucking his designer wallet inside his suit jacket. The bracelet was paid for. It was hers. A small bracelet was nothing to his immense wealth. And that wealth meant not a thing if it couldn't be enjoyed with others. Coworkers, friends, family.

Maryan was none of those to him. And yet she'd helped raise Zara. He owed her more than a pretty trinket.

"Can we talk?" he asked in Somali.

She briskly nodded and turned to answer Zara's reaching hands and clamoring cry to see the second shopping bag.

"I want to see your present, Maryan!" She bounced for a look but stopped when Maryan handed her the bag. They lingered in the shop until Zara talked her nanny into wearing the bracelet. Then Maryan helped Zara with her necklace. Both of them walked out of the shop wearing smiles and their new accessories.

Faisal had to capture the moment. "Wait. Can I take a picture?"

Maryan was shaking her head when Zara exclaimed, "Yes, please!"

Zara posed with Maryan, who allowed him to take their pictures.

Once he was satisfied, he slipped his phone in his pants pocket and waved Burak over to them.

"Take Zara to the restaurant," he said to his friend and security head.

Zara began protesting, but he crouched down to her level and squeezed her hands. "I need to talk to Maryan quickly."

Maryan helped by stepping up and stroking Zara's braids. "We're right behind you."

"Promise?" Zara asked them, her bottom lip not trembling as noticeably.

"Promise," he said with Maryan. They traded a quick look before Burak accepted Zara's outstretched hand and led her away from them.

"If this is about you being late *again*…" she began.

"It is, but let's talk elsewhere." He guided her through the populated centuries-old bazaar, down winding alleys, past ancient crumbling sections of walls and under the canopy of arched ceilings decorated with blue mosaic tiles. They emerged out of one of twenty-one entrances into the Grand Bazaar.

Breathing the fresh air outdoors was always a treat. Especially when the breeze was tinged with aromatic flavors of spices, herbs, meats and tea.

"Would you like a cup? It won't spoil our appetite."

With their tea in hand, they found a bench in the square across from the bazaar. Nowhere near as crowded, it was the perfect place to talk to her, and he hoped to plead his case of tardiness. He didn't know which would be more challenging to do: to lay bare his heart or give her the rundown of how he'd failed to secure his coveted partnership deal for Umar Capital Group.

"Where did your security guy take Zara exactly?"

Faisal's heart-stopping grin put her at ease as much as it set up her guard.

"Ever heard of the internet-famous Salt Bae?" He mimed sprinkling salt and laughed breezily. "He's got a restaurant inside the bazaar and it's very popular. And since he's somewhat of a national treasure and this is a tour of Istanbul…"

The mention of the tour reminded her why they were outside and away from Zara.

Trusting his judgment that his daughter was safe in the care of the tall, muscled bodyguard Burak, Maryan focused on delving into what she expected was his apology.

Might as well get this over with.

If it was going to be a half-cocked attempt at an apology, she wanted it done and over with, and preferably before her refreshing pomegranate iced tea grew too warm.

"I'm sorry about being late. I am." He sighed and unbuttoned his suit jacket. Shifting on the bench to face her more, he launched into an explanation. "Something came up last-minute at the office. I couldn't leave it to anyone else. All my staff were expecting me to be there. I... It didn't feel right to abandon them."

Without thinking it through, she blurted, "But abandoning your daughter was okay?"

He pulled his handsome features into a grimace. He had to have known he walked *right* into that one. It stung, she bet, but it couldn't be hurting any more than her bruised ego. She'd really believed him—*trusted* in him to come through for her and spend the day with Zara. This wasn't about the tour, she'd told herself, but about whether he could be there for his daughter the way she deserved.

For four years she'd been a rock to Zara. She'd nurtured her confidence and protected her whenever possible.

And now she was passing that long-held torch to Faisal. *But he's failing.*

He was also doing a terrible job at trying to meet her tall expectations. Even the short ones, like arriving on time, were eluding him right now. If he was going to apologize, would he be passing the blame on to some ambiguous work-related problem that had cropped up conveniently at the last minute?

"The deal's been postponed." Faisal looked down into his paper cup, both hands holding his tea. His face crumpled as he said, "After everyone's effort and hard work, it all managed to fall apart anyway."

She only learned of this deal yesterday, but he'd made it sound important to his company.

And to him.

She felt bad for him. Sympathy held her irritation at bay.

"It was going so well, too. The two brothers who own majority holding of this Turkish natural gas and oil company were happy with the partnership my company would offer."

"They must have explained why," she said.

Faisal barely sipped his cup. He touched the rim to his lips and pulled back to answer her, embarrassment coloring his tone. "They did."

She didn't rush him to elucidate. Looking miserable, he glanced at the passersby in the square. Whatever it was that put the brakes on his hard-sought business deal must have been bad. Especially when it was obvious he was working up the courage to rehash the humiliating explanation.

"I'll show you what went wrong," he finally said, his phone in hand. He pulled up his email and opened attached photos.

"These are recent photos from a magazine. A popular gossip rag published all through Europe. They'd sneaked a paparazzo into the party." He turned his phone for her to have a look at the photos attached to the email. Each photo had him in a compromising position with a different woman. The last one had him pressed between *two* waifish brunettes in skimpy bathing suits.

"Where were you when this was taken?"

"A pool party I attended last week." He tucked his phone away.

She'd read about him being a playboy. It shouldn't have surprised her that he would be partying the week before his daughter arrived to live with him forever.

Stuffing down her misplaced annoyance, and the more frustrating twinges of jealousy at seeing the photos of him embracing other women, she asked the next most logical question. "Why do they care what you do in your spare time?"

It shouldn't have been anyone's business. Certainly not hers to judge what he did to unwind after a long day's work.

"The host was one of the Turkish brothers. Erkin is his name, and he loves partying. More than me, evidently." His self-deprecating smile plucked her heartstrings. "I know what they call me. A playboy."

She didn't confess to having believed the epithet.

"It's okay," he murmured, his piercing gaze frozen on her. "It's true. I like partying. I work hard, play harder sometimes. Not always. When it's deserved."

"You didn't answer me. Why should you have to explain what you do in your free time?" She wasn't lauding his playboy reputation. She just didn't feel he should be penalized for it. And he wouldn't suffer alone. There were people he might be able to help in Somalia with his oil and natural gas project. Families and communities who would benefit from a healthy economy. Families like hers.

"That was my mistake. I didn't think it'd be polite to refuse the younger brother's invitation. But it seems his older brother is more traditional than I was led to believe. They don't want their company image tarnished by photos like the ones I showed you."

"So, is there hope left to save the deal?"

He heaved a sigh. "There might be, but I'll have to win back the older brother's trust. Prove that I'm not just partying all day and debauching my company's reputation."

"Is that all you wanted to say to me?" Maryan sensed there was more he hadn't let her in on.

Sighing again, he said, "Besides begging you to understand that I normally don't break promises?"

"Yes."

"I don't want you to think I can't work all of this out. Fatherhood and running my business. I'm capable of doing both and not drowning."

His vehement statement was impressive.

It also wasn't enough.

She needed to *see* him putting in the same effort she had no doubt he'd shown to secure his gainful business.

Faisal turned into her a little more, the heat coming off him closer.

"My parents moved from a small town outside of Mogadishu to Turkey thirty years ago. They were business owners in Istanbul. We lived next door to our small family bakery. On weekends, my sister and I would help them by doing whatever we could.

"I watched them juggle us and their business, and they juggled successfully."

"And that's why you believe it'll work for you." She hugged a bare arm around her stomach and narrowed her eyes. Everything he said about his family was a step in the positive direction.

But it's still not enough.

"I have to believe it will." He gazed at her with an intensity that made her heart pang.

Softly, she said, "On your boat you said you wanted to try, and I believe you. But you have to *actually* try to be here with Zara."

"I will," he vowed.

"I'm not going to dictate your schedule to you." She

wasn't here to tell him how to spend his time. "All I'm asking is that you find more time for Zara."

"I swear I will," he repeated, a smile relaxing his face and making him painfully handsome.

She gulped a bigger sip of her tea than planned and coughed.

He leaned in, his hand falling on her shoulder, his fingers pressing gently. "Are you okay?"

She had cool tangy sweet tea shoot up her nose, but it might be worth the spine-electrifying contact with him. Maryan felt a telltale blush, her dark brown skin warming to the touch and her cheeks aching in her battle to stop from smiling goofily.

"Fine," she murmured. "But we should head back to Zara."

Faisal stood and offered her a hand to help her up from the bench. As they walked back together, he shattered the silence.

"I also hope you'll let me give you that tour of Istanbul while you're here with us?"

He framed it as a question, giving her a chance to refuse. It was a brownie point for him.

"We've seen the bazaar," she said, barely recognizing the good-natured taunt in there. Who was she? Faisal's flirty nature was rubbing off on her obviously.

He laughed and smiled. "I know you don't mean *all* of the bazaar."

"Some of it," she teased.

He guided her past the metal detectors at the bazaar's entrance and drew close enough to bump arms with her and rattle the silver mother-of-pearl bracelet on her wrist. The bracelet he'd gifted to her.

She turned her head and discovered his face inches from hers. Naturally a kiss wasn't far from her mind.

He closed the gap to her ear in a heartbeat and whispered, "Then allow me to show you more."

CHAPTER FIVE

A FEW DAYS AGO, Maryan hadn't believed Faisal's promise to change all too much. She had learned through life experiences not to trust twice. First with her parents promising they'd see her soon before sending her off to live in America on her own, and then when her thieving ex-boyfriend, Hassan, robbed her and her family.

She hadn't placed stock in his vow to be more present and spend time with Zara.

If she'd been a betting person, she would've lost a lot of money by now. Because Faisal surprised her. Not only had he shown up regularly and on time for their outings the past three days, but he'd shown them plenty of Istanbul. Never taking them to the same place twice. Always showing them a new and beautiful side to the metropolis he called home.

And Maryan had already known this, but Istanbul wasn't merely a concrete jungle. Pockets of green spaces were to be found all over the city. Çamlıca Hill was one of those places.

"Let's go on a picnic," Faisal had said that morning.

Zara had been more than happy with the idea.

After Maryan had wondered whether they'd be distracting him from work, Faisal had assured her that everything that needed his personal attention was seen to before he'd asked them on the impromptu picnic. His exact words echoed in her mind.

I'd rather spend the day outside with you and Zara than be cooped up in my office.

It sounded like he was turning a new leaf.

I don't even know him.

Certainly not well enough to know whether he had changed or not over these five days. And if the change was truly for the better or otherwise. But he hadn't been late again. And he had managed to keep any promises he made to Zara. It didn't matter what she thought outside of that.

Zara was happy, and that was enough to quiet her doubts about him.

"Maryan, look," Zara whispered in her ear and wrapped her arms around her neck. She surprised her by coming up from behind.

Maryan had been sitting by Faisal while Zara wandered off to explore nearby. She was enamored by the pretty rows of flower gardens lining the footpath. The path wended through the hilltop park. Zara hadn't been alone in exploring it, either. Plenty of children loitered near the flowers, their parents and families sheltered under the umbrage of the trees scattered through the park.

They were under one of those trees now. Sunlight pierced weakly past the net of the wild maple's thick foliage. Even with the shade protecting them from the midafternoon sun Maryan hadn't taken any chances. She'd packed suntan lotion to protect them all. The last thing she wanted ruining their perfect day was a sunburn.

"Daddy's sleeping," she said in Maryan's ear with a giggle.

Maryan looked to her right to find that Zara's reporting was true. Faisal *had* fallen asleep.

They had been chatting about the city, and she'd gotten the sense that he loved Istanbul. But then they'd lapsed into a peaceful silence. She had looked away for what had felt like a handful of minutes, so it was surprising to see him sound asleep.

He was lying on his back on the grass, his arms tucked under his head and his T-shirt stretched tight against his sculpted chest. He was nothing but lean, clean-lined muscle under his finely tailored business suits. She'd discovered over the course of the day that it was more challenging to look away from his hotness when he was wearing a casual T-shirt and denim "manpris" than it was when he was in his work wear.

She raised her eyes up from his body to his gorgeous face. The man could've been a model or actor and given Salma a run for her money. Though now, Maryan understood how they'd been an item once. Two breathtakingly beautiful people gravitating to each other was a tale as old as time.

That wasn't jealousy souring her tongue. Rather the bitter dregs of the spices from the freshly made Turkish tea Lalam had packed for them in a thermos.

It was pointless to be envious when Faisal would never see her like that.

I wouldn't want him to, anyway.

Nothing would come from a relationship right now. And one-night stands had never been her thing. Her friends had *urged* her to have meaningless rebound fun after she and Hassan broke up. She wasn't up to it. Even knowing that it would feel good to hurt Hassan. He'd been a cocky jerk. Once she'd believed his charismatic personality was the most attractive part of him. That was before she had realized how toxic his overconfidence could be to her.

Looking at Faisal, she couldn't help but compare his charming persona with her ex's.

That isn't fair. He isn't Hassan.

But it didn't change the fact that it would spell trouble for her to mingle with someone equally as magnetic as her ex-boyfriend. The thought alone soured her mouth. It made it all too clear to her that she wasn't ready for romance yet. She wasn't in the headspace to tangle hearts with anyone. Even someone as attractive and good-natured as Faisal.

"Do I wake him up?" Zara moved her arms off Maryan and sat carefully by her dad.

"No, we'll let him sleep." Maryan pressed a finger to her lips and watched as Zara mimed her. She shared a smile with her before glancing at Faisal's relaxed facial features. And because she couldn't stare at him forever, she forced her attention to her phone.

She hadn't answered any of her friends' messages with any details about her trip yet. Any replies to their questions had been vague. But she knew that couldn't last forever. She'd posted more photos to her social feed, and they had gotten plenty of hits. Hundreds of hearts and comments from friends, family and even random people who had followed her over the course of the last few days.

The hashtags she'd been using were new to her but popular in travelers' circles: *#istanbul, #travelbug, #travelgram, #travelwithme.*

One of her favorite photos had the most buzz.

It was a photo of her and Faisal atop Galata Tower. They went to the popular tourist spot yesterday. The line into the tower at sundown snaked so long she hadn't thought they'd ever make it to the top. Though after waiting half an hour—and following Faisal's teasing suggestion of using his company's helicopter to see both Galata Bridge and Tower from above—they were admitted inside.

Maryan tapped the photo for a closer look…again. She'd looked at it enough when she had been alone last night.

Faisal kept his arms at his sides, but his posture was relaxed. He leaned on the stone railing at the top of the tower and pulled into her right before Zara snapped the photo. She couldn't help noting they looked *cozy*. And she wasn't alone in thinking so. All she had to do was scroll down to see her friends echoing the same thought.

It seemed *everyone* in her life wanted to know whether Faisal was her rebound after Hassan.

Her aunt and uncle weren't hooked on social media as most people were these days. A blessing in this instance, as they still hadn't caught wind of the online speculation of her love life. And the *only* reason she was 100 percent certain of that was that they'd have texted or called about it by now.

She'd have to burst everyone's bubbles eventually. Crush her friends from hoping that there was anything happening between her and Faisal.

Nothing has and nothing ever will.

She posted a new picture. A photo of the snaking garden footpath on Çamlıca Hill. Adding the appropriate tags, she tapped to post. No sooner had she when her notification bell alerted her to new activity. Maryan sighed. Apparently even a safe, Faisal-free photo like the one she posted warranted curiosity from friends.

Maybe I should clear the air and tag him.

Faisal had suggested it on the first day. Now it wasn't looking like a bad idea.

Before Maryan could give it any more thought, Zara pulled her out of her thinking with a question.

"When you leave, will it just be Daddy and me?"

Her heart thumping a little faster, Maryan hummed softly, tucked her phone away, and scooted closer to where Zara sat by her father. She squeezed both of Zara's small shoulders before pulling her back into her open arms. Zara fell gently and willingly into the comforting embrace.

With Zara's head tucked under her chin, Maryan sought to calm any doubt in the young girl.

"Unfortunately, I can't stay forever." In fact, she was due to leave in a little more than a week. She gulped at the reality. Somehow her time in Istanbul was coming to a speedier close than she'd hoped it would.

When she spoke next it seemed as though she were convincing herself of her encroaching departure as much as Zara. "It's going to take some getting used to. But I hope you try for your dad's sake."

"Will you miss me?"

Maryan rocked her side to side, her voice a hoarse but emphatic whisper when she answered, "Yes. Of course I will."

"Do you think Nadia and Simone miss me?"

Nadia and Simone were her school friends. The trio were inseparable. Maryan had spent countless days planning playdates for Zara and her friends, minding the children when the other girls' parents couldn't spare time away from their jobs.

"I'm sure they do. But you have their numbers. You can call them on your phone." She hadn't approved of Salma giving Zara a phone, but now it would come in handy. "And you can always call me, too."

In the smallest voice, Zara glumly stated, "That's not true. I tried calling them today, and they didn't answer me."

"When did you call?"

"Don't be angry." Zara turned in her arms, her bottom lip protruding and her wide brown eyes begging Maryan's forgiveness. "I stayed up last night to call them."

"Oh, honey," Maryan began, tamping down the instinct to scold her. Sleep was important, but Zara was clearly hurt that her friends hadn't answered her call even when she'd phoned them at an appropriate time. Maryan had explained the eleven-hour time difference from Istanbul to Los Angeles, and Zara had been listening well. Still, despite her effort, she was disappointed by her friends.

"Why didn't they answer, Maryan?"

She chose to ignore that Zara had stayed up past her bedtime. There was a time and place to chastise her behavior later. Now wasn't it.

"I don't know, sweetheart." She stroked Zara's cheek and smiled to soften the blow. "Sometimes people can disappoint us."

Zara sniffed and burrowed her face into Maryan's shirt. Her quiet sobs shuddered through her small body. The anvil pressing down onto Maryan's chest crushed her heart as she held Zara through her tearful display.

It wasn't fair that she should be feeling this way.

Worse, it felt so familiar to her. She wasn't much older than Zara when she'd been sent away to live in America. The confusion of assimilating into a new culture, of making new friends and adapting to a whole new life apart from everything and everyone she'd known in Somalia, had been the toughest part.

No, she corrected sharply. Because eventually she *did* adapt. With the help and support of her aunt and uncle, Maryan had survived. What she hadn't recovered from was the painful knowledge that her parents could live without her.

She couldn't quiet the idea that they'd used her.

Like Hassan had used her for a job and then after their breakup didn't have the shred of decency to walk away but robbed her and her family instead.

Now here was Zara feeling lonely and adrift. And she was leaving her, too, so it wasn't like she had a leg to stand on. But she'd meant it about never forgetting her. Trouble was, Maryan wasn't certain her promise made any impact.

Absorbed with comforting Zara, she forgot about Faisal.

It was an upsetting surprise then when he sat up suddenly.

"What's the matter?" He phrased it like a question, but with his steely eyes and gruff tone, it was unmistakably a demand. She couldn't blame him for it, either. What parent wouldn't be annoyed to wake up to find their child distraught in the arms of their nanny?

Zara saved her from a response.

She pulled out of Maryan's arms and turned to her dad, sniffling loudly before clutching him like she had Maryan.

He hugged her tightly. As though his arms were shield enough from her big worries.

"I'll stretch my legs," Maryan said, a yearning flourishing in her. For what, she couldn't name.

At least she couldn't until Faisal gave her the tersest of nods.

Dismissed, she rose to her feet, an epiphany dawning on her. She'd wanted him to stop her. The farther she walked from them, the more she longed for him to call her back, to ask her to stay while he took over assuaging Zara's fears. Fears he might not fully understand or appreciate. She had the unique perspective of being dumped in America by her parents. It wasn't so far off from Zara's situation. Cultural shock, a loss of friends, a sense of displacement—she'd experienced all of that.

Faisal doesn't know that, though.

Because surely if he had he wouldn't have accepted her leaving…

Would he?

Faisal began doubting whether it had been a wise choice to let Maryan leave. It was difficult to ask her to stay when he recalled their conversation from a few days back outside the Grand Bazaar. She'd said she believed he could be there for Zara. She had also challenged him to prove it.

And that's what I'm doing. Proving that I can be more than enough of a parent for Zara.

Letting Zara's nanny walk away had to be done, no matter how panicked he felt in doing this alone.

Gulping, he hoped this went well and cleared his throat. "Zara? Can you look up at me, sweetheart?"

She pulled back but kept her small hands latched onto his shoulders. She sat on his lap, looking smaller now that her bottom lip trembled and her eyes and lashes were darker for her tears.

"Why are you crying?"

He'd woken up to her sobbing in Maryan's arms. It was a startling sight to open one's eyes to. Naturally, he'd immediately asked for answers. But he realized snapping at Maryan wasn't fair. She hadn't made him sleepy. He hadn't thought a nap would make him miss a crucial moment relating to Zara. It had, though, and now he hadn't even had the forethought to ask Maryan to catch him up to speed.

Zara sniffed, her head lowering, eyes downcast.

"I can't help you if you don't tell me." Softening his voice, he then added, "I know it's hard, and I can't promise that I'll be able to fix whatever's bothering you, but I'd like to try."

Zara's chin wobbled, and her sniffling grew louder.

He resisted the impatience rising. Remembering that this was a new experience for her in some ways, he tempered the need to rush her through to an explanation. After all, she was ripped away from her mom and home in LA, and she'd been too young to recall living her early life in Istanbul with him and Salma. He couldn't assume any part of this long-distance change was easy on her.

Eventually his forbearance was rewarded with a response.

"My best friends forgot about me."

Why hadn't he thought of that earlier as being a problem? *She's seven!* Friends were at the top of her list of values at that age. What child wanted to be pulled away from their friends?

In a whisper, she said, "I called them and they didn't call me back."

"Was it late for them when you called?"

Zara snapped her head up for a spirited headshake. "I know the time is different here. Maryan told me."

He suspected her brilliant nanny would. Maryan wouldn't have let Zara assume her friends were ignoring her for a simple fact such as time zones.

"Okay, so why do you think they didn't answer your call?"

Zara knit her brows, her consternation carrying into her voice. "I don't know. They don't like me anymore?"

"Did they like you before you left?"

"Yes. They threw me a party. Maryan helped them surprise me, and Mommy brought me to the party, and everyone jumped out with *confeffi.*"

"Confetti," he softly amended. "And?"

"And we had cupcakes and cookies. Then we played games like capture the flag and freeze tag, and we pinned a sparkly horn on a unicorn!" Zara regaled him for a bit, painting a picture of that afternoon in sunny Los Angeles, one of her last among friends and family.

And Maryan.

Maryan had been by her side then and she still was for now.

He'd thought he was grateful to her before, but that sensation intensified into a hot, bright point that tore open an ache inside him to see her.

Nearly breathless by the end of her story, Zara looked… happier.

That happiness dimmed when she seemed to remember why she was in his lap. Dropping her head, she muttered, "But now they hate me."

"No one hates you," he assured her.

"How do you know?" she shouted. One stern look from him and she sulked again, mumbling, "Sorry, Daddy. Maryan says I shouldn't yell when I'm angry."

"She's right. *But* I also understand you're upset right now."

She bobbed her head and sniffled.

He embraced her for a moment, letting the sadness be what it was. His mother had taught him that life skill. Sometimes a low mood was just that and nothing more. Chemicals in the brain acting funky. A bad day spoiling a week or more. Most times it passed, and he knew with Zara that it would. But he had to help her through it, and the first step was showing her how to be proactive about her problems.

"When was the last time you spoke to your mom?"

"She left me a voice message yesterday. Maryan played it for me before bed."

His heart did a jig at the mention of her nanny. It had been doing that too much lately.

"Why don't we give your mom a video call later? We can ask her about your friends."

Zara's shy smile told him that she was in, but he teased her.

"Is that a 'yes'?" He tickled her sides.

She shrieked into laughter, the peals of joy floating up into the perfectly cloudless sky. He wrapped her in a bear hug and hauled her up into his arms, her legs dangling around his sides. To see her smiling again meant more to him than he'd ever thought because he had put the smile there on her face. It was a sign that he'd done the right thing by bringing her to live with him.

"Why don't we go find Maryan?" he suggested.

Zara nodded, her enthusiasm for her nanny more innocent than the heated excitement rippling over him whenever he thought of Maryan.

Faisal had their picnic packed up in the backpack slung over his shoulders. Zara skipped by his side, more carefree after their little heart-to-heart. She spied her nanny first and tugged at his hand to get him to move faster.

Maryan was watching tourists and Turkish citizens streaming toward the Çamlıca Mosque, her back facing them.

She turned when Zara called her name.

"Hello," she said simply, her gaze flitting from him to Zara, and he guessed as to why when her expressive dark eyebrows furrowed closer. She couldn't mask her worry for his daughter. And given that he'd sent her away when Zara had still been upset, he realized he needed to fill her in on what happened. Though that would have to wait until they were alone.

"Is this all of the masjid, Daddy?" Zara asked, using the Arabic word he'd just taught her for the mosque. She didn't hold a trace of sadness in her innocent expression. Only curiosity gazed up at him. Faisal was relieved to see she was back to her normal self.

"The masjid is one part. There's an art gallery, a library and a museum." And an unencumbered view to the Bosporus that he wanted to show them.

"It's so big! Is it the biggest masjid ever? The biggest in the whole world?"

Zara's barrage of questions lightened his heart as usual. Answering her calmly, he flickered glances at Maryan and found her watching them. Surprised to feel an insistent tug of attraction for her in the moment, he concentrated on Zara and decided to untangle his complicated emotions later.

But it wasn't long before Zara pointed to the nonfigurative sculptures in the mosque's expansive courtyard, where other children played.

"Can I go play over there?" she asked.

Faisal nodded, and she wrapped her arms around his legs for a quick hug before doing the same to Maryan and rushing off.

"Walk, please, Zara," Maryan called after her, shading her eyes from the sun and watching Zara move farther away from them.

It left him and Maryan to stroll the courtyard of the newly built mosque.

Since it wasn't a Friday, the holiest day of the week for Muslims, the grand mosque wasn't packed to its capacity of sixty thousand. Still, there were enough tourists and visitors in the courtyard for Faisal to guide Maryan to a quieter section of the mosque's grounds while they watched Zara play. They stood outside the shade of the grand mosque with its domes, half domes and six minarets. Maryan gasped pleasingly at the sight of the city below the valley. He'd shown her Istanbul from many heights now. From his home, Galata Tower and Çamlıca Hill, and now from the mosque. It was what he had promised her: a tour of Istanbul. Taking her to his favorite places in his beloved city was only one small way he could thank her for everything she'd done for Zara up to that point.

Everything she continued to do.

All that was left was to thank her in person.

"She's feeling better as you might have noticed." Faisal

gazed around Maryan to where Zara had found a group of kids her age to play with. Smiling from a rush of fatherly pride, he reported, "She misses her friends."

"Yes, she does," Maryan agreed. She folded her arms, the gesture more protective than defensive. Casting a look backward at Zara as well, she said, "She's young. It's going to be harder for her to adjust, but she'll make new friends soon enough. She's more resilient than I ever was."

That was an interesting way to put it. He cocked his head, intrigued to know what had caused the melancholy in her voice.

"What do you mean?" he asked.

Maryan snapped her head to him, her pleated brow and frown touched by bafflement. As though she were only piecing it together right then that she'd spoken aloud. And that she wasn't alone when she had.

A shutter rattled in place over her open features. "It's nothing."

"It sounded like *something.*" He hoisted the rucksack full of their picnic essentials higher onto his back. "Does this have to do with your family?" She'd mentioned they lived apart from her. The Somali diaspora had scattered many families, rending them apart. It hadn't occurred to him until that moment that she could be a victim of this dispersion. His heart pulled out its next few beats distressingly sharp.

She stroked her tongue over her bottom lip, watching him with a wary slant to her eyes.

Seeing as he couldn't wipe all her worries away with a flick of his wrist, Faisal tried the next best thing.

"I told you my parents left Somalia three decades ago. They were fleeing the civil war and wanted a better life for me." He was turning thirty-eight next month, and a quick calculation reminded him he'd been Zara's age when he'd fled their homeland. No more than seven or eight when he had lost everything he knew and had it replaced with the place he now called home. "It was hard at first. I didn't speak Turkish and my English wasn't good, yet my parents enrolled me in school immediately. They hadn't wanted me to fall behind on my studies. It took some getting used to, a new life here in Istanbul. That's why I know it'll be challenging for Zara."

For a while Maryan remained silent. Then she was quiet for so long, he resigned himself to getting nothing in return for his vulnerability. Not that he'd expected her to reciprocate.

Still, it would have been nice to hear from her.

Surprisingly, she finally dispelled the silence with a breathy sigh.

"My parents sent me away because they couldn't feed the whole family. My father owned a corner store, and he'd taken on too much loan from the bank. It was causing an immense strain on them. Then my aunt Nafisa called my mother and suggested that I live with her and her husband, my uncle Abdi, in California."

"How old were you?"

"Twelve. Old enough to be asked an opinion on whether I wanted to go or stay."

He heard the sharp bite to her words. She'd been hurt by a decision that clearly hadn't been fully hers to make. A choice that had altered her life immensely. It was making more and more sense to him *why* she was fiercely protective of Zara. She was fighting for the little girl she'd been who had no voice.

"To be fair, I didn't tell them how I felt." She spoke quietly, a decibel above a whisper if it could be called that. Lowering her arms, she huffed a brisk sigh and angled her head to the sky, her chest rising and falling with her even breathing. "At the time I couldn't think but how selfish it was to speak of my own feelings. My younger brothers and sisters needed my help. That was how I saw it. That, and my parents were relying on me to do something they couldn't do themselves. *They* had to stay behind and care for my siblings, and I had to go."

"Still, it's okay to feel hurt, too."

Maryan slowly lowered her head, blinking the sorrow clear from her eyes.

He knew she was done when she steered the conversation back to Zara.

"For someone who was so sure he couldn't do this on his own, you handled that well."

A blush brightened his face, her compliment lighting up places he didn't know could be lit. "I understand why she's upset. I'd be, too, if I were in her position right now."

"It's good for her to know that she can talk to you when she's feeling down."

"I know that. I'm also well accustomed to sadness." Given how he'd been raised, he had to be. He hadn't thought he was going to tell Maryan this, as she'd be gone in another week, but he was opening his mouth and talking faster than his brain was processing. "My mom lives with depression."

Maryan didn't say anything, and it was different from what he was used to. Usually, the few people he'd told in the past tripped and tumbled over themselves to try to fill the air with condolences, apologizing as though they'd been responsible for his mother's mental health turn. It was the strangest response. But apparently the most natural or obvious one.

It wasn't helpful, though. None of those people had stuck around by his side.

Salma had been one of them. Like most of the women he'd dated, she'd listened, gone through her rote sympathy, and moved on to the glitzier parts of what his wealth could offer her. Such as access to an elite nightlife and a leg up in networking to expand her career. They'd gone after him for his money. His chest pulsed around the spectral dagger stabbing his heart and hammering the hilt to drive the pain home. He struggled to speak around the emotional suffering.

"My mom's one of the strongest people I know. My father comes in a close second."

"She sounds inspirational. They both do."

Faisal smiled, his pride for his parents rivaling that for Zara. He could talk about them for ages. But he spared Maryan the boringness of it. "She's the reason I'm successful today. When I couldn't kick this idea of starting my own business and, seeing as my parents knew a thing or two about being entrepreneurs, I'd gone to them for advice. It was my mother who suggested I go for it. She never liked it when my sister and I held ourselves back from achieving whatever we set our minds to, not especially when her depression was stronger. She talked my father into early retirement. They sold the bakery and invested half of its sale in my company. All without my knowledge or input. They knew I'd stop them because I wasn't convinced that I would be fortunate in my endeavor."

"They believed in you and your vision."

He liked that Maryan got that. And it reminded him of what she'd said the day she arrived in Istanbul, about how she trusted in his ability to raise Zara alone. She had repeated herself at the bazaar a few days ago. His family knew him. They loved him. Their support meant the world, and he didn't take it for granted, but he expected it.

Because that was what family was. A steadfast support unit.

Unlike his family, Maryan didn't owe him her encouragement.

She'd given it freely.

Faisal pulled a hard swallow. "I never did get to thank you."

"For?" She raised her brows, looking appropriately perplexed.

"I'd given you reason not to trust Zara's care to me." He'd arrived late to the airport, and late to the bazaar. He had confessed about his fear of being a single dad when he'd been a bachelor for too long. He'd been the kind of bachelor who'd lived and seen many parties in his lifetime and all the sin that came with it. Showing her what the media thought of him as a so-called playboy had taken courage because…

I care what she thinks of me.

Despite falsely convincing himself he didn't at first.

Faisal couldn't say what it was he felt around Maryan, but it was harder to remember why bottling his emotions was the best recourse for so very long.

Feeling his throat closing from a sudden spike in anxiety, he babbled out the rest of what he wanted to tell her. "It might not seem like much, but to me, it was kindness. A kindness I didn't feel I deserved at the time because I couldn't see where the trust in me was coming from. Now that I do, it means even more."

Maryan's lips parted slightly, presumably to reply.

He tensed his muscles in anticipation.

Whatever her response might have been was swallowed up by the call to prayer, the undiluted sound of the muezzin's voice reverberating through the courtyard. The crowds thronging around the mosque split into two groups, those who weren't religiously observing and remained unruffled by the call, and those who hadn't entered the mosque earlier but were now moving toward it to observe prayer indoors. They fell into the latter group.

He'd be separated from Maryan now.

"I'll need my hijab, and Zara's, too."

He held still while she stepped behind him, opened the backpack, and rummaged through for the shawls they'd need to enter the mosque. She looked the same with a hijab on. Just as beautiful in the pearl-and-lace headscarf as she was without it.

"Is it on crooked?" Maryan's hands rose automatically to her head to right an imagined wrong.

And he was to blame because he'd been gawking at her rudely.

Embarrassed, he shook his head quickly. Too quickly. "No!" On his second attempt, he managed a more subtle, albeit hoarse, "No, you look…perfect."

It was her turn to color from shocked to abashed. She looked as flustered as he felt.

Zara raced over to them, her cheeks glowing from her run, her eyes wide with wonder. "Daddy, Maryan, can we go inside the big masjid now?"

Maryan helped Zara wrap her hijab, then pulled the small girl into a side hug and smiled quickly at him before turning them toward the mosque for their tour. As they walked before him, he noticed they appeared like a family.

One big happy family.

Stricken by how perfectly normal that thought felt to him, he rid it from his mind and forced it from his thundering heart. Because as much as he liked Maryan, and as wholly unlike the women he'd been romantically engaged with as she was, she couldn't mean anything more to him.

For that he would have to risk his heart.

And he'd decided love wasn't worth its weight in joy *and* pain.

CHAPTER SIX

Two days later, Faisal arrived home late, exhausted from working overtime but his spirits soaring at the thought that he'd be seeing Maryan and Zara soon. He hadn't liked breaking their plans today to tour more of Istanbul, but he'd had no choice in the matter. His board had called for an emergency meeting. They'd had questions about his leadership and direction in steering investors. Springing it on him hadn't made it any easier. Though in the end he'd been able to talk them into his confidence again, the onus fell on him to handle his board's fragile trust delicately. They wouldn't give him a second chance to secure this oil and natural gas partnership.

Groaning softly, he keyed in the pass code to his security gate when his driver pulled up. Faisal thanked his driver from the back seat as the car slowed and parked in his drive. Instead of heading up above his garage to his apartment for a much-needed workout, shower and change of clothes, he walked toward the main house.

Funny how nothing had changed at work. He was still flogging this same horse.

And yet everything has changed at home.

He no longer arrived at his house and anticipated spending the short hours of night into dawn trapped in his office, where he'd squeeze in more work. Nor was he answering any of the invites from his usual social circle to meet up at their typical haunts. He'd pushed all that aside these days, knowing full well that he would be winding down the evening with Maryan and Zara. They'd taken over his life in a way that had him smiling more and more. Even now he felt his lips spreading synchronously to the warmth pouring out from the center of his chest. If he'd gulped a big cup of black coffee, he would feel the same lively jolt.

The jolt peaked when he opened the front door. Voices rang out from deeper inside the house. It sounded like Maryan and Zara weren't alone.

"Maryan? Zara?"

He followed the voices to the kitchen.

Maryan and Zara were there, along with his diligent housekeeper, Lalam.

Zara noticed him first, her loud, cheery, "Daddy!" grabbing the attention of Maryan and Lalam.

He approached them slowly, curious as to why their faces and clothes were covered in flour. Zara appeared the messiest, her small cheeks caked white from the flour, and even the ends of her braids were chalky white from the stuff.

"What are you baking?" he asked, his intrigue intensified.

"Maryan's teaching Lalam how to make Somali candy, and I'm helping."

"Somali candy?" He looked to Maryan for clarification.

"Kac kac," she said, wiping her hands with a tea towel. A towel she soaked the end of before swiping it over Zara's cheeks. She cleaned her up as best as she could, but the damage required Zara to shower. She'd need to wash the flour from her hair.

"We're not done yet, Daddy. You have to wait to eat it," Zara was telling him.

"I'd like that." He hadn't had *kac kac* in a long while.

Less of a candy and more doughnut, the soft, subtly sweet Somali fritters had been a staple in his house, especially during Ramadan.

"You look tired," Maryan remarked, her hands kneading into her portion of the dough. Beside her Lalam rolled out a second portion. Zara clung to the edge of the counter and stood on tiptoes to watch them work. It was a wonder how she managed to get the most flour on her when she wasn't doing much.

Scooping Zara up and helping her to a seat on the counter, Faisal said, "That's putting it mildly. I've certainly had better days. But it's nice to see friendly faces." He tickled his daughter then, and she broke into a fit of breathless giggles.

Maryan was frowning at him when he glanced in her direction. "You've got flour on you now, too."

"I guess I do." He regarded his shirt front and navy blue herringbone suit jacket. Flour dusted parts of his sleeves. It hadn't occurred to him that it'd be a problem. It wasn't like he didn't have a walk-in closet full of similar-looking costly suits. Zara's laughter and happiness were worth so much more. "I think we'll all need to clean up after this."

"Actually, I'm almost done here. I'll take Zara up for a bath."

Lalam stopped Maryan. "I will help Zara." The housekeeper slipped off her apron and lifted Zara off the counter. They left the kitchen hand in hand, Zara still wearing her apron and her flour-caked braids bouncing up and down as she skipped beside Lalam. Their carefree chattering floated farther away until silence filled the kitchen.

"Isn't it Lalam's day off?" he asked, shrugging off his suit jacket and rolling up his sleeves.

"It is, but she came in to bake with us."

"I see. Who taught you to make *kac kac*?" He washed

his hands at the sink and dried them before taking up the dough that Lalam had been rolling. Feeling Maryan's questioning gaze, he laughed softly and said, "Don't worry. I know what I'm doing. I won't make the dough too thin." He rolled precisely, pressing on the rolling pin lightly and evening the dough to a quarter-inch thickness. Just about the right size for it to puff nicely in the frying oil.

"I could ask you that question."

He laughed again. "My parents owned a bakery, remember?"

She flashed him a small smile. "My *hooyo* taught me."

Faisal wasn't surprised to hear her mother had passed on the essential skill. In Somalia, women handled much of the cookery. It was thought to prepare a young girl for when she was old enough to be married and manage her own household. His parents had raised him in Turkey, though, and they'd expected him to know his way around the kitchen as much as his sister, Yasmin, did.

Not that this was about him or his opposition to patriarchal society's inherent sexism.

Anything he learned about Maryan was good information in his books.

"Your mom must have been a great teacher."

"She was." Maryan pressed her dough between her hands and the counter, flattening it into a round shape before accepting the rolling pin he passed to her and rolling it as he'd done. She worked faster than him and achieved the same result. Clearly, she'd practiced more than he had.

She swiped flour onto her cheek, the curly black strand of hair she'd been trying to unstick from her face persistently remaining fixed to her. She had her hair in a messy bun, yet she still was attractive to him. Her beauty was unblemished by the flour spotting her cheek and the sheen of perspiration making her forehead glow. He wished he felt differently about her. His life was complicated as it was without throwing in the odd thoughts he'd had lately of family, love and romance.

None of it worked for him before. He'd tried family with Salma when she'd sprung her pregnancy on him, and then he'd depleted his endurance for dating seriously—with all intent to marry someday—on his heartless past partners. Without his money, he'd have meant nothing to them. It was tiring to pretend like the vultures hadn't chased him out of the dating scene. He'd gone from being hopeful to a cynic in a short time after hitting his first million. And for years he had been happy to date for pleasure instead. One night or a few months, it didn't matter because it never lasted long-term. Salma had given him pause only because their short-term pleasure had resulted in the miracle of new life.

When she arrived in the world, Zara held his heart alone. His adorable little girl.

Considering his rocky history with romance, it sat oddly with him whenever his eyes strayed to Maryan. It was a hard feeling to fight, too. She captivated him. He had this strange compelling urge to watch her work the dough evenly on the counter.

She wore a pale green petal-sleeved tee and black jeans that molded to her thick thighs and shapely legs.

He tracked his eyes up to find her looking back, her lips tilting downward.

Groping for words, he ended up bumbling, "You're good at being a nanny, good at baking, what else can you do?"

"Yoga."

"Yoga?" he parroted, images of her in fitted workout gear flitting through his mind and warming his body. He wished she hadn't answered. He *wished* he hadn't asked. Harmless as it sounded, it was wreaking havoc with his senses. A familiar yearning heated his groin. Disgust curled above his lust, rising like froth to the top of his simmering emotions. He'd been raised better. Objectifying her felt… perverted. Disrespectful. Wrong.

It was worse because he knew nothing more could come of it were they to fall into bed together.

And Maryan came across as faithful. The type who'd want chocolate hearts and commitment, and flowers and wedding vows. Family.

The things he couldn't give her.

He didn't want to give *anyone*. At least that was what he'd believed until she came into his world.

"I relax with yoga. What do you do to unwind?"

Her question pinged off him. "What?"

She paused in rolling the dough. "I asked what your hobbies are. Work doesn't count."

This he could answer. Chuckling, he replied, "I read when I can."

"I've seen your library. Zara loves the fairy-tale collection you chose for her."

"They were the ones my parents used to read to me and my sister when they weren't telling us the old Somali folktales."

"The fox and the hyena?" She grinned knowingly.

He laughed. "I think it's a rite of passage."

"They were violent, though. Humorous, but more Grimm than Disney."

"Good point. It won't hurt Zara to grow a little older to hear them."

"What else?" she encouraged, brushing flour from her hands and reaching for a paring knife. She sliced the dough into quarters. Each piece was then transferred to a clean, dry plate.

"Well, you've met my Turkish drama addiction."

They'd been going through his collection of Turkish

films every night. Action-packed thrillers, to mysteries, and even the occasional romance. Zara never lasted for very long, her bedtime early. It left him and Maryan to watch more of the films together. He'd grown to cherish the time more than he felt he ought to. Attachment was a dangerous thing.

"Do you watch Salma's films?" Maryan asked.

He'd told her about Salma beginning her acting career in small Turkish roles. She picked up the language quickly when she'd been living with him.

"Only small clips, but I'm saving them for Zara."

"She loves watching her mom on TV," she approved.

"I bet she does." He checked the fryer, seeing that she'd had the oil changed and readied for the fritters. That time allowed him to sort and organize his thinking. "One thing that we'd agreed on is to keep Zara in both of our lives. I'd never hold her back from her mother."

"It's a solid rule for co-parenting." Maryan rolled and sliced her second piece of dough. She had one left, and she was making quick work in completing it.

He found tongs for her to use. Fetched a cooling rack and cookie pan to drain the fritters once they were done. He did all that he could do until he ran out of errands to run around the kitchen. She noticed, too, her eyes having followed him while he'd moved around his kitchen and helped her in his own way.

"She thinks pretty highly of you, too."

"Does she?" A sense of unease shivered through him. He didn't want to stand there and talk about Salma, not when he kept stealing glances at Maryan's lips and wondering what they might feel like against his. The air in the kitchen was growing to be stiflingly hot—

"Why aren't you together?"

A coldness showered over him, her query the trigger

to the ice flooding his veins and the frost seeping into his heart.

It wasn't her fault. She didn't understand how loaded the question was, how complicated the response to it would be if he allowed it. He stuck to the simplest answer. "We aren't together because we don't want to be. And we didn't want to pretend to be, either."

"*Do* you ever plan to marry someday? Give Zara a step-mother? Maybe brothers and sisters?" She plated the last of the dough and switched on the fryer. Working and talking and avoiding his eyes all at the same time. "Billionaires are a catch, aren't they?"

"Funny thing about money. It attracts all sorts of people." And it was difficult to distinguish between who was with him for his wealth and who wanted him.

None of which he said aloud to her, fearing he'd come across pathetic. Like she'd have any sympathy for him.

The poor billionaire can't reel in a serious relationship. Boo-hoo, he thought derisively.

Tired of the spotlight being on him, Faisal shifted gears and focus.

"And you? Has your ex jaded you beyond the point of no return?"

Maryan should have known. She couldn't even fault him for asking, not after she'd pried into his love life. It didn't stop her from stalling with her response. Luckily the fryer was ready. She popped in a few pieces of dough, the crackle and scent of fried oil diffusing in the kitchen. It took all of thirty seconds. Seconds she relished before she faced the one-man firing squad.

Faisal's good looks dulled some of the pain murmuring through her heavy chest.

She breathed in deep, expelling as much of the negativity as she could. What she couldn't shake off she carried into her story.

"I wouldn't call it 'no return.' Just a long, *long* vacation from the warfare of dating."

He snorted. "That bad?"

Hassan's betrayal had cut deeply. But he hadn't been her first boyfriend. She'd dated duds like him through high school and college. Enough men to know she had a type. A rough-around-the-edges but charming type. Hassan had been that. His confidence and winsome personality had lured her in. He seemed a perfect fit at her aunt and uncle's restaurant. Working his way up from busing to the kitchen. When their old sous-chef retired, Maryan talked her aunt and uncle into taking a chance on Hassan.

She'd liked him.

But it had taken a while—nearly most of their three years of dating—for her to realize she didn't *love* him.

Breaking up felt appropriate. Even the kind thing to do. She'd thought Hassan understood why she had to do it. She never would have guessed he was angry enough at her to steal from the restaurant and flee before he was caught.

The two-faced idiot.

Maryan turned the fritters over in the crackling oil, tucking her anger away where it couldn't leave her unguarded in front of Faisal. For some reason still unknown to her, she didn't want him to see her weakened. She liked that he thought her strong, a fierce lioness, and someone who'd protect his daughter to the ends of the earth. It was the exact opposite of how she saw herself when she looked in the mirror. After all, to be strong meant to be willing to fight for one's values…and she hadn't done that. With her parents, she'd allowed them to do as they wished, and it resulted in her being shipped off to grow up without her family. Then Hassan used and abused her trust, robbing her and her family blind, and leaving her feeling like his accomplice. She'd brought him into the confidence of her aunt and uncle. They had relied on him, and only because they placed their faith on her word.

If Maryan hadn't vouched for him, her aunt and uncle wouldn't have taken the hit to their finances. Once she was done in Istanbul, she owed it to them to return and help them earn what they'd lost and assuage her persisting guilt.

She brooded and nearly missed the pastries turning the right shade of golden brown.

"Here." Faisal held a spider skimmer under her nose.

She'd completely forgotten she would need the long-handled spoon to fish the fritters out.

Their hands touched when he passed her the handle. She froze at the same time he did. They stared at each other, and then she took hold of the kitchen tool and scooped the fritters out into the safety of the colander at the end of the handle.

As she added the second batch of *kac kac*, Maryan sensed Faisal's eyes on her.

He reached over to the freshly baked fritters. "A *kac kac* for your thoughts?"

"Careful, they're hot," she warned, her sternness melting when he grabbed a fritter, bit into it and groaned his pleasure, his eyes fluttering shut. She didn't think eating could conjure such a sexual picture. And yet Faisal had her imagining a dimly lit bedroom, slippery silk sheets and heated limbs intertwining in passion.

Maryan blushed furiously when he opened his eyes and stared at her with an altogether different hunger.

The emotion flashed briefly in his half-lidded gaze before blinking out of existence.

"Damn. I think this might be the best *kac kac* I've had."

"You think?" she taunted, watching him demolish the

fried delicacy. Surprised she could flirt when he left her feeling breathless physically and emotionally.

He smirked and licked his fingers slowly until they were crumb-free. "It's definitely the best I've had."

A pleasurable shudder rippled through her at his double entendre. Flushed all over, it felt like, she cleared her throat and muttered, "Thank you."

She popped the latest batch of fritters out and placed the last set into the cooling oil. Cranking up the heat slightly, she glanced up to his intense stare.

"I'm sorry to have asked about your ex."

Maryan shrugged. "It's only fair. I asked you about Salma." She'd done more than ask; she'd poked and prodded him for information, convincing herself it was to help Zara when she wanted the details for herself just as much.

"Still, I didn't mean to make you sad."

He'd noticed the change in her mood then. What he didn't have was the full story to work with, otherwise he would know that nothing he'd asked had deliberately instigated her turn in mood.

Before she thought too much on it, she said, "He stole from us."

Faisal's jaw hardened visibly, his face transforming into steel.

"It wasn't that much." A few thousand out of pocket. The restaurant was doing well enough for the stolen money not to cause a massive problem. It was just the principle. The fact that they'd been betrayed by Hassan. Taken for fools.

I'd been the fool.

And now she felt foolish when she heard it said aloud. "He didn't like it when I broke up with him. I'd thought that it was mutual…"

She'd been wrong.

"How is that your fault?"

"I should have figured he was upset."

Faisal pulled in a loud breath, his hand quicker to the spider strainer on the counter. He flipped the fritters, saving them from being scorched on one side. Frown in place, he looked at her. "You're shouldering blame senselessly."

She sputtered, bouncing between whether she should be annoyed he'd butt in with his opinion, or relieved that he could see how ludicrously tough she was being on herself.

In the end it was near impossible to remain irritated when he plucked a fritter from the plate and waved it in front of her face.

"Indulge yourself," he urged. "I can't think of anyone who's more deserving of a treat right now."

She accepted the soft fried dough, gaining immediate comfort from biting into it.

He snagged another one, too.

"Feeling better?" he asked her when they finished eating in silence.

"A little." She was feeling silly that he even had to ask. Sighing, she said, "It's a trust issue. I trusted my parents, and it brought me to America. I trusted my ex, and he stole from my family."

Maryan let that truth settle over her. She'd thought it plenty of times before. Registering Faisal's empathetic smile wedged open room for growth beyond that circular thinking. Like she'd found in him a kindred spirit.

"Trust is fickle," he agreed gruffly.

"Mine is close to nonexistent."

Rather than ridiculing her for being dramatic, he dipped his head. "On that, we can agree."

"Are we talking from experience?" She quirked an eyebrow, checking on the slowly frying fritters.

"Yeah."

His monosyllabic response should have persuaded her

away from the subject, but she recalled how he'd lifted her up when she had been hard on herself. And when he turned his back on the plate of deep-fried pastries, she had to speak up.

"Bad breakup, too?"

"A string of them, actually."

Her mouth flopped open. She should have known. Faisal was hot. His model-worthy good looks had to be reeling in all sorts of interest. Mostly her surprise was because he'd had more bad luck it seemed than she did. *Not* that she likely dated as much as he had, or that any of her dates were internationally renowned like his former partners were. Really, there was very little comparison to go on between the two of them. Worlds apart as they were.

"I mentioned money being a problem."

He had.

"It's a real thing. There are loads of deceptive people who would date me for my net worth. Loads who have."

"Sorry."

"Then there's the paranoia." His brows scrunched, deep brackets framing his scowling mouth, his eyes looking ahead but his features revealing the pain his dating experience had taught him. "The overthinking is the worst part of it. It's ruined a date or two...or three. I keep asking myself if I'm who they want, or if I'm a package deal. And if they'll take the money someday and run."

"Have you tried dating online? It'd be easier to hide your identity. At least until you could get to know someone."

He shook his head and didn't look like her suggestion made him any happier. "It won't change that there will always be a part of me that questions, wonders, *doubts*. And I can't enter anything serious and long-term with that hanging over me. It wouldn't be fair. I wouldn't be true to myself."

She pulled the fritters out one by one, flicked off the fryer and closed its lid.

"Guess we're both jaded in similar ways."

"Trust," he echoed her unspoken thought, his laugh raspy and joyless. "Where does that leave us?"

"Clinging to hope?" she offered.

Faisal tipped his head to the side, his eyes boring into her, face closed to any emotion. "How old are you?"

"Why?"

"You look young enough for hope." He raked a hand through his silky-looking black curls, the longer ones on top clinging to his fingers and distracting her more than they should. His huff of indignation grounded her. "But I'm thirty-eight next month. Old enough to be worrying my mother that I'll never properly settle down and give her another grandchild."

"I'll be twenty-seven this September."

"I'd have guessed your mid-twenties. I was right, then. Young enough for things like hope."

She oscillated from flattered to puzzled, to finally landing on insatiably intrigued.

"Where are you going with this?"

"Don't you want to get married? Have kids?" He answered her question with a question, but it was a *good* one. Annoyingly so.

"Possibly. Someday. Though not anytime soon."

"Because you have plans after you head home. For your aunt and uncle's restaurant."

She nodded. "That, and I'll likely take a second job."

"Where?"

"Before Salma hired me, I used to teach cooking classes at my neighborhood's community center." Maryan smiled at the fond memories of working alongside her students of all ages. Young and old, novice and aficionado, and from a variety of backgrounds. Everyone had shared one thing in common: a passion for making tasty meals. Reminiscing had her thinking of her aunt and uncle and her obligations back home.

"They've been talking about renovating the restaurant's dining room for a while now. But that means they'll have to close shop temporarily." And they were already a little tight with money after her ex's stupid stunt. That was where the job at the community center would come in handy. Maryan's boss had liked her, and she'd left on good footing. She made a mental note to reach out for job prospects soon as she returned to California.

Which was sooner than she liked...

But it's not like any of this with Faisal and Zara was permanent.

"That explains a lot." Faisal lifted the plate of fritters, holding it between them when he angled his body to face her fully. "These are phenomenally good. Have you ever considered opening your own business?"

"A bakery, you mean?"

"Sure," he said, all lopsided smile and irresistible charm. "I could be your first investor. You could pay me in baked goods."

She swatted his hand before he reached another fried pastry. "Save some for Zara."

"No fair. You two cleared out my baklava stash."

Noting her confusion, he traded the plate of pastry to open a top cabinet and pull down a nearly empty container.

Maryan recognized it and realized where he was going with this. "My stash. You've demolished it."

"We didn't 'demolish' anything. We've had a few," she lied.

Faisal shook the nearly empty container at her.

"Okay, we ate a little more than that, but there wasn't much left in there."

Chuckling, he said, "Try harder to convince me."

"First the tea stash, now baklava. This secret snacking is concerning, Faisal."

"Don't turn this around on me." He laughed. "I'll negotiate for another one or two *kac kac* to stock more baklava."

She pretended to think about it before nodding. "You have yourself a deal."

He offered her a hand.

Maryan hesitated a second, and then she grasped his hand, his long, strong fingers holding hers in an even-pressured grip.

Their hands remained clasped longer than necessary.

Longer than she'd have normally liked.

But Faisal had made her feel like she wasn't alone. Like her troubles were his in a way, and she'd come out of this baking and talking feeling lighter, calmer.

Happier.

"Maryan." He spoke her name in a breathy whisper; a reverence pulsed from those two syllables. So much so that it sounded less like her name and more like a prayer. She shivered visibly, unable to help the reaction. Her body temperature rose when he closed the short gap between them and his hand brushed up her arm before moving to cup her too-warm cheek. It was a simple touch that set off a firework of desire in her.

"Thank you for listening. For asking. For pushing to know."

He spoke her mind. Those were the exact words she wished to utter to him. And she would have, had she had a voice to do it with.

His next breath was drawn out, the heat of it brushing her cheek when he planted a quick kiss there.

She stood frightfully still, the pressure of his soft mouth, the emotion behind the gesture, forcing open an ocean's worth of yearning for him. When he slowly drew his head up, almost reluctantly, Maryan made her choice.

Or maybe he'd made it first, and she went along for the ride.

Because when his eyes regarded her, and his face pushed in closer again, their noses brushing, she pulled up onto her toes and connected their lips in an intimate play of his chaste kiss on her cheek. A hunger accentuated their lip-lock. It colored the moan rumbling through his chest and the heated press of their bodies as he backed her into the opposite counter.

Resurfacing for air was expected but unwanted.

Maryan would've gladly allowed Faisal to steal another kiss and rob her of breath again. A clanging alertness took hold of her when he growled, "Maryan," and splayed his heavy, warm hands on her hips.

This time she knew who made the decision for them.

She pushed him away first. Gently, pleadingly. She didn't have the strength to do it twice.

"We *can't*." And they really couldn't. They had to think of Zara. What would she wonder if she caught them kissing?

And I'm leaving in a week.

A week wasn't a good enough reason to jump into bed with the first good-looking billionaire who swept her off her feet. Chemistry or no chemistry, sleeping with Faisal would be a stupid and dangerous move. Stupid because there was no chance it would become a meaningful relationship, and dangerous for the very same reason.

She backed away, her shaking hands giving up on untying her apron.

Abandoning the kitchen, she hightailed it to her room and didn't look back until she closed her door.

She counted the seconds that lapsed from the time she left him.

When no knock came from the other side and no footsteps down the hall, she pressed a hand to her thumping heart and analyzed what happened downstairs with Faisal.

He'd kissed her.

Correction: *they* had kissed.

She'd been an active participant in it. That, and she couldn't kid herself that she hadn't thought of kissing him before then.

As Maryan stood there, her body more alive in that second than it ever was, two things were clearer now about her and Faisal. Their hearts were both closed off to love, and their attraction was a potent force of nature that went against everything she thought she could feel with another human being before.

CHAPTER SEVEN

"TONIGHT'S PERFECT. I'LL see you both then."

Faisal pulled his Bluetooth from his ear and dropped it on top of the blueprint of an oil rig overtaking his office desk. Rukiya had been sitting across from him; her eyes, glued to her tablet, sprang up to him as soon as he ended his phone call. She looked as he'd felt before he had taken the call: nervous.

Thankfully he had good news for her.

"They're willing to discuss our original terms for the partnership over dinner."

All wasn't lost after all. The Turkish brothers he'd hoped to partner with were reconsidering their hasty decision not to sign their deal. Faisal's grin edged on manic as he realized what that meant; his board wouldn't have anything to hold over his head, and his company's hard work and effort wouldn't go to waste. Moreover, the people of Somalia stood a chance at being uplifted by this project. Assuming his dinner went smoothly, and everyone walked away happy.

"Shall I look into restaurants?"

"No, they've already made their reservations." Which was more than fine by him. He had enough on his plate to think about. Zara...

Maryan and our kiss.

He'd thought of Zara's nanny plenty since yesterday. Now, nearly twenty-four hours later, Faisal still didn't feel any better about how their explosive brush of intimacy ended. She had run away from him.

It's not a good sign, he thought glumly.

And for once he didn't know what to do around a woman.

It wasn't like he had to fight for the attention and affection. Women liked him. He liked them, too, well enough to hook up when he needed an itch scratched. He hadn't had any of them push him away after a kiss.

Or flee from him.

Once again, for what had to be the millionth time, he tripped over that fact and fell flat on his face. All the thinking he'd done left him with no answer to solve the riddle that Maryan had become to him overnight. She was a beautiful enigma. One he wanted to kiss again over and over until they were both breathless.

What wasn't a mystery was their chemistry.

He'd been right about his instinct. They were mutually attracted to each other. It was enough for him to hope by the time they spoke again yesterday's worst parts would have been forgotten. And they'd be speaking sooner as his evening plans were now changed. But first he'd clear his office and end another long day of work.

"Feel free to leave for home, Rukiya. Thank you for staying longer again."

His executive assistant nodded her acknowledgment. "If that's all then," she said, standing. "Have a good night, Mr. Umar, and enjoy your dinner."

Before Rukiya reached the exit of his office, a knock at his door had Faisal calling out, "Come in."

Burak opened the door and remained on the threshold as he explained his presence.

"One of the secretaries has a message for you."

Rukiya managed his messages at her desk primarily. She'd been with him most of the day, researching alternative partners for their foray into the oil and gas industry. Naturally, she appeared clueless when Burak forwarded this news.

"I can look into it," his efficient EA commented.

"That's fine. Have the secretary call my office." When Burak lingered, Faisal asked, "Was there another message you had to deliver?"

Burak flickered his eyes to Rukiya, his expression brightening. "I was on my way out. Shift change in the security office. Would you like a ride home?"

Faisal couldn't see Rukiya's face, but she sounded bashful when she assented, "I'd like that, thank you."

They left together, his office feeling emptier without them.

Good on them.

He wished them a peaceful night. They'd done enough for him as it was. Everyone in his company, from his top executives to his middle management and line employees, had striven equally hard for each of their investments. His dream project in Somalia transformed from a personal goal into a community one, shared by his colleagues, employees and investors alike. Any win now would be a win for all of them.

His office landline rang. He answered, knowing it'd be the secretary with his message.

"Mr. Umar, your daughter called."

"My daughter?" Recovering from the surprise, he hurried the secretary off the line politely. Fitting his Bluetooth back in his ear, he pulled his phone from where his suit coat hung on the back of his chair and dialed Maryan.

She answered after only a ring. For that alone he could

kiss her. He didn't think he could stand another second of suspense.

"I just heard word that Zara called me."

"Typically, people start with a 'hello' first." Maryan's dry humor warmed his unease. She wouldn't sound so relaxed were Zara in any real danger or harm. He should have known that she would care for his daughter. Maryan might have confused him with her reaction after their steamy kiss, but he was confident in trusting her with Zara's well-being.

"Sorry. I had a long day."

"Will you not be coming home?"

Home. She'd called his place home. It wasn't his imagining. Wiping the burgeoning smile from his face, he said, "I've been invited to dinner to salvage the hope of my company's partnership deal. It's tonight, though."

"That's great news. Sudden, but good."

"It is," he agreed, grinning from ear to ear. He could feel it overtaking his face the second her praise came through the line. "I was calling to let you know I'm on my way now. I know it's late, but is Zara awake?"

"No, sadly. She was calling to ask you to come home to read to her. She prefers your ogre voices over mine."

Their bedtime routine had quickly grown to become his favorite part of the day.

"You can still creep in and kiss her. She's a deep sleeper."

"Good suggestion," he said, his heart galloping now as he stood and cleared his desk. He had one other thing on his mind, and there wasn't a better opportunity than to do it now, when her end of the line grew quiet. "Maryan?"

She hummed. "Yeah?"

"About dinner… Would you want to be my plus-one?"

Faisal's explanation for inviting her was sound.

He didn't want to go alone when everyone else in the

dinner party would be coupled up. Saving him from being a fifth wheel, Maryan agreed to the short-notice dinner. It was the kindest thing to do for him.

It wasn't like the sparking, fizzing delight at having been asked was her *only* motivator.

She just had to remember not to be lulled into a delusion. This was a one-off. They weren't dating for real. And it would be easier not to be tempted if the scent of Faisal's cologne weren't so dreamy. Thinking straight was proving improbable when the peppery spice of his aftershave wafted under her nose teasingly throughout the evening. Mostly when he leaned in to check in on her. Fighting against the instinct to draw closer to him, inhale his essence and commit it to memory for when she left Istanbul, Maryan focused on the faces around the table.

Faisal's hosts…and hers as well.

It wasn't long, though, before she was drawn back to him. A moth to a flame. A fly snared in a web. Only instead of the fear of a fly or a moth, every time she looked at him, an undercurrent of immeasurable pleasure overtook her. And in the pleasure, there was an assurance in knowing he hadn't asked anyone else to be his date.

He kissed me yesterday.

Naturally she'd thought of their kiss first when he asked her. She had to be realistic, though. For Faisal, finding women and getting them to spend an evening with him surely wasn't a trying task. He could probably do it with his eyes closed.

If his handsome face didn't lure them, then his money. He'd said so himself: he had trouble trusting his romantic partners and questioning their motives for dating him.

Still, even with his reservations, he'd chosen to be with her tonight. Maryan had little doubt he could've found another woman to fill her wedge heels. Had she declined his invitation, he'd likely have gone that route. Replaced her easily.

Her heart felt like it skipped a beat when he glanced at her, his conversation with the two men sitting across the table flowing freely up until that moment. She guessed that he'd seen something on her face.

He stopped talking and turned into her, leaning closer to whisper in Somali, "Are you doing all right?"

The Somali rang to her as more intimate. Mostly as no one else at the table understood them. And there was the bonus of being able to talk freely.

"It's getting late, that's all." The sun had set, but the sky nearer the horizon glowed soft yellows and oranges. It looked more magical from where they were sitting. She hadn't thought a rooftop restaurant could feel very romantic. Certainly not when a chilly breeze kept nipping at her bare shoulders whenever her shawl slipped to her elbows. The floral embroidered cocktail dress was a favorite of hers, and the only thing she considered suitable for a semiformal dinner. But now she wished she'd worn something warmer.

A shiver strummed through her.

"Are you cold?" Faisal pulled his jacket off quicker than she could stop him.

He covered her shoulders, his body heat and cologne blanketing her. It was like he was hugging her.

Blushing when his face remained close to her, she ducked her head and muttered, "Thank you." She kept her head down, unprepared to face the rest of the table but sensing their eyes fixed on her and Faisal. Their attention was warranted. Faisal had introduced her as his daughter's nanny. Bringing her as his plus-one made enough of a statement. They had to be wondering what a billionaire was doing with an ordinary salaried worker.

Unperturbed, Faisal faced the table and continued his

conversation as if it were perfectly normal to drape his jacket over her.

She wondered if that was why he hadn't mentioned their kiss.

It would make sense, wouldn't it? He's likely kissed many times.

One kiss with her wasn't an earth-shattering event. Whatever she might think or feel, she had to remember that Faisal was far worldlier than her. Romanticizing a single, inconsequential encounter wouldn't be something he would do.

She barely tasted her dessert after that. The rosewater and lemony flavor of the Turkish delights no longer bloomed as vibrantly on her tongue. It tasted more of its cornstarch dusting than its beautiful flavors and robust chewy texture. She chewed, swallowed, bit and repeated until she drained her pear-shaped glass of traditional Turkish coffee.

The sand-filled pan warming their coffee sat in the middle of the table. It had fascinated her when their waiter joined them and shuffled the sand closer to the sides of the pot with a metal scoop. Faisal had explained that the pan sat over an open flame and gave the waiter complete control over the heat. The coffee would never be too hot or too cool.

Another thing she had to get used to about Turkish coffee: the fine-ground coffee beans were not filtered out of the cup. This method resulted in a thicker, stronger brew.

She gagged on the first sip, admittedly. But by her second cup she felt more like a pro. More like she belonged by Faisal's side, among these beautifully dressed people.

There were four of them. The two Turkish brothers who Faisal mentioned to her. Aydin and Erkin. Erkin was younger and was the other purported playboy seated at their table. Impressively tall, he was also incredibly thin and his face was all bony angles and lines. But his broad smile and booming voice made up for his gaunt, emaciated appearance. His older brother, Aydin, was the traditional-minded brother of the two. Faisal had warned her that Aydin was the one they had to impress. He called the shots when it came to the partnership deal. Shorter than Erkin, Aydin made up for his height difference by perfecting a dour-faced expression that kept her on edge all through dinner. Aydin spent half the evening stroking his long wiry beard thoughtfully, and the other half he spoke in an even tone that masked his true thoughts.

She realized it was a tactic. Acting uninterested when they talked business and carrying that indifference to small talk about the weather, sports games, politics. Faisal mirrored his blasé attitude. It gave her a glimpse into how he'd managed to amass billions in such a short span of time.

There was a seductive power to his no-nonsense voice. An energy that abounded in his every little movement.

She could watch him work all day… He was that magnetizing when he was in his element. He brokered multimillion-dollar deals, negotiated with equally powerful businessmen and looked incredibly sexy when his singular focus and passion collided.

"Maryan?"

Maryan was startled when she heard her name.

She swiped the back of her hand over her mouth for lack of a napkin. Still worrying that she had cornstarch powder dusting her mouth, she faced the woman beside her on the cushioned floor sofa.

Aslihan was one of the two other women at the table. She'd come as Erkin's date. Hatice was Aydin's wife and she sat by her husband. Unlike Hatice, Aslihan was… catty. Maryan had learned why soon after she and Faisal arrived for dinner. Aslihan and Faisal had a past. They'd been neighbors as children before Aslihan and her family had moved to Turkey's capital, Ankara. But Aslihan had to jog Faisal's memory when he hadn't recognized her immediately. She'd been ready to sink her claws into him. Only Maryan's presence had stopped her from it.

Because of that she'd had to deal with Aslihan's passive-aggressive comments most of the night.

Like the one Aslihan uttered right then. "So, how long are you staying in Istanbul, Maryan?"

"I have a week left." One more week with Faisal in his home. Seven days before she had to leave Zara forever and pick up her life in California.

"I suppose you'll miss Faisal's daughter." Aslihan looked past Maryan, presumably to Faisal. She'd been watching him like a hawk stalking its prey all night. The longing in her eyes made it hardest for Maryan, especially as Aslihan was a far better fit for him.

Jealousy dragged its claws over Maryan's insides.

"My job would have ended someday," she said through a gritted-teeth smile. "It's only unfortunate that it's ending sooner." And then because she hated the sting of tears sparking at her eyes, Maryan shoved a bigger piece of Turkish delight in her mouth to keep from answering any more questions.

Aslihan took the hint and struck up a chat with Hatice.

Eventually the evening wound down, and Aydin and Hatice stood for their departure.

Faisal held a hand down to Maryan. "We'll walk them out," he said with a coaxing smile.

She slipped her hand in his, not caring that he assumed she wanted to go with him. The excitement at touching him again coiling electric pleasure through her heated blood.

Aydin's brother Erkin waved them off. He had asked for a hookah to be brought to the table. He smoked from the single-stem pipe, the fumes of the shisha rising over their heads. Aslihan remained seated as well, her envious eyes narrowed and pinned on Maryan and Faisal's hands. It was enough to remind Maryan to pull her hand away. She was blushing as they walked out of the restaurant, tailing Aydin and Hatice.

They took the stairs wrapping the side of the building, the long flight of stone treads coming to an end at the bottom of a narrow residential street.

Under the orange glow of streetlamps, Aydin and Faisal faced off.

The niceties traded at dinner were well behind them by the determination hardening their expressions.

Aydin spoke first. "I'm speaking for my brother as well when I say that we've had our reservations about partnering with your company. I won't lie. I still have my doubts."

No disappointment registered from Faisal.

Suave as ever, he replied, "I thought dinner was going nicely."

"It was very pleasant." Aydin's eyes cast over to Maryan before focusing on Faisal again. "Friendly company makes all the difference."

His wife murmured her assent.

"However, the dinner hasn't settled my...indecision."

"You don't want your company's image besmirched by the indiscreet photos taken of me." Blunt as the end of a hammer, Faisal dealt his blow. Maryan thought it a very brave move. Charge at the problem rather than cower before it. She couldn't say if Aydin would see it the same way, though.

"I'll remind you that your brother was in some of those glossy pictures."

Aydin's eye twitched, his hand palming his beard quickly. "I've spoken to Erkin. He understands my sentiments. We both have businesses to run, and bad press can be very damaging."

"Let's bury the bad press then."

"With a partnership," Aydin hedged.

"Nothing like the good press to offset an unseemly story." Faisal folded his arms after his clever suggestion, his feet spaced evenly apart and his whole stance projecting his steadfastness to this plan for Somalia's dormant gas and oil sector. Best of all, he looked good in his black long-sleeved polo shirt, slim dark-wash jeans and leather spiked high-tops.

As much as she would love to admire him all night, fatigue was sparking from her feet in her wedge sandals and creeping up to weaken her.

The back-and-forth parrying was getting to be too much.

Shuffling her weight, Maryan hugged her arms to protect herself from the coolness riding the twilight. They'd be out there all night if this kept up. Neither man appeared to be budging from his perspective, and they overlooked that they had an audience.

When a shiver raced through her and her teeth clenched from the chill oozing into her bones, Maryan looked to Hatice.

The other woman shared a quick, sympathetic smile. They were in this together, suffering because these two pigheaded men couldn't look past their egos to notice their dates were freezing.

I'm not Faisal's date!

No, she wasn't. Which made it worse in a way, as she had no proper reason to be enduring the cold when he'd seemingly forgotten about her.

Maryan heard herself speaking over the isolated sharp throb in her chest, directly over her heart.

"Stop! Please stop."

Both men swiveled their staring to her. Their gazes mirrored identical stupor. As though she'd grown an extra head in the short time that they'd been quibbling over their business dealing.

"Isn't it obvious that you should work together?" She looked between them, doling out her exasperation fairly between them as they both deserved it. "I won't presume to know you, Aydin. However, I've since gotten to know Faisal better this last week. With confidence I can promise you won't find a partner as passionate in a project as him. He's talked nonstop about his hopes for successful drilling offshore Somalia.

"What you probably haven't seen is how his eyes light up when he speaks of helping the families and communities in Somalia, or how he smiles brightly at the positive economic and social changes that could come of a booming oil and gas trade in a developing nation.

"I know money is important to the both of you. You each have people who work for you and who rely on your business expertise and professional decision-making for their livelihoods. But this partnership wouldn't only affect the people nearest to you. It'd brighten the futures of many children and their families.

"Families like my own." Maryan ended her speech with a swift, deep inhale that soaked her lungs with much-needed air. She hadn't meant to talk that long. Hadn't known she held all of that inside until it came spilling out. Like projectile word vomit.

She shook that image out of her head. It was bad enough she was queasy from embarrassment. She didn't need to be picturing it. Shrinking back beside Hatice, Maryan directed her sight down to her wedges and envisioned a massive hole opening beneath her and transporting her far, *far* away.

Far enough not to wonder what Faisal was thinking of her.

Did he hate that she'd stepped onto a soapbox in front of Aydin? What would it mean if he was upset with her? Would she still be welcome in his home?

"She's right," Faisal's voice boomed loudly in the hushed street.

Maryan raised her head slowly, afraid her ears were deceiving her, shocked to find Faisal's smirk matching his bright voice.

"Everything she's said is true. This project is near and dear to my heart. I've…sacrificed time with my daughter for it these past couple of days. I don't want my sacrifice to be in vain. And as confident as I may be in moving forward with my business, a partner for this large undertaking would make my workload easier."

She blinked at his every word, as if she might awaken from a dream.

Surely, he wasn't *praising* her for butting in with her opinion. Possibly humiliating him. *And* destroying any chance he might have had at gaining this partnership.

But as many times as she looked, he was still looking at her fondly.

She returned his smile uncertainly at first, and then bashfully when he winked at her.

"Your family lives in Somalia?" Aydin persisted in wearing his stony expression, his voice emotionless and his hand no longer making sweeping gestures at his beard. "Are they poor?"

"They are," she said hoarsely.

"And do you truly believe the future of a new frontier lies deep in the Indian Ocean near Somalia?"

Time slowed when she glanced at Faisal.

He nodded, his smile benevolent and communicating exactly what she needed to see: his trust in her.

"Yes, I do." She didn't recognize her voice, full of a quiet but powerful self-confidence. It resonated through her and filled the quiet air in the street.

Aydin studied her for an unnerving moment and then he jerked his head at Faisal, looking to have forgotten her again.

"Erkin and I will have to review a few clauses with you and your team. Does tomorrow morning in your office sound good to you? We can teleconference our legal team in Ankara as well then."

"I'll arrange for it," Faisal agreed.

They shook on the promise of tomorrow before Aydin called to his wife.

Hatice fit perfectly at his side, her demure face glowing now that she was the prize of her husband's attention. Aydin looked different, too, smiling for what had to be the first time that night.

It wasn't long after that when a sleek white town car pulled down the street, looking massively out of place among its mundane surrounds. Limos weren't a part of her world, but Faisal hardly blinked as he raised a hand to bid the couple farewell. As soon as they were gone, he turned for the restaurant.

Pausing once he noticed she wasn't following.

"Are you coming?"

She clutched his jacket, swimming in his scent, feeling his warmth mingling with her own body heat. "What happened?"

Faisal's chuckle rubbed her deliciously raw in a way that had a second heartbeat pulsing between her legs.

"You helped secure my partnership deal."

Maryan craned her neck to look back into his eyes, disbelief still rooting her four-inch wedges to the pavement. She saw nothing gleaming down at her but unfiltered awe. It wasn't the world swaying but her body tilting closer to his.

Faisal molded his hand to the curvature of her cheek, his attention hers and hers alone. It jarred her to think they might look like Aydin and Hatice.

The difference being that the other couple were married *and* in love.

Meanwhile, they were nothing more than passing ships. Here together today. Parted forever tomorrow.

Faisal's mouth sealed over her other cheek, his hot breath steaming her flushed skin.

"I'm glad you're here."

He was?

"I wouldn't be if you hadn't asked," she reminded him quietly, still awe-stricken by what happened just now.

"And I'm happy you chose to come." Faisal dropped his hand from her, making her yearn for a second before he held his palm out for her to take once more if she wished it.

And she realized with a startling clarity that she did. More than anything she ever wanted.

She grasped his hand, praying that the night didn't end anytime soon.

Never had he wanted to kiss a woman as much as he did Maryan.

Faisal ached to taste her again, breathe her hunger in, worship her as she deserved to be worshipped. He slowed as he walked her direction, fresh cups of tea in hand, his eyes riveted on her.

She sat unaware of his longing stare, her head lowered to the phone in her hands, the glow of the screen illuminating her face while an abundance of traditional lanterns brightened the rooftop.

He wasn't holding out for the possibility of another kiss, no matter how much it killed him.

This is enough.

Just having her with him for the night. He wouldn't be greedy and beg for more. *Hope* for more.

Absorbed by her, Faisal missed the sharp click of heels behind him. Aslihan materialized by his side.

"I know it's been a long while since we've spoken, yet I can tell when a man is in love."

"I don't know what you mean," he grumbled in Turkish, annoyed and befuddled and embarrassed all at once. *Love?* What did she mean that he was in love?

Aslihan's laughter was shrill and loud.

Loud enough to rouse Maryan's attention from her phone and to them. Her eyes found his immediately, her brows pinching at the center and making him feel as though he'd been caught sneaking one of her delicious Somali beignet-style desserts.

He didn't know why it mattered that he was standing close to Aslihan. Only that it felt wrong. An urge to rush over and explain himself to Maryan barreled into him with its overwhelming power.

"You *love* your nanny."

"She's not *my* nanny." She technically wasn't. Salma had employed her. And in a short matter of days, Maryan would be no one's nanny. She'd be unemployed and free to go wherever she wished to go. Free to do whatever she wished…and with whomever she wished.

Aslihan sniffed. "Fine. If that's the case, you won't mind me asking you to dinner."

"I…can't," he said quickly, softly, his eyes still locked on Maryan.

Aslihan could have prodded him as to why he'd rejected

her. Instead, she slipped a business card into his shirt's breast pocket.

"What's that?" he asked.

"It's for the boarding school. Aydin mentioned you were considering the school for your daughter. My father's stepped down as headmaster, but my ex-husband's taken over. We're on good enough speaking terms for me to get you and your daughter an appointment."

Faisal had forgotten he'd been considering this route of schooling for Zara. The past week had been dedicated to sightseeing. With Maryan leaving soon, he'd have to get back to reality eventually.

This was his wake-up call.

"I'll leave you two alone then." Offering a parting smile, Aslihan marched off in her tall, clicking heels, freeing him to uproot his feet and walk toward Maryan.

"You two looked cozy," was Maryan's first words as he grabbed the soft, colorful cushions beside her. The floor seating was meant to encourage comfort and the chance to take memorable photos of the backdrop.

Faisal sensed the change in her instantly. She sat beside him, an aura of suspicion drawing her shoulders up to her ears and fixing her eyes on her phone again.

"She was saying farewell." He placed their teacups aside where they couldn't be knocked down. "And she was also handing me this."

Maryan took the business card from him.

"It's the boarding school I attended. Aslihan's father helped me secure a scholarship to enroll there." The older man had been a family friend of Faisal's parents. "I started late, but I went to the school for the last three years before graduation." Then he'd graduated and gone to one of Turkey's top universities. Again, on scholarship, but it had been enough for him to know that he had a chance at securing a well-paying job with his premier education. Anything to help his family, especially after his mother's diagnosis of depression. What he hadn't expected was to discover his passion along the way. It happened when he'd secured an internship position at an investment firm. He had studied and put to practice what he had learned in school, building a powerhouse network source and a portfolio of transferable skills. And when he was finally ready to strike it out on his own, he had done it with a confidence that paid off, first a million times over and then a billion more.

"It's in Ankara," said Maryan.

"Would it help if I said that the children have a week longer for summer and winter holidays? Also, Zara would have a top-tier education and a chance to study with peers who could later be a good network for her."

"She's seven. Networking is the last thing on her mind."

"I don't know who I'd be without that opportunity." He looked at Maryan, saw her weighing her thoughts before uttering them.

Then the fight seeped out of her with a soft sigh. "I know I have very little say on what you choose to do." She paused, looked into his eyes, and then gently noted, "Zara won't get to know you from afar. It might seem like the best option for you, given your busy schedule, but ask yourself what it means for her."

He swallowed, promising, "I will." And he meant it, too. He'd consider what she told him. She hadn't steered him wrong with her advice yet.

"Did you call Lalam?" Maryan's moving on was a good sign that he wasn't persona non grata.

"She messaged not too long ago. Zara's asleep, and she's happy to stay longer to watch over her."

"She's an angel." Maryan voiced his sentiment for his

housekeeper. "I don't know how you managed to rope her into babysitting last-minute."

He smirked, laughing low. "I gave her a raise."

"You didn't," Maryan said, her tone disbelieving and her laughter sparkling in the night air and rivaling the warmth of the lanterns near them.

"It was the least I could do on short notice. She deserves it, too."

"She does," she agreed with an approving hum.

Grabbing her a cup of tea, he handed it to her. Their silence after was natural, easy, nothing he hastened to disrupt.

"It's getting chillier." Maryan huddled into his coat and shuddered. He'd hoped the tea would warm her up. "Maybe now's a good time to leave."

"Let's take a photo first."

He took their cups again and placed them a safe distance away.

When he turned to her, it was to find Maryan much, *much* closer to him.

It was a repeat of yesterday's scene in his kitchen. With a throat-clearing cough, he pulled out his phone and arranged his arm over the back of the cushions behind her. They were pressed together comfortably, nearly nose to nose, when he glanced over to her. He fell into the deep brown pools of her eyes, her black lashes fluttering lower, her gaze peeking out from under them shyly when she dropped her chin. Behind her the blue-black sky and the city glowing with lights. The shadowy domes and spotlighted minarets of the famed Blue Mosque and its *külliye*—its complex of buildings—hung in the backdrop of their seating. Pigeons that normally haunted the Sultanahmet Square below had retired for the night.

All these observations rushed into his mind, one after

the other, until they were a blur because her luscious mouth hovered temptingly closer.

"Are we going to take the picture?"

Nodding dumbly, he held his phone up and touched his cheek to hers, his arm rising from the cushions to fold over her shoulders and curling her into his side where she fit snugly. They snapped low-light photos, their figures illuminated with the aid of his phone's high-resolution front camera and the lanterns sharing the rooftop with them.

He could stay pressed against Maryan like this forever.

For as long as it took to understand what it was that he felt for her.

What had Aslihan called it? *Love.* It couldn't be that.

"Zara will love seeing this photo," she murmured near his ear, her cheek still warming his.

Thinking of his daughter made him think of taking Maryan home. *Home?* Since when had he gotten to thinking of it as her home as well?

"Ready to go?" He lurched to his feet and grasped her hand. Pulling her up against him, their bodies aligning briefly, he thought of kissing her again. Leading her away from their secluded place to the restaurant's exit, he passed Erkin and Aslihan smoking shisha at their table.

Once they were alone again, he hurried to whisk Maryan to his car.

He had no driver today. It'd be just the two of them on their ride home.

Home.

The word settled deep in his heart, comfortably, naturally.

He was taking her home.

CHAPTER EIGHT

FAISAL SET A record driving them home.

Thankfully, he hadn't been stopped for his breakneck speed. The important thing being they were home faster for his risk-taking.

Maryan exited his sports car, not waiting for him to open the door for her this time. She had her sparkly black clutch pressed to the front of her floral see-through bodice. All night she'd tempted him with sneaks of her through the sheer material. It was a miracle he hadn't rushed them back here faster.

"I should head in…" Trailing off with her obvious intent, she glanced at the main home.

He didn't want her to leave him.

It seemed the universe wanted the same thing because his phone chimed with an incoming text. "It's Lalam," he said, skimming the short messages she'd sent, a wide smile lifting his cheeks. "She's asking to spend the night in one of the guest rooms. She's got an exam tomorrow, and it's quicker to catch a ride with my driver to her university."

"That's generous of you," Maryan said, a smile fighting its way onto her rosy cheeks.

"You say generous. I say selfish."

"Selfish?" The smile veered into flirtatious territory with her sultry tone.

Pulling closer into her, he inhaled her springtime scent. He singled out mouthwatering citruses and fresh notes of herbs, along with her own natural fragrance. Something that was wholly a blend of her shampoo, body wash, and... *her*. Just her.

"I'd be lying if I said I didn't want you to stay with me longer."

Maryan looked away, murmuring, "I wouldn't be opposed to it."

"Will you come up and have a nightcap with me?" A grin fighting its way out. "I have a second stash of baklava upstairs."

Her lips twitched from laughter. "More baklava. You've been holding out."

"No, I haven't. Just waiting for the perfect time to tell you."

"To lure me in, you mean."

"Is it working?" he joked.

"I'll let you know...upstairs." She marched straight for the stairs up to his garage apartment.

Completely enchanted, Faisal followed her and wondered exactly who lured in whom.

Maryan sat enthralled watching Faisal take command of the kitchen.

"Is herbal okay with you? Chamomile?"

"Chamomile's good," she said, blushing when he stared at her a little too long. "Can I help?"

"I've got this." Shrugging his jacket off, he rolled up his shirtsleeves and grabbed a double kettle. She'd seen Lalam use one while making traditional Turkish tea. Faisal caught her staring this time when he flung a smile over his shoulder at her.

"It's called a *çaydanlik*. We use the smaller pot for a

stronger brew, and the larger pot for boiled water to dilute the tea." Once he had the kettles on the stovetop, he circled the island to grab the stool by her. "Now we wait."

She'd ask him how long, but the wait time for the tea was the last thing on her mind. She hadn't come up for a nightcap or the sweet promise of baklava.

I came up for him.

Maryan allowed that admission to wash over her. Suddenly, a deep fatigue set into her bones. She was drained and done with fighting an unending battle of desire for Faisal. She'd wanted him for more than half this trip. Wanted him more than she had any man. It was a carnal, raw emotion and completely unfamiliar to her. She'd spent all of her life setting aside her wants and needs, for her family. For Hassan. Even for Zara. For everybody else but for herself.

Enough. She'd had enough.

Just this once she wanted to do something for herself. She deserved a moment's taste of selfishness.

"So…" Faisal drawled, his smile full of sexy confidence. "I never properly thanked you for accepting my invitation."

"I thought that was what the baklava was for."

He laughed, low and inviting.

Right then, Maryan felt powerful. Unstoppable. She leaned into the delirious power trip and acted in a way she normally would never dare to act. She cupped her cheek and fluttered her lashes lower, teasing, "Okay, then why am I here?"

"Because I didn't want you to leave me just yet."

His seriousness eked a gulp from her.

The atmosphere in the room shifted. It reminded Maryan of the electrified air right before a thunderstorm. You could taste and smell the heavy rains draping the atmosphere, feel it in your soul, know it was coming and be helpless to stop it from downpouring over you.

"What do you want?" She forced the question out into the open.

Judging by the way his eyes widened slightly, she'd shocked him.

"Am I that transparent?" He laughed sheepishly. When she didn't join in, he nervously rubbed his hands down the legs of his jeans and plodded through a response. "I l-like you."

Her heart pulsed. "You like me?"

"I'm attracted to you, yes. Very much. More than I wanted at first, and then I didn't see a reason to fight it."

"Zara," she blurted as though that were a barrier. It should have been. At least it *had* been for her the other night when he'd kissed her, and she'd commended herself for dredging up the strength to stop them. None of that same vigor to fight this was in his apartment with her now.

"I've thought of that. Believe me, it's all I've thought of." He grimaced and then amended, "That's a lie. I have also thought of you. But I said that. Implied it at the very least—"

"One night."

Faisal goggled at her, his jaw falling open.

She'd laugh at his comical reaction, but it would betray the solemnity in the air, and she didn't want to lose momentum on her thoughts. Lose grip of her sudden flare of courage to take what she wanted.

And I want him. I do.

"It has to be one night." She had no heart to risk anything more.

"One night," he assented softly.

"Because my family needs me." The explanation bubbled out of her, fear that maybe he wouldn't perceive why she was setting a limit. She'd told him about helping her aunt and uncle. Then there was her dread of leaving Zara behind. She would miss his daughter when she left for California. Picking at that emotional scab by building something real and honest with Faisal was pointless. And she wasn't a glutton for punishment. A boundary of one night would save them both grief in the long run.

"I understand and respect your reasons." His smile was as gentle as his tone, his words sincere and pulsing of his heart.

In that instant, she knew she could trust him unreservedly.

They sat there gazing at each other after, the same breathlessness claiming her seeming to affect him.

Faisal rasped, "I keep thinking about our kiss." He gazed at her mouth, his attention riveted there.

"What about it?" she whispered.

"I want to kiss you again."

She couldn't help the laugh now. "Faisal, we just agreed to a night. That includes kissing… I hope."

"May I kiss you?" He hadn't lifted his eyes from her lips, his one-track mind adorable and unbelievably sexy when *she* happened to be his singular point of concentration.

"Yes," she gasped.

Faisal pulled in and touched their mouths gently. He stayed still a second before moving, his intimate caress thorough but tender. She parted her lips with a sigh when his hands settled on her thighs, his strong, warm fingers kneading her as they moved higher to her hips. He slid his hands behind her, tugging her deeper into his embrace.

The kettle rattling on the stove ripped him away from her.

"Sorry," he panted, slinging her a weak grin and leaving to give the stove his attention.

She followed him with her eyes, her fingers playing over her tingling lips, her body shining from his kiss.

One night, she vowed. *Just this once. One little time won't change anything.*

Why did it feel like that was a lie? Shaking off the odd sensation, she watched him slowly prowl around the kitchen island, his eyes unblinking and resolute in keeping her in his sight.

He grasped her hand, and she marveled at the ache in her core splashing out to all parts of her body. Her breasts grew heavier, her face and neck were warm to the touch, and her legs weren't as steady as they were before she entered his apartment. Before he dropped the mask and looked at her with this unrestrained hunger.

"Kiss me," she implored huskily.

She needn't ask him again. His lips landed on hers and a happy blankness wiped clear her thoughts and other emotions. Everything and everyone but Faisal were pushed out of her mind. She didn't think of her thieving ex, her kind-hearted aunt and uncle, her last few days with Zara, her life after her job as the nanny officially ended, her family back home in Somalia. She didn't even think of what came after this, now that it was so clear she'd given a little more of her heart than she intended to Faisal.

Faisal's hot mouth lifted off her and he growled, "I *need* more," and swept her feet out from under her. He carried her to his bedroom and settled her on his bed.

He undressed hastily, his chest bare and all that warm, tensing muscle open to her trailing hands and curiosity. She traced his pebbling dark brown nipples and grew bolder when his breathing puffed out faster.

She tracked her fingertips over his pelvic bones and followed the line of coarse dark hair vanishing beneath his belt.

Faisal caught her hand over the fly of his pants.

"Not yet. Let me pleasure you first."

She wasn't going to deny him that.

He claimed her lips again, her mouth pliant to his heavier, hotter techniques. He kissed her masterfully. She didn't think anyone should be allowed to kiss so sinfully. He'd ruin her for other men. Other kisses. Any hope she'd had with someone else puffed out of existence. In a blink of an eye. A stroke of his tongue inside her mouth. He tasted better than flaky baklava or any Turkish delight she'd enjoyed that night. Maybe because she could taste the robust Turkish coffee on his tongue, the sweet lemon of the traditional Turkish confection, and something that was wholly him and made her crave more.

"Kiss me again and again." She moaned the command when he lifted his head to give them both air.

"With pleasure," he growled, taking her lips with his, his body echoing the hungering passion crawling up from deep beneath her the longer he held her in his strong arms.

She laced her fingers at the back of his neck, wrapped her legs around his waist and gasped into their open-mouthed kiss when his hands skimmed her thighs and cupped her backside.

Dark eyes glittering, he broke their lip-lock and gazed tenderly down at her. "Do you want this?"

"I do." Her heart and head were united in the desire. Still, an insidious hesitance crept over her trust in him. What if he changed his mind and was looking for a way out? And what if he didn't want her as much as she desired him?

As though feeling her doubt, he covered her with his warm, hard-muscled body and kissed her long and deep. Nuzzling her nose with his, he groaned, "There's nothing I want more right now. Nothing I *need* as much as you."

And she believed him.

CHAPTER NINE

MARYAN SPENT THE next day in a palace. An honest-to-goodness palace—yet all she could think about was Faisal's body atop hers, her nails sinking into his back, his hot lips peppering kisses from her leaping pulse at her throat to her heaving breasts…

What happened last night was a result of a week's worth of pent-up lust. On her part *and* his.

She still couldn't believe he desired her. That she'd made him quake and shudder uncontrollably during their intimate coupling. She'd felt powerful. Like a goddess. But also like a slave to her passion. Faisal the master of her body. And he had given her incomparable sensual bliss. That moment in his arms relieved her of the pressures that'd been weighing on her over the last week and longer.

She hadn't given a thought to anything but rocking and meeting his every thrust.

Embraced the exquisite pleasure he was offering with the whole of her body.

Her limbs continued sparking all through the day. She was a bundle of joyous electricity; her smiles felt infectious, her laughter rolling out easier, her heart as light as air and dancing in her chest. She'd even viewed their private tour of Dolmabahçe Palace in a different light after spending the night with Faisal.

Dolmabahçe's renowned Crystal Staircase shone brighter, and its vast collection of chandeliers gleamed like constellations swinging from gold-framed high ceilings. Luxurious silk, wool and cotton woven Hereke carpets flowed from halls into salons, and hundreds of oil paintings elevated the cultural history of the grand 285-room palace. They'd taken a leisurely tour, stopping and admiring the magnificent architecture and decor, and discovering the history of the six sultans who called the palace their private residence.

She had worried they would get lost when Faisal had them separated from the regular tour group scheduled to go in with them. And when he'd guided them to the closed-off areas of the palace, her paranoia that they'd land in hot water with palace administration and security bounced off him like pebbles.

"I called and asked for a private tour," he'd said, all cheeky smiles. "This way it's just the three of us."

Zara had been delighted. This stop of their tour was her choice. She'd wanted to see one of the many Ottoman-era palaces in Istanbul. After leaving her behind from yesterday's dinner, it was the least Maryan felt she and Faisal owed his daughter.

That was why she hadn't uttered a complaint when her legs ached from walking the extraordinarily colossal palace from end to end. Faisal had noticed her slowing even when Zara held most of his attention. Without casting focus on Maryan, he'd stop them to rest at convenient intervals. To let *her* recuperate from the long walk.

His kindness resembled his tenderness from their night together.

He had made love to her body gently, slowly, exploring every inch of her trembling, sweat-soaked skin with his hands, his lips and tongue. And after he'd driven their passion wild from the foreplay, they had joined fast, hard and explosively.

She couldn't stop thinking of him in the palace, and her head was still full of the same thoughts as they stepped into the sunlit courtyard.

The palace's cool air-conditioning disappeared. She shivered at the abrupt temperature change and rubbed her bare arms. But it wasn't long before sunshine poured into her the way it flooded the palace courtyard. She dropped her hands from her arms when Faisal's voice called her out of her woolgathering.

"Do you want to grab tea to warm up? There's a café on the other side of the *sarayi*—the palace, I mean." She was getting used to his Turkish slip-ups. Almost as much as she was growing used to his small, kind acts. Soon she'd be an addict to them…

And his smiles, his laughter, his kisses.

"I know they have dessert," Faisal said.

Zara's eyes widened with her glee, a bounce in her step as she begged, "Can we please have dessert?"

"It's up to Maryan," said her dad, his eyes twinkling because he knew he had her there.

How could she refuse when Zara pinned her with those puppy-dog eyes?

"Oh, all right." She threw up her hands and laughed when Zara slammed into her for a hug.

She ran a hand over Zara's natural coiling curls, her hair held out of her face with a sparkly purple headband. As her fingers brushed the curls and avoided tangling them, Maryan's heart panged at how she missed Zara's braids. And how she would miss the little girl when they had to part ways.

She had just six more days in this perfect vacation bubble of theirs.

Then she'd have nothing to hold her to Istanbul. Not even one fabulous night with Faisal was enough.

Not unless he…

Unless he what? Wants me? Actually wants to date me?

Maryan hated to entertain that train of thought, especially because it sounded as crazy as it had when she'd been lying in his arms, ravished by postcoital bliss. Last night she *had* wanted him to *want* her enough to ask her for more.

To ask her to stay in Istanbul for longer, maybe. Stay and explore what lay beneath their intimate and immediate connection. He hadn't brought it up, though. That left her with a decision of her own. Pining over him and their night of passion, or letting it be what it was: one night with a sexy billionaire.

She still hadn't reached a verdict yet.

"How was your day as a princess?" Faisal nudged her with his elbow playfully, his body heat making her think of their explosive night together.

Zara skipped ahead of them, the lure of dessert before lunch too powerful for her to contain her thrill.

"I think Zara was the real princess. She'd have the sultan's harem wrapped around her little finger." Maryan wagged her pinkie at him and gasped lightly when he caught her hand. His thumb caressed the soft inside of her wrist, his touch creating that coiling, striking heat in her lower belly. She burned supernova when his mouth hovered over her ear.

"So, is that a 'yes' then? Did you enjoy your day, Maryan?"

She choked through a reply, sputtering, "Not as good as it might have been if I were a sultana."

The joke didn't land as well as it might have had she not trembled under his provocative touch.

Had he not growled back, "I'll make you a queen for another kiss," and made her body grow weak.

They both knew that kissing was impossible for them right then. Public displays of affection in Turkey were not as frowned upon as in other Islamic-dominant countries, but the nation was a study of contrasting histories and opinions. Namely traditional and modern ideologies and lifestyles.

They weren't risking jail time, just jeers from strangers…and queries from Zara. She'd want to know why her dad and nanny were practically embracing.

And if all of those weren't deterrents to toss caution to the wind and kiss Faisal again, Maryan revisited their choice of making this a one-night deal and nothing more. They'd both agreed to it. For the obvious reasons that neither of them seemed ready for a serious relationship. She hadn't needed Faisal to say it; his trust issues were his own and hers were…well, they were her problem.

The fissure of yearning for him shouldn't alter her plan to keep their night what it was: a one-night stand.

The hottest one-night stand ever. Her friends would be pleased that she'd finally cracked and had a rebound after her awful ending with Hassan. So, why did it feel like it was *anything but* with Faisal?

"Zara will see us." She whispered her admonishment. She couldn't bring herself to remind him of their deal from last night.

That appeared to cool him off. Backing away to a safer distance, Faisal tucked his hands in the pockets of his chinos and cast an adorable apologetic look at Maryan. They left it at that, but when they pulled in close again as they entered the café, their hands bumped, and they linked pinkies.

The secret contact was destructive to her willpower against his charm…and yet as deliciously pleasing to her as kissing him.

Faisal suffered when Maryan ordered Turkish delight ice creams for her and Zara.

The waitress delivered the ice creams quickly.

Zara dived in, making a mess of the lower half of her face. She had sticky pink ice cream and pistachios stuck to her chin, but she beamed toothily at him and Maryan, the picture of contentedness.

After helping wipe Zara up, Maryan tasted her ice cream, her mouth closing over her spoon, her eyes widening as she moaned her satisfaction. It was a soft, low moan, appropriate for their setting, but it lanced a bolt of desire through him. He shifted awkwardly in his seat and watched her all the while.

He was torturing himself and couldn't stop.

She licked and sucked her spoon, unaware of his perverted fantasizing.

When his chicken breast pudding arrived, Maryan paused from eating her ice cream and looked at the delicacy on his plate curiously. She stroked her tongue over her bottom lip and drove him to a fantasy of their lips meeting again.

"Want a taste?" He held out his spoon, knowing perfectly well he could have asked the waitress to bring a second spoon.

"What is it, Daddy?" Zara leaned over her ice cream, equally intrigued by his chosen dessert.

"Chicken breast pudding."

Maryan raised her brows. "How is it made?"

"My mom used to make it, and I've watched her do it enough times. You tenderize the chicken until it's soft, then you add milk and sugar, a flavorful thickener like broken rice, and a dash of cinnamon for taste and garnish. It's thick enough for you to shape onto a plate." He gestured to the cinnamon checker design atop the square piece of pudding.

Zara pulled a face and poked out her tongue at the description. "Ew! That doesn't sound very good."

"Zara, we don't say that about food," Maryan chided.

"Sorry, but I don't want any chicken pudding, please." And then as if to avoid any pudding finding its way to her mouth, she shoveled a spoonful of ice cream until her cheeks puffed.

Faisal smothered his laugh with a cough. He didn't want to humor Zara when Maryan was attempting to discipline her.

"So, do you want a bite?"

Maryan eyed his spoon, keeping him on tenterhooks until she nodded. She took his spoon, their fingers touching, his heart beating faster.

She spooned a small bite and tasted the unusual pudding. "It doesn't taste like chicken."

"It's not supposed to. The name is misleading." He accepted his spoon back from her and tasted the dessert, aware that Maryan's luscious lips had been around the spoon crossing his mouth. That naughty thought combined with the delectably sweet and creamy bite of pudding had him stiffer below the belt than he'd been in a long damn time. So long, in fact, he didn't recall ever getting hot and bothered over dessert shared with a beautiful woman.

Maryan isn't any woman, is she?

He was starting to believe that more with each passing day. The conundrum being that she had six days left with him and Zara. Six days before she left his world, his life… and any chance at sharing his bed again.

It shouldn't have changed anything. They'd had a perfect understanding last night.

One night.

Maryan said it herself, giving him the best out a man like him could want. A man who wasn't in the market for a ring, a white picket fence and all the other trappings that were expected with a vow of forever.

And yet he'd flirted with her *and* tried kissing her outside the café. If she hadn't stopped him, he would have. No questions asked. No doubts. No care as to how it flung a wrench in their plan to seal their passion away in one night.

So much for my self-control...

Faisal lingered in the café after they were done to pay their bill and leave a tip.

Maryan had taken Zara outdoors. Zara's giggling was the best music to his ears. Maryan was twirling her. She danced around her nanny, spinning and laughing, and looking so heartwarmingly happy. He dropped enough liras on the table to please the waitress and hurried to join them.

"Where to next?" Maryan asked once he was standing by her.

"I thought we could go check out a park nearby. We'll have to take the car." He'd dismissed his driver again, preferring to chauffeur Maryan and Zara himself. It gave them time alone. Time he cherished more than he had ever thought he would. It was a scary but thrilling feeling.

Like experiencing the heights of their pleasure last night.

Maryan had made him feel *alive*. In a way he hadn't felt when his business plans flowed smoothly. With her in his arms, Faisal felt indomitable. All-powerful. Like he held all the world's good fortune in the palm of his hands. Swept up by that flurry of emotion, he'd had a private thought— what if Maryan *didn't* leave? What if she stayed with him and Zara here in his home, in Istanbul?

He swallowed to no effect, his anxiety floating to the top of the mire of his feelings.

That morning he'd considered asking her to stay longer and not leave them just yet. One look at her blissful expression and his courage evaporated. What if by asking her to stay he ruined the extraordinarily delightful mem-

ory they'd just created together? Then he'd have nothing
to remember her by.

And it wouldn't be fair of him to ask when she'd been
adamant about the limit being one night.

She needed to go home to her aunt and uncle. She'd said
it herself. The obligation to her family was greater than his
desire to keep her in Istanbul. He had to be selfless, no matter how it pained him to be.

"Are you coming?" Maryan was looking back at him,
Zara's hand in hers and a question in her eyes.

He forced a smile for them and nodded his assent.

She gave him a fleeting look of curiosity and then turned
to walk away with his daughter toward where he'd parked
his car.

Faisal trailed them slower, his head and heart at war
over what to do about his growing attachment to Maryan.
If he asked her to stay, it'd be a selfish request, but it would
also make him happy. But if he let her leave him and Zara
he had no doubt in his mind they would lose her forever.

And forever… Forever was the problem.

Maryan had no guess as to what Faisal could be thinking.

They didn't speak while he drove them to their next
destination.

He parked his ultra-fancy sports car near the gates of
an urban park sharing the grounds of the Topkapı Palace.
Another place she'd meant to visit before leaving Istanbul. Before she asked what he was thinking, and whether
their plans had changed, Faisal grabbed Zara's hand and
stepped up to her.

"We'll go through Gülhane Park and head west first.
There's another mosque I'd like to show you."

So far Faisal hadn't disappointed her with his city tour.
It helped that Istanbul was new and welcome to her. The

city was a paragon of splendid views, friendly citizens, and appetizing foods and drinks.

And Gülhane Park was enchanting.

Wonder-struck, she admired the forested park, its well-tended gardens full of tulips and a tranquil creek. Zara stopped them at a colorful signpost of the park's name to take a photo with her phone, all three of them. Faisal asked a passerby to help them with the picture. While the friendly stranger waited for them to get into position, Zara instructed Maryan and Faisal to sit on either side of her.

"Daddy, you sit here. And Maryan, you sit beside me this way."

Her bossy attitude inspired a laugh from her father and an indulgent smile from Maryan.

The stranger snapped a couple of photos before handing Zara's phone back and leaving.

They took more pictures at Zara's behest in front of the Column of the Goths, an ancient Roman victory column. Once they passed the gate out of the park, Maryan sensed Faisal dropping back to match pace with her. Zara was absorbed with her phone and the photos they'd taken on it and walked ahead of them.

"We should talk." Faisal brushed his hand along hers as they walked closer together.

"About?" she asked.

She had a clue of at least one thing they could discuss, but she wouldn't put words in his mouth. She'd rather hear what he thought without any more suppositions.

"Last night," he said, his voice dropping to a tantalizing whisper. "Being with you was…"

Mind-blowing? Soul-shattering? Exquisitely and incomparably *perfect*?

"Fun."

"Fun?" she repeated, a hollowness setting in all over her body.

He slowed and stopped her with a hand to her elbow. Staring down at her, he frowned, confusion touching his attractive face. "Wrong word?"

"No," she said, forcing herself to say it again when he tilted his head to the side and appeared unconvinced, "*No*, you're right. It *was* fun." *Fun* came out fast and harsh, and with a thread of a growl in the one syllable.

Faisal pulled his fingers through his long curls. She slipped her arm out of his hand and met his troubled eyes.

"You're angry," he said, regret roughening his voice.

"I'm not," she flung back, and walked away.

He caught up quickly, his strides matching her clipped pace. Zara had left them behind when they'd stopped, but she was within visual distance. At least Maryan didn't have to worry about losing her. Clearly the same couldn't be said for Faisal.

He wasn't yours to begin with. One night was all it was supposed to be.

She blinked fast to stop the tears. Crying now would unleash all sorts of problems. Faisal would feel guilty and have even more power over her, and Zara would wonder what had gotten her so upset.

Don't cry. Do not. Cry.

"Maryan." He beseeched softly and touched her shoulder.

She jerked out of reach, stopped fast and whirled on her heel to finish confronting him. She'd get the last word in, and then they would close the book on this chapter and move on.

But before she said anything, Faisal blurted, "Fun wasn't the first word that came to mind. It really wasn't."

She sucked her lips in, wanting to believe what he said

yet still feeling raw and awfully vulnerable. Keeping silent felt the best course of action. Sure enough, her quiet roused him into continuing his speech or apology or whatever it was.

"Spectacular. Unlike anything I've experienced before. Chemistry off the charts." He shuffled in place then, his palm curling over the nape of his neck and a shyness overtaking him. "For lack of a better word, it was *perfect*. I can't think of any other way to describe it."

"Perfect," she said softly. So softly it was a wonder that he heard her.

"Perfect," he rejoined with a crooked smile. "Are you still mad?"

She shook her head, and his smile spread wider and crinkled his eyes. She turned his words over in her head, her heart lighter and her body shrugging off the frosty remains of her crushed ego and heartache.

They walked then, lapsing into a peaceful silence and following Zara out of the park toward their next stop in that day's leg of the tour.

The New Mosque offered a brief respite from the heated moment in the park.

Pigeons flocked to the square at the foot of the steps into the seventeenth-century imperial mosque. Maryan had done some research on the Ottoman-era structure. It was only one of many mosques constructed by the women closest to the all-powerful sultans of that era. Their wives and mothers.

Faisal purchased three cups of wheat from an elderly merchant working a mobile stall and handed Maryan and Zara one each.

"The pigeons have come to rely on the food," he said, showing Zara how to feed the birds without upending her cup and spilling the wheat inside.

Maryan flicked her wrist, showering wheat grains on the square. A herd of pigeons fluttered nearer to her to scavenge the ground for the fresh wheat. She tossed them more, laughing with Zara when the pigeons brushed their legs in a mad dash to peck the ground clear of food.

When Zara finished her cup, Faisal replenished her with his. He hadn't fed the pigeons, appearing satisfied with watching his daughter experience it for them both.

Eventually he left Zara to continue scattering small handfuls of wheat to the hungry pigeons and wandered over to Maryan.

She sensed he wanted to pick up where they'd left off speaking.

"I am sorry if I made you think anything else," he said. "It's just we decided that it would be a night…"

"I know."

"Can you tell I'm regretting it?"

She couldn't believe her ears. Did Faisal want her for *more* than one night? Not that it changed anything. She had a responsibility to help her aunt and uncle. They were family. Family helped each other. She'd been helping hers all her life.

A promise of countless more sultry nights with Faisal wasn't enough to keep her in Istanbul.

And the one thing that possibly could cause her to waver from her plans would never, *ever,* not in a million years happen. It didn't stop her from thinking it.

If he loved me…

But, as she knew, *that* was an impossibility.

Faisal pushed his hands into his pockets, gazing at her with an intensity that manifested an ache all through her body. "Am I wrong to assume that we should revisit our terms?"

What would be the point?

Maryan clued in that she'd asked the question aloud when Faisal's eyes grew larger, his brows vaulting higher. *Crud*, she thought, cursing her runaway mouth.

"You're right," he said with a slow nod and the saddest smile. "I shouldn't have even brought it up. No, we were smart to have kept it to one time only. No strings, no commitments and above all else: no complications."

No hearts broken. No lives irreversibly changed, for better or worse.

She left those thoughts to herself. It was hard enough recalling why they'd chosen to limit their passionate attraction.

Harder to do it while falling deeper into his eyes and glimpsing the same longing she had for him staring back at her with equal force.

Faisal's ringing phone took that moment to interrupt. Maryan watched him pull it out and stare at it before he looked up to her with an apologetic expression. Figuring it had to do with work, she nodded dismissively before he asked, and he walked away to answer the call.

Maryan went to Zara and found them a spot on the staircase of the mosque to watch the pigeons being fed by passersby.

When Faisal returned to them, he still had the phone in his grasp.

"What's the matter?" Maryan asked, sensing the change in him. There was a pep in his step. A joyous gleam in his eyes. And a curl to his smiling mouth that had her lips pulling up in return.

"It's done. It's really done. Aydin and Erkin have agreed to the deal, and my team's just received their signed preliminary documents." He shook his head, the bewilderment taking hold of his handsome face. "There's still the finalizing of the contracts to complete, but then that's it. We're officially partners."

"And you're building your oil rig and helping Somalia," she added encouragingly.

He looked at her then. *Really* looked at her, his smile softer, his eyes suspiciously glassy. "I couldn't have done it without you."

"What did I do?"

"Aydin was impressed by your speech. I know he was."

"You don't," she argued, losing the battle when his boyish grin dazzled her into silence.

"I just do."

Maryan nudged her chin at his phone and hugged his daughter closer. "Is that what the call was? Do you have to go in to work to oversee your team?"

"No…"

She pursed her lips, not liking that he trailed. Last time he'd done this they'd ended up going to dinner together—

And having the hottest, most perfect sex of my life after.

"We've been invited to a party the day after tomorrow to announce the partnership officially."

Before Maryan could give him the third degree, Zara sprang up and hugged her father's legs.

"Do I get to go to the party, too?" she asked sweetly.

Faisal laughed. "Yes, you're coming with us, too." He met Maryan's eyes when he said that last part. She strayed from her doubts, her worry falling off the edge of a cliff, and her memory of their wickedly hot night playing in her mind again. A part of her still couldn't believe their lovemaking meant more to him as well. She never wanted to come down from her cloud nine.

Maryan was riding that emotional high when he said, "I have to make some calls, though, so I'll be a little while. That won't be a problem, right?"

Any red flags that might have been triggered were quashed by her good mood. A mood that Faisal had greatly contributed to.

Which was why she said, "Make your calls. We'll be here waiting for you."

Faisal sneaked a private smile full of heat at her. Planting a kiss atop his daughter's head, he left them then. Maryan watched him go, Zara tucked against her side again, the two of them waiting for Faisal's return. She pushed aside the foreboding sense that she should be worrying. She trusted him. Cared for him.

Loved him.

Maryan stiffened and then relaxed into that truth.

She did love Faisal.

She didn't know when it had happened. Probably when she felt perfectly safe in his tender and passionate embrace. Or perhaps it was whenever she watched him with Zara— watched him be playful and loving with his daughter. Then again, now that she gave it her full attention, she must have fallen in love with all of him. And not all at once. *Yes.* That's how it happened. Gradually, as she stripped each layer to the hidden truth of him, down to the most secreted parts, her attraction and attachment to him grew stronger and the love sprung forth naturally.

She loved every side of Faisal she'd witnessed in the past week. Every side of him he'd shown her.

She loved him. Full stop.

CHAPTER TEN

BUT WAS LOVE ENOUGH?

Maryan grappled with that thought more than twenty-four hours later. More than a day since she'd last seen Faisal.

After their trip to the New Mosque, Faisal's phone wouldn't stop ringing. He had barely been present mentally when he'd dropped them off at his home and left for his office. And that was the last time she and Zara had seen him. He had called late last night, right after Zara's bedtime, to ask after her. Maryan had him on the line in hopes that he would want to talk more, but then, citing another boardroom meeting before promising to call her tomorrow morning, he'd hung up faster than she had liked.

He hadn't called but texted her and Zara a short morning message. Apparently "good morning" was his idea of a conversation. He hadn't even responded to her text yet. She'd asked if he was doing all right.

Now several hours later she was entering his home, shopping bags on both her arms, and a few more in Burak's hands as he shadowed her and Zara indoors.

Lalam took the bags from Burak. Freed of his task, Faisal's security man left with an acknowledging nod.

"Do I take bags upstairs?" Lalam offered.

"Please, thank you," Maryan said, smiling weakly. She wasn't surprised when Zara yawned big. The young girl had woken up earlier than usual to start their busy day. Though none of Zara's earlier enthusiasm was present now. She looked as worn out as Maryan felt.

Noticing that Lalam hovered nearby, appearing as if she had something to say, Maryan regarded her with another fatigued smile. "I'll come up and organize the bags later."

"Yok," said the housekeeper.

From her limited Turkish, she understood that to mean no.

Then Lalam pointed out through one of the glass panes in the front doors. Her finger was directed at Faisal's garage apartment. "Mr. Umar is home."

"He is?" Maryan would've muffled her shock, but it sprang out of her.

"He came home not so long ago."

Maryan thanked her, her mind more alert with this bit of news. Lalam grabbed the bags her hands could carry and headed for the stairs.

"Let's go see your dad."

Zara gripped her hand and they veered out the door, leaving the main home behind and covering the distance to the garage quickly. They climbed the stairs and tried the door. Knocking, Maryan waited with Zara, her thoughts spinning faster the longer it took Faisal to answer his door.

When it opened, he stood there with his earpiece and gestured for them to enter.

She tried not to let her eyes linger where his dress shirt hung open. His fingers made rapid work of buttoning himself up, his hair wet from a shower she presumed, and his woodsy bodywash and aftershave trailing him into the kitchen like a sensual banner. He was pulling out mugs and refilling a kettle. Moving and talking at once, he arranged baklava on a plate and brought it to where they sat on the sofa in his living space.

"It's all set then. Perfect," he said, returning to his call. "I'll have the last few documents delivered in the next hour. Also, send the list of media representatives over to my executive assistant to double-check."

Maryan nibbled on her baklava roll, the flaky dough dissolving on her tongue and bringing her an immeasurable amount of comfort. Watching Faisal work was nerve-racking. Burning the candle at both ends had to be stretching his limits—even billionaires needed a break, didn't they? And, of course, she had to think of Zara. She deserved to be Faisal's topmost priority. Not his company's stocks, or his shareholders, but his daughter.

And me?

No, not her. Most definitely *not her*. She wasn't anyone to Faisal. Pining for him to beg her to stay had consumed her enough. It was starting to feel obsessive.

He finished with his call right as the kettle burbled its signal that tea could be served.

"Zara, you look beautiful," gushed Faisal the second he had their mugs in hand. Once he had the cups safely deposited atop the coffee table, he hugged Zara and held her. "I love your braids and these gold beads."

"Maryan said they would look pretty with my dress," said Zara, her adoration in her eyes when her father pulled back from hugging her and she glanced up at Maryan.

Maryan smiled back down at her. "But Zara chose her own dress, and it's a wonderful choice."

"I can't wait to see it," Faisal praised.

"You will tomorrow, Daddy." Zara yawned then, rubbing her eyes and dropping forward into her father's arms.

"She needs a nap," Maryan told him, their eyes meeting over Zara's head. For a beat they stared at each other silently, and then he broke eye contact and scooped Zara into his arms.

"I'll take her to her room."

"I'll come with you." Faisal stood with Zara, leaving Maryan no other option. Secretly she was pleased that he was putting Zara before his many work-related duties. To think she'd been doubting him. Her concern was unfounded, obviously. She did tell him that he could do it. Be a dad to Zara. Be everything his daughter needed once it was just the two of them.

Overlooking the pain married with that thought, she followed Faisal and Zara back to the main house to do her duty. She was still the nanny, after all.

Only this time it was clear to her, and very quickly, that she was unneeded.

Maryan faded into the background as Faisal carried Zara inside their home and up the stairs to her bedroom. Without having to tell him what to do, he had Zara in the bathroom, running a bath for her, while he rummaged through her dresser for a clean pair of pajamas. Maryan waited outside while he bathed her. Pacing. Worrying, not for Zara but over her unsteady head and heart. They warred with each other. One wanted to tell Faisal of the love for him she'd recently discovered. The other wished to bury any trace of it, smother it with cold dirt and forget it ever flourished to existence.

Which part of her could she trust? Her head warning her from eventual heartbreak, or her heart pulling for love and its restorative magic? The kind of magic bundled in the fairy tales Zara loved to hear.

The bathroom door opened on a flourish of steam. Faisal trotted a sleepy Zara out and to her bed.

She didn't even beg for a bedtime story, snuggling under her bedcovers and falling asleep instantly.

Creeping for the exit together, Maryan came face-to-face in the hall with Faisal.

"Out like a light," he observed, chuckling softly.

"We had a busy day, and an early start."

"I can see that." He studied her, a slow, appreciative sweep over the length of her, his tongue pulling out and dragging over his bottom lip. On anyone else she would have been creeped out. With Faisal, her body grew warmer, and her head jumbled any sense of speech she might have had prepared.

"You and Zara matched."

She ran her hands over her microbraids, the waterfall of long black extensions seamlessly woven into her natural hair and curling softly at the tips. It had taken hours to perfect the look, but she'd been in good hands with Faisal's executive assistant.

"You'll have to thank Rukiya for me. I wouldn't have known what salon to go to here."

"I'll let her know her service was appreciated."

They stood there, on opposite ends of the wide hall, with only the vibrant runner between them…

It might as well be a chasm with my nerves.

Maryan pushed her hands into her belly, anything to relieve the pressure of the knots forming inside. She couldn't do this—she wasn't ready to tell him. She'd chosen one night to avoid muddying their situation. And now… Now she wavered between her choices. Should she stay or leave? Should she tell him she loved him, or should she let the distance between Istanbul and Santa Monica erode her love?

She was itching to leap out of her skin, indecisiveness clanging in her brain.

Standing across from him wasn't helping her settle on a decision once and for all.

"I'm going to do yoga while Zara's asleep. I haven't stretched and exercised today." The physical exertion would clear her mind. "I'll be outside if you need me."

"Maryan?"

She paused and spun back to him, her heartbeats so fast she swore she tasted every pulse on her tongue.

"I'm looking forward to seeing your dress, too." Faisal winked and grinned saucily, striding off in the opposite direction, back toward his apartment and office no doubt.

Maryan watched him leave, his flirting giving rise to hope. And that hope eclipsed all her panicked fretting. This whole time she'd thought *she* had to decide. But it struck her that the decision would affect them both. That he had a say, too.

If he asks me to stay—

She'd stay. Sort it out with her family but stay in Istanbul with Faisal and Zara.

And if he didn't ask her…

Lucky she was covered there. She had plans for when she landed in California for renovating her aunt and uncle's restaurant, and her job hunting at the community center. This way she'd keep busy with a broken heart.

Faisal attempted working.

But it was pointless. His head was full of Maryan. Something in her eyes earlier had taken hold of his curiosity. She had looked like she wanted to get something off her chest. And it was enough to pull his attention away from the press release announcing his partnership with Aydin and Erkin that his PR team had sent over for his explicit approval. If not that, he had at least a few other tasks on his to-do list for the day, and many more that would need to be completed over the next couple weeks. Not that his busy schedule was anything new.

The distraction from his work *was* a novelty.

He pushed from his chair and paced his office. Then

he latched onto the excuse for tea and decided to leave his apartment to head toward the main house for a cup.

The kitchen was eerily quiet. Faisal figured Zara was still sleeping as he'd been gone from the house for an hour. Maryan had told him she'd be doing her yoga. Which meant she would either be in her bedroom...

Or his backyard.

Faisal slowed as he opened his bifold patio doors and passed through the seamless transition into his garden-rich outdoors. His feet had their own agenda, and he was along for the ride.

Walking out into his carefully architected oasis never failed to calm him.

Several large pots housed palm trees, their recognizable fronds swaying to the warm winds that passed through the garden. A plethora of colorful, vibrant tropical flora encircled the garden and its water features. A two-tier fountain was the focal point. The fountain's bowls were held up by a pride of three lions, their gaping maws and sharp teeth lifelike and a testament to the sculptor's skill. Further in the recesses of the garden, the rippling shallow waters of a man-made pond was at the foot of a crafted waterfall. The trickling water from both fountain and pond completed the tranquil mood of the cultivated garden. Most thrilling of all, the full-foliage shade of two massive oak trees lent a privacy to the space and separated his vast manicured lawn from his garden paradise.

Normally, escaping to his terrace was a joy in and of itself.

Only it was tenfold more gratifying now that Maryan was in his backyard.

She was under the gazebo and in the middle of a complicated yoga position that had her hands and arms supporting her lower half. She had her back to him and had no clue when he stood a foot from where she exercised, blissfully clueless to her audience of one.

Her very mesmerized audience of one.

He wiped his mouth, fearing drool.

She lowered to the yoga mat and stretched her arms up before transitioning gracefully into her next position. Before she raised her taut rear up again and he lost his train of thought forever, Faisal coughed loudly, sputtering from the force. He coughed for real, tears pinching the corners of his eyes, while Maryan dropped to the mat and whipped her head around to him. Shock morphed to concern on her lovely face.

"Are you okay?" She reached for her water bottle on the gazebo bench, looking prepared to offer him a sip.

"Just a tickle in my throat," he croaked with a blush he could feel warming his face.

Maryan didn't argue, letting it go and saving him from fumbling through more of his embarrassment.

"Is Zara awake?"

"I don't think so." His daughter was a bundle of energy, as most kids her age were. She'd have been downstairs, tearing the house apart, if she were awake. He was confident in this. "I came for tea."

"What happened to your stash in the apartment?"

He rubbed his stubble-heavy jaw, a chuckle rolling out of him. "Okay, you got me. I had a need for company. Nothing makes tea sweeter than enjoying it with someone else—or so my parents say."

"I wouldn't mind a cup of herbal."

"Would you settle for green? I hear it's good…er…post-workout." This was the part where he didn't allow his eyes to trace down her wrap sweatshirt—envisioning her body under the drapey top. Or to her scrunched leggings that accentuated her round backside and thighs and reminded him of the strength he felt in her legs when they'd been wrapped around his waist.

And now I know where she's getting that strength.

"I'll grab the tea for us," he said, desperately needing the time-out to get his head on straight.

He'd come to her for a reason.

It was only as he was pouring their green tea into their cups did Faisal understand what that reason was.

I want her to stay.

More than he wanted to give in to his fear that she'd turn out to be like one of the many money-hungry dates he'd had in the past. Taking his heart out of the equation had done wonders for his peace, even as it reinforced the idea that he'd never find love. Not with his wealth luring in the wrong kind of women.

And Maryan didn't feel wrong. She felt crazily, miraculously *right*.

That was why he had to speak up. Say something. Give voice to the wild but wanted emotions she'd inspired in him.

He carried their cups on saucers back to the garden, an eagerness to get back to her in his hurried steps.

"...perfect dress! It cost a lot, but Faisal's generous. You'd like him, Habo."

Habo. She was talking to her *aunt*.

Faisal stepped behind the giant potted palms before the gazebo. Under their cover, he listened at the cost of his breaking heart.

"My hair is beautiful, too. I'll take a picture for you at the party, show you all the fun times I'm having."

Was that what he was to her: *just* fun times?

His shoulders slumped, his grasp on the saucers tightening, the cups jangling louder when he backed up at her nearing voice. He miscalculated one step. The next few seconds happened fast. With a startled grunt, he fell back, the hot tea flying and dumping onto his lap and the front of his dress shirt.

Maryan turned the corner, phone pressed to her ear and with eyes as large as a full moon. Faisal imagined he looked a sight. The teacups and saucers scattered on the lawn, his shirt and pants drenched at the front, and his pain and misery finding company in his humiliation.

"I'll call you back, Habo." She hung up and rushed to him, quick on her feet, her hands gripping one of his arms and helping him from the ground. "What happened?"

"Lost my footing," he grumbled, hating that he already sounded as miserable as he felt.

She looked to where his shirt stuck to his chest, a wrinkle in her brow. "Does it burn?"

"I'll be fine. Only my ego's hurt," he lied.

Cowardice had him stooping to pick up the cups and saucers, a chip in one teacup eliciting a groan—Lalam wouldn't be happy. She prided herself on preserving his tableware. Cleaning up kept him busy for a minute or two, and then he had to meet Maryan's eyes again.

She was worrying her bottom lip with her teeth.

Did she know that he'd overheard her? He hadn't meant to eavesdrop. But it was what it was. Still, he didn't want to do this now if he could avoid it.

Before he could wrestle with his choices on what to do, Maryan got ahead of him with whatever was clearly bothering her.

"I was talking to my aunt."

"Oh?" He aimed for nonchalant, testing the waters with what she knew and what she didn't.

"She's been calling me, and I hadn't had the time to call back last night."

"I bet she misses you."

"Well, I miss her, too." Maryan chewed her lip again, her brows slashing lower.

Faisal hardened his jaw, refusing to give in to the instinct to make her worries go away. "Two weeks is a long time. I suppose you're happy it's coming to an end?"

She frowned. "I'll miss Zara."

What about me? he wanted to ask petulantly.

"My aunt was confirming my flight time again. My uncle wants to pick me up at the airport."

He swore a thread of hesitation skirted her voice at the end. Not that it softened the blow of her words. And they were like a punch to his juddering heart.

This was it. She's leaving.

And he had to let her go. He promised he wouldn't hold her down past one night. She'd bared her heart to him in a short time, trusting that he'd understand—and *he did*, but it didn't change the fact that he burned achingly to beg her to stay. But the plea dried up on his tongue.

It would be cruel to ask her. She'd told him how her parents had planned for her to make a life in America alone. Then how her ex-boyfriend abused her confidence. Robbing her of this decision to stay or leave would be betraying everything they'd shared.

The only thing that might solder her by his side was the very thing he'd avoided thinking too hard on. *Love.* Faisal let it breach his mind, but all he could think was how very wrong it would be to use the power of deep affection on her. Not when he wasn't certain of it, and when he didn't know if love would be an unquestionable fact.

"It's always nice to see family at the airport." He spoke slowly and over the rushing blood in his ears.

His chest stung where the tea was cooling on his clothes, and his backside ached from his hard fall. A strange bitterness filled his mouth, and a sweetness tainted the air he breathed—it was either Maryan's fragrance or the garden. In the end he settled on it being a little bit of both, her scent and the greenery circling them. But soon her scent would be gone from the space.

Too soon she'd be gone.

"It'll be good to see them again," she said softly, tacking on, "Though I mean it. I'll miss Istanbul. Even the parts I haven't seen yet."

Those words should have been a remedy reversing his unhappiness. But all he processed was her tense, fake smile. There was something she was holding back from saying. Did it have to do with what she'd been saying to her aunt? What did Maryan tell her about him?

He stopped his overactive mind from churning out conspiratorial theories, all centered on his immense personal wealth.

She isn't like that.

He just knew she wasn't after him for his money. Even so, she couldn't want him. He was a bundle of trust issues. And she had explained why love wasn't for her. Knowing this and then subjecting her to his mistrust would be cruel.

It's me. I'm the problem.

Faisal stood taller at that unnerving revelation. Because it was, no matter how he looked at it. He wanted her to stay, but he wasn't willing to lower his defenses and let her in. And if by some chance they did last forever, it would be a forever spent with him always on guard—always doubting—always vigilant for the first sign she'd unravel his heart.

"Faisal?" Maryan's voice wrenched him out of his thoughts.

"We still have some time to squeeze in a few more landmarks." He smiled forcibly, rattled by his self-reflection. "Unless…you'd like to stay on as Zara's nanny?"

He knew the tasteless joke wouldn't land. He bargained on it. There was too much between them now, and the sex had been both a blessing and a curse. A blessing because he'd found someone he genuinely liked, and a curse as he couldn't in good conscience have her work for him and pretend that she meant nothing to him.

She'd never be just the nanny to him.

Because she never was.

Maryan's face fell.

"We both know I couldn't."

"Maryan, I was kidding…"

She hummed as though she believed him, her tight-lipped smile filling the pained silence that followed.

"I should go in, get changed, showered, check on Zara." She listed her excuses, her feet moving for the patio doors.

Faisal heard himself mutter, "Of course," his head lowered, shame keeping him from looking her right in the eye.

This was best for them. He couldn't hold her down with a false promise of feelings he was still sorting through. Maryan deserved a clear answer, and he didn't have it for her right then.

He didn't know if he ever would.

Maryan didn't stop until she reached her bedroom.

She headed out onto the balcony, the air fresher outside, her lungs no longer ready to burst from lack of sufficient breathing. Faisal had made her breathless—again. But in a way that also made her feel like the smallest, most insignificant being in the whole world. She wanted to cry. And cry. And never bother reaching out and grabbing what she wanted most, no matter how promisingly close and deceptively hers it felt.

He wasn't ever mine.

Accepting that with a torturous swallow, she let free the first sob of many.

She cried quietly, curling down to a crouch and squeezing the stone balusters for support. Waking Zara next door wouldn't help, and alarming Lalam would bring forth questions Maryan wasn't ready to answer.

The tears felt endless. She let them out with soft hitched breaths. Crying because she *wanted* to stay. Maryan understood that clearly now. She had made her decision, and then she'd prayed that Faisal would show her some sign that he felt the same about her departure. That he wanted to see just how far this electric attraction between them could go.

But…she should have known it was too good to be true.

She'd just told her aunt about him. And although she hadn't mentioned any romance, her Aunt Nafisa had teased her anyway. The warmth and hope she had felt earlier was gone.

Why hadn't he asked her to stay? They had grown close over a short span of time. Faisal had listened to her. They'd talked. Shared their hurts and fears, and then connected on a physical level that outshone her previous relationships. The only thing that seemed off the table from the start was a possibility of forever.

But she still stupidly hoped.

And now her heart was broken.

And…and…she wiped under her stinging eyes and brushed her hot cheeks, a rush of anger overtaking her. She had four more days. None of them *had* to be spent in Faisal's home. Seeing him every day would be a special kind of torture for her. And she wasn't a masochist. Maryan did think of Zara, and her anger cooled slightly, a sorrow filling the spaces it left vacant. If given the option, she'd have wanted to keep Zara close to her forever. She loved Faisal's daughter. No distance would change that for her. Not ever.

Packing her suitcase was something she'd known she had to do eventually. Even when she had deigned to be silly and hope to stay, a part of her had resigned herself to this being a possibility. She placed the last few items in, closed the lid on her luggage and rolled it by the door, before going in search of Lalam. On the way, she stopped by Zara's room, her feet unbudging. She touched the door with a trembling hand, her eyes filling up again, and her heart tugging down, down, deep down into her stomach.

Pressing a kiss to her palm, she touched the door one last time and left in search of Faisal's housekeeper.

Lalam's voice drifted from a slightly ajar bedroom door.

Faisal was in there, too. Maryan slowed at the sound of his deeper voice. Nothing he said was discernible, though, so he must have been farther in the room. Too far for her to eavesdrop.

She waited nearby for Lalam, and not for long.

"Miss Maryan? Is something wrong?" The amiable housekeeper caught sight of her only after she closed the bedroom door behind her.

She glanced down at the first aid kit in Lalam's hands, recalling Faisal burning himself in the garden. *Is he hurt badly?* she wanted to ask, but bit the inside of her cheek. She'd see for herself when she spoke to him.

"Nothing's wrong," she fibbed, offering what she hoped was a reassuring smile before pointing to Faisal's closed bedroom door. "Do you think he'd mind if I knocked? I need to speak with him."

Lalam gave her an encouraging nod before walking off, seeming none the wiser of the turmoil in Maryan's heart.

"Come in." His voice was muffled but loud enough to answer her rapping knuckles.

Faisal was stepping out of a massive walk-in closet opposite his king-size bed. He tossed the tea-stained dress shirt in his laundry hamper when she walked in. He slowed and stopped, staring at her. The curtains were drawn to his room, the natural light showing her the glamour of his master bedroom *and* the clear alarm in his widening eyes.

He dropped his gaze suddenly, fixing it on the carpeted floor. "Hey. I thought you were Lalam."

"I saw the first aid kit. Are you hurt badly?" The question blurted out of her. Funny how even after he'd knocked her heart into despair, she was concerned for him. She blamed love. Stupid, silly, maddening love.

"The burns sting a little, but I was just about to take pain reliever for it."

The fact that he kept his eyes glued to the carpet spoke the kind of volumes that made her eyes water again. Maryan blinked furiously, glancing up at the ceiling with its pretty pendant lighting and willing the watery heat from making an appearance. She didn't want to cry in front of him. She wasn't certain how he'd react, not after he hadn't made any move to ask her to stay. She couldn't be sure of anything between them anymore.

"I'm leaving," she said, glad her voice was strong, crisp, full of the certitude she hadn't felt a moment ago.

That snapped his head to her. *Finally.*

"As grateful as I am to have been able to be close to Zara in your home, I've overstayed my welcome."

"Maryan, you don't have to go yet."

But she had to go eventually, so did it matter when she walked away?

"If it's not a bother to you, I'll wait until Zara wakes up. I want...*need* to tell her myself." She knew what it felt like when adults made decisions for children and expected them to follow along. She wouldn't leave like a thief in the night and shatter any trust Zara had in her. "Then I'll book a hotel and grab a taxi."

Faisal scowled. "No way. If you're intent on leaving, my driver will take you where you please."

She could've argued, but then they would be standing here longer, and she couldn't fight to hold back the brunt of her emotions. The tearful anger, the disheartenment, and above all, the disappointment. In him. In herself.

"Do you have to go…now?" he pleaded.

She wasn't so naive anymore to read more into his plea. It was on Zara's behalf that he was persisting on changing her mind. He'd made it loud and clear that none of this begging was him wanting her.

"Sorry. I should respect your wishes," he apologized quickly.

But it isn't my wish! I want to stay here, with Zara. With you!

She clamped her teeth over her bottom lip to stop from shouting the words out into the open.

Faisal's pinched brows, downturned mouth and hard jawline—all of it registered to Maryan as his way of building a wall between them. It gave her more of a reason to walk away while they were still being civil. Instead, she waited, expected him to address the elephant in his expansive bedroom, and then opted to do it herself.

"Also, I won't be attending the party."

"This is because of me," he said in a low, rasping voice. "Zara will hate that you won't be there."

She wouldn't be guilted into going, and he must have realized that because he apologized a second time.

"I'm sorry. I don't know what's wrong with me." He sucked in a whistling breath and scrubbed a hand down his long face. She wasn't sure why *he* looked so unhappy. Wasn't her leaving what he wanted?

Faisal sighed then, interrupting her quiet bafflement as he continued.

"This is my fault. I'd expect nothing less. I just wanted you to be comfortable here, with us. Obviously, I haven't been the best host in the past hour or so." He smiled weakly. "Thanks for staying to explain to Zara. She'll take it better hearing it from you."

Maryan had thought she'd feel gratified at hearing his misery. Far from it, she battled her weakening determination as she left his room to hide out in hers again. She wanted to feel like this was how it should be. He hadn't asked her to stay longer. He'd made her feel miserable. It should have felt good to see him just as downcast.

Newsflash: it didn't.

Worse, she was rethinking whether this was the right choice for them after all...

CHAPTER ELEVEN

SOMEHOW, HE'D SURVIVED the events of yesterday.

Maryan left for her hotel after she spoke to Zara, and with a terse farewell to him, abandoning them to experience their first night without her.

And what a night it was. He hadn't slept long enough to dream. After a tousle with his sheets and some fitful rest, he awoke for an early start to his day. He was only beginning to feel the sleep deficit now. Faisal rubbed his tired, aching eyes, a toe-curling yawn taking him by surprise. But not nearly as surprising as a call from his mother, first thing in the morning. He blinked at the missed notification on his phone, puzzling as to what her call could be, and then panicking as his imagination spun the worst-case scenarios as to why she'd phoned him outside her regular hours.

"Mom? Are you all right?" He stopped himself from asking if her new treatments were not helping with her depressive moods.

She quickly assured him of her good health, and then she heaved a put-upon sigh. "Why is it that my son does not call me when good news has happened for his company? Why is your sister the one to tell your father and me first?"

With everything that happened, his memory had lapsed in informing his family. But the news would have circulated online and reached his sister. He knew she liked to keep tabs on him whenever she wasn't actively interrogating him about his life.

Still, the thought of his bossy little sister teased a smile from him. "How is Yasmin?"

"She wants to see her niece." His mom tsked good-naturedly. "And your father and I want to see our sweet-faced Zara, too."

"I promise you'll see her soon. Actually, I'm hoping we can visit sometime next week." He had it all set up, but his planning had fallen by the wayside when Maryan arrived. And then again when she checked out of his home early to finish up her final few days in Istanbul in a hotel. Just like she would have if he hadn't interceded and talked her into staying with him and Zara.

His mother didn't know that, though, so he couldn't unload his troubles onto her.

Perceptive as always, his mother stated, "You sound like you are very busy."

"I am, but never for your calls. You know that." For his family, he'd drop everything. They were all he had. All he could trust.

Especially now that I pushed Maryan from me.

"Are you eating well? Do I have to come for a visit and make you all your favorite foods?"

God, would he love that.

"Zara's nanny made *kac kac*. It tasted like yours." The highest praise from him. Maryan had given him a taste of his childhood.

"She can cook?" His mother harrumphed. "And you let her go?"

Faisal let out a belly laugh, but the tears in his eyes were not solely attributed to his mirth. There was a despondency left after the laughter stopped. It ate away at any remaining joy until he had to fear that nothing would be left soon.

"I warned her about your matchmaking."

"You should have brought her with you, that's what you should have done."

His mother's teasing was a healing salve to the wounds afflicting his soul. *Self-inflicted*, Faisal noted sternly. He could've kept her with him. Or tried to. Instead, he'd thought he was doing the right thing by letting her go.

"I will have to test her *kac kac* myself."

"She's gone," Faisal said gruffly, short with himself and forgetting who he was talking to.

His mother latched onto this with silence first, and then a soft, "This is what's upsetting you," nailing him to the wall with a truth he'd preferred to have dusted under his office rug.

"Mom…"

"No," she spoke with a sharpness that stilled his tongue, "you like this nanny."

"Her name's Maryan…and, yes, I do. *Did.*" He huffed, "It doesn't matter. She would have left at the end of her two-week stay."

"Love doesn't have a measure of time," exclaimed his mother, her exasperation clear as a bell.

There it was again. She'd be the second person to call him out on loving Maryan.

"I didn't say I *loved* her." He grunted when he bit his tongue, his confusion about his feelings physically harming him now. Guess it was what he deserved after the way he treated Maryan in the end. She'd done so much for him. She could be humble all she wanted, but she'd instilled a confidence in him with Zara, she had believed in his dreams for Somalia, and then she had stuck up for him in front of Aydin. All of that on top of the body-melting pleasure she'd given him in bed.

No one had to tell him he was a fool to let her walk away.

"I did not raise an idiot for a son."

"Hooyo…" he began affectionately, snapping his mouth closed when it didn't work and she tsked louder.

"You love her, and you have made a big mistake when you let her leave."

"She wanted to leave, Mom. I wasn't going to lock her in her room." He stopped breathing as soon as the words tumbled from his mouth. He didn't even argue this time on whether what he felt for Maryan was love or not.

"She was staying with you?" His mother's incredulity had him drawing the phone from his ear and face-palming. He pulled his face out of his hands when she finished lecturing him about the impropriety. And he only knew it was safe to place his ear back on the receiver when a silence dawned on her end.

"Mom?"

"Do you love her?" she asked gently and with none of her chagrin at his indecorum.

Without thinking, Faisal avowed, "I…think I might."

"It is never an easy thing to undo our faults. Much easier to make a mistake than repair one."

"I don't know if I *can* fix this."

She was quiet long enough for him to worry that the line had cut off. But then his mother said, "You will. My son may be an idiot—he's also zealous for the things he loves most."

Faisal brushed the back of his hand over a cheek, coming away with a wetness that matched the love he was feeling from his mother. And not just her. He had a chance to speak to his father, and then his sister, both in congratulatory moods over the news of his lucrative partnership. After he bade them farewell, he rubbed his chest above his heart and relished the tremendous weight that vanished sometime during the call to his family. Their support was all he ever relied on. Their love strong enough to banish the negativity that had been weighing him down.

And keeping him from realizing that his mom's advice aligned with his heart's deepest truth in that moment.

I love Maryan.

He saw that so clearly now and wanted to thump his head over his desk at the obviousness. Everything he'd been feeling. All the confusion surrounding his emotions when he was near her, the clawing worry of what she thought of him, the heartache at her departure, and the surety that *nothing* would feel right for him without her. Each was a sign that he loved her.

But she had no idea of how he felt about her truly, and he'd have to remedy that first.

CHAPTER TWELVE

MARYAN THOUGHT SHE'D settled the matter of the party.

But she was exiting Faisal's luxury sports car, lifting the voluminous, tiered skirt of her crystal-and-tulle designer ball gown, and climbing the endless stone steps to the opulent mansion at the top. Behind her Burak shadowed her dutifully. He'd come bearing the handwritten note from his boss, along with the expensive dress in its dress bag. She had left the gown behind when she fled Faisal's home for a hotel.

I might be the last person you want to see, but I would love if you could attend the party tonight.

Faisal had been right about her not wanting to see him. At least that was how she felt when the note and dress arrived at her hotel suite by way of his security. Then as the day passed, and she reread his message, she sensed a shifting in her heart. It wasn't as stony and unimpressed by Faisal's quiet plea.

Then her curiosity ran away with her.

Had he changed his mind possibly? Did he, in fact, not want her to leave Istanbul? And if so, why?

She was resolute that she wouldn't be a booty call to him. Fantastic as it was, sex alone wasn't fulfilling for her. She wasn't in the market to be an au pair, either. As much as she loved Zara, being her nanny with Faisal as her boss was a recipe for disaster. She'd abandoned one unhealthy relationship, and she wasn't trading her ex-boyfriend for fast, fun times with Faisal.

I'm not asking for a proposal, either.

She wasn't ready for that leap of faith. Marriage was serious business. When she imagined her wedding day, it was opposite the man she loved and felt confident was her soul mate. She didn't know if Faisal could be that—and she realized she wouldn't ever know because she hadn't *told* him she loved him.

That was why she'd come to his party.

She needed to get her truth off her chest, once and for all. He had to know.

It doesn't matter if he feels the same.

All her life she'd learned to not question the people she cared about and who supposedly cared for her. She had done it with her parents when they'd packed a small suitcase for her one-way trip to America. She hadn't loved her ex-boyfriend, but she'd trusted him, and she hadn't thought to question that bond of trust.

They had made their decisions. Left her with the mess. And now—

Now Maryan had a chance to speak up where Faisal was concerned. And if he didn't reciprocate her love, then at least she'd get to see Zara in person one last time…

"Is he inside?" she asked Burak, looking back to find him waiting on her. For once he had his sunglasses off. Possibly as the sun had long set, and it wouldn't make sense to wear shades right then. But with nothing obscuring his eyes, Maryan could see him squinting through a study of her. He almost looked as though he had something to tell her. "What is it?" she wondered.

"It's not my place to say anything, but he's not been himself today."

"Pardon?" She could tell herself whatever she wanted, but her heart wasn't beating loud enough to drown out Burak's observation.

Not elucidating on what he informed her, he simply said, "Yes, he's inside, waiting for you."

With a look down at the line of luxury vehicles snaking up to the front of the waterside mansion, their headlights shining brighter alongside the Bosporus's dark, still waters, she fortified herself for what awaited inside the shining windows of the mansion.

And who, she thought with a nervous gulp.

"A toast, to our partnership. May it see us weather the challenges and celebrate the victories ahead."

A chorus of clinking glasses spread through the spacious salon from the dais in the center. Faisal raised his glass of raki after his speech, first to his new business partners, Aydin and Erkin, and then to their guests, including a curated group of media representatives. This was one piece of news they wouldn't doctor into a scandal of his personal affairs.

Stepping down from the dais, he smiled wide and laughed on cue, working the room as he was expected before he found refuge in the corner where Zara waited with Rukiya. Nodding his thanks to his executive assistant, he abandoned his untouched drink and lifted Zara into his arms and spun with her in place, thrilling in her laughter.

"May I have this dance, little princess?"

She bobbed her head, but the luminous silver flower crown threaded to her braids didn't budge.

It was as Maryan said. Faisal thought Zara adorable in her cap-sleeve dress and strappy party shoes. He set her down and showed her how to balance on the ends of his feet, not caring if her shoes scuffed his. Then he duck-walked, turning circles carefully to the music and creating their own beat when the couples around them swayed to a different melody. When the band switched to a lively folk song, Faisal popped Zara off his feet and he twirled her around and around, her glee casting out the darkness glooming his mind, but also forcing him to face what he'd lost.

He didn't mean to think of her, but it was hard not to see Maryan in every part of his life now.

At his home, at work—when he couldn't stop from thinking about her—and now, here, at this party that she refused to come to, while he was dancing with his daughter and crafting another amazing memory.

He'd sent her a note and had Burak deliver it.

But it wasn't enough, he surmised bitterly.

None of the bitterness targeted at Maryan. This was on him. And now he had to nurse his hurt and disappointment alone.

"Daddy?" Zara tugged his hands to get his attention. Once she had it, she gestured for him to crouch. Then when he did that, she hugged him, her small arms squeezing around his shoulders and prompting him to embrace her just as tightly.

"What was that for?"

She touched her hands to his clean-shaven face, looking as solemn as an energetic seven-year-old could. "You look sad, Daddy."

"Do I?"

He hated that it was obvious even to her.

"Are you sad because of Maryan?"

They'd discussed her nanny's departure, and Faisal comforted Zara as best as he was able. Finding that he wasn't half bad at it without Maryan to guide him.

"It's okay to be sad. I miss her, too."

"I know you do, sweetheart," Faisal murmured, kissing her forehead. "I also know that she misses and loves you very much."

"Can I talk to her tonight?"

"Remember what she told you? She said you can call her whenever you like." It was exactly what he expected from her. Maryan had to be grieving the change of not seeing Zara every day as well. And he'd caused their pain, unnecessarily so. All he had to do was tell Maryan how he felt. Tell her that he loved her, and though marriage was far from his mind still, he had a strong feeling that with time it could be in their future.

Not that it mattered now. That ship had long sailed. Her flight home three days away. And she hadn't spoken to him when she'd called Zara earlier today. Besides a short text letting him know she'd arrived at the hotel safely, she hadn't reached out to him at all.

The worst part being she didn't respond to his note.

Since leaving to deliver the note an hour ago, Burak hadn't reported anything, leaving Faisal with the understanding that he'd have to learn to live without Maryan because she wasn't willing to forgive. Regardless of his efforts to make his grand declaration of love and try to sweep her off her feet.

"Daddy, don't be sad. I'll love you for both me and Maryan."

Zara's proclamation earned her another bear hug from him. At the end of it, his daughter wriggled free and grinned, asking, "Can we spin again?"

He spun her a few more times before swinging her up into his arms and swaying with her in his embrace.

"Maryan!" It wasn't so much Zara squealing in his ears or her bouncing in his arms that stopped Faisal. It was what she said and who she called to.

Sure enough, when he turned his head to where Zara

smiled, he spotted her nanny walking past. Maryan seemed not to have heard Zara over the din of the party, her back to them as she retreated deeper into the mansion. These old Ottoman-era waterside houses were sprawling and maze-like. Throw in a guest list of nearly two hundred people and the sinking dread of losing her was in the realm of possibility.

Setting Zara on her feet, he walked her back to Rukiya. Burak was there, too.

"Is she here?" Faisal knew what his friend's answer would be, but he was further reassured that he wasn't imagining Maryan when Burak nodded.

"She wanted to explore the house."

Of course she did. It sounded just like her.

Leaving Zara to their care, Faisal went to search for her. Having Maryan so close, knowing that she had come after all, was the kick in the pants that he needed to see his mission through. By the end of the night she'd know that he had fallen in love with her, and if she deigned to have him, he would seriously attempt to be the man she desired. A man who was worthy of her, body, heart and spirit.

Scouring the house for a sign of her was more of a challenge than he had prepared for.

People crowded every room and corner. Erkin had overseen the guest list, and with Aslihan, they had seemingly invited the whole of Istanbul's elite. Faisal encountered politicians to pop stars, and even an actor or two from one of his favorite Turkish dramas. Stopping to chat wasn't an option for him right then, no matter how much the idea of an autograph was appealing. Finding Maryan was his single-minded pursuit. She wasn't in any of the lavish salons, their gilded ornamental walls and theatrical furnishings lovely, but nowhere close to being lovelier than her face. The roof-top terrace shone with countless string lights, but their radiance was dimmed without the presence of Maryan. He even tried the Turkish hammam with no luck. The resplendent architecture of the bathing rooms standing empty.

Naturally, as his search area dwindled, his concern of having lost her again began to set in. By the end of his tireless searching, he walked slower, dejection slumping his shoulders. That was it. He'd looked high and low, *literally*. Maryan wasn't in the splendid waterfront Turkish manor hosting his party.

Faisal brushed a hand over his head, remembered he'd had his curly hair shaved for a cleaner, professional look, and groaned loud, his frustration echoing off the darkened walls of the lonely room he'd ended his search in. He couldn't even indulge in tugging at his hair. Missing his curls, and missing Maryan even more, he gazed mindlessly out the floor-to-ceiling windows wrapping the far side of the room. The view was of the front of the house, the obsidian strip of the Bosporus separating the row of Empire-style waterfront properties from the rest of Istanbul on the opposite side of the strait's waters.

No natural lighting gleamed off the ink-like surface of the waterway. Instead, it reflected the lights from the mansion's many narrow windows and the lampposts irradiating the private port…and Maryan.

Faisal did a double take, but she didn't vanish from where she paced alongside the Bosporus down below.

He pulled himself away, realizing that he had to seize this opportunity while fate was so generously offering it. Getting down to her was another obstacle to surmount. It took a while to cross the more crowded areas of the mansion before he strode out a back door and into the night. Then it was all about how fast he could jog to where he'd seen her last.

It felt like an age had passed when he halted a few feet

from her, her back to him again, his heartbeats pounding in his ears from a combination of his jogging to her and from the exuberance that he hadn't lost her.

Not yet.

A series of vibrations from his phone hummed in his inner coat pocket. Faisal halted his movement forward just as Maryan whipped around to face him. Her eyes rounder than ever before, one hand clutching her phone and the other her sparkling sequin clutch.

"Faisal?" She sounded as if she couldn't trust that her eyes weren't deceiving her. As though he were a figment of her imagination.

He knew that feeling all too well.

"You came," he said.

"I did."

"That means you received my note." He had asked her to come, leaving out everything of import that he wanted to tell her. Chiefly that he loved her, and he didn't want her flying from Istanbul without knowledge of how he'd grown from simply admiring her to adoring her completely.

"You look wonderful," he noted, his gaze roving her curvaceous figure appreciatively. He hadn't expected any less. Maryan could likely transform a paper bag into a couture gown in his eyes. She wore a dress of burgundy clouds, her bodice twinkling as if inlaid with the stars that were missing from the light-polluted night sky, and her jewelry challenging the effulgence of the sun itself. A goddess. That was what he was made to think when he looked at her. His reverence for her pairing with that glorious image.

"Zara liked this one best." Maryan slid her phone in her clutch and then pressed the purse with both hands to her center. "What are you doing out here?"

He could ask her the same. "I needed a breather. What about you?"

"Same," she uttered quickly.

A quietude closed over them, and then Faisal grasped for his straws, a now-or-never mentality rearing up in his head.

"I thought you left."

She frowned lightly, the corners of her mouth drooping but her eyes dark and clear and reflecting the lighting around them. "Why would I leave?"

A few reasons popped into his mind, but he said, "I haven't given you a strong reason to come, that's why. I wouldn't have held it against you if you didn't stay."

She shrugged bare shoulders prettily. "Your message was vague… I was curious why you invited me after we decided that I wasn't coming."

"I never wanted you to stay away," Faisal said.

"You *didn't* say that," she snapped, and then breathing herself to a calm state, she continued, "I don't want to argue."

"Neither do I."

She lowered her clutch, looking far less defensive and far more curious. "Why did you invite me?"

"I wanted to see you."

Her clutch rose again, higher this time, above her heart.

"And I needed you to hear something," Faisal clarified. Taking courage that she wasn't running away or shutting him down, he relinquished the final traces of doubt about this approach and opened his heart to her.

"I tore this mansion apart looking for you. When I couldn't find you, I thought I'd lost you twice over. I felt double the anguish for my loss. Seriously, I thought the pain of losing you once was bad." He blew a shaky breath. "Then I saw you and it was like being given one last chance to set everything right.

"Because I realized as soon as you left my place that I shouldn't have let you leave us. That I was a fool to allow you to walk away. And I'd be a bigger fool not to tell you that I do care about you. Far more than I've let on. Vastly more than you'll likely believe.

"The thing is, I wasn't sure I could love you freely without mucking it up with my trust issues. But that's the thing: I *love* you."

Maryan was frightfully still, looking prettier than any painting by an old master, but appearing as though she'd checked out of his short speech.

Fear wormed its way into his blood and gouged his heart.

"Maryan?" he called out, taking a step closer to her.

She mirrored him, her eyes bigger, her mouth slightly open, her throat shivering with fast pulls of air and her chest heaving. She'd have scared him with concerns for her health if she didn't whisper, "What did you say?"

"I love you," he repeated.

"You do?"

He smiled fully, exquisite relief eradicating his worries. "Yeah," he drawled, laughing huskily, and saying it again for both their certainty, "I love you, Maryan."

He loved her.

All her hand-wringing and heart palpitations to make the same declaration, and he'd beat her to it.

Does it matter who said it first? He loves me!

"I'm not proposing marriage…*yet*," stressed Faisal, his eyes soft with the love he professed.

No, he was right not to propose. She didn't want to be married—at least not yet.

"I *am* asking you to give me a chance." He stepped closer, the gap between them sealing quickly when she met him halfway. "I want you to stay if you want, but if you need to be in America, I'll let you go. Whatever you desire, I'll try to be that for you."

"You want me to stay?" She was finding it hard to process all that he was telling her.

"I do. And not only because Zara wants you to stay, too."

Maryan blushed when his soft, sexy laughter washed over her.

"I thought I needed you as the nanny, and then you showed me that I could be Zara's father. Then I thought I needed you for a night. I haven't been wrong about much in my life."

She believed that. He was a billionaire. A fortunate entrepreneur, and a big-hearted one who was using his money for any good he could bring to the world. Somalia would be lucky to have him steering one of its first successful oil and gas businesses.

"But I've been wrong about this." He brushed a hand over her arm, taking that final step and bringing them as close as they'd been in the tangled sheets of his bed. Shivers broke out over her as his warm palm rubbed over her arm, up from her elbow to her shoulder, and back down to her wrist, his fingers interlocking around hers. "You're wearing the bracelet."

She looked between them where her other hand gripped her clutch, the mother-of-pearl bracelet he'd purchased for her from the Grand Bazaar shimmering like it knew it was being admired.

"It paired well with the dress," she said, laughing softly when he chuckled.

He lowered his head then, and Maryan understood what he was after, meeting him naturally. They kissed gently and faster than she would've wanted. Faisal explained, "We'll be seen. I don't want any media ruining this," before kissing her again, pecking her mouth with feathery brushes of his lips, breathing harsher with each short, fervent kiss. "I should stop. Before we get caught. But it's so hard."

He swallowed her laughter with a longer kiss.

When she went to grip his head, she remembered that his curls were gone. "You cut your hair."

"Do you hate it?"

She rubbed his shorter hair, the bristles tickling her hands, the sides shaved close while the top was darker and thicker. Shaking her head, she replied, "It's still very you." Then, feeling mischievous, Maryan teased, "I just won't have much to grip on to when you're——"

Faisal smacked a kiss on her lips, a warning growl heating her trembling mouth, "Don't make me regret having to stay at this party longer."

He hugged her then.

She held on to him tightly, unable to separate the sound of her heart from his.

When he drew back, his hands on her shoulders, his eyes darker, she sensed the direction of his thinking even before he voiced it.

"Do you...like me?" He didn't say *love*.

Maryan sighed. So, he'd noticed that she hadn't given him a response yet. There was a reason for it. He had gotten to say his piece.

I need to say mine now.

"I did want to run away at first," she confided quietly.

Faisal's brows pulled down, a frown storming over his darkly good looks and taking away the pleasure they'd just enjoyed. She knew he had to be wondering where she was going with this. But she'd had enough time to think this through, and she wasn't going to let fear hold her down any longer.

Cuddling his love close to her beating heart, she launched into this brave, new territory with him.

"Yesterday, in your garden, I told you that I was confirming flight scheduling with my aunt. The truth is… I've been wanting to stay."

She saw surprise flit over his face, but he didn't interrupt her.

"But then you didn't invite me to stay, and I got the sense that you might not want me to stick around."

"Which isn't true," he said roughly, shame supplanting his surprise. "I *should have* asked. I *should have* known what I felt for you wasn't leaving with you. I was a colossal idiot…"

"*You* were protecting yourself. I was, too. Otherwise I would've told you all of this sooner."

Faisal moved his hands from her arms to her hips, the comforting squeeze there meant to fan the flames of her courage. That wasn't sexual heat in his eyes, but a promise that he'd be there to catch her on the other side if she stumbled and fumbled her way through this important step.

"I've learned through my life that it's easier to accept the way things are, rather than yearn passionately for the things I wanted."

She swallowed, this part the hardest to say and hear aloud. "I wanted to stay with my family in Somalia. I wanted my parents to bring me home. I wanted my ex-boyfriend to understand why I couldn't be with him and not retaliate with petty theft. I wanted to stay with Zara for…well, forever. I love her, and it hurt to know that I'd likely never see her again."

Faisal framed her cheek with one of his big hands. "She loves you, too," he confirmed what she already knew.

"I *wanted* you. But I thought you didn't want me—*need me* beyond our physical chemistry."

"Now that you know I want *and* need you, too…"

She pushed up to kiss him quickly, sweetly, smiling against his lips, laughing away the last of her terrible unease.

"Tell me, Maryan."

So she did. "I love you, Faisal."

He kissed her until they were breathless, her lips sore and likely chapped, but her heart—her heart was with him. Nothing could pull her out of Faisal's arms, it felt like. Nuzzling noses, she imagined their night could be spent out there, just the two of them.

Rudely, his phone vibrated and forced them apart briefly.

It was only when he had his phone in hand that she remembered what she'd been up to before she noticed him behind her.

"Faisal, there's something else…"

She blanched when he looked up at her from his glowing phone screen, one eyebrow rising slowly, a stunned expression slackening his jaw.

"I *might* have posted some pictures," she began with a shy, nervous smile. And when he didn't respond, she backed away.

Faster than she could get away, his arm hooked around her waist, and he hauled her in, looking unfazed when she yelped.

"I can see that," he rumbled sexily. "You finally tagged me."

"I'm sorry!"

She expected to do more groveling, but he sealed their lips in a hot, lingering kiss, before whispering, "For what? Remember it was my idea from the beginning."

She did remember that first day in Istanbul; Faisal tried to get her to tag him in the photos of them together. She hadn't wanted her friends to bug him…but now they were bugging them, and she couldn't separate it from her happiness.

"Although your grand gesture has mine beat."

She snorted. "It might have ended badly, though." If he didn't love her.

Thinking the same, Faisal said, "It didn't."

He hugged her tighter to his side and angled his phone so they could both see the comments that were beginning to trickle in, and fast. Support from her friends and followers, and from his. Everyone either wanted to know the nitty-gritty details or wanted to know when the wedding was happening. The photo was of them on the rooftop restaurant, their love for each other glowing from their faces even then.

"I'll have to explain to Salma."

"Worried?" Maryan asked, knowing that Zara's mother wasn't in love with Faisal, and she wouldn't stand between them. Yet she sympathized with any concern Faisal might have. Especially as there was someone else who would have to know about them. "We'll have to tell Zara as well."

He touched his lips to her temple. "Afraid of what she'll think?"

"A little. Aren't you?"

Faisal stared into her eyes, and she knew that he had her full, unwavering trust whatever he said. "It's only been a day and she misses you terribly. She loves you. Still, I won't pretend that it won't require adjusting on all our parts, but I know she'll be happy for us."

Trusting him, Maryan leaned in as his arm settled over her shoulders and read more comments until Faisal shut off his phone.

"Since you're staying in Istanbul for longer now—"

"Am I staying longer?" she teased.

"If you *choose* to extend your stay, I'll happily charter a flight for you whenever you wish to leave for America."

She laughed, kissing his cheek, finding his lips, and nearly losing track of her thoughts before she pulled back to mock gasp. "A plane? I knew a billionaire was a catch." She giggled when his mouth brushed the heated tip of her ear.

"Is that a 'yes'?"

"I'll have to call my aunt and uncle to let them know about us. Though I can't stay long. I still have to help them…"

Faisal kissed her sweetly and touched their foreheads together. "Whenever you want to go, you let me know. Distance won't be a problem."

She believed him. And not only because he had a private jet at his disposal. She didn't think her heart could feel so dangerously full before, but he surprised her with better news.

"Guess now is a good time to tell you that someone else will be happy for us."

"Who?"

"My family. My mom especially. Fair warning in advance, she might talk you into marrying me."

She snorted a laugh.

"Seriously though, Zara and I will be leaving to visit them in a few days. I want you to come with us."

He didn't need to twist her arm. Nervous though she was, meeting his family would be exciting and meaningful.

"And maybe one day we'll get to visit yours?" Faisal hedged.

"Actually…after I left you yesterday, I got to thinking that I should visit them soon. Likely before the end of the year. There's a lot I need to say to my parents. A bunch of healing that needs to be done."

He pulled her in and bussed her cheek. "That's big of you."

She blushed, feeling like she'd never react any differently when he praised her so warmly. And she wasn't any less bashful when broaching the final topic they had to discuss.

"What happens after I leave Istanbul?" She hadn't settled on where to live, mostly as this was still fresh to her. They'd only just confessed their love to each other.

Faisal seemed to have thoughts on it, though. With one of his winning smiles, he hugged her closer, turned her to the magical Bosporus, and vowed, "No matter where we end up, here in Turkey, or America, or Somalia, I'll love you always."

"I'll always love you, too."

"Even when I'm running late?" he laughed.

Grinning, she promised, "Even then."

*   *   *   *   *

COMING SOON!

We really hope you enjoyed reading this book.
If you're looking for more romance, be sure to
head to the shops when new books are
available on

Thursday 9th
June

To see which titles are coming soon, please visit
millsandboon.co.uk/nextmonth

MILLS & BOON®

Coming next month

BAHAMAS ESCAPE WITH THE BEST MAN
Cara Colter

The smile that had been tickling the wickedly attractive curve of his mouth formed fully, revealing the full straightness of his teeth, as white as the towel around his neck.

Then he threw back his head and laughed. The column of his throat looked strong and touchable. The sound of his laughter was more intoxicating than the rum.

She, Marlee Copeland, had just made a very attractive man laugh. That felt like a cigar-worthy reason for celebration!

"The cigar matches your start on your career as a criminal. People sometimes lick them before they light them."

"What?"

"They're usually wine-dipped."

She flicked the cigar with her tongue.

"Here," he said, gently. "Let me take that."

And just like that, his hand brushed hers, and a few more rocks crumbled from that cliff.

He took the cigar.

His eyes lingered on her lips.

A fire leaped to life within her.

"I wonder if there's really a wild, train-robbing outlaw under all that green fluffy stuff."

"It's not green." Her voice was hoarse, a choked whisper. "It's sea foam. Chiffon."

He held up the cigar and his tongue slipped out and licked it, exactly where her own tongue had been. His eyes were steady on hers. It was shockingly sensual.

"I need to get out of this scratchy dress," she said. What had made her say that? It was totally inappropriate. Did it sound as if she wanted to get out of the dress with him? Did it sound like an invitation?

Why did she always have to be so socially inept, blurting things out awkwardly?

Why did men like this always make her feel like a tongue-tied teenager?

Fiona had been right. This dress did suit her.

On the other hand, what would a train-robbing, cigar-loving, rum-drinking outlaw do? She could be that. For just a few minutes in time, she could. Maybe just for one night.

She took a deep breath. She felt as if she was on the edge of a cliff, trying to build up her nerve to jump.

"Want some company for your swim?"

Continue reading
BAHAMAS ESCAPE WITH THE BEST MAN
Cara Colter

Available next month
www.millsandboon.co.uk

MILLS & BOON

THE HEART OF ROMANCE

A ROMANCE FOR EVERY READER

MODERN

Prepare to be swept off your feet by sophisticated, sexy and seductive heroes, in some of the world's most glamourous and romantic locations, where power and passion collide.

HISTORICAL

Escape with historical heroes from time gone by. Whether your passion is for wicked Regency Rakes, muscled Vikings or rugged Highlanders, awak the romance of the past.

MEDICAL

Set your pulse racing with dedicated, delectable doctors in the high-pressure world of medicine, where emotions run high and passion, comfort a love are the best medicine.

True Love

Celebrate true love with tender stories of heartfelt romance, from the rush of falling in love to the joy a new baby can bring, and a focus on th emotional heart of a relationship.

Desire

Indulge in secrets and scandal, intense drama and plenty of sizzling hot action with powerful and passionate heroes who have it all: wealth, status good looks…everything but the right woman.

HEROES

Experience all the excitement of a gripping thriller, with an intense romance at its heart. Resourceful, true-to-life women and strong, fearless m face danger and desire - a killer combination!